Thanks to

Debbie, for the memories

Bas, for your love and patience, everyday

"She stood in the storm,
and when the wind did not blow her way,
she adjusted her sails." Elizabeth Edwards

Chapter 1

May 1985

Shelley Charlton had a headache; it was pounding. She'd taken two paracetamols about an hour ago, but they hadn't touched it. The mist of Insette hairspray and the heat from the dryers wasn't helping matters and Shelley realised that her only option was to go home to bed. It was years since she'd suffered a migraine but for her, lying in a darkened room was the only solution.

'Dawni,' Shelley mumbled, in a sheepish voice. 'Don't be mad but, I've got to go home. I'm getting one of my, headaches and I need to go to bed.'

'Oh hellfire, Shelley. You've got to be kidding me,' Dawn replied in an alarmed voice. 'You've got Mrs Coombes in for a perm at 1pm.

'I know, but my head's pounding. I can hardly see straight, and I feel really sick,' Shelley continued, adopting a meek tone. The type which people automatically develop when reporting a sickness to their boss. 'I'm sorry, Dawn, but I've got to go,' she added a little more firmly. 'It's a migraine and it's only going to get worse. I don't let you down often, do I?' she protested.

'Well no, I suppose not,' Dawn sighed. 'I just wish it wasn't today, that's all. We're fully booked and as well you know, Tracey's on day release at college.' 'Anyway,' she shrugged, 'if you're ill, you're ill. I suppose it can't be helped.'

Shelley had worked in her cousin Dawn's hairdressers since she'd left school at sixteen. Dawn, now thirty, was so proud of the fact that she was running her own salon by the age of twenty-five, taking over the shop that she herself had worked in since leaving school. Her then boss, Marian Coleman, decided at fifty-five that she'd had enough of the 'shitty English weather' as she'd put it, and was selling up. She and her Arthur were moving to Spain. As her top stylist, Dawn was offered first refusal of the salon. So, after sweet talking the bank manager and with a little help from her parents, she bought the shop and never looked back.

Soon, followed the transformation of the blue rinse parlour into a much trendier salon, with an all-round younger clientele. Dawn had loads of ideas and was forever browsing glossy magazines, checking out the latest styles from London, Paris and Milan. She was even considering branching into the beauty sector, after reading that salons were opening throughout the bigger cities. Why not here in Lancashire?

'Hey, you're not pregnant, are you?' Dawn questioned, with wide eyes.

'Am I heck. Chris always pulls out. He says, we've plenty of time for kiddies. He says, we should be enjoying ourselves whilst we're young, taking holidays abroad and concentrating on the house,' Shelley replied, smiling at her vision.

Shelley's house was her pride and joy. It was on a new estate in the small Lancashire town of Shaw, at the foothills of the South Pennines. With its driveway and neat little gardens, front and back, the modest semi-detached had cost them just over thirty thousand pounds. At the time, Shelley couldn't help but worry about the mortgage repayments, as she only earned a pittance, hairdressing. Chris contributed the lion's share of the household finances, meaning that they could afford to live in their dream home. Although he would often remind her that they were a team and just because he earned much more than she did, that didn't make her any less equal.

On moving into their new home, Shelley had ordered the Eternal Beau range of crockery from the catalogue, and had velvet curtains made to measure, with swags and pelmets. Keeping her home spotlessly clean was so important to her and every Monday, on her day off, she'd Shake and Vac the whole house. Never had she owned anything so lovely and she treasured it immensely. It was a far cry from the council house she'd grown up in, which was less than a mile away and where her mum and dad still resided.

Sharing a small bedroom with her elder sister Jackie, the girls had adorned the walls with posters of their favourite bands of the time, constantly arguing over space and the borrowing of each other's clothes. Back then, she'd never realised how run down their house was. Shelley's mum, Carole wasn't particularly house proud and managing three jobs hadn't left her much time for cleaning. It wasn't until she bought her own little palace, that Shelley appreciated the importance of owning nice things.

Her dad Gerry, who was somewhat work shy, spent most of the money her mum slaved away to earn, down at the bookies, or in the Commercial Inn. After being made redundant from his job as a sheet metal worker in the early 80's, he now, at forty-nine felt that he was too old to be working ten-hour shifts, and a sceptical bad back saw the end of his working life, as they knew it. Shelley and her sister had been brought up, like many of their friends, on a shoestring budget, but they had been happy.

-

Getting off the bus near her house, Shelley couldn't wait to get home. The nausea she felt was growing and she craved a darkened room and the comfort of her bed. Turning the corner of cul de sac, she was surprised to see her husband's Ford Capri sitting on the drive. Chris had recently landed himself a job at a solicitors firm in Rochdale. He was on the up, and his studies and hard work were beginning to pay off. He was constantly telling Shelley that computers were the future and that there was big money to be had if he were to pursue a career in I.T. He was determined to study hard and work his way up the ladder.

Shelley was in total awe of him. As a backstreet hairdresser, she had no ambitions to 'make it big'; her goals were to keep a tidy home, be a good wife and hopefully, become a mother. She was more than content working at the salon and her life, as far as she was concerned was perfect. She did, however, admire Chris's enthusiasm, and she loved how he never made her feel inadequate, even though she wasn't ambitious like he was. Moving into their new home had been the icing on the cake for Shelley and she hoped that in the next year or so, they'd be starting a family.

The young couple had met one another at the tender ages of eighteen and twenty. They were married two years later, with many of their family and friends commenting on how young they were to be taking such a big step. However, no one doubted that they were perfect for each other. No one, that was, apart from Chris's mother, Vivien Charlton.

Vivien was a snob. A curtain-twitching busybody who loved nothing more than gossiping with her equally snobby friends. She looked down her nose at those less privileged than herself and felt that her darling boy was marrying beneath him. There was no doubt she considered Shelley to be a pleasant and very pretty girl but in her heavy heart, she couldn't deny that in her opinion, Christopher could do better for himself. She hadn't sent him to the best schools and paid for maths and English tutors, in order for him to marry the first pretty girl that batted her eyelashes at him.

In Vivien's view, there was no getting away from the fact that Shelley was from a rough council estate, with no ambitions to become anything more than a two-bit hairdresser, with a brood of snotty nosed children trailing behind her. Vivien kept her own counsel, but she gave the marriage two years, maximum. Her Christopher was worth so much more, and in her own late mum's words 'a mother's instincts are never wrong.'

Turning her key in the front door lock, Shelley was relieved to enter the house. As she was about to call out Chris's name, she heard his voice coming from upstairs. Her head felt fuzzy and she couldn't comprehend whom he might be talking to. His voice was muffled, and she was unable to distinguish his words. Shelley began climbing the stairs towards the voice; towards their bedroom. It was quiet now, apart from the distant sound of the radio in the kitchen and Chaka Kahn singing, 'I Feel For You'.

Shelley briefly wondered if Chris was with a workman. He'd talked about them having fitted wardrobes in their bedroom. Maybe he was discussing the measurements with the chippie. However, a nagging feeling was preventing her from calling out his name.

Reaching the top of the stairs she caught sight of herself in the landing mirror. She looked awful: scared even. Shelley was usually immaculately gorgeous, with her streaked blonde hair and Michelle Pfeiffer features. Her looks were envied by many women. But right now, she looked pale and worried.

As she walked along the landing towards the bedroom door, the seconds seemed to pass in slow motion, and it was with a flicker of hesitation that she reached for the handle. Pushing open the door; two shocked faces turned to stare up at her. Their entwined bodies lying together in a loving embrace. Shelley felt in that instant as though time stood still.

'What the fucking hell's going on here?' she screamed. 'You, fucking, cheating bastard!' she spat at Chris, hearing herself screech the obscenities, in a voice that didn't even sound like hers.

'Shelley, Shelley, I can explain. Oh fuck, Shelley,' Chris yelled, jumping out from beneath the duvet and grabbing his boxer shorts.

The sight of her naked husband suddenly shocked Shelley; it was as though she'd never seen him hard before. She couldn't believe she was seeing him now, naked and aroused, whilst he was in their bed, with another woman. The pretty brunette who had been draped over Chris was now sitting bolt upright, with the duvet covering the ample but perky breasts she'd been happy to expose only moments before. With fear and shock written all over her face, she was clearly alarmed, and wondering what course of action her lover's wife was about to take.

But Shelley was in shock at the scene before her, and with the bile beginning to rise in her throat, she turned and ran down the stairs, just managing to escape out of the front door before her vomit spewed all over the driveway, splattering Chris's beloved Ford Capri.

Chapter 2

Tina Doyle stood in front of the long mirror in just her underwear, staring at her underweight frame and the bruises, old and new, that covered her body. Her face crumpled and she began to cry. Dropping to her knees, her cries turned into racking sobs. How had she let this happen? How had her happiness turned to misery in such a short space of time?

Finally, when she was totally spent and drained of all her tears, she composed herself, took a deep breath, and rose to her feet. Opening the wardrobe, she reached for the small tatty suitcase, and opening it out on the bed she began to pack the few clothes and belongings that she owned. Just eighteen months ago, she had been the happiest girl in the world. That now felt like a lifetime ago.

Darren Doyle was known as a catch. With his smouldering good looks and naturally muscular physique, he was on every girls 'I'd do him' list. After serving an apprenticeship as a mechanic, he was earning a pretty decent wage, working in his brother-in-law's garage. He was never short of female company and was an all-round popular guy. Spotting him most weekends in the town's local pubs, Tina thought he was an absolute dreamboat, and although she had enough confidence for every female in the pub, she turned into a nervous wreck when Darren was in her vicinity.

Tina was stunning, with green eyes, an olive complexion, and naturally wavy chestnut hair, falling down her back. At five-foot one, she was tiny in stature with a curvy size eight figure. She was adored by the opposite sex, meaning she could have her pick of men; but a guy really needed to make an impression on Tina, if she was to consider giving him the time of day. And that was just what Darren Doyle had done. What was even more frustrating to Tina was that she wasn't used to being ignored, and as hard as she tried, she'd never even caught Darren's eye, or so she thought. That all changed, on a warm August evening in 1983.

'Bloody hell, Shelley,' Tina squealed, nearly choking on her lager and lime. 'Darren's coming this way.'

Shelley giggled. 'Act natural, he's looking right at you.'

Tina and Shelley had been best mates since their first day at Royton and Crompton High School, when Tina had stood up to a couple of third year girls who were trying to steal Shelley's lunch money. Since that day, she and Shelley had been inseparable. With Shelley's laidback nature and Tina's feistiness they complimented each other's personalities perfectly, getting on like a house on fire.

'It's Tina, isn't it?' smiled Darren, as he gazed down at her with his deep brown eyes. He looked even taller against Tina's tiny frame and with his tanned arms bulging from his white T-shirt, Tina thought she might melt. She gawped up at him with a soppy grin, replying, 'Tina Firth, at your service.'

Shelley snorted a laugh and Tina wanted to die on the spot, realising what she'd actually just said. She wished for the ground to open up and swallow her whole. Darren smiled a wide grin, trying to ease her embarrassment, as he offered to buy both girls a drink.

'I'm fine, thanks,' smiled Shelley, and giving Tina, a quick wink, she made her excuses to go to 'The Ladies.' It was an unspoken rule that the girls had; if one of them was being chatted up by someone she fancied, then the other one would do a disappearing act.

Tina felt as though she was under a spell and, as Darren chatted freely to her, she hung on his every word. She didn't want the night to end. The music was loud and when Darren leaned in to speak in her ear, she could feel a tightening in her nipples. No one had ever had this effect on her and with the feel of his warm breath against the side of her face, it took all her willpower to stop herself turning to kiss him.

The next thing she knew, the bell was being rung for last orders and she was left wishing that she could relive the last two hours. When Darren offered to walk her home, she was thrilled and could hardly contain her excitement. She went to find Shelley, to tell her the good news.

'My God, Tina, calm yourself down, love! He'll think you're a right easy lay at this rate,' giggled Shelley, trying to compose her friend.

'I know but I've fancied him for months, and right now, Shell, I'd be an easy lay if he wanted me to be, I fancy the pants off him. Just talking to him is getting me going.'

Both girls burst out laughing. They were totally on the same wavelength where their humour was concerned.

'Hey, I best get myself back out there before he leaves without me.'

'Will he 'heck', Shelley grinned, 'he's well into you. Ring me tomorrow with an update. And be careful!' Shelley called after her friend, as Tina was halfway out of the door.

As Darren gently kissed her lips at her front door and asked if he could see her again, Tina felt like she was on cloud nine. If she'd known what the future held, she would never have agreed.

Chapter 3

Mandy Allsop liked a good time and she liked to get her own way, at any expense. She was a hit with men of all ages, a fact she often used to the best of her advantage. This was mainly due to her tiny waist and large breasts, which she was more than happy to display in the tightest of tops. She often told her best friend Judy, a rather plain and plump girl, 'if you've got it, flaunt it', and boy did she practise what she preached.

Mandy often found that men spoke to her chest rather than her face – it was quite an attractive face, but nonetheless her breasts were her best asset. She didn't mind this at all. Her 'bosom buddies', as she called them, had opened doors for her on many occasions.

Since her recently ex-boyfriend Mark, commented on how much she reminded him of the glamour model Linda Lusardi, Mandy had been dreaming of becoming the next big, page 3 model. She often stood in front of the long mirror in her bedroom, posing and pouting, pretending to be at a photoshoot.

Mandy ditched Mark when his job as a builder became unreliable, due to bad weather. There was no way she was paying on their dates. Mark was a nice lad and he'd been great in the bedroom, but Mandy had her sights set higher. So, the big elbow came into force. Judy, her long suffering, best friend, was secretly pleased to hear that Mandy had finished with Mark, as she'd had a silent crush on him for ages. But any time they'd bumped into him around town, it was always Mandy who got his attention, just as she did with most men, with Judy left standing in the background like a spare part.

-

Starting a new job can be nerve-wracking.

Fortunately for Chris, the team at Cuthbertson & Foster Solicitors were a very friendly bunch. They'd recently come into the computer age and Chris had been taken on as their one-man I.T. department.

It was on his second day, whilst standing at the photocopier wondering what the cause of the paper jam was, that he first encountered Mandy Allsop.

'You okay? You look lost,' Mandy smiled.

'Oh, I'm just wondering what P-5 stands for,' said Chris. 'The paper's stuck and I've pressed every button I can think of and nothing's happening.' He scratched his head, ruffling the blonde hair that Shelley had streaked for him. He had squealed like a pig when she'd pulled his hair through the streaking cap. She'd affectionately laughed, telling him, 'if you want to look good, Chris, you're going to have to take it. No pain, no gain.'

It was at that moment that Chris first noticed Mandy's impressive breasts, and however hard he tried he could not avert his eyes from them. Mandy was well aware of this, and often played on the power she held over men. It amazed her that a pair of tits could turn them into quivering wrecks, whom she could manipulate into doing almost anything she wanted.

It was the same when she came for her interview at Cuthbertson & Foster. She'd heard there was an opening as a trainee secretary for Mr Cuthbertson, from her Aunty Joan, who was the cleaner there and had given her the heads up. Joan had also informed Mandy that old Mr Cuthbertson was a bit of a letch and he would be sure to appreciate a secretary with Mandy's assets.

Mandy attended the interview looking smart, wearing a black suit from Principles. However, the blouse accompanying the suit was extremely fitted, with one too many buttons undone at the cleavage, leaving little to the imagination. Poor Kenneth Cuthbertson's eyes had nearly popped out of his combed over-head. After a brief overview of her recent college course he'd given Mandy the job there and then, much to the dismay of his senior secretary, Doreen. Who, apart from being a brilliant typist and loyal employee, was on the wrong side of forty and did nothing to brighten his day. Kenneth Cuthbertson had rubbed his hands with glee after Mandy left. Deciding to finish early for the day, he would take a drive to the private 'club' he frequented, where he could pay for a lovely young lady to fulfil the desires Mandy Allsop had stirred in his loins that afternoon.

Following their first meeting, Mandy made it her mission to get to know Chris Charlton better. There was something about him she really liked. Mandy usually dated the grease monkey type, but in his trendy suit, Chris was different, and he smelled so good, doused in Paco Rabanne aftershave. She'd noticed his wedding ring at their first meeting but that wasn't an issue to Mandy, after all it was only flirting, and as far as she was concerned the chase was usually better than the catch.

It started with trips to the pub at lunch time. Chris told himself that it was all harmless fun and that was how he justified it. But Mandy was like a drug, and as he sat facing her, in Yates's Wine Lodge, watching her luscious lips as she laughed at his jokes, he just wanted to kiss them with all the passion he could muster. Mandy Allsop made his pulse race and his cock hard and he wanted more of her.

Old Edna Roberts had contacted Mr Cuthbertson about making her will, and as she was housebound, her appointments were made by home visit's. On the day that Mr Cuthbertson had arranged to have the will signed and witnessed, he'd come down with the flu and was unable to come into work. Telephoning the office that morning, he asked Mandy if she could call on Mrs Roberts with the necessary paperwork. She would need to take someone else from the office, to drive her there and witness the signing. Mandy was only too delighted to skive off work for a couple of hours and knew exactly who would be accompanying her.

On leaving the old lady's house and getting into Chris's Ford Capri, Mandy turned to him with a big smile.

'Would you mind driving me to my house please, Chris? I've forgotten my gym kit.'

Chris replied, with a sly grin, 'Not at all. Show me the way and you can also show me your bedroom at the same time.'

'Hey cheeky, I'm not that kind of girl,' Mandy giggled, knowing full well that she was, as she hitched up her skirt a little to show her tanned legs.

Mandy invited Chris inside, knowing that her mother would be at work. No sooner were they through the front door, than she grabbed him and kissed his eager lips with her hungry mouth. Chris had been dreaming about this moment and it was even better than he'd imagined. The pair raced upstairs to Mandy's room, where he ripped open her blouse to reveal what had to be, the best pair of tits he had even seen. He thought his pants were going to explode and he knew he had to have her there and then. The vision of Mandy's buxom breasts bouncing up and down whilst she rode him, was too much for Chris, and with one final thrust they both climaxed together.

Lying in an exhausted heap, Chris suddenly began to feel guilty. He loved Shelley and he'd hardly given her a second thought. They had a good marriage and a great sex life, but he just couldn't help the hold that Mandy had over him. He made a vow to himself that sleeping with Mandy had to be a one off, and now he'd got it out of his system, it couldn't ever be allowed to happen again.

That, however, was three months ago, and they'd been sleeping together on a regular basis ever since.

Chapter 4

Picking up her suitcase, Tina took one last look at the peach and grey decorated bedroom she'd shared with her husband. She felt numb. She used to love this little terraced house, but now she hated it, along with all its painful memories.

She afforded herself a painful smile as she remembered how happy and full of hope she was when they first moved in on a frosty day in January 1984. The young couple had only been together for five months, but Tina had been so excited about their future. With their wedding date quickly approaching and the new life growing inside her, Tina Firth couldn't have been happier. It certainly wasn't the way she'd always planned her wedding would be, but she was sure everything would be perfect, and that her parents would eventually come around to the idea.

Her mother had been furious upon hearing about her impending pregnancy. 'You bleeding what? Run that by me again young lady,' Beryl Firth had shrieked, staring at her daughter, as though she had grown another head. 'Donald, Donald, you better get in here, now. Donald!'

'What's all the commotion, woman?' Donald Firth grumbled, shuffling into the kitchen in his string vest, peering over his glasses, with the Racing Post and a biro in hand.

'Oh God, Donald, she's only gone and gotten herself bloody pregnant by that flamin' idiot she's going out with,' Beryl cried, shaking her head in dismay. 'I'm presuming it is that bloody wide boy and not some other fool you've got yourself involved with?'

'Of course, it bloody well is, Mother. What do you think I am, some sort of tart?' Tina retorted, rolling her eyes.

'Hey, don't be so bloody cheeky to your mother, ya brash little mare,' Donald responded, sternly. 'You're not too big for a bloody good hiding.'

Tina knew her Dad's words were empty threats and that he was only trying to save face in front of her mother. She could, however, see the disappointment in his eyes, and for that much she was sorry.

Donald was a hard-working man, who always put his family first. Tina loved him dearly. She was the apple of his eye and she hated hurting him. She thought the world of her mother too, but theirs was a love-hate relationship. They were far too alike, and their slanging matches could be heard at the other end of the street, when they were in full swing.

'So, what do you presume you're going to do about your belly full of arms and legs?' Beryl huffed, standing there in her apron with her arms folded.

Tina suddenly realised the seriousness of the matter, but nerves made her want to laugh as she took in the look on her mothers' face. She resembled a bull waiting to charge. From seeing pictures of her mother in her younger days, Tina knew she bore an uncanny resemblance to her. But twenty-seven years of marriage and three kids had taken their toll on Beryl Firth. Tina vowed she would never end up the same way.

'So, what are you going to do about this mess then?' Beryl repeated. 'And where the bloody hell, is he, your wonderful boyfriend? He's gotten you in the family way, yet he's not even here to face the music with you, is he?'

Replying in a much smaller voice, Tina suddenly felt foolish. 'He's on a stag do, and we thought it would be better if we both spoke to our parents alone,' she muttered.

'Well he'll be attending his own bloody stag do very soon,' Beryl shrieked, 'cause I'm not having you bringing shame on this family. Do you hear me, lady?' And with that Beryl broke down in tears.

Donald cradled his wife in his arms, gently stroking her hair until her sobs subsided.

Chapter 5

Shelley stared down at the tea and toast her mother Carole had placed before her.

'C'mon, love, it's going cold. You've got to start eating something.'

'I can't, Mum. I just can't stomach anything.' Shelley looked up at her mum with tear-filled eyes. She seemed to have been crying for five days solid, showing no signs of stopping.

After finding her husband in bed with his bit on the side, she'd run the mile to her mum's in her bare feet. Arriving in a hysterical state. Carole Barnes had thought her daughter had been in some sort of accident or, even worse, been attacked. It was a good five minutes before she could get any sense out of her. On hearing the full story, Carole couldn't believe her ears.

'The two-timing little rat. How wrong can you be about someone?' she said aloud.

Carole had always thought the sun shone out of Chris's educated backside. She was so proud of how well, her Shelley had done for herself and never missed an opportunity to brag to her friends at the bingo about her youngest daughter, her son-in-law, and their beautiful home on the new housing estate. She was, however, going to be keeping this little snippet of information to herself. Hopefully, it was just a stupid mistake that Shelley could forgive him for. She would soon take him back and in the future, her husband would learn to keep his overactive dick in his pants. Although Carole hated seeing her daughter upset, she felt that Shelley was dragging it out a touch, and that she could do with getting her arse back up to her little palace, to sort this sorry mess out.

The kitchen door burst open and in came Shelley's sister Jackie, with her four-year-old twins, Ben and Carly Ann.

'Aunty Shelley,' shrieked Carly Ann, running up to her. Will you play Barbie dolls with me?'

Shelley loved her little niece and nephew like they were her own, but right now she couldn't even be bothered to eat, never mind play.

'Not today darling, but I'll play with you next time.'

Carly Ann was like a miniature version of Shelley and Jackie and, even at four years old, she knew when something wasn't as it should be. Reaching up, she gave Shelley a big hug which made Shelley start crying again.

'Come on you two,' said Carole, beckoning to the children. 'Let's go in the front room and I'll put some cartoons on for you.'

Four years older than Shelley, Jackie was very similar in her looks but not as striking. She was like a watered-down version of her younger sister. She was also considerably heavier since getting married and having the twins. She'd married Kevin Jenkins, her childhood sweetheart, when they were just nineteen. Kev worked at the local paint factory, putting in all the hours God sent to feed and clothe his family. They didn't have a pot to piss in, but Jackie and Kev were as happy as any young family could be. Shelley had always been glad that she was with someone ambitious like Chris and not a plodder like Kev, but right now she'd trade Jackie's life for hers any day of the week.

'Any updates, Shell?' Jackie asked.

Shelley shook her head miserably. The first two days that Shelley had been at her mum's, Chris had been ringing the house phone non-stop. Her dad, Gerry, had told him in no uncertain terms to piss off, and that he'd be in for a good hiding if he showed his face around there again.

That was never going to happen; Gerry couldn't fight his way out of a paper bag, but he was defending his daughter's honour and for that Shelley was grateful. She'd felt as though she never wanted to face Chris again, but for the last three days she'd heard nothing at all from him, and she was beginning to panic. She loved him so much her heart ached, and without him, she felt as though it was actually breaking. She missed his smile and his voice and of course, the affection they shared.

Gerry came into the kitchen to see if there was a cup of tea going spare and whilst she had them all together in the same room, Shelley decided it was time to say her piece.

'I'm going to take him back.'

'What? Are you bloody mad?' Jackie stared in disbelief. 'Oh Shelley, don't, you'll regret it. He'll do it again,' she continued. 'Once a cheat always a cheat.'

'Over my dead body you are,' Gerry chipped in. 'You can't just give in, and forgive him for such an indiscretion,' he added, sounding concerned.

'Er, excuse me Gerry Barnes, but you'd have been down the road long ago, if I'd never forgiven you, for your bloody indiscretions. Have you forgotten that?'

Sheepishly, Gerry looked at Carole and knew he'd be wise to shut his trap and leave the women to it. He realised his opinion wouldn't count anyway. Picking up his builder's tea, he shuffled back to his greenhouse.

'Look Jackie, if the girl's made her mind up then we should respect her decision,' Carole said, putting her arm round her daughter. 'She loves Chris and that beautiful little home of hers. She'd be giving up so much if she just walks away without fighting for it. Yes, he's been a silly little git, but I'm sure it was just a stupid mistake.'

Shelley smiled up at her mum and decided there and then that the next time Chris rang she would arrange to meet him, to talk over their relationship. As if on cue, the shrill bell of the telephone startled them all. Carole went to the hall to answer it. Holding it up, she shouted,

'Shelley, it's for you. It's Chris.'

Chapter 6

Tina was afraid that on the mention of marriage, Darren would run a mile, but she was pleasantly surprised to find that he was truly happy to make an honest woman of her. What Tina didn't know, was that Darren had set out to make her his own from the first night they'd met. Wanting her to become his personal property – and what better way to do it than by getting her knocked up? Having never been a fan of condoms, Darren had refused point blank to wear one. When they were intimate, he assured Tina that withdrawing was just as effective. Darren had also insisted that Tina shouldn't consider going on the pill, telling her how his sister had put on loads of weight since she'd been on it. Tina had no intentions of losing her svelte figure and was more than happy to agree to whatever Darren wanted. She loved him so much and would do almost anything to keep him happy.

Her hottest topic of conversation with Shelley had immediately been the new love in her life. It was Darren this and Darren that, and if Shelley herself hadn't been so wrapped up in her own love for Chris, she might have started getting a little pissed off with it. She was really pleased that Tina was happy and in love, but she wasn't altogether Darren's biggest fan. She thought him a cocky lout, and she didn't like the way she'd spotted him eyeing up other women. Not wanting to upset her friend, Shelley hadn't mentioned this to Tina, but secretly she hoped that her best friend would soon see sense and ditch him, before things got too serious.

Upon hearing the bombshell that Tina had just dropped, she now feared it was now a little too late for that.

'How far gone are you'? Shelley asked, still in shock.

'About seven or eight weeks,' Tina grinned.

'Are you going to keep it?' Shelley quizzed.

'Of course, I bloody am.' Tina replied, wide eyed. 'God, Shelley, I thought of all people you'd be happy for me.'

Shelley's face broke into a false smile. 'I am, love, honestly, I am. It was just the last thing I expected to hear, that's all,' she replied, trying to sound more convincing.

'Well there's more,' grinned Tina. 'We're getting married at the register office, three weeks on Saturday!' she squealed excitedly. 'It's a bit of a rush job I know, but they had a cancellation and I wanted to get married before I start to show,' she continued, unable to hide her glee. 'Shelley…' she paused, smiling at her best friend in anticipation. 'I want to ask…would you be my chief bridesmaid? Say you will,' she pleaded.

'Bloody hell, Ti, you don't do things by halves do you? Of course, I will. I'd be honoured.' Shelley grabbed her friend and hugged her tightly. Tina thought it was because she was as excited and as happy as she was, but Shelley's face couldn't hide the worry she felt, as she anticipated what the future held for Tina.

Chapter 7

Sitting on the single bed listening to the top 40 and sharing a bottle of white wine, Mandy giggled with her friend Judy.

'I can't believe she walked in on you, whilst you were at it with her husband!' Judy exclaimed, taking a gulp of her wine.

'Well we weren't actually on the job, we'd just finished,' chuckled Mandy.

'Still, you were naked right, lying there, in her bed?' Judy stared, wide eyed in disbelief.

'Well yeah, we were I suppose,' Mandy shrugged.

'Bloody hell, that must've been a shock for the poor cow. And she'd never even suspected a thing before that?' Judy asked, shaking her head in disbelief.

'Nope. She thought he was the perfect husband! Cheating bastard,' Mandy sighed, nonchalantly. 'They're all the fucking same. You're better off on your own, Jude,' she added, raising her glass.

'I suppose,' Judy sighed, pouring herself a top up.

Judy was a plain girl, with a rather plump frame and straggly, mousy, shoulder-length hair. She was not exactly what you'd call a head turner. She'd been best pals with Mandy for years and would do anything for the glamourous friend, that she was in total awe of. Whenever they went out it was Mandy, with her good looks, fabulous boobs, and cracking figure that got all the male attention, whilst Judy was left in the background to chat awkwardly to the weird mate. So, she'd resigned herself to being Mandy's plain friend, and she assumed that's how everyone else saw her.

Judy was always there for Mandy at the drop of a hat, whilst Mandy would shit on Judy from a great height, if a better offer came her way. There were plenty of times that Mandy would ring Judy up at the last minute, letting her down for a date with some bloke. Never holding it against her, Judy would say it was okay, and tell Mandy to go and have a good time.

'How are you getting on at the slimming club, Jude?' Mandy asked, looking over at her friend pityingly.

'Yeah, two pounds off this week. But this wine's not going to do me any good, is it?'

'Oh, you've got to have some fun, babes, but yes, I agree, we do need to start being good if we're going to look hot in our bikinis this summer when we go to Ibiza. I'm going to have to stop eating junk, I'm getting a right gut on me,' she stared down at her tiny waistline.

As much as Judy loved Mandy, it really annoyed her when she came out with such comments. She'd look good in a bin bag, never mind a bikini. Judy was dreading the holiday they had planned, knowing she'd resemble a stranded whale next to Mandy on the beach.

'Hey, have you had any replies back from the modelling agencies?' Judy quizzed, changing the subject.

'D'ya know, Jude, I've not heard a dicky bird. You did put the correct postage on, didn't you'? Judy worked at the Post Office and Mandy knew she could send her modelling pictures without having to pay for the stamps, so she'd left it in Judy's capable hands.

Judy nodded. 'Yeah, course I did.'

'Well, I really don't know why I've heard nothing then.' Mandy shrugged. 'It's been weeks since we sent them and those pictures Lenny did looked dead professional, even if I do say so myself. Lenny said I was a natural,' she added, flicking her hair from her shoulder with her hand.

Lenny Dobbs was a creep; he'd done photography at college and, to be honest, he would've told Mandy that the sky was green, and the grass was blue if it meant he'd get to take pictures of her. When Mandy had asked him to take some topless shots to send off to glamour model agencies, Lenny had been only too happy to oblige. Explaining that she didn't really have much cash to pay him with, but that she'd make it worth his while, Lenny had felt a tightening in his jeans. Licking his lips and smiling to himself, displaying teeth that resembled a rack of burnt toast, he'd arranged a time and place with her right there and then. The venue was his front room and the time was to be the very next day.

As a photographer, Lenny was well equipped, but when it came to experience, he was a little more than vague, claiming to Mandy that he'd taken lots of glamour shots before, which was complete and utter bollocks. Mandy wasn't shy in the least and had no problem revealing what the good Lord had blessed her with. Lenny did his best topless photographer impression, telling Mandy to pout, then look shy, then give him her best, come and get me look. Mandy's tits were superb. Lenny had never seen breasts of that size that stood to attention as hers did.

After the session, Mandy handed Lenny a fiver and when he protested at how much the development would cost him, she'd dropped to her knees, taking out his already, rock solid cock. She then proceeded to give him the best, deep throated, blowjob that he could hope to receive that decade. Satisfied with his payment, Lenny told Mandy the pictures would be ready in a week and that if she ever wanted any more taking, then he was her man. Advising her that it was always good to have an up-to-date portfolio. Mandy had smiled wryly; she was no fool. This little photo session would hopefully be the first step to catapulting her into the fame and fortune, that she craved.

Chapter 8

With the wedding just over a week away, all Tina could do was think about hers and Darren's new life together. She was so excited to wear her ivory, satin wedding dress and to experience what was sure to be the best day of her life.

Tonight, was their hen and stag nights, and even though she couldn't drink, Tina was really looking forward to seeing Shelley and the rest of her mates. Deciding to go to Rochdale, the girls met up in the Flying Horse and the night went on from there. They all had a great time and danced to everything from Karma Chameleon, to Uptown Girl. But in the early stages of pregnancy, tiredness soon got the better of Tina and was home and in bed by 11:30.

In Oldham, Darren's stag night was quite a different affair. His mates had decided that as his last night out as a single man, he deserved a treat. As they all stood laughing and joking in the Hare & Hounds, a woman police constable approached the group.

'I'm looking for Darren Doyle,' she announced, with a tone of authority.

Placing his pint on the bar, a worried look clouded over Darren's face. He'd done a few dodgy deals in his time, but he couldn't for the life of him, think of why the, law would be coming in here for him. On his stag do of all nights. Then suddenly he twigged as he saw his mates sniggering. Realising that the WPC was flashing a little too much chest and thigh, he began to grin.

'Argh, you got me, you set of bastards,' he laughed to his mates, as the music to Irene Cara's Flashdance began.

The stripogram sat him down and handcuffed him to a chair, before proceeding to dance sexily in front of him. She began to strip, whilst all Darren's mates chanted a chorus of 'get your tits out for the lads.'

As Donna the stripper wiggled her pert little arse in front of Darren in her high heels and suspenders, he could feel himself getting hard. Even under the influence of alcohol, Darren Doyle never had problems getting a stiffy.

When the time came for Donna to remove her bra, all that could be heard in the Hare & Hounds was 'off off

off off'. Donna flung her bra off to reveal a fine pair of bouncy breasts, and as she leaned forward and rubbed them in Darren's face, she gave him a kiss on the cheek, wishing him well on his forthcoming marriage. Taking a bow to the crowd and with all the lads still cheering for more, she blew them all a kiss and was on her way.

After a few more drinks, the lads decided to go on to a club, and with the night's earlier show, of tits and arse, Darren was in the mood for a little bit of female company, other than that of his pregnant wife to be.

He soon spotted a petite redhead and had been watching her dance for the last ten minutes. Knowing it would be a piece of cake, Darren went over and turned on his usual charm. As luck would have it, her parents were away that weekend and it wasn't long before they were sharing a taxi back to her place.

Arriving home at six in the morning, Darren informed Tina that the lads had locked him in one of their garden sheds as a stag prank. Tina bought the whole story, and as far as Darren was concerned, no harm had been done.

-

The day of the wedding arrived. Tina stayed at her mum's the night before the big day and her last words to

Darren had been, not to be late and that she loved him, and she couldn't wait to become his wife.

She was so nervous she could hardly stomach any breakfast. But Shelley, who'd also stayed at Tina's mum's, told her she had to eat something, that it was going to be a long day, and that she needed to keep her strength up for the baby's sake.

'Bloody hell, Shell, I'm a bundle of nerves. I could do with a ciggie right now.'

'No fags or booze for you, lady,' said Shelley, smiling and playfully wagging her finger at her friend. 'I bet this wasn't what you thought your wedding day would be like, hey, Ti?'

'Nah, it's not, but you know, Shell, I love him so much and I'm so happy. I wouldn't have it any other way.'

Shelley was in turmoil. She'd heard through her cousin Bryn, who was on the stag do, that Darren's 'being locked in the shed story' was a pile of crap, and that he'd been seen doing a disappearing act in the early hours, with a pretty little redhead. But Shelley didn't know the full extent of what had happened or how truthful the story was. So, she didn't feel that she had enough evidence to say anything to Tina. Who was she to burst her best mate's bubble without any hard facts?

A couple of hours later, Tina came downstairs in her wedding gown and everyone turned to stare.

Clasping her hand to her mouth, Beryl gasped. 'Oh my god, girl, you look an absolute picture, you really do! Donald, Donald, pass me a bloody tissue before all this makeup gets cried off.'

Beryl still wasn't happy about the situation, but she'd now come around to the idea of becoming a grandma and, even though she'd never admit it, she was secretly looking forward to it. She still couldn't stand the sight of Darren but the fact that he had readily agreed to marry Tina, after getting her in the family way, had at least earned him some brownie points. Little did she know that Darren had his own reasons for wanting Tina as his wife and getting her away from her family and her overbearing mother was one of them.

The cars took Beryl, Shelley and the rest of the bridesmaids to St James's church, whilst Tina was left alone with her dad, to wait for the Daimler.

'You okay, sweetheart?' Donald asked softly, putting an arm around his only daughter.

'Dad. Watch my veil,' Tina cried, turning to look at her dad and catching a tear forming in his eye. 'Oh Dad, I'm fine, honestly,' she smiled. 'I'm really happy. I love

Darren and I know how much he loves me. We're going to be perfect together.'

He nodded. 'Listen, sweetheart, I love you. You're the most precious thing in my life and your happiness is everything to me. If he ever hurts you, he'll have me to deal with.'

'I know, Dad, and I love you too. Now come on, the car's here.' Tina paused, then turned to him and smiled. 'Thanks, Dad.'

The reception was in full swing and all the usual wedding songs were playing. The DJ, Dave 'Decks' Davies, one of Darren's mates, was taking requests and everyone seemed to be having a great time. Everyone, that was, except Tina. She was sober as a judge, her feet were killing her, and she'd hardly seen Darren all day. He'd done yet another disappearing act and she felt as though he might as well be married to his mates. He'd turned up to the church late and her car needed to do two runs around the block, before she could get out. When she got to the altar, she was mortified to find that Darren was red-eyed and stinking of booze. She was sure the vicar could smell it and she was so, embarrassed.

Right, she thought, *I'm going to find him, and he can spend some time with his new wife.* The first dance would be anytime soon and the last thing she needed was her mother questioning his whereabouts.

Walking into the foyer, Tina spotted Darren chatting to a couple of young girls who must've only been about seventeen. It was clear they were hanging on his every word and, feeling annoyed, Tina's pregnancy hormones went into overdrive.

'There you are,' she called, sharply. Darren spun round to find a, none-too-happy Tina with her hands on her hips. 'What's going on here?' she questioned. 'I've been looking all over for you.'

'Sorry, babes, I was just getting the latest on Finchy. You know, my mate, who's in the army? This is his kid sister,' he said, nodding towards the blonde, doe-eyed teenager.

'Well, I don't really give a shit who she is. You're, supposed to be with me, and I've seen nothing of you all night.'

With that the two young girls scuttled off into the ladies. Darren was not at all happy at his new wife's outburst, and he walked over to her with a face like thunder. Grabbing her roughly by the arm, he moved his face to within an inch of hers. So close that she could smell the stale beer on his breath.

'You ever fucking embarrass me or speak to me like that again, and I'll knock your fucking teeth down your throat, do you get that?'

Stunned, tears immediately welled up in Tina's eyes and she quickly nodded. She'd never known Darren to get angry with her before and she immediately blamed herself for pushing him too far; after all, he was only catching up with his mate's sister. At that moment, Shelley and Chris walked into the foyer.

'Oy mate. Get your hands off her, that's no way to treat her,' Chris called out, with concern in his voice.

Darren turned, his face twisted in a snarl, seeking out whoever'd got the guts to tell him how he should treat his own wife.

'Who the fuck, do you think you're talking to, you, snobby ponce?' Darren snapped, pacing over towards a suddenly very nervous Chris. 'I've seen the way you look down your nose at us, thinking you're better than we are. Well let me tell you, mate,' Darren glared, poking Chris in the chest with his finger. 'Yer not. And, if you ever interfere with me and my wife again, you'll wish you'd never met me. Now fuck off home, this is my wedding and I don't want the likes of you here. And you can take her with you,' he nodded towards Shelley.

Shelley was in total shock and gestured to Tina.

'Are you okay, Tina, do you want us to go?'

Tina, now staring at the floor, shook her head. 'No, but I don't want any trouble, so maybe it's best.'

Shelley was absolutely livid: but for her friend's sake, she didn't want to antagonise the drink-fuelled Darren. So, with that, she and Chris left.

One of Tina's mates popped her head around the door.

'Come on, you two. DJ Dave is calling for you. It's the first dance!'

Darren turned to Tina and, stroked her face.

'C'mon, babes, let me have this dance with my gorgeous wife. It's just you and me. Just the way it should be.'

Tina uneasily half-smiled as Darren led her to the dancefloor and held her tightly, whilst they danced to True, by Spandau Ballet.

After they got home, Darren spent most of the night vomiting and the rest of it asleep on the bathroom floor. Tina woke up early the next morning to feel a warm, stickiness between her legs. As she threw back the blood-drenched covers she screamed for Darren's help.

Later that day at the hospital, the doctor confirmed that the baby had miscarried. Tina cried solidly for a week.

Chapter 9

Shelley's nerves were shot. She felt as though she was going on a first date, not meeting up with the husband she'd known for years. Chris had suggested she came to the house, but she still felt the situation was a little too raw for that.

Even though she'd already decided she was going to take him back, she didn't want to give him that impression. No, she was going to make him work for it, with plenty of grovelling.

She looked at herself in the mirror and was pleased with what she saw. Even though she'd lost her appetite, she hadn't lost too much weight and still had her curves. She wasn't blessed with much up top, but what she did have suited her slender frame, and Chris had always said, that more than a handful was a waste. Choosing to wear some tailored white shorts that were very much in fashion and a candy pink off the shoulder T-shirt, she finished the look with some peep toe heels, which accentuated her shapely legs. Her streaked blonde hair was piled up high with tendrils hanging down the sides of her heart-shaped face, and the back of her head.

On entering the kitchen, Carole gasped. 'Oh Shelley, you look absolutely lovely, you really do. When he sees you, he'll realise what an absolute idiot he's been,' she said, shaking her head and raising her eyes to the ceiling. 'Sometimes though, you have to make the effort girl. Remind 'em of what they've got at home. Every time I see you these days, you're in those bloody ski pants and your hairdressing tunic,' she sighed.

'Oh, bloody hell, Mum,' Jackie chipped in, shooting her mum a look. 'Talk about a back handed compliment.' She looked over fondly at her younger sister. 'You do look lovely though, Shelley, and even though I don't really agree with you taking Chris back, I'll always stand by your decision. Just remember, you are beautiful, inside and out, and he's lucky to have you, not the other way around.'

Shelley set off on the short walk to Dunwood park, where she'd agreed to meet Chris. It was a glorious day and she remembered fondly the times they used to meet there in the early days when they were dating. They would take picnics and go for long walks and sometimes go into the woods off the beaten track, where Chris would make love to her. He was so good with his hands and knew exactly how to please her. She'd had a couple of boyfriends before Chris, but no one had ever made her feel the way he did. All Shelley wanted was her life back with her husband, exactly how it was before.

As she approached the bench where Chris was sat waiting, her heart lurched, and all the old feelings came flooding back. He looked just as good as she remembered, in his Don Johnson, turned up chinos and moccasins. Shelley loved this man so much and she needed to have him back in her life, so she could be the wife he needed her to be. She would love him with every ounce of her being and do her utmost best to make sure he never wanted to look at another woman again. But first, she needed to be cool, calm and collected. She must make him think he was on the verge of losing her forever.

'Hi,' she said, softly.

Chris looked up and smiled at her. 'Hi, please – please sit,' he stammered, nervously. 'You look beautiful, really stunning,' he said, meaning every word. Taking her by the hand, Chris looked deep into her eyes. 'Shelley...' He paused. 'I can't tell you how sorry I am about what happened. It was a really shitty thing for me to do and it must've been such a shock for you, walking in on me and Mandy like that.'

Shelley was a little taken aback. Yes, she'd expected Chris to be extremely apologetic, but she certainly hadn't expected him to bring up that tart's name, as though she actually meant something to him.

'Yes, it was an awful thing to see, Chris, and if I'm honest I'm still having nightmares about it. I don't know if I'll ever get over it,' she sniffed.

Holding her hands in his, he caressed the surface of her skin with his thumb, staring down for an age before he spoke again.

'I can't tell you how ashamed I am, putting you through that,' he said. 'I'm really, really sorry, I honestly never meant to hurt you.' Pausing again, Chris took a deep breath before he continued. 'Look, Shelley, I've been doing a lot of thinking. I realise that you're unable to make the mortgage payments by yourself, so I am prepared to buy you out. I've passed my probation at work and I've been given a pay rise, so I can take the house on by myself, no problem.'

Shelley looked at him in total shock. This was the last thing she'd been expecting to hear.

'What are you saying, Chris?' she gasped.

He turned to face her. 'I think we should get a divorce, babe,' he said, in a voice no more than a whisper. 'I love you, I do, but I love you more as a friend, you know, like a sister. I think it's for the best, babe.' He shrugged.

Swiftly pulling her hand away from his, the usually placid Shelley cried out, 'Don't you fucking "babe" me! You cheat on me, want to turf me out of my own home, then have the cheek to ask me for a divorce? You're a fucking class act you are, Chris Charlton. Then you have the fucking nerve to tell me I'm more like a friend or a sister to you?' she bellowed, shaking her head in disbelief.

Shelley's voice was getting louder and Chris was well aware that passers-by were staring at them.

'No wonder you wanted me to meet you at the house,' she continued. 'Was that so I could pick up the rest of my things and you'd never have to clap eyes on me again? Or is she there getting your tea ready, using all my stuff?' With that image torturing her mind, Shelley broke down.

Chris put his arm around her, in a bid to comfort her, as she sobbed.

'How could you do this to me, Chris? I thought we were forever. What did I do wrong?'

He shrugged awkwardly. 'You did nothing wrong. I just love her. I can't help it.'

On hearing this last statement, Shelley saw red. Pushing away Chris's arm she got up from the bench and grabbed a slush puppy from a youth who was walking past.

Apologising to the startled young teen, she turned and threw the lot over Chris's head. With that, Shelley turned and ran the short route back to her mum's, with the devastating realisation that her marriage to Chris was over for good.

Chapter 10

Tina dragged the case with all her worldly belongings in, down the narrow staircase of the small terraced house, resting it by the front door. Walking into the kitchen diner, she fished in her handbag for a small slip of paper. Staring at the name and number on it, she took a deep breath before reaching for the telephone.

As soon as she dialled the number, she replaced the receiver. Her heart was hammering in her chest and even though she knew that making this call would be the first step to changing her life for the better, she was still scared. No longer was she the confident, self-assured young woman she had been only a couple of years before. A shadow of her former self, she was constantly living on her nerves, in fear of what mood her husband might come home in. Taking a deep breath, she redialled the number on the scrap of paper, that she'd kept folded and hidden away in the inside pocket of her handbag.

Upon hearing the soothing voice on the other end of the line, Tina immediately relaxed and knew that contacting the domestic abuse, women's refuge had been the right and only option left to her.

As she waited in the kitchen for her taxi to arrive, she watched the minutes tick by slowly. She had tried so hard to be the best wife she could be to Darren. Running around, picking up after him, whilst maintaining all the domestic chores, as well as holding down a full-time job at the factory. She had run herself ragged. Being made redundant a few weeks ago had meant that money was tight, and Darren's moods were even blacker. Without her family and friends around, Tina was so isolated, feeling like a prisoner in her own home. She cooked all the meals and waited on her husband hand and foot, whilst Darren didn't lift a finger.

Looking around the kitchen, Tina shuddered as she remembered the first time, she fully realised that Darren was not the charming man she'd thought she'd married.

As he'd walked home from work that night, Darren had called in to the Moulders for a pint, which had turned into five. It was March, but the weather was particularly cold for the time of year and the windows on the parked cars he passed were already beginning to freeze up. He was swaying a little as he walked due to the alcohol and the fact that he'd had nothing to eat. As he entered the little two-up, two-down he shared with Tina, the heat immediately hit him, and the smell of food made his hunger go into overdrive.

Tina had no way of knowing what time Darren would arrive home from work. Each day varied, depending on how many beers he fancied. She'd once rung the pub to ask him if he was going to be long, and what time could she expect him home that night. Later, he had told her in no uncertain terms that if she ever rang him at the pub again, she'd be more than sorry.

Lately, Tina had become increasingly more nervous around Darren. One minute he was the perfect husband, loving and gentle, and the next minute his temper would rage, and he was like a completely different person. Never the shrinking violet, Tina had always been able to hold her own in an argument, but she was wary of pushing her luck with Darren. His temper scared her and although she was sure he'd never hurt her, she didn't want to provoke him. She'd seen his anger flare on several occasions, with other men in the pub, and she never wanted to be on the receiving end.

After being married a couple of months, the honeymoon period was officially over. Tina was still upset over losing their baby and, emotionally, she was not coping well.

She cried most days, and Darren didn't understand why she was still so upset.

'It wasn't even a proper baby,' he scoffed. 'How can you cry so much over something that's not even formed? There'll be plenty of time for more sprogs.'

Shelley had called round to see her a few times since the miscarriage, to offer her support, but after the incident between Darren and Chris at the wedding, things seemed strained between the two women. Shelley knew Darren wasn't happy with her visiting; he totally blanked her when she called round, making it quite clear that she wasn't welcome. In Shelley's view he acted like a caveman, with his old-fashioned ways. Not like her Chris, who was happy to help with the housework. Chris was also openly loving and caring, whilst Darren behaved like a chauvinistic brute.

On one visit, whilst Shelley was having a cuppa with Tina, he barged into the living room.

'Haven't you washed my fucking Levis, Tina?' he bellowed.

Tina looked embarrassed at being chastised in front of her best friend.

'I'm sorry, Darren, I didn't know you wanted them,' she answered, sheepishly.

'It's Friday friggin' night, of course I want them. You're fucking useless, you are,' he tutted, storming upstairs to find another pair of jeans.

He then slammed the front door shut on his way out, without even saying goodbye. Shelley was dumbstruck and couldn't believe what she had just witnessed.

'Bloody hell, Ti, you're not going to put up with him talking to you like that, are you?'

'He doesn't mean it,' Tina replied, blushing. 'He's had a really stressful week at work. He's just letting off some steam.'

'Well don't be letting him treat you like shit, it's not right. The Tina I know wouldn't put up with that.' Shelley smiled at her friend to try to ease her embarrassment. 'Hey, you know what you need? A good night out with your mates. I know it's been tough lately, you know, since the baby and all, but I think a night out will do you the world of good. What d'ya say?'

Tina smiled. 'You know what, Shell, I think that's a great idea. Speak to the girls and we'll arrange it for next Friday.'

'Good girl. It'll do you a power of good.' Shelley winked.

But when Tina mentioned to Darren that she was planning to go out the following Friday, he put the blocks on it.

'Tina, you're a married woman now, leave all that drinking and clubbing to your slaggy mates.'

'My mates aren't slaggy, none of them. They're decent girls,' Tina retorted.

'What, with their skirts up their arses? Oh yeh, really decent that, in't it?' he sneered. 'Tina, I've told you, that Shelley is a bad influence and she's trying to turn you against me.' Softening his voice, he continued, looking deep into her eyes. 'I'm your husband and you should be standing by me, instead of choosing your mates,' said Darren, attempting to seem hurt.

'Okay,' Tina relented. 'If it means so much to you, I'll call the night out off and maybe do it some other time.'

Darren smiled stroking the side of her hair. 'You know I'm only looking out for you, babes. I love you so much and I don't want anyone trying to come between us.' Turning away, Darren smiled to himself, triumphantly.

By the time he came home that night at 8.30pm, Darren's Holland's meat and potato pie, chips and peas were a little on the dried-up, side. Tina had tried her best to judge when to start preparing his meal, but as she had no way of knowing what time he'd roll in, she had to just hope for the best. If Darren came home and his meal wasn't ready, she knew he'd start a row and the last thing she needed was him in a foul mood.

'I'm just doing the gravy, love,' Tina said, smiling. *Keep it light-hearted*, she thought.

She'd long since given up asking him why he was home so late. She figured if she was in a good mood with him, he'd reciprocate it. But Darren was already in a bad mood that evening; he'd lost on the slot machine and he'd lost big time. After ordering his first pint, he put a pound in the slot machine and straight away won a tenner.

'Get in, you, beauty,' he'd said, punching the air. But three hours later, after putting the tenner back in the machine, along with another £60, Darren had accepted defeat and given up. Slamming the dregs of his last pint on the bar, he'd walked out into the cold night air to make his way home.

Tina placed the meal in front of him as he sat at the small pine dining table. As she reached to get him the jug of gravy off the side, he erupted.

'What the fuck do you call this shit?' With her back to him, Tina froze, sensing Darren's anger. 'I can't eat this shit, it's dry as a fucking bone,' he barked, his voice getting angrier.

'I'm sorry, Darren, you're later than normal and I was trying to keep it warm for you,' Tina tried to explain. 'Maybe if you pour the gravy on it, it'll be okay,' she nervously suggested.

Lifting the jug from the table, Darren paused, just shaking his head at the plate in front of him. Then, slamming the jug down on the table, spilling the gravy and making Tina jump with fright, he bellowed,

'Are you for fucking real? You stupid bitch.'

Tina took a deep breath and, mustering some courage from somewhere, answered him back.

'Well if I knew what time you were going to come home then maybe your food would be fit to bloody eat!'

Almost quicker than her mind could comprehend, Tina felt herself being lifted off the floor, as Darren's large hand wrapped around her neck. Her head was slammed backwards against the tall cupboard behind her – the pain was instantaneous, and with Darren's menacing face contorted in front of hers, Tina had never before felt such sheer terror. He then grabbed the back of her head and shoved her sideways, onto the open door. She fell, banging the side of her face on the hard frame. Falling to the floor in a daze, she then felt the full force of Darren's boot in her right kidney.

Frightened for her life, Tina curled herself into a tight ball, waiting for Darren to stick the boot in once again. But instead, he crouched down beside her, speaking in a low and menacing voice.

'If you ever dare to speak to me like that again, Tina, I'm telling you now, I'll make you, fucking sorry. Do you hear me?' And with that he smacked her around the head with the flat of his large palm, before standing up, grabbing his coat and slamming the door on his way out.

Tina was brought to her senses by the beep of the taxi outside the house. She rushed to open the front door as the taxi driver took her small case and put it in the boot of the car. Without a backward glance, Tina closed the front door, scanning up and down the street to check if any of the neighbours had spotted her. No one was about and, as the taxi pulled away, Tina slumped back into the seat, taking a deep, relieved breath.

The cab stereo was playing 'Invisible' by Alison Moyet, and as she listened to the words, which echoed most of her time spent with Darren, a silent tear ran down her cheek. She felt relief at the nightmare she'd escaped from, but also a deep sadness at the failure of the marriage she'd tried so very hard to save.

Chapter 11

Riding the, 403 bus home from work, Judy Smythe could hear her stomach rumbling. She was starving and couldn't wait for her tea. She'd been trying so hard with her diet, but she wasn't really in the zone and was finding it hard to focus, especially as there were always cakes and sweets going around at work. She'd lost 5lbs in three weeks at the slimming club but knew she had at least another two stone to shift if she was going to look half decent on her holiday to Ibiza with Mandy.

The summer weather had been glorious so far, but Judy didn't feel that she could wear the little tops and skirts that her friends were parading around in. When she'd cautiously appeared downstairs in the new summer dress, she'd bought a couple of weeks before, her fourteen-year-old brother Dan, had nearly fallen off his chair laughing at her. His cruel taunts about Moby Dick in a dress had sent Judy fleeing back upstairs in tears and gotten Dan a clout around the head from their mum, Sheila.

Wearing big baggy clothes to hide her frame and with the summer temperature soaring, the bus ride home was a hot one, and Judy was sweltering. She hoped that her mum had prepared them a salad for tea. At a dress size 28, Sheila Smythe would also definitely benefit from it.

Walking through the back door straight into the kitchen, the smell of chips frying instantly hit Judy's nostrils, immediately sending her hunger pangs into overdrive. Looking through the smoked glass oven door, Judy turned to her mum.

'Oh, bloody hell, Mum, not Findus crispy pancakes and chips again! You know I'm on a diet.'

'Listen, lady, if you think I'm cooking different meals for everyone, you've got another think coming,' Sheila Smythe said, wiping her chubby hands on a tea towel.

'Yeah, I know. I'm sorry, Mum, I'm just bloody starving and with the heat today, I thought you might have done us all a nice salad or something,' sighed Judy, sitting down at the kitchen table.

'Judy, love,' her mum said, smiling at her, 'you look lovely as you are. Men don't want skin and bone to cuddle, they want a real woman. Look at me and your dad, he loves my curves. He wouldn't want me any other way,' she said, gesturing at her enormous frame.

Malcolm Smythe was as thin and wiry as Sheila was large. He worked as a delivery driver and his diet consisted of smoking forty Embassy cigarettes a day and drinking copious amounts of strong tea. What Sheila didn't know was that Malcolm had been having an affair with a woman called Brenda from the same council estate, for the past five years. He'd always preferred his women on the larger side, but Sheila had taken it to the extreme. She was now double the size of when he'd married her, and these days, she got a sweat on merely getting herself dressed in the morning. All this was making it increasingly difficult for Malcolm to find anything remotely attractive about her anymore.

Brenda Hodder, meanwhile, was a sweet, timid woman. She'd been a widow for over twenty years. after losing her husband in a motorbike accident. Brenda never made demands, or nagged him, and she was always pleased to see him. So as far as Malcolm Smythe was concerned, life was pretty good.

Sheila served the food and sat down to eat with Judy and her brother. Dan ate like a horse. Luckily for him, he had inherited his father's metabolism and never gained an ounce. With a plate full of buttered bread piled high on the table, it took all the willpower Judy had to refrain from making herself a big fat chip butty.

Halfway through her meal, she glanced up at her mother and watched with disgust as Sheila greedily shovelled large portions into her mouth. Judy saw the grease from the butter dribbling down her mother's chin and the bingo wings on Sheila's fat, flabby arms swing in motion with the cutting of her food. The sad realisation hit Judy like a train; if she carried on eating the same food her mother cooked, that was what she'd have to look forward to, in years to come.

Slowing placing down her knife and fork, Judy made the excuse that she was suddenly feeling unwell. Leaving the table to go to her room, she made her mind up, right there and then, that there was no way that she was going to turn out like her mother.

Like a flick of a switch, Judy's mindset changed. She couldn't carry on this way. Not only did she yearn for a slender frame, she wanted to feel fitter and healthier too. She'd worked hard all year and she was really looking forward to relaxing on holiday. Even if she didn't have Mandy's knockout figure, she knew she could look half decent if she put her mind to it.

Having just a couple of months to go before they jetted off, she now had the drive and determination she needed to succeed. Judy had waited months for this holiday, and she owed it to herself to have a great time. She was no longer dreading it and, who knew, she might even have herself a holiday romance. With that thought in her mind, she smiled to herself and suddenly began to feel truly positive about the future.

Reaching under the bed, she pulled out the A4 brown envelopes containing Mandy's modelling photos. She studied them admiringly. Mandy had such a fantastic figure, with curves in all the right places. Judy had always put her on a pedestal. She longed to look half as good as her friend and now she felt really inspired to push herself, to achieving her goal.

Mandy had entrusted Judy to post the photos out to various modelling agencies, and Judy suddenly began to feel guilty for failing to fulfil her friends request. Mandy continually got what she wanted in life, always coming up smelling of roses.

It had been a tough blow for Judy when her so called best mate began dating Mark Devine. Mandy was aware how much Judy fancied him, but she'd gone out with him anyway. She treated him like dirt, then dropped him from a great height once he'd served his purpose. In fact, that was how she treated Judy on a regular basis, and it hurt.

Even after Mandy ditched Mark, Judy knew he would never look twice at her. Not after he'd sampled the delights of the exquisite Mandy. She wasn't normally vindictive, but Mandy had abused her good nature once too often. She treated people like crap, but still seemed to have it all.

Judy had kept hold of the pictures as payback, but she was beginning to feel guilty. There was no point holding a grudge, and she decided she would post the envelopes the very next day. She was sure that Mandy would get some positive responses, so no real harm had been done.

About an hour later, Dan popped his head around her bedroom door.

'Oy fatty. Your mate big tits is on the phone,' he called out, grinning at his own humour as he ran out of the room, before Judy could chastise him.

Still in her good mood, Judy picked up the phone.

'Hi, Mand,' she almost sang.

There was a long pause before Mandy replied. 'Er, hi Jude, you okay? You had a good day at work?' Mandy enquired. She didn't seem her usual chirpy self, but Judy just thought she'd probably just had a bad day at the office.

'Yeh, I'm good, but I'll be even better eight weeks today, when we're in Ibiza,' Judy squealed excitedly.

There was another long pause from Mandy, then she hit Judy with a blow she wasn't expecting.

'Yeh, er, about the holiday, Judy. Well I, well me and Chris actually, were wondering if you fancied selling him your ticket?'

Judy was stunned, but before she could say anything, Mandy continued to ramble on, about how she felt that Judy wasn't really looking forward to going and how Chris could really do with a break after the split from his wife.

Judy's voice quivered, 'Chris left his wife to be with you, so why does he need a break, when the split was his own doing?' Judy's voice was low, and her lips were beginning to tremble.

'Yeh, well, his wife's being a complete bitch,' Mandy lied. 'She's ringing the house at all hours, demanding money and threatening him with court. You don't know what it's been like for him, Judy. There's, loads of stuff I've not even told you. I actually think he's heading for a breakdown. This holiday could be just what he needs,' Mandy added, trying to sound convincing. 'You know I would never ask you unless it was an emergency, Jude.' There was a long silence between the pair, which Mandy eventually broke. 'Judy. Are you still there?' she asked.

Silent tears were falling down Judy's face, and she tried to compose herself.

'Yeh, yeh I'm still here.'

'So, what do you say, Jude?' Mandy asked, trying not to sound too impatient. 'Me and you can do something else together to make up for it. What d'ya think'?

Judy knew only too well what she thought, but where Mandy was concerned, she could never quite find the right words.

'Okay, that's fine, he can buy my ticket,' she said, replacing the receiver.

As Mandy put the phone down at her end she turned to Chris, throwing her arms around him.

'Yay, we're going to Ibiza, baby!' she shrieked.

Shaking his head, Chris grinned. 'Come here, you sexy little thing,' he purred. 'How the fuck did you pull that off? Your mate must be a right pushover.' He gave Mandy a sly grin. 'You could've won a fucking Oscar for that little performance. Now, get yourself up those stairs where I can take a closer look at that bikini body.'

Judy's mood went from high to low in two minutes flat. Walking into the kitchen and opening the cupboard, she grabbed a full packet of chocolate digestives, which she took straight up to her room. Closing the door behind her, she sat on the bed and let the tears flow.

When she finally dried her eyes, Judy took Mandy's photos and tore them up one by one. There was no way she'd be posting them now, after the stunt Mandy had just pulled. Tearing open the biscuits, she devoured them one by one.

Stuff the fucking diet, she thought. *Who needs a bikini body? Not fucking me, that's for sure!*

Chapter 12

Blasting out Madonna's, 'Like a Virgin' LP, Mandy pouted her full lips in the mirror as she applied her favourite lipstick, Boots 17, Twilight Teaser. Its shimmering lilac shade matched her Rara skirt perfectly. She teamed it with a T-bar crop top that made her ample chest look even bigger, and doing her best Madonna impression, she finished the look with strings of pearls and a diamante encrusted crucifix chain. Slipping into her white court shoes, she admired herself in front of the long mirror.

'Mwah,' she said aloud, blowing herself a kiss. This was an outfit she usually saved for special occasions, but Chris had asked her to meet his mum, so Mandy decided that she wouldn't disappoint.

Chris was woken from his dream by the phone ringing. He ran downstairs naked in a rush to get to it, hoping that it would be Mandy. Picking up the receiver, he answered the phone breathlessly. Unfortunately, it was his mother, Vivien.

'Hello darling, just thought I'd give you a little tinkle and see how my boy is doing.' Vivien's naturally high-pitched voice made Chris's Saturday morning hangover suddenly kick in with full force.

Insisting that Friday was girl's night, Mandy had told Chris in no uncertain terms that she was going out with her mates. So, rather than stay in, Chris also decided he'd make a night of it, with a couple of the old crew, Ross and Shane. They'd been mates since school and had kept in touch through the years. Both lads had been ushers at his wedding to Shelley, and the two of them, like everyone else, thought the couple were made for each other.

Towards the end of the night, things had gotten a little heated between Chris and Ross. Both his mates had told him from the off that they thought he must be mad to have cheated on Shelley. They agreed that she was a lovely girl and gorgeous with it, and that this Mandy he'd told them about had to be something really special for him to give up a girl like Shelley.

At first, Chris had taken it on the chin, as banter, but after a few pints he was getting sick of their jibes. Ross pushed Chris too far when he said that he didn't deserve a girl like Shelley, and that he must be mad to give her up for some tramp who was just offering sex on tap. With this, the usually placid Chris snapped, taking a drunken swipe at Ross.

At six feet-three, Ross, who could hold his drink much better than his mate, stepped backwards, and instead of hitting him on the chin as intended, Chris punched the air, falling to the ground in a drunken stupor. Luckily, there were no hard feelings as far as Ross was concerned, and the lads bundled Chris in a taxi and sent him home.

'Christopher?' Vivien's voice sounded shrill in his delicate ear. 'I'm putting on a special afternoon tea today and I'd like you to bring your new girlfriend, Amanda to meet Daddy and I.'

'Oh Mum, we've only been going out two minutes, you can't be expecting me to bring her round to meet you so soon. And it's Mandy, not Amanda,' Chris sighed.

'Look, Christopher,' said Vivien, her tone becoming exasperated. 'If you've left your wife for this girl then she must be special to you, and I for one think you owe it to daddy and me to bring her to meet us. After all, this is a serious matter, darling. I've had to explain to my friends at the amateur dramatics society that you've split up with your wife and have a new partner. The least you can do is let me meet her. I want to put my mind at rest that she's a nice, decent girl.' She paused, feigning a teary sniff that Chris knew only too well was for his benefit. 'This has been a very upsetting time for your daddy and me. We worry about you, my dear,' she continued.

Chris was now moving from one foot to the other, stifling his desperate urge to pee. He would've said anything at that moment to get his mother off the phone.

'Okay Mum, what time do you want us?'

'Two o'clock sharp, please,' Vivien answered, with satisfaction in her voice.

'Right, we'll be there, bye,' said Chris, hurriedly putting the phone down on his mother, who was still chattering away.

Mandy was none-too-pleased when Chris rang her ten minutes later to give her the news.

'But we're supposed to be going shopping for holiday clothes, Chris, you promised,' Mandy said, in her whiny, childlike voice.

'I know, sweetheart, I'm really sorry, but my mother insisted and she's putting on a special afternoon tea, so I could hardly say no.'

Chris decided not to mention the fact that his mother only wanted to vet Mandy, to see if she was suitable enough for her only son.

'I tell you what,' he said, 'we can go shopping next week and I'll buy you something really special. I get paid on Friday and I get my quarterly bonus this month too, so I'll be able to buy you something really nice. How does that sound, babe?'

Mandy smiled slyly, seeing the pound signs in front of her eyes, and knowing she could work this to her advantage.

'Okay darling, we'll go shopping next week,' she said, in a sickly, sweet voice. 'Sorry, I was being a brat. I don't mind if we go to your mum's today. In fact, that would be lovely.'

'Okay great, I'll pick you up at 1:45pm,' Chris suggested.

'No need, I can come to you. I have to call at a friend's, on the way so I can kill two birds and all that,' she replied, before they said their goodbyes.

Leaving her house at 12:15pm, Mandy made the short walk to drop in on the 'friend' she had mentioned. Nudging open the paint-flaked gate with her shoe, she walked up the unkempt path to Lenny Dobbs' ground floor flat.

He opened the door before she had the chance to knock and, smiling, he flashed her his brown, stained teeth. Mandy felt quite nauseous at the sight, but putting on her best false smile in return, she entered the flat.

After having no success so far with the photos she'd asked Judy to post to the modelling agencies, Mandy had decided to widen her search for fame. She was going to send her pictures to some of the soft porn magazines, in hopes of getting some recognition. There was no way she was prepared to do porn, but if she could get her foot in the door and get noticed, it would be the stepping-stone she needed to achieve fame and fortune.

She'd told Lenny over the phone that she wanted the negatives to the pictures he'd taken of her. With the negatives, she could get as many copies of the photos as she needed, so she wouldn't have to go through this rigmarole every time she wanted a set. Lenny had been reluctant; he knew Mandy would probably be back for some more copies and planned to get as many blowjobs from her as he could. If he gave her the negatives, he realised that it would probably be the last time she visited him. After much deliberation, Mandy had decided to call his bluff, telling him he could take it or leave it and that she'd get herself another photographer. He'd decided to take it. It was the best offer Lenny Dobbs was likely to get and he'd thought of nothing else since she'd last been to see him. Fortunately for Mandy, she didn't have to put much work in before Lenny Dobbs was entering seventh heaven.

Leaving the flat, carrying the brown envelope that held a set of her photos along with the negatives, Mandy breathed a sigh of relief, thanking the Lord that, that was the last time she would ever have to endure Lenny Dobbs.

Back inside, Lenny moved the pile of cushions from the settee, that had hidden his video camera. Checking that he'd captured the important parts of Mandy's fifteen-minute visit, he grinned, once again showing his brownish yellow teeth. Now, he could be sure that there would always be something good to watch, on TV.

Chapter 13

Mark Devine paced up and down the corridor of the Cardiology unit at Boundary Park Hospital. His mum, Marian, sat on one of the, orange, plastic chairs, staring at the ground with a glazed look in her eyes. Always a well-presented woman, Marian Devine looked good for her forty-nine years. But in the last few hours it seemed like she'd aged another ten. Her daughter, Cassie, handed her a cup of sweet tea from the vending machine. Its, colour was reminiscent of dirty dishwater, but hopefully the sugar would give her mum the strength she needed, to get through the tough night that lay ahead.

As the doors to the specialist unit swung open and the young doctor in the white coat appeared, all three of them turned to look to him, for the news they so desperately wanted him to deliver. Unfortunately, they were all to be disappointed, and from that moment on their lives would change forever.

'Mrs Devine,' the doctor said, in a quiet voice. 'I'm really sorry, we did everything we could for your husband, but the cardiac arrest he suffered was fatal.

'Your husband has passed away.'

Marian Devine fell to her knees and wailed, creating the sound of an injured animal. Her children rushed to her, with Mark lifting her to her feet. Holding onto him for support, she managed to sit down, and there, Mark cradled her for the next half an hour whilst she sobbed.

Devine and Son Builders Ltd had been founded over forty years before, when Dave Devine's father had established it. Back then, it had just been known as Devine's, but when Dave joined his dad as an apprentice in the 1950's, his father had changed the name to Devine and Son. After his father passed away, Dave had eagerly waited for his only son to join the firm. Mark had finished serving his apprenticeship the previous year, but he had a natural flare for the job and his dad never worried about leaving him with work that many builders took years to perfect.

The company had gone from strength to strength recently, despite the country's poor economic climate. Trusted builders were hard to come by, and Dave

Devine's reputation as a quality tradesman, whose prices were always competitive, preceded him. The firm had recently landed a big contract working on a brand-new housing development on the edge of the town. They now had several more, first class men working for them and the company was definitely growing in stature.

It was more recently that Dave had commented on how well Mark was doing and how he'd have no qualms about leaving the company in his capable hands one day. Mark could never have known that that day was much closer than he could imagine, and that he would be heading the business at just twenty-three years of age.

Chapter 14

Wednesdays were always the quietest day of the week, at Culture Cut, hair salon. Dawn asked Shelley to give her a trim before her next client was due.

'My God, Shelley. Put your bloody face straight, will you? You're going to drive all our customers away at this rate.'

'Oh, I'm sorry, Dawni,' Shelley mumbled. 'I can't shake off this sadness. I'm so lonely without Chris, I just cry all the time.' She bit her bottom lip as she spoke. 'I hate him, and I hate what he's done to me, running off with that trollop and having an affair right under my bloody nose. But in the same breath, I love him too. I can't just switch my feelings off like a tap. The ache in my chest, makes it feels as though my heart is actually breaking. I understand that might sound daft to you, but I feel like I'll never be happy again.' Tears appeared in Shelley's eyes, and she turned her face away from her cousin's view.

'Aw Shelley, darling, I do know what it's like to be hurt. Remember my Ray, leaving me for that Pauline Snape? He's still with her to this day. But I'm well past all that now. I see them out sometimes, when I'm doing my big shop. He's fat and bald now and she's got a greasy head of hair, that you could fry an egg on. The scruffy buggers. They always look miserable as sin together, and I'm glad I'm out of it. Honestly, I am. When I think of what I've got here, with my own business, not to mention, my own home too. I couldn't be happier,' she added, triumphantly.

'And if, sometime in the future, I do ever meet Mr Right, well it'll be on my terms,' she continued. 'Look, I know you miss him but honestly ask yourself this, my love. If he came back with his tail between his legs, begging you for a second chance, would you take him back, knowing what he's done to you? You could never trust him again Shell. Mark my words, if there's one piece of advice I can give you it's this, a leopard doesn't change its spots. He'll do it again, I guarantee it."

Shelley shrugged. 'Maybe, but I just wish my life was back to how it was before.'

Always a straight talker, Dawn Barnes told it like it was. 'That, my girl, is never going to happen. You've got to look forward now, not back. Look, I wasn't going to tell you this just yet, not until I got confirmation. But as my cousin, and of course my best stylist, I might as well let you in on my little secret.'

Shelley's eyes widened, with eager anticipation.

'I'm extending the salon!' announced Dawn, proudly. 'I want to introduce a beauty studio, using some of the spare rooms upstairs.'

'Wow, that's exciting,' said Shelley. 'Who's going to manage it?'

Dawn grinned. 'That, my love, is where you come in.'

Shelley gave her cousin a confused look. 'But I don't know the first thing about beauty. Plus, I'm your best stylist. When will I find the time to do beauty treatments?'

'You'll know everything you need to know, when you've trained as a beautician,' Dawn answered. 'You, my girl, are going to college.'

'College?' Shelley cried, worriedly. 'But I'm a hairdresser, Dawn, it's what I love. I don't think I'd be any good at being a beautician.'

Dawn put her arm around her cousin. 'Look, Shelley, I'm moving this business forward and I think this could be just what you need right now. Something to get your teeth into and focus on. If I didn't believe in you, there's no way I'd be putting you forward for it.'

Shelley shrugged, not feeling totally convinced.

'There's one more thing,' Dawn added. 'I'm hiring a new stylist.'

'What?' shrieked Shelley. 'No way, Dawn. You can't just replace me.' Her voice quivered, as though she might burst into tears at any moment.

'Don't be daft.' Dawn sighed in exasperation, at Shelley's dramatics. 'But like I said, I'm extending, and we're rushed off our feet as it is. You'll still be doing hair, but I need another pair of hands for when you're busy doing beauty treatments. Also, of course, for when you're on day release, at college.'

Shelley was not happy, one bit. She was extremely territorial where her clients were concerned and she did not like the thought of a new stylist, muscling in on her patch.

'I've got someone coming in soon for an interview, and they've come highly recommended. So, when they arrive can you hold the fort, until your next client turns up?'

'Yeh, I suppose,' Shelley replied, sullenly.

Normally a very friendly girl, Shelley couldn't help feeling animosity towards her future, new colleague. She knew she wouldn't like her, whoever she was. Shelley worried that the new girl would take her place as head stylist.

Just then, the salon door was flung open and breezing in like a flurry of autumn leaves, came Jason Barrie. Mincing over to the counter, he introduced himself.

'Hey honey, I'm Jason, he said in a friendly and camp voice. I'm here to see Dawn, for an interview.'

Wearing turned up three quarter length chinos, with a white vest top and a pale pink Lyle & Scott sweater, draped over his shoulders, Jason was hardly dressed for an interview. Shelley couldn't help but smile. She liked him on sight, with his blond streaked hair and sunbed, tanned complexion, Shelley knew she'd have no trouble getting along with him.

After a ten-minute chat with Dawn, Jason was hired. As he was leaving, he flashed Shelley a smile of his perfect pearly whites.

'Ciao for now,' he beamed, blowing her a kiss and leaving the salon, as theatrically, as he entered.

Shelley's fears faded instantly. She knew she was going to have lots of fun working with Jason Barrie and that, there would never be a dull moment in the salon again.

Chapter 15

Opening one eye, Darren attempted to lift his head off the pillow. Groaning slightly, he lay back down, cautiously turning to his left. On spying the mousy blonde that was gently snoring next to him, he grimaced, taking in her blotchy foundation and smeared eye makeup. She'd looked so much more attractive, the previous evening.

Leanne Dagger liked a good time and never regretted the morning after. She'd been used and abused for most of her life, and one night of affection, was better than nothing at all.

Fuck me, Darren thought to himself, *I'm really lowering my standards here. I need to sort my act out, before my reputation slips.*

It was three weeks since Tina's departure and he'd spent the majority of it on the piss. He was on a final written warning at work and it was only due to the fact that his sister was married to the boss, that he'd held on to his job by the skin of his teeth. He knew he needed to sort his head out but admitting to himself that his wife was gone for good, was too much to take in right now. Getting blind drunk and bedding any woman that made herself available, was the only way he could deal with the situation, which he hadn't seen coming.

Deep down he realised that he'd treated Tina badly at times. Closing his mind off to those parts of his marriage was his way of justifying his actions. He wanted to believe he was the injured party. No way could he admit that he was in the wrong. Even to himself. He still had no idea where Tina was and the thought of her being shacked up with another bloke was, driving him mad.

He'd made enquiries with all the contacts he could think of and no one, had either seen or heard from her. She'd been laid off from her job a couple of months before, so he had no leads there, and none of her friends knew where she was. Not that she had many, these days. It was as though she'd disappeared into thin air. She wasn't back at her mum's, and to be honest, he knew Tina had burnt her bridges with her family after turning her back on them, when he'd made her choose between them. He was at a loss as to where she could be. She'd have to turn up at some point and when she did, he would make it his business to find out exactly where she'd been.

The day Tina walked out on their marriage, Darren arrived home from work on time, for once. He was in a good mood and had decided he was going to take his wife to the pub with him, for a rare night out. What he wasn't going to tell her, was that his Friday night crew had gone to Magaluf for a week. He would let her believe it was because he wanted to spend some quality time with her. That way, he would win some brownie points, that he could bank for the future. If he could've taken the time off from work, Darren would've been joining his mates on the boozy lads' holiday. Unfortunately for him, his brother-in-law and boss, Ian Kennedy, was also a regular at the Moulders Arms and would know only too well where Darren was if he went AWOL for the week. Darren hated Ian with a passion and the fact he was married to his sister Bernie, was the only reason, he hadn't chinned him by now.

As it was a lovely, warm, summer's evening, Darren thought that Tina would be more than thrilled to be spending a night out with him. These days, the most Tina saw of the pub, was when she got off the bus outside it with her heavy bags of food shopping. Nights out were now a thing of the past for Tina. The majority of the time she was treated like a skivvy, and a punching bag for the rest.

When Darren arrived home from work and Tina was nowhere to be seen, he couldn't for the life of him think where she might be.

But if she thought she could do a disappearing act during the day, then she could think again. With his mood suddenly turning black, Darren vowed he'd make Tina pay when he caught up with her later. He left for the pub, only to find that when he returned a few hours later, his wife was still missing.

Half-pissed, he opened the wardrobe doors to confirm his worst fears. Her clothes were gone, along with the tatty suitcase she owned. In a rage, Darren proceeded to smash up anything he could get his hands on. Only calming down, after a neighbour called the police.

In his own way, Darren did love Tina, and he missed her presence terribly, but he still couldn't see that it was him, and him alone, that was totally responsible for her unhappiness.

Leanne Dagger made a grunting sound, beginning to stir from her slumber. With a stretch and a yawn, she turned to Darren.

'Mmm, hello handsome,' she purred, feeling her way under the covers for Darren's prize package.

She cupped his ample balls and began to stoke his length with an experienced hand. Sex had been the last thing on Darren's mind when he woke up, but he didn't need much persuasion once his loins began to stir. Never managing to stay faithful to any of his girlfriends, Darren didn't change when he'd married Tina. He loved sex and was more than happy to sample the delights of a multitude of women. He liked to think he had certain standards but after a few pints too many, he'd been known to have bedded a few double baggers in his time.

When he was at full length, Darren swiftly flipped Leanne over, so he didn't have to look at her face, as he entered her with expertise. After only a few thrusts he released his load, quickly detaching himself from Leanne, who couldn't have been less impressed with Darren's speedy performance. 'Is that it?' she muttered under her stale morning breath.

With a light slap of Leanne's scrawny arse-cheek, which was still in the doggie position, Darren responded dispassionately.

'C'mon love, I'll ring you a taxi.'

'Okay, babes, if you say so,' said Leanne, a little miffed as she reached for her once white underwear, which was now grey in colour.

Dialling the local taxi number, Darren asked her, 'Where to, love?'

'Bowler Street,' she told him, as she stepped into her jeans and stilettos.

My God she's rough, he thought, *I need to get her out of here, asap*.

He recalled that she'd looked much prettier the previous night, when he'd pulled her in Jaspers night club. Darren hoped she lived at the top end of Bowler Street rather than the bottom end where his mate Wayne lived. He reminded himself that he would have to have his wits about him, next time he paid Wayne a visit.

The Datsun Cherry from Motown Taxis pulled up outside Darren's house and he handed Leanne a fiver, ushering her out of the door and praying that none of his neighbours were about. He wasn't concerned that anyone would judge him for having a different woman round, almost every night since Tina left. It was rather his choice of women, that was the issue. Darren was meant to have standards and tramps like Leanne were not supposed to be on his radar. In the future, he would need to ensure that he didn't let his beer goggles cloud his vision.

Closing the door, Darren looked around him. The kitchen was a total bomb site, and the front room was full of empty beer cans.

Fucking hell, I shouldn't have to spend my Saturday mornings, cleaning up this shit, he thought. Never, did he once consider that it was all his mess and that he was now responsible for himself. Grabbing his jacket, he decided to go to his mums for a full English, before meeting the lads for a game of pool.

Chapter 16

Sitting on the large bay windowsill, hugging her knees to her chest, Tina admired the view from the sitting room. It was lovely, and she could've sat there for hours, transfixed by the tranquil serenity of the mature gardens at Copley House. She'd been there for three weeks and was already taking massive steps forward, in a bid to get the old Tina back.

Following her arrival at Copley House, Women's Refuge, she instantly knew she was in safe hands. On entering the large Victorian building, Tina was accompanied by the manager, Dianne, whose calming voice and pleasant demeanour immediately put her at ease. She just had a presence that aided instant relaxation.

As a previously battered wife herself, Dianne knew the fears that Tina held, and one of the first things she instilled in her was the belief that she was completely safe now.

'No one will ever find you here, Tina. I met you at a secret location before bringing you here, so unless you tell anyone where you are then there's no need for you to worry.'

'I definitely wouldn't tell anyone,' said Tina, urgently.

'Then you're totally safe.' Dianne assured her.

Before long Tina was issued with a case worker, who counselled her, encouraging her to talk openly about her feelings, without judgement. She was helped to understand that her situation with Darren, was not her fault and nothing she could've done would've prevented her husband treating her the way he had.

She was going from strength to strength, and even in the short time she'd been there she was beginning to look like her old self. She had gained a few pounds and almost all the bruises had now faded away. The colour had returned to her cheeks and her eyes seemed much brighter than they had. The dark circles beneath them were no longer visible and Tina felt more alive than she had in years.

'Here you go, coffee two sugars, just how you like it,' Marsha smiled, handing her a mug.

'Oh, thanks love. I was just thinking about making a brew,' Tina replied.

All the women she'd met at Copley House were lovely, each with their own sorrowful tale to tell. But Tina had become especially close to Marsha. At twenty-five, Marsha Campbell was stunning. A mixed-race girl who was tall and slender, standing 5"11, bare foot. Tina commented on how she could easily be a model, with her height, figure and not to mention, her killer high cheekbones. Marsha had just smiled, raising her eyebrows, and Tina immediately realised she must have been told that, many, many times before.

Escaping her boyfriend of eight years, Darnell Brown, Marsha had arrived at the refuge in a very sorry state. Following one particularly brutal beating, where she lost the baby, she'd been carrying for over six months. The attack had landed her in hospital on a life support machine, and her chances of ever conceiving again were now less than slim. She'd taken Darnell's beatings for many years but losing the innocent baby girl, she was nurturing had been like a light bulb moment, for her.

She'd always been able to take what he dished out to her, but the loss of her precious child enabled her to see things in a different light, realising she must get away from him before he eventually killed her. It would take time and patience to gain the confidence she needed to pick up the pieces of her life and start again with her young son, Jerome, who at four years old was her world and, as she'd said herself, the reason she was still alive today.

One thing she was sure of, she could never again return to her old town of Gorton in Manchester. Darnell finding her was not an option. If that were to happen, she would never be free of him. She did, however, want to be close enough to her beloved mum, Deana. Maybe Droylsden or Denton would be okay. She would speak to her social worker before finalising her decision. As the girls chatted, they watched Jerome playing, with his Etch-a-Sketch.

'He's the double of his dad, you know,' said Marsha. 'But I can't hold that against the poor little mite. Thankfully though,' she added, in a more serious voice, 'his personality is as different to his dad's, as day is to night and for that I'm so grateful. I'll teach him to always respect women and let him know that it's never acceptable to raise your hand to them.'

Tina smiled. 'I don't think you'll ever have a problem with him on that score, Marsha. He's such a placid, well-behaved little lad. He's a credit to you.'

'Listen, Marsha,' Tina spoke, looking intently at her friend. 'I need your advice. I want to contact my mum and dad, but I'm scared. I've got some bridges to build with my family, and the sooner I do it the better. They're sure to know by now that I'm missing. God knows what they must be thinking. But we left things on such bad terms the last time we spoke.'

'Tina, sometimes family's all you've got left. Life's too short to hold grudges, against the people we love. People who would fight, tooth and nail for us.' Marsha's words were wise, and Tina realised she was right.

'That's it then, my mind's made up. I'm going to ring my mum and see how the land lies. I love and miss them so much. I've got a lot of ground to make up but I'm sure, knowing them like I do, that they'll turn up trumps for me.' Tina's words were full of hope.

'I'm sure they will.' Marsha grinned. 'Hey, you'd better stay in touch with me and Jerome when we leave.'

'You try and stop me,' said Tina. 'I've found a true friend in you, Marsha Campbell, and that's one thing I haven't had for a long time.'

Chapter 17

To say Vivien Charlton was upset was an understatement. It was Tuesday now, and ever since Chris and Mandy's visit on Saturday afternoon, she'd been stuck like a broken record. She'd moaned repeatedly to her husband Spencer about how their beloved Christopher was making a humongous mistake, getting involved with a gold digger like Mandy.

It was a completely different story before their arrival. She'd prepared vol-au-vents, egg and cress finger rolls, French fancies, and a beautiful homemade Victoria sandwich. Everything was arranged on doilies, along with her best china crockery, which was laid out on her solid mahogany dining table.

Vivien was like a cat on hot bricks, pacing up and down in front of the living room window. Every couple of minutes she'd twitch the lace curtains, awaiting Chris and Mandy's arrival.

'You're going to wear the carpet out at this rate,' remarked Spencer, peering above the Telegraph, over his steel-rimmed glasses.

Pursing her thin lips and shaking her head at her husband, Vivien quipped, 'Obviously, Spencer, you don't have the same concerns that I do regarding our son's welfare. He's finally seen the light, as far as that Shelley was concerned, and now, hopefully, he's found himself a credible suitor. Someone we can invite to social gatherings with our friends. Someone, who we won't mind him one day producing offspring with. Heaven knows what type of children he would have had with that Shelley. If her family's anything to go by, they would have been council estate tearaways, you mark my words.'

Spencer sighed; his wife was a snob and to hear her talk you'd honestly think she was related to the Queen herself.

'He's in his twenties now, Vivien. He's a grown man. He doesn't need to be tied to your apron strings for the rest of his life. He knows his own mind and it's up to him, whom he chooses to be with. In my opinion, he's been a fool throwing his marriage away on some young bit of stuff. I for one, thought Shelley was a nice girl. He could do a lot worse. She's also very pretty too I might add.' He added the last bit just to wind Vivien up, as he was aware she was already on high alert.

'I have a good feeling about Amanda,' she remarked, nodding in approval at her own words. 'She's working towards becoming a legal secretary, at the company where Christopher works. That, I believe speaks volumes, about the type of girl she is.

It was almost 2pm and Vivien was getting more anxious as the minutes ticked by. She insisted on punctuality and in her book, being late just wasn't an option.

'Come on, Spencer, put your newspaper away and move your feet from the pouffe, they'll be here any minute,' she urged impatiently.

Without giving her husband the chance to do as he'd been told, she was already whipping the newspaper out of his hands and folding it away in a drawer.

By 2:10pm, Vivien was not impressed to say the least. She was huffing and puffing and repeatedly questioning her husband on their son's whereabouts.

'Where could they have got to?' she said, directing her glare at Spencer.

Spencer shrugged. 'How the heck should I know, he's probably having car trouble.'

'This is a disgrace,' Vivien tutted. 'Christopher knows how I feel about punctuality.' She paused. 'Oh, you don't think they've had an accident, do you?

'There's no answer at his house,' she said worriedly, replacing the receiver.

-

Chris and Mandy were speeding the couple of miles to his mother's house. Knowing how much she hated poor timekeeping, Chris was panicking, as they were already ten minutes behind schedule. He'd been all ready to leave the house when Mandy arrived.

On opening the front door to her, she insisted on coming in to use his bathroom. He was not at all impressed. She was later than she said she'd be, and it was already time to leave. Chris was very conscious that they didn't have a moment to spare.

Breezing her way down the stairs, Mandy studied Chris, waiting by the front door, in his fashionable clothes and his trendy streaked hair. She suddenly had the urge to give him one of her Mandy specials. Chris tapped his watch to let her know that time was getting on, but Mandy just pulled him towards her and began to kiss him passionately with her full lips. Mandy didn't do kisses by halves, and Chris's mouth was soon responding to hers. She guided her hand towards his crotch, where she could feel him getter hard.

Dropping to her knees she opened the zip of Chris's chinos. As she held his length and guided it towards her mouth, she let her tongue tease the tip, making Chris groan aloud with pleasure.

Mandy's blowjobs were legendary, and Chris could not get enough. Right now, he didn't care how late he was to his mother's tea party. What he felt was extreme pleasure, and there was nothing on Earth that could stop him now. Mandy knew how to take him right to the edge of an orgasm and then pull away, just enough to control the inevitable eruption. She knew this technique gave her complete power and that provided her with as much satisfaction as if she was being pleasured herself.

Needing to feel him inside her, Mandy turned around and leant over the telephone table, waiting for Chris to enter her. Just as he was about to ease his way inside, the shrill sound of the telephone made them both jump, catapulting Chris back to reality. He lost his hard on within seconds, realising that it would be his mother phoning to check where the pair had got to.

'Shit, we have to go, babes,' Chris said, with panic in his voice. 'That'll be my mum ringing, and you don't know what she's like. If we're late, she'll play bloody hell.'

Mandy was not impressed to say the least. She was ready for a good seeing to and her boyfriend would rather pass up a session with her, for cucumber sandwiches at Mummy's house. She decided there and then, that she instantly disliked Vivien.

'Bloody hell, Chris, surely she won't mind if we're running a few minutes late? This is ridiculous,' Mandy huffed, straightening her skirt.

'I'm sorry, sweetheart. I am. She's just a bit, well, funny about certain things. Come on, I promise I'll make it up to you later, honest.' Chris gave Mandy's bum a reassuring squeeze.

'Okay,' she sighed, raising her eyes. 'Let's get this over with then.' Inside she was fuming and wondered if she was losing her touch. She decided she'd put it to the test, later.

-

'They're here, Spencer. They're here.' Vivien shrieked, the octaves in her voice, becoming increasingly higher.

Their car pulled onto the drive and Vivien swiftly moved away from the window before she was spotted. Standing at the ready, she waited until she heard footsteps on the gravel, approaching the front door. Swinging it open eagerly, the wide smile she was wearing immediately dropped at the sight of the crop top, which tightly hugged Mandy's ample breasts. Quickly composing herself, she beckoned the couple inside and into the living room.

'I was terribly worried when you weren't on time, darling,' Vivien said, directing her concern towards her son.

'Oh yes, sorry, Mum. I forgot I needed petrol, should've been better prepared,' Chris lied.

Vivien squinted her eyes, looking at their flushed faces. She didn't believe a word of it. Eyeing Mandy up and down, Vivien disliked her on sight. She could tell trash when she saw it and it was quite obvious to Vivien, that there were two big reasons why Chris was attracted to Mandy, and they were staring her right in the face.

'Would you both like a cup of tea?' she asked, smiling falsely.

'I wouldn't mind a glass of wine if there's one going spare.' Mandy knew exactly what Vivien was thinking and decided to play her at her own game.

'Er, yes dear, I'm sure we have some in the fridge. Spencer, would you pour Mandy a small glass of Chardonnay?' Vivien instructed.

'I'll have a beer too please, Dad,' Chris added, getting up to help his father with the drinks, oblivious to the tension between his mother and his girlfriend.

'But you're driving, Christopher, I'm not sure you should.' 'Oh, he'll be fine' Mandy grinned. If he gets drunk, we can always stay over.'

Shocked at this statement, Vivien had to sit down and compose herself. She felt as though her worst fears were coming true. Chris now had a girlfriend who was much worse that his wife had been. She couldn't believe what was happening.

The afternoon tea passed slow and painfully, although Mandy was thoroughly enjoying herself. She knew she was no Princess Diana, but if this pompous woman thought she was going to look down her nose at her, she decided she'd give her good reason to.

After their food, Spencer, also oblivious to the women's distaste for one another, was making small talk with his son, when Mandy announced aloud, 'Oh, Chris I'd love to see your bedroom and all the old posters you told me about.'

Vivien's jaw dropped open at the brashness of the hussy her son had presented to them. Taking Mandy by the hand, Chris replied,

'Great idea. We can have a go on my old Scalextric too, if you like. Bagsy being blue.'

Vivien's face was like thunder as the two of them strolled off, hand in hand.

'Spencer, what are you going to do about it?' she hissed.

'What?' He raised his eyes to the ceiling. 'They're only going to his room. They'll be back in five minutes. What's wrong with you?'

'She is a tramp, Spencer, she's worse than the other one.'

'Look, dear,' Spencer said, placing a reassuring hand on his wife, knowing her only too well. 'I'm sure Mandy will just be a fad and Chris will no doubt find someone more suitable before too long. She's seems a little feisty for our Chris, and somehow I think she may tire of him soon enough.'

'Mmm, well, I hope you're right, and before she cleans him out, too. I can spot a gold digger like her a mile away,' she replied, looking as if she was about to cry.

As Chris and Mandy entered his bedroom, she turned and kissed him before he had the chance to utter a single word.

'You're not getting away this time, Chris Charlton.' *No one puts their mother's bloody tea party before Mandy Allsop*, she thought, as she lifted her up crop top, to reveal her magnificent breasts.

Chris's manhood stiffened immediately, and Mandy knew she had him right where she wanted him. As Chris entered her from behind, Mandy let out an almighty pleasure-filled groan, fully aware that it was likely to be overheard by his parents. Trying to shush her, Chris put his hand over her mouth, which made Mandy smile to herself. She made sure she gave out one more load moan as Chris finished. Turning to him, she giggled. 'I'm really sorry about making so much noise, Chris, but you were so good. I just couldn't help myself.'

Always happy to receive praise on his performance, Chris grinned, 'Well hopefully we weren't heard.'

'I'm sure we weren't,' Mandy smiled, knowing full well that she'd left the living room door wide open behind her. The satisfaction she felt was not from having sex with Chris but knowing that she'd got one over on his snooty mother. That fact alone, made her entire weekend.

Chapter 18

Locking the bathroom door and removing her dressing gown and slippers, Judy stood naked in front of the bathroom scales. With her eyes closed she slowly stepped onto them. Peeping from one eye she hesitantly looked down. When she saw where the scale dial had stopped, she quickly opened both eyes, staring in disbelief.

Surely that isn't right, she thought.

She stepped off the scales to make sure the dial was on zero, before getting back on. Confirming that it was, she stepped back on them again. No, she wasn't imagining it, she had lost just over a stone. A wide smile spread across her face and as she looked up catching sight of her expression in the bathroom cabinet mirror, she shook her head in disbelief. It was five weeks since she'd last weighed herself. Five weeks since she'd decided that her life needed to change and now, she was seeing the results; the hard work was paying off.

Waking up to find the empty packet of chocolate digestives she'd devoured following the unforeseen upset Mandy's phone call had caused, about Chris and their holiday to Ibiza, Judy felt guilt, shame and hatred for herself, all in one go. But she didn't hate herself half as much as she hated Mandy at that moment in time. There and then she decided that she was no longer going to allow Mandy to use her as a doormat. She was sick and tired of being used and let down by her so-called best friend. Enough was enough. She needed a break from Mandy and decided that she might just make it a permanent one.

But first, she needed to get this whole holiday business out of the way and there was no time like the present. She decided to ring Mandy before setting off for work, instructing her to bring Chris and meet her in town the following day, so they could all go to the travel agents to swap the names over. Mandy was surprised, at Judy's early morning call. Her tone was assertive, and she was also straight to the point. This seemed so unlike the meek and mild manner that her friend usually possessed.

After replacing the receiver, Judy heaved a sigh of relief. She had not been as confident as she sounded but she was proud of herself for holding her own. Now she just had to get tomorrow's visit to the travel agents out of the way and she could get Mandy out of her life for good. She suddenly felt as though she had an inner strength to succeed. It was time to rid the bad from her life and introduce the good things she deserved.

From that day onwards things had been going from strength to strength for Judy. She was eating healthily and instead of letting her mum put her a pack lunch together, which usually consisted of cheese or spam on thick white bread, with crisps and a biscuit, she was now making her own. She didn't even feel as though she was sacrificing too much either. She never realised how much she enjoyed fruit, because she hadn't really eaten much of it before. Judy even joined the gym and attended the aerobics class, twice a week.

It was at this class that she met Kath and Jenny, two lovely girls who worked together in the accounts department at Platts Engineering. They all enjoyed a giggle together and Judy felt that she could totally be herself around them. They had no hidden agenda and weren't constantly bitching about people, which made such a refreshing change. The two friends, often tried to persuade Judy to join them on one of their weekend nights out, but as a naturally shy girl, Judy had so far declined. However, her confidence was growing, and she eventually agreed to go. It made such a difference having friends that seemed interested in her, rather than the leading subject constantly revolving around them.

Dealing with Mandy and Chris at the travel agents wasn't a pleasant experience. Judy just wanted the whole sorry episode over and done with as quickly as possible. True to form, Mandy turned up bold as brass, acting not one bit sorry for letting her so-called best friend down, in the worst possible way.

On first impressions, Chris was exactly how Judy had imagined. Certainly not Mandy's usual type. He was a pretty boy, and anyone with eyes, could see that he was also a mummy's boy. He was good-looking, there was no denying that, but he had a weak chin and Judy could tell from a mile away that Mandy was running rings round him. His demeanour reminded her of a limp lettuce. She afforded herself a smile, thinking about how Mandy would be taking him for everything she could get. Some things would never change.

Another reason for Judy happiness, was that for the past three weeks, Mandy's ex, Mark Devine had become a regular at the post office. Judy had heard through the small-town gossip grapevine about Mark's father recently passing away and that he was now heading the family business. He'd been coming in to pay the business cheques into the company's account and knowing that she would be seeing him on a regular basis had given

Judy a real lift. She did, however, feel very sorry for him under the sad circumstances. She couldn't imagine how difficult it must be to lose a parent at such a young age. Shy and easily embarrassed, Judy had so far managed to avoid him coming to her counter. Just seeing him was enough for her. He was so good-looking, in his rugger boots and jeans, with bits of cement and dust on his tanned arms and face. His dark glossy hair was the colour of treacle and perfectly matched his kind eyes. She wished that she could sit and stare at him all day.

Judy got into the shower and with the dreamy thoughts of Mark in her mind, began to lather herself. She didn't normally take much notice of her body. Its size and shape usually repulsed her. But with the knowledge that she had lost over a stone, Judy felt suddenly more attractive. As she washed herself with the bar of Imperial Leather, Judy's hands moved over her waist and up to her breasts.

She closed her eyes and let the warm water drench her as she massaged her breasts, gently tweaking her pink nipples. With no experience of ever being pleasured before, Judy let out a slight moan at the sensuous new feelings she was experiencing. She moved a hand down between the top of her thighs and hesitantly allowed the tips of her fingers to touch the soft mound of flesh of her private area. As her middle finger explored the crease of her vagina, connecting with her clitoris, she felt an instant, electrifying sensation of pleasure shoot through her body, making her gasp.

Letting her natural instincts take over she continued to feel her way around the most intimate areas of body, until she finally brought herself to a magnificent orgasm. With her whole body trembling, Judy realised that she now, finally knew what all the fuss was about. Steadying herself, she carefully stepped out of the shower, wrapped herself in a large towel, and lay down exhaustedly on her bed.

Happy in her being and feeling sexually fulfilled for the first time in her life, Judy was sound asleep within minutes.

Chapter 19

Shelley and Jason had been working together in the salon for a month now, but Shelley felt like she'd know him for years. He was the funniest, most likeable friend she'd ever had and the reason she no longer didn't want to get out of bed in the mornings. In that month alone, she felt that he had single-handedly got her back on the road to happiness. She now looked forward to work every day, knowing that Jason would fill each day with fun and laughter. Shelley stopped dwelling on losing Chris and began looking forward to the future.

About to enrol on her September college course and with summer in full swing, she now felt she had something to aim for. She obviously thought about Chris from time to time but the fact that she'd heard nothing at all from him, since the day on the park bench when he'd asked her for a divorce, had made it so much easier to continue to live her life without him.

It was Saturday morning and the salon was as busy as ever. Radio One was blasting out and Shelley and Jason were singing to Wham's hit song, Freedom. Using their hairbrushes as microphones, the pair re-enacted the back to back Abba stance, as they belted out the tune. They finished in fits of giggles whilst their customers gazed on, unable to hide their smiles at the pair's obvious great friendship and camaraderie.

Dawn had nipped to the newsagents and they took every opportunity to have some fun whilst their boss wasn't around; not that Dawn minded them having a bit of fun, a happy workforce was very important to her. The junior stylist, and the Saturday girl were busy washing the hair of the next two clients and were enjoying the atmosphere, just as much as the others were.

As Shelley finished taking payment from one of her regulars, she turned to Jason and mouthed, 'thank you.' He wrinkled his tanned nose.

'For what?' he questioned.

'For making me smile again. You're so kind and funny and I'm so glad I met you. I can't wait for our night out later, we're going to have such a laugh.'

'No, thank *you*, my gorgeous girl. At last I've finally found someone who loves George Michael just as much as I do,' he grinned, blowing Shelley a kiss. 'Listen, princess,' Jason added, holding up his colour pot. 'I'm nipping in the back to mix this colour, if our Ross calls in let me know. He's bringing me a set of keys to the flat today.'

'Okay, will do,' Shelley called as Jason turned on his heel.

She smiled to herself at the prospect of seeing Ross again. Ross Barrie was Jason's cousin. The pair were like chalk and cheese. As different as two lads could be. Growing up together hadn't always been easy. Jason was often bullied for his camp ways, but Ross had always been there to stick up for his cousin.

Throughout high school there were many times that Ross had intervened, when bullies were giving Jason a hard time. At six feet-three Ross had willingly been his saviour and as word spread that the boys were cousins, the bullies left Jason alone. Ross was a keen Judo enthusiast and had achieved his black belt, although he never flaunted the fact and rarely used it to his advantage. He had however, taught Jason some important self-defence techniques as he knew that being gay would always make him a target for narrow-minded bigots, and he wouldn't always be there to protect his cousin.

Until now, Jason had been living with his parents. It was easy at home. Everything was done for him by his mum.

It was also cheap. He only had to tip up £10 a week, but of late Jason, in his early twenties felt the urge to spread his wings. He needed more independence and more importantly he wanted privacy. Jason was openly gay, which his mother had secretly always suspected, and she didn't have a problem with it when he finally confirmed her suspicions. Being as camp and flamboyant as he was, it was difficult to come to any other conclusion about him.

His father, on the other hand accepted the fact, as he loved his son unconditionally, but he made it clear that he did not want it flaunted in front of him. Jason realised that he would never be able to openly love whom he wanted whilst he was still living at home. He and Ross had always been close. More like brothers than cousins. So, when Ross's flatmate Aaron, got married and bought a house of his own, it seemed like the obvious solution to them both for Jason to move in.

As a firefighter, Ross worked shifts so there would be plenty of opportunity for Jason to live his own life, seeing the friends he chose without judgement. The flat was behind the Railway Pub in Royton. It was nothing fancy, but he felt comfortable there and knew he would be happy. He and Ross had spent the past few days moving in his belongings and today he was dropping a key off at the salon.

Ross had first called at the salon the week before, to give Jason a lift home. When he walked through the door at closing time, Shelley had done a double take.

'Er, oh, hi Ross,' she'd said, recognising him instantly as one of Chris's old friends. Ross was as surprised to see Shelley, as she was to see him.

'Have you come to make an appointment?' She asked, as numerous thoughts ran through her mind; *why would Ross be calling at the salon? Had Chris sent him? What other reason would he have for being here?* Her heart began to hammer in her chest.

'Bang on time Rossi boy,' announced Jason, flouncing in from the back.

Now Shelley was even more confused. 'Shelley, meet my manly cousin Ross,' Jason smirked, winking at his cousin.

'No need for introductions Jay, I know Shelley of old. I met her through her husband, Chris.'

Eyes widening, Jason put his hands on his hips.

'Oh, spill the beans then. Small world isn't it? And, it's ex-husband now,' he corrected.

'Oh, yeah sorry. I did hear that you guys had split,' Ross acknowledged.

As the three of them chatted, Shelley felt Ross's eyes studying her intensely. She'd always been aware of his good looks, though she hadn't seen him since her wedding. She couldn't help thinking how much he reminded her of Rob Lowe from the Hollywood, Brat Pack and she liked what she saw.

Ross too felt instantly drawn to Shelley. He'd always thought she was a stunner, but as his mate's girlfriend he'd never looked at her that way before. She had a real presence about her, and he found her intoxicating.

Waving their goodbyes as they left the salon, Shelley couldn't help but smile. It was the first time someone had made her feel as though there could be life after Chris and that she would eventually move on. Of course, Jason had not been oblivious to the exchange between his cousin and his new friend and he delighted in the thought that he may have a chance to match-make with two of his favourite people.

The very next day, Jason couldn't wait to let Shelley know exactly what Ross thought of her. Not wanting to appear too keen, Shelley didn't say too much, but from the massive grin on her face Jason could see she was pleased. She secretly decided that if Ross was to ask her out then she'd go on a date with him. What did she have to lose? She had to start living again.

As lunch time approached and there was still no sign of him, Shelley figured she was going to have to take her half hour break. She'd spotted a dress in Chelsea Girl the week before and she desperately wanted it for the night out she and Jason had planned. If she was quick, she could be there and back in twenty minutes. As long as they had her size.

Leaving the salon and briskly walking down Union St in the midday sun, she felt happier than she had in ages. Entering her favourite clothes shop, Shelley made a beeline for the off-the-shoulder, drop waist jersey dress she had seen the week before. It came in three different pastel shades – yellow, pink and blue – and she was torn between them. Shelley was a definite size eight and she could tell just by holding it to her that it would fit perfectly. She decided to go with the blue one to match her eyes, and she also had a banana clip that was the same shade.

Heading towards the counter to pay, she stopped in her tracks as her eyes locked on the person in front of her, who was holding up the skimpiest of bikinis. Mandy had already spotted Shelley, making it her mission to ensure she clocked her in return. Chris was standing beside her, in a world of his own, unaware that his estranged wife was just meters away from them.

'Oh, babe, what do you think of this one?' Mandy exclaimed, making sure that Shelley could hear her as she waved the tiny polka dot bikini in Chris's face. 'Isn't it sexy? I can't wait to wear it when we go to Ibiza!'

Shelley froze on the spot; her heart was pounding, and her legs had turned to jelly. She wanted to get as far away from them, as quickly as possible but she couldn't move. It was at that moment that Chris looked up and saw her. As she caught his eyes, she felt terrible sadness, along with a hatred for the brazen bitch who was flaunting their new romance in her face. Dropping the dress, she was holding Shelley turned and ran out of the shop as quickly as she could. Her chest felt tight and the sights and sounds around her were swimming in a haze. As she left the shop, she heard Chris's voice call to her, but she carried on running without looking back.

Tears streamed down her face blurring her vision as she headed back up Union St to the salon. Turning the corner, she bumped straight into Ross. Seeing her tears, he was instantly concerned for her.

'Shelley, whatever's happened, are you okay?' he asked.

Shelley blurted out the scene that had occurred in the clothes shop, allowing Ross to hold her in his arms while she sobbed. Guiding her into the salon, Dawn took her into the back and made her a cup of sweet tea. Handing Jason a key to the flat, Ross shrugged.

'I guess it's too soon to ask her out. She's obviously still hung up on that cheating bastard.'

Running his fingers through his golden quiff, Jason shook his head.

'I honestly thought you'd have a chance, mate. She's hardly mentioned him lately. Never mind, hey?' He shrugged.

With that, Ross left the salon. Deciding for now, it was best not to pursue Shelley.

Chapter 20

Finishing his second pint in the Moulders Arms, Darren turned around to see his mates, Bryn Barnes and Dave 'Decks' Davies, entering the bar, closely followed by his friend Wayne.

'Whoa, Casanova's already here,' Bryn announced to the others, as he gestured towards Darren.

Grinning, Darren shook his head.

'Fuck off Bryn,' he laughed, 'just cause the only thing you can pull is your knob.'

At Darren's response, the others started laughing and so did Bryn.

'Yeah well, I'd rather wake up alone than with Leanne 'double bagger' Dagger.'

At Bryn's quick return, Wayne and Dave couldn't contain their laughter, which was echoed by Darren and Bryn as they chuckled at one another's banter.

'He's right though,' Wayne added. 'She's not much cop her, Daz. She wouldn't look out of place in the Star Wars bar.'

Everyone sniggered.

'Any hole's a goal after ten pints,' Darren replied, trying to defend himself. 'Plus, they all look the same from behind,' he joked, continuing the usual Saturday afternoon pub banter.

After his first encounter with Leanne Dagger, Darren had sworn it would be his last. Lately though, his drinking was spiralling out of control and despite his good looks, most decent girls in town were giving him a wide berth, after seeing the states he'd been getting himself into.

Leanne could always be relied on to be somewhere in the vicinity when it was chucking out time at Henry Afrika's or Jaspers nightclub. Knowing he was guaranteed a jump, it was the easier option for Darren to take Leanne back to his and have his fill, rather than spend the night buying drinks and chatting up some dolly bird, only to get a knockback when it was time to get a taxi.

True, Leanne was no looker, but she was up for anything. She didn't hassle him about getting his number or going on future dates. It seemed the situation suited them both. He wasn't about to broadcast it, but so long as he was on a promise, he was happy enough with this arrangement. As far as the lads were concerned, last night with Leanne was a one off. He'd be sure to be more discreet in future. Tina seemed to have fallen off the face of the Earth and even though he was secretly cut up about her absence, he would never admit it. The drink was doing its job in masking the hurt.

'Are we going to town tonight then lads?' Darren asked, looking round at the others.

'Oh, I don't know,' replied Dave. 'I'm only just recovering from last night and my wallet's taken a right battering. I had three days on the sick last week, so my wages are down.'

'I'll sub you a tenner,' Wayne offered. 'I won on the bandit last night.' He grinned.

'Oh, go on then, cheers mate. I'll see you right next Friday,' Dave nodded, raising his pint to Wayne. 'A couple more of these and I'll be back in the saddle and ready to strut my stuff on that dance floor,' he added, winking. 'Hair of the dog, it works every time.'

'Let's try Rochdale tonight,' Darren suggested. 'See what the talent's like there. I've heard there's a new club. Bit of fresh meat never did anyone any harm,' he chuckled rubbing his hands together. 'You never know, we might get lucky. Even you, Bryn.'

At this they all began laughing again.

'Well they can't be any worse than Leanne Dagger,' Bryn smirked back. 'Anyway, I can't get too rough, I've got a family BBQ tomorrow for my mum's birthday.'

Shaking their heads, the others all replied in unison, 'Pussy.'

Chapter 21

'Slow down doll. We've got all night,' Jason said, reaching to take Shelley's glass from her. 'That's the third vodka and orange you've downed in an under an hour. If you carry on at this rate you won't get to see the dance floor.'

'Oh Jase, I just want to get wasted and forget all about today. I don't want to be all maudlin on our night out. I need to have a good time.'

'I know you do princess, but neither do you want to be puking your guts up by midnight,' Jason advised, giving Shelley a look as if to say, *You're not going to take a blind bit of notice of me, are you?*

'Oh Jase, I love this one. Let's dance!' Shelley shrieked, as Dead or Alive, *You Spin Me Round* started playing.

'No need to ask twice angel,' he replied, as his eyes lit up and he downed the remains of his Black Russian. 'Lead the way baby.'

After the day's earlier events, Jason really had his work cut out, persuading Shelley to still go on the night out they'd planned. Dawn calmed her down in the back but had also given her a stern talking to.

'Look, as horrible as it was, at least you've seen them together now. The first time was always going to be difficult, my love.'

'Dawni, it was dreadful. They were just there, right in front of me. He's taking her on holiday too. It should be me going instead of that tramp!' Shelley sobbed.

'Right lady. Look at me,' Dawn's voice became hard and her face serious. 'You've got to get over this. He's made his choice and you need to accept it. You've got a shop full of clients out there and they're relying on you, to make them look gorgeous.' Dawn's voice softened once more. 'Come on sweetheart, you're better than this. Now wash your face and I'll see you out there in five, okay?'

Digesting Dawn's advice, Shelley nodded.

After supplying Shelley with words of encouragement as the afternoon dragged on, Jason was more than happy to say goodbye to the last client of the day.

'You'll feel loads better when you've got your glad rags on darling,' he winked.

'I'm not really in the mood Jay. I'm sorry. Plus, I didn't end up buying that dress, because I fled the shop in such a hurry.'

Turning on his heel, Jason went into the storeroom and waltzed out holding up a Chelsea Girl bag. 'I nipped out between clients and picked it up for you,' he grinned at her. 'You've been going on about it all week, so I knew which one you wanted. I also heard you tell Dawn that you were about to buy the blue one, so I thought I'd do the gentlemanly thing and buy it for you.'

Throwing her arms around him, Shelley squealed with delight.

'Jason Barrie, you are without doubt the best friend any girl could wish for,' she beamed.

'I know,' he winked. 'But it's because you deserve it.' Holding her chin up, he looked directly into her beautiful blue eyes. 'Listen to me, Shelley doll. You are a stunner and you're certainly nobody's backing singer. Now let's go out, have a ball and paint this town every colour of the rainbow.'

Chapter 22

Standing in the driveway of Copley House, on a drizzly August morning, Tina and Marsha held each other tightly. As they broke away, they both had tears in their eyes.

'Look at the state of us,' Marsha laughed. 'The way we're acting, you'd think we were never going to see each other again.'

'I know,' sniffed Tina, 'we're a soft pair, aren't we?' Bending down she gave Jerome a big hug, as he stood by his mum's side patiently waiting. 'Now, be a good boy for your mummy Jerome, and look after her,' she smiled, giving him a gentle kiss on the cheek. 'Are you sure you have everything?' she asked, looking back up at Marsha.

'Yes, we're all set and if I need anything, I'm sure my mum will be able to provide it. She's really looking forward to our arrival. She only has a one bedroom flat herself, so it's good of her to put us up for a few days, until my place is ready.'

'Promise you'll ring me as soon as you get settled, so I can come and visit?' Tina asked, as she gave her friend one last hug.

'I will, I promise,' Marsha replied, as she and Jerome got into the waiting taxi. Winding the window down she waved as the taxi pulled away. 'Look after yourself Tina. I'll see you soon.'

Frantically waving back, Tina called after the cab which was now halfway down the drive, 'Don't forget to ring me! See you soon!'

Making her way back inside, Tina's mind was made up. She dialled the number with a trembling hand. On the fourth ring, it was answered.

'Hello.'

Before she could back out and change her mind, Tina blurted,

'Hello Mum, it's me. Tina!'

Chapter 23

Waking up with a mouth like the bottom of a budgie's cage, Shelley blearily opened her eyes in the dimly lit room, trying to focus on the large paper lantern style lightshade hanging from the ceiling. Through the thin, paisley cotton curtains, she could see that the sun was shining outside. In her confusion, she wondered for a couple of seconds where she was.

It was only then that reality sunk in and the blurred memories of the previous night crept into her mind. Listening to the gentle snores coming from the body lying next to her, Shelley hardly dared to breathe, in fear of waking them. Pondering her next move for what seemed like an eternity, she gently lifted her head to see if she could locate her dress and shoes. Peeking under the covers to find herself completely naked, Shelley felt as though she might cry. If she could only slide out of the bed without disturbing her sleeping partner, she could get her stuff and be out of there. A sudden rapping at the bedroom door made her rapidly sit up, clutching the duvet up to her neck.

'Wayne, d'ya want a cup of tea and a bacon butty?' the female voice on the other side asked.

Waking from his slumber, Wayne turned to look at Shelley and back at the door.

'Er, yeh, cheers Trace, I'll be down in five.' Sheepishly smiling at Shelley, Wayne whispered, 'Morning.'

With an extreme look of worry on her face, Shelley whispered back, 'Who was that?' she nodded towards the bedroom door, as though the voice behind it may barge in at any moment.

'Oh, don't worry, that's my sister Tracy. She'd never come in without asking. Would you like some brekkie? She won't mind,' said Wayne, nonchalantly.

'Do I heck,' Shelley's wide eyes looked shocked. 'I need to get myself home. I shouldn't be here. I don't even know where I am.'

As tears began to well in Shelley's eyes, Wayne could see that she wasn't like the usual birds he occasionally brought back, on a Saturday night.

'It's okay love. Don't fret, I'll get you home safely. Where do you live?'

'Rushcroft. You know, near the Commercial Inn?' Shelley sniffed, wiping a tear and feeling rather foolish.

'Okay, I'll go to the bathroom whilst you get yourself dressed, then we'll sneak out of the front door. They'll all be in the kitchen, so we won't be seen. No-one'll ever know you were even here. You'll be home, safe and sound in no time,' he smiled, reassuringly.

Feeling more relaxed and truly grateful to hear Wayne's plan, Shelley breathed a sigh of relief. 'I've never done anything like this before, honest. I don't know what came over me,' she said, feeling the need to explain her reason for ending up in a total stranger's bed.

'I'd say about ten vodka and orange,' Wayne grinned. 'You were downing 'em for fun.'

Shaking her head in dismay, Shelley continued making excuses for her behaviour. Wayne couldn't help thinking how beautiful she was, even with her hair stuck up and her makeup smudged. Her vulnerability made her seem even more appealing. Five minutes later, they were sneaking out of the front door of the end-terrace house, where Wayne lodged with his sister and her husband.

'Here'll be just fine,' said Shelley as they reached the edge of the estate, where her mum's house was.

Not wanting the neighbours or her parents to see her being dropped off, Shelley was more than happy to walk the couple of streets to her mums. Even if she was still wearing the clothes she'd gone out in the night before. Worrying about doing the walk of shame was the last thing on her mind, right now.

Switching the engine off in his mark 2 Cortina, Wayne turned to her.

'Can I have your phone number then?' he asked, hopefully.

'Oh, I don't think that's a good idea. My life's a little bit of a crazy at the minute,' she replied, her voice trailing off, knowing how lame the excuse sounded.

'It's okay, I know a brush off when I hear one.'

Looking at Wayne's kind eyes, Shelley did feel a bit sad about letting him down, but the last thing she needed right now were complications.

'Thanks again for the lift,' she smiled, as she stepped out of the car.

'Yeh, see you around then.' He drove away feeling a bit miffed at not getting Shelley's number, but he soon began to smile to himself at the memories of the wonderful night they'd shared.

Dancing the night away at Tiffany's nightclub, Shelley and Jason had been having a whale of a time. Seeing some old school friends, Shelley left him on the dancefloor whilst she went to have a catch up. Being a regular at Tiffs, Jason was well known and accepted as the flamboyant, camp young man that he was. Happy to dance with anyone, he continued to strut his stuff as the DJ played a session of golden oldie tracks, commonly known as the 'mad half hour.'

Nudging Bryn on the side-lines and pointing towards Jason, Darren shouted to his mates over the loud music.

'Look at that fuckin' puff.'

Smirking, Bryn shook his head. 'Shouldn't bleedin' allow it. It's a disgrace. Don't know what the world's coming to these days,' he tutted.

Realising he was currently the topic of ridicule and insults. A very drunken Jason turned and blew Darren a kiss. Like red rag to a bull, Darren launched himself onto the dancefloor at his taunter. As drinks flew and handbags were trampled on, the men were quickly pulled apart by the bouncers, before any real damage could be done.

Chucking Darren and Bryn out, they took Jason into the back, whilst he straightened himself out. Being a regular at the club and also a great hairdresser had its advantages; in his intoxicated state and with his lip bleeding, Terry the head bouncer called him a taxi. In a drunken blur and without a thought for Shelley's whereabouts, he staggered into a waiting cab and was on his way home.

After walking around the club three times, Shelley once again stood scrutinising the dance floor, in hope of seeing Jason, or a flash of his purple silk shirt.

'Have you lost someone?' the voice beside her enquired.

Turning to answer Shelley couldn't help liking what she saw. With his floppy dark hair and pale grey, smiling eyes, Wayne had a striking resemblance to the lead singer of A-ha, Morten Harket. Since the band's recent chart success, Wayne's appeal with the ladies had dramatically increased. He played the compliments down, but he was somewhat grateful for the Norwegian band's new popularity.

As a schoolboy, Wayne was overweight and suffered from acne. He was also easily embarrassed and rather shy. Even though he was now a fit and muscular young man who had certainly grown into his looks, he never forgot how it had felt to be an ugly duckling. Although he was a lot more confident these days, he never saw women as notches on his bedpost, and he certainly didn't treat them the way Darren did. He still had one-night stands, but he wasn't prepared to take any sort of girl back to his, just for the sake of getting his leg over.

Immediately recognising Shelley's description of Jason, Wayne decided it was best that he didn't tell her about the fight between his best mate and hers. He did, however, say that he'd seen the lad in question leaving the club about half an hour earlier. He was absolutely sure it was him, due to the flamboyant attire she'd described.

Under normal circumstances, this information would've really worried Shelley, but as she was very tipsy and already attracted to Wayne, she relaxed and freely carried on chatting as they headed to the bar to get some drinks.

An hour later, still engrossed in conversation the slow dances began, signifying that the night was drawing to a close. Wayne and Shelley both looked at their watches in disbelief, wondering where the night had gone. He suggested they dance.

Holding Shelley in his arms, Wayne could smell the sweet lacquer in her hair. He couldn't remember ever being with a girl as beautiful as Shelley before, and he hoped she fancied him as much as he fancied her. As the lights came on and the crowds made their way to the exit, Wayne thought he'd try his luck, asking Shelley back to his. To his amazement she readily agreed.

As they kissed in the taxi on the way back to his, Shelley felt happy. She was drunk and lost in the moment. She didn't have a care in the world. Wayne was the first man she'd kissed since she'd separated from Chris but that thought didn't even enter her head. Wayne's kisses were hungry, and as they entered his bedroom and continued the passion, their intimacy lasted into the small hours.

Chapter 24

Mandy had been working at Cuthbertson & Foster Solicitors for over a year now. For the most part she enjoyed her job and got on well with everyone who worked there. Everyone that was, except Doreen, Mr Cuthbertson's senior secretary.

At forty-eight, Doreen had been a loyal employee of the company for almost twenty years. She was a first-class typist, whose skills in shorthand would take a lot of beating. When Mandy was first employed as junior secretary, Doreen had not been pleased with the decision and there was still no love lost between the pair. Fiercely protective of her position, Doreen took every opportunity to criticise Mandy's work. True, Mandy had no real office experience when she'd began her employment, but since completing the first year of a day release college course in secretarial skills, she had mastered typing and letter writing and was proving to be an asset to the company.

Therefore, Mandy was none too pleased when it came to her twelve-month review and Doreen insisted on sitting in on it. It had gone as expected; Kenneth Cuthbertson had praised her in completing her first year with the company and was glad to hear that she had ambition and was happy there.

Not as happy as you are, Mandy thought to herself, when she pictured him leering at her when she brought him his morning coffee. She also recalled the numerous times he had asked her to remove the dead files from his office floor, to take down to the cellar of the old Victorian building, for archiving. She knew full well that he'd be trying to get an eyeful up her skirt.

It was Doreen, who a few days later delivered the bad news to her, that she would only be receiving a £2 a week pay rise. Mandy was not happy. After all the hard work she'd put in at college, she felt the measly sum unfair. But protesting to Doreen was a waste of time.

Haughtily replying to Mandy's complaint, Doreen announced, 'Mr Cuthbertson and I have decided, that until you've completed next year's course, your salary will remain at a junior's rate. Now take these letters to him for a signature and be sure to get them in tonight's post,' she added, with sneering authority.

Absolutely seething Mandy collected the letters, whilst delivering Doreen with one of her sweetest smiles. There was no way she would let that bitch see how annoyed she was. She was in no doubt that Doreen would've been the one to persuade Mr Cuthbertson to keep her on the junior salary. Well, Mandy had other ideas. She could play dirty too. It would take some planning, but she would make Doreen wish she'd never met her. Though right now she had to get out of that office, before she blew. She was so annoyed she could've happily strung the smug cow up by her American tan tights.

Chapter 25

As the enormous, heavily pregnant woman moved down the line, revealing the next customer, Judy's heart lurched. She hadn't seen Mark Devine in the queue and now he was heading straight towards her counter. Issuing an awkward smile, she was unable to make direct eye contact with him.

'Hi, can I pay these cheques in please?'

Taking the cheques with trembling hands, Judy was sure that her heart could be heard hammering outside her chest. She was only glad that she was seated, as she felt that her legs may not hold her up, had she been standing. They had turned to jelly, and it was all she could do to concentrate on the numbers on the cheques before her.

'Can't believe we're still having this heatwave,' Mark said, making friendly conversation.

As though she were a mute, Judy found she was unable to open her mouth to speak. Staring blankly at Mark, she finally managed a small smile before rapidly diverting her doe-like gaze from him. Wishing she'd not been running late that morning and had managed to wash her hair as planned; Judy could only hope that Mark didn't notice that it was a little greasy. She'd sprinkled some talc on it before deciding to scrape it up, and although it was highly unlikely that any young man would be interested in this fact, Judy was well aware that she wasn't looking her best.

'Have I seen you before, around town on the weekend?' Mark asked, carrying on his friendly chit chat.

Taken aback by his direct question, all Judy could do was nod.

'I thought it was you. The band that was on in The Coach and Horses last week were really good. Did you see them?' he continued.

Finally finding her voice, Judy quietly answered, 'Yeh,' managing a shy smile, before looking back down at her counter.

'Well, I'm sure I'll see you around then,' Mark replied, as she handed him his cheque book.

Watching him casually walk away, Judy's heart was still pounding. She was mesmerised by his perfection. He had actually spoken to her and she couldn't believe she'd acted so dumb. At the same time though, she couldn't help feeling happy. He had made her day and she was on cloud nine. She vowed to herself that she would set her alarm fifteen minutes earlier in future. Next time he came to her counter, she would ensure she looked her very best.

Chapter 26

Taking the letter from the typewriter, Mandy studied her handiwork, grinning.

'Perfect,' she murmured, praising herself as she gathered up the remainder of the documents.

'Come in,' the intimidating voice bellowed, as she knocked on the door of Kenneth Cuthbertson's office.

'I just need your signature on these letters Mr Cuthbertson, please,' said Mandy, making sure she made eye contact with him. Handing him several letters, Mandy waited in anticipation for his reaction.

'Who's typed this?' he asked, with a look of dissatisfaction on his saggy, jowly face.

Knowing he would be sure to see the deliberate typing errors, Mandy smiled slyly to herself. A stickler for perfection, Kenneth Cuthbertson could make no allowances for careless mistakes. Seeing Doreen's initials in the reference, he soon realised the answer to his question.

'Where's Doreen?' he asked, in a rather impatient tone.

'She's gone to the dentist, Mr Cuthbertson,' Mandy answered.

Looking over the next couple of letters, Kenneth began to shake his head, tutting loudly.

'Have you seen this?' he grumbled. 'Such shoddy work. This is not acceptable, at all.'

Seizing her chance, Mandy decided that now was as good a time as any, to stick the boot in for Doreen.

'Actually Mr Cuthbertson, I'm glad that you've seen this for yourself. I felt it was time to bring it to your attention as I was unsure that I could keep it from you any longer. I just didn't want it to look like I was telling tales.'

Looking up at her with confusion, Kenneth's voice softened.

'What is it, dear?' he questioned.

Studying her in more detail, his eyes couldn't help being drawn to her huge breasts, which looked as though they were desperate to escape from the very fitted blouse she was wearing. The subtle amount of cleavage that Mandy displayed, was enough to make Kenneth Cuthbertson feel a hardening in his trousers. Stifling his embarrassment with a cough, he turned his gaze back to the letters.

Aware that she had his full attention, Mandy continued. 'I'm afraid that Doreen has been making these errors on a daily basis for some time now. I have been retyping the letters on my lunch break for weeks, so that you wouldn't notice. I'm worried that her sight may be failing. Or God forbid, something much worse may be affecting her,' Mandy added, her voice full of fake concern for her senior colleague.

'There have been other things too,' she continued, revelling in the shocked look on her boss's face as she revealed more of Doreen's misdemeanours. 'She's been forgetting things a lot lately. She even forgot our address the other day, when she was on the phone with a client.'

Kenneth Cuthbertson's face was a picture and Mandy found it difficult to hide her glee. Taking the letters from him, she informed him that she would hastily retype them in time for that night's post. Leaving the room and allowing him time to digest all that she had told him, Mandy grinned to herself. Her little plan was coming together nicely.

'One nil to Mandy,' she said, quietly under her breath.

Chapter 27

Riding the number 59 bus from Manchester to Oldham, Tina stared out of the window. She watched the outside world going about its daily business; everyone seemed to be acting so normal. Mums pushing prams and a window cleaner scrubbing away the grime of the traffic, from the windows of the houses on the busy main road. Life hadn't changed at all whilst she'd been away. Why would it?

Checking her watch for what must've been the fourth time in the last ten minutes, Tina felt the nervousness of her clammy palms. It had been months since she'd last spoken to her mum. Let alone seen her. Darren had made sure of that with the control he'd instilled over her life. But making the call to her parents only two days before had alleviated any fear she might have had, over a difficult reunion with them.

Beryl Firth was overjoyed at hearing her daughter's voice over the line. She sounded crystal clear. As though she was in the next room. The relief was too much for Beryl to hold inside. Instantly breaking down she clasped her hand to her mouth in shock, calling out to her husband.

'Donald. Oh Donald. It's our Tina, she's alive.'

Never doubting his daughter's mortality, Donald had endured weeks of his wife's over-dramatic imagination and anxiety, believing that Tina would eventually be found dead in a ditch somewhere. But still, he had empathised with his wife every step of the way. Her child, her only daughter was missing, and she was bound to believe the worst.

Due to their love/hate relationship, Tina had never been one to confide in her mum. It was her father who knew her better than anyone, and he knew his girl would be safe. He knew the strength she had inside and her ability to stand on her own two feet.

Many facts had emerged since his daughter had left her husband and gone on the missing list. In a small town such as theirs, someone, somewhere was always willing to disclose the truth. Of course, the rumour mill started but Donald wasn't stupid. He had already begun to see things for himself months ago.

When Tina married and left home, it had become a regular occurrence for her to visit her parents on Thursday evenings, straight from work. That was the day her mum always made a potato pie. Beryl's tater pie was legendary and was always accompanied with red cabbage, mushy peas and brown sauce, making the Lancashire dish complete. It was a time to catch up with her family and she always looked forward to it. It had been difficult at first; Tina was grieving for the child she'd lost and although the subject wasn't really brought up as such, it had been a great comfort to her, knowing that her family were there for her should she need them.

Marrying Darren and losing touch with her family and friends had somewhat isolated Tina. It was clear from day one that he didn't like Shelley and her other girlfriends. He had a devious, manipulative way of making her think that he was just looking out for her. That he had her best interests at heart. But eventually, one by one, her friends began to fade away, and after months of Tina breaking planned arrangements, Shelley too, finally let her be.

It was not easy for Shelley. She could see what was happening. She could see the effect that Darren was having on her best friend and she didn't like it one bit.

The Tina she knew had always been so feisty, with a zest for life. But the Tina who was now in her place was a doormat. A shadow of the girl she once knew. Shelley's instincts told her that it was more than just the miscarriage that was making her once so vibrant friend, now so withdrawn and insular. So, as her best mate she felt she had the right to say her piece.

It had been the third time in a month that Tina had broken plans with Shelley and her excuses were wearing thin. Banging on the door of the terraced house, Shelley had decided to get to the bottom of things, and she wasn't leaving without answers.

'I knew you'd be in. I knew you were bloody lying to me,' Shelley yelled at the startled and now sheepish-looking Tina, as she answered the door. 'Fancy making up a story like that, Tina. Saying that your own niece had been taken to hospital! That's bloody wicked, that is. I've just seen little Stacey with your mum on the swings. She didn't look like she'd broken her arm to me!' Shelley added, shaking her head, her face now red with anger.

As annoyed as she was, Shelley couldn't help but notice how gaunt Tina looked and how tiny her frame was. Under normal circumstances, Shelley would've been full of concern for her, but in her rage, she could only think of her own hurt at being lied to by her so-called best friend, and probably not for the first time.

'If you didn't want to see me, you should've just said,' she continued. 'This is the third time in as many weeks that you've let me down. I can't believe the change in you lately, Tina. All since you've been married to…him!' Off on a tangent, she continued to barrage her friend. 'You're just letting him rule you. You need to get yourself a bloody backbone, girl.'

Feeling close to tears and knowing every word was true, the normally confident Tina felt defeated. But with Darren in earshot, she knew she had to stand her ground. Taking a deep breath, she started back at Shelley.

'What the fuck gives you the right to come around here, to my house, and insult me on my own doorstep?' she bellowed at a gobsmacked Shelley. 'If you want the truth, I'll give you the fucking truth, shall I?' she continued, pointing her finger in Shelley's direction. 'I'm sick of hearing you, going on about your toffee-nosed, posh fella and telling me how much this cost and how much that costs. Swanning around in your trendy new clothes, trying to rub my nose in it all the bloody time and bragging about all the things you're getting for your new house.

'Well I couldn't give a rat's arse how much your bloody new curtains cost you, Shelley. It doesn't matter to me, because true love doesn't cost anything, and that's what

I've got right here with Darren. So, you can take your pelmets and shove 'em where the sun don't shine for all I care! Now piss off from my doorstep and don't come back,' she shouted, as she slammed the door in a stunned Shelley's face.

Storming upstairs with the tears streaming down her face, she heard Darren's voice commending her.

'That told the snooty bitch. Well done Ti, you gave her what for there, love.'

Putting her head in her hands as she sat on her bed, Tina sobbed. Shelley's words had stung her. She knew there was more than a grain of truth to them. But she'd vowed to love Darren, for better, or worse and she would try to make this marriage work, if it was the last thing she did.

Tina had thought of Shelley many times since that sad day when their friendship ended. Although they lived in the same town, they now moved in different circles and that was the last they'd heard of one another. Tina pictured Shelley now. Imagining her blissfully happy with Chris, in their beautiful home. She would probably have a child by now, maybe even two. The thought made her smile, but at the same time she felt sadness, at the loss of the best friend she'd ever known. Tina realised she'd since learnt a valuable lesson, which was to never put a man above such a friendship again.

As the bus pulled into the stop outside C&A, Tina got off, instantly feeling the warm August sun on her bare shoulders. Waiting for the large orange and white vehicle to slowly move past, clearing her view of the buildings in front, she took a deep breath of anticipation.

Furiously waving at her from the other side of the road was the familiar figure of the mother she loved so dearly, and who she had missed so much. As they ran towards each other, the sight of Tina's beautiful beaming smile was too much for Beryl to bear and her tears flowed once more.

'Oh, Tina love. I've missed you so much. It's so good to see you,' she cried, joyously.

The pair hugged each other, tightly.

Composing herself, Beryl held Tina at arm's length, so she could get a good, long look at the daughter, who seemed to have been gone from her life for so long.

'You look wonderful love. Now come on, let's go and get a pot of tea and an egg custard and you can tell me all about it.'

Chapter 28

Nosy Noreen Crosby stood behind the lace curtains of her front room window, in the two-bedroom bungalow that she shared with her husband Glynn, on Duchess Park Close.

'Hey, there's movement across the road,' she exclaimed, with sudden excitement in her voice. 'Glynn turn that bloody TV down,' she ordered, nodding towards the television in the corner of the room. 'All I can hear is Keith Chegwin squealing like a bloody pig.'

Glynn was laughing as Cheggers was once again plunged into a gunk tank, on the popular kids' programme, Saturday Superstore. Cheggers' fate hung in the balance as his co-presenter, Sarah Greene, posed pop trivia questions to some kids from a school in Bristol.

'Shh. If there's going to be another argument, I want to be able to hear it,' Noreen said, grinning, pointing up at the small open panes of the front bay window.

'Come away from that piggin' window will you woman? All I can see is your baggy arse, in those god-awful leggings. You're putting me right off my bacon butties,' said Glynn as he took another big bite, oozing brown sauce from the sides of his mouth.

Opening the gap in the curtains a little more, Noreen responded in protest, 'I'm not missing round two. Not if last night was anything to go by. She's trouble with a capital T, that brazen little mare that he's taken up with. There was none of this when his wife lived there. I'll be making sure our Julie hears about all this. She's one of Shelley's regulars. She'll be sure to inform her about all the goings on that are taking place. In her own home too, I might add. It's bringing the neighbourhood down, this type of behaviour, you know,' she tutted.

'Will you put a sock in it, woman? I can hardly hear the telly now,' moaned Glynn, shaking his head. 'Anyway, never mind "bringing the neighbourhood down", you'd rather look out of those nets than watch bloody Coronation Street, and that's saying somat.'

-

The Bulls Head, in High Crompton was renowned for its Friday night disco. Right on the outskirts of the town, in an almost rural setting, the pub boasted many of the same regulars for years. But the popularity of the Friday disco, held in the tap room, had really taken off. It was only a small venue and often full to capacity, with people coming from all over town to attend. There was hardly ever any trouble though, as the landlord Ken, wouldn't stand for it. At an imposing 6'4", he was a well-known and respected figure in the community. If any fracas were to erupt in his pub, it would soon be extinguished, with both parties being chucked out by Ken, single-handedly.

The local hard men, brothers Micky and Clint McKinney, were transfixed on the sexy body gyrating in front of them, to Phil Collins and Philip Bailey's, *Easy Lover*. Both with faces like a bag of spanners, they couldn't ever be described as good-looking lads, but this didn't affect their popularity with the female of the species. Their battle scars and reputations, and the fact that they were highly feared and respected, made them even more appealing to women.

Wearing the shocking pink, lycra mini dress that she was supposed to be saving for her holiday with Chris, Mandy continued to dance in front of them. With the material clinging to every curve she had, it wasn't just the McKinneys, that couldn't take their eyes off her. Mandy absolutely loved the attention she was getting. Raising her arms above her head as she danced, she continued with the show.

As the bell rang for last orders, Clint, the quieter of the two, made his way to the bar with their empty pint glasses, for a refill. Seizing his opportunity, Micky made his way towards Mandy, putting his arm around her waist as they began to move together as one to the music. Believing he was on a definite promise, Micky moved his large hand to rest on Mandy pert buttocks. When she didn't protest, he gave his brother, who was returning with the drinks, a sly grin.

Suddenly looking up, Mandy stopped dancing and her relaxed body stiffened, at the sight of Chris. On spotting her, he almost dropped his pint. As Micky took in the scene, he immediately realised what was happening. Releasing Mandy after giving her a peck on the cheek, he turned back to Clint who handed him his pint. Usually this type of situation would've ended in a brawl, but after one look at Chris in his pale-yellow shirt, adorned with a thin black leather tie, there was no way Micky would waste his energy on this mummy's boy.

Trying to play down the scene, Mandy gave Chris a wide carefree smile and flung her arms around her him, pretending that she couldn't be happier to see her boyfriend. Peeling her arms away from his neck but trying not to draw attention to himself, Chris turned and walked out of the pub. Though not before shaking his head and throwing his wayward girlfriend a disgusted look.

Chasing Chris in her 4" heels, whilst trying to stop the tight, lycra dress from riding above her knickers as she ran was no easy task, and Mandy was finding it very difficult to keep up with his wide strides, as she tottered behind him. Under normal circumstances Mandy would've just let him go, calling time on the relationship as she had done with many of his predecessors. But with their holiday only a few days away, there was no way Mandy could afford to do that.

'Babe, Chris wait, please! What's wrong with you? Babe…come on, wait, please!' she wailed.

After a few minutes of trying to catch up with her boyfriend and with her pleas falling on deaf ears, Mandy began to get angry. She was not used to being ignored and it was the worst form of punishment that could be dished out to her. As they approached Chris's house Mandy decided she'd had enough of his sulking.

'Chris, I've done nothing wrong. If you think I'm going to start begging you, then you can just fuck off,' she shouted at him.

Stopping in his tracks, Chris turned to face a breathless Mandy, whose feet were now killing her.

'How about you fucking off, back to Lancashire's answer to the Krays?' Chris spat in response.

Realising that this was going to be more difficult than she thought, Mandy changed tactics. 'It looked worse than it was, Chris. As if I'd go with a bloke like him. Especially when I've got someone like you,' she added, her voice softening as she reached out and touched his arm.

He shrugged her off; Chris was not going to be persuaded that easily. 'You're unbelievable, Mandy. You told me you were staying in tonight, and there I find you, in the arms of some…thug. Wearing the dress that I bought you. You wouldn't wear it for me last week. Said you were saving it for the holiday. I'm beginning to think it's right what my mother says about you.'

Seething at the reference to his mother's thoughts on her, Mandy glared at him.

'And what exactly is it that your mother says about me?' she demanded.

As the argument continued, on the doorstep for the next ten minutes, Nosy Noreen was having a field day at her front room window. She'd just sat down with a cup of tea and some digestives, ready to watch Brookside on her

VHS. She taped it religiously, as Glynn wouldn't let her watch Coronation Street as well as the Scouse soap, all in one go.

'One dose of daily crap's enough for me to deal with,' he groaned. 'I'm not having a full hour of this shit you call entertainment.'

So, she was forced to record Brookie and watch it on Friday night, when he went to his local. When all the commotion begun outside, Noreen had been up and out of her seat before Sheila Grant, had time to get Bobby's tea out of the oven. Pressing pause on the recorder she ran to the window, in time to catch the full-scale row between Chris and Mandy, before they eventually took the argument indoors, much to Noreen's dismay.

When their front door finally opened the following morning, Noreen had been only too eager to see if the argument was going to continue. Unfortunately for her, she was only subjected to a long passionate kiss between the couple as Mandy grabbed Chris towards her when they stepped outside. Chris got into his Capri and as Mandy walked to the passenger side, she turned towards Noreen's house, pulling up her stretchy top to reveal her enormous breasts. That gave Noreen something she was definitely not expecting. Then, before she got into the car, Mandy blew her spectator a kiss. Dumbfounded, all

Noreen could do was to turn to face her husband, open-mouthed.

As the car pulled away, Mandy giggled to herself. Who was that nosy cow fooling, thinking she couldn't be seen behind her net curtains?

If it's a show she wants, it's a show she'll get!

Still, Mandy was shattered and couldn't wait to be dropped off at home, so she could go back to bed. The previous night's activities had left her exhausted. After realising that her only option was to back down to her boyfriend, she'd spent a couple of hours allowing him to sound off, whilst she grovelled. Then the next couple of hours giving him the best sex she could muster. She was finally back in his good books and once again in control. Next time she was up to no good, she would ensure that she knew exactly where her boyfriend was. She wouldn't be getting caught out again in a hurry.

Chapter 29

Walking home from work past the Dolphin chippy was pure torture for Judy. The smell of the freshly cooked fish and chips was to die for, and she would often try to get past the shop without breathing in. She'd had an absolutely shit day and even though it was Friday, she wasn't looking forward to the weekend.

Mandy would be flying to Ibiza with Chris that evening on the holiday that she was originally booked on, and although Judy couldn't give two hoots about Mandy, she could really have done with taking a holiday. A break away from work and her mundane life in general, was just what she needed right now. Her new friends, Kath and Jenny had gone to stay at their Aunt's caravan in Pwllheli and she would have no alternative that night, but to stay in and watch, Play Your Cards Right with her mum. She just hoped Sheila was in a better mood than when she'd left her that morning.

Screeching at Dan to get out of his bed and get ready for school, the normally jolly Sheila Smythe was in a raging temper.

'What's up Mum?' Judy asked, giving her a puzzled look.

'What's up? I'm sick of that lazy little shit, that's what's up,' Sheila snapped. 'He went to bed last night, after raiding the bloody fridge and left the door open. Now the milk's off, so I can't even have a brew. Plus, he's left all his dirty pots on the side and I'm just about sick of it.'

Studying her mum's bright red face, Judy wanted to laugh. She looked like an enormous red balloon that was about to burst, after being blown up just that bit too much. Her jowls wobbled as she shook with rage and Judy had to turn away in order not to snigger. After composing herself she turned back to her mum.

'Come on Mum, sit down and calm yourself. I'll make sure Dan gets himself up and ready, and I'll get Dad to have a word with him tonight about the other stuff. Let me nip next door and get some milk from Dorothy and Bert's. They won't mind. You'll have a brew in no time.'

When Judy went to the neighbours, Sheila sat at the kitchen table and put her head in her hands. She wanted to break down and cry, but she knew she had to hold it together. Although keeping to herself the information she had found out a week ago, was killing her. Every day was getting harder. At the mention of her husband, Sheila's thoughts had once again switched to their marriage, which she, in her blind ignorance had thought was perfect.

As usual, Thursday was bustling with shoppers in Shaw town centre. It was market day and the sun was shining. A sure-fire combination to attract those who loved to browse the stalls for their wares and others who saw it as a weekly opportunity to catch up with their fellow townsfolk, for a general gossip. As Sheila was coming out of Greggs with her favourite cheese and onion pasty, accompanied by a chocolate éclair, she'd bumped into an old work colleague, Mavis McReady.

'Hello Sheila,' said Mavis, beaming. 'I've not seen you for a few months. How are you keeping, love?'

Smiling politely in return, Sheila could not believe her bad luck. This was all she needed. With her hands full, from her market purchases and her pasty begging to be eaten, Sheila hoped Mavis would keep it short and sweet. Otherwise she'd be forced to make her excuses and depart. She wanted to be home by 12:30 for The Sullivan's and Pebble Mill at One. But being a pleasant woman, it was not in Sheila's nature to cut someone dead.

Mavis was well known for her acid tongue and she would keep her audience for ages, whilst she gossiped about every man and his dog. However, today Mavis's attention was focused on Sheila herself.

'How's the family, Sheila?'

'Yeah, they're fine. And yours?'

Without answering, Mavis continued. 'How's Malcolm? He's working long hours I see.'

'Er, yes I suppose he is,' Sheila responded, feeling puzzled as Mavis's beady eyes squinted at her, for a reaction, to the mention of her husband's name.

Briefly pausing, before delivering her long-awaited bombshell, Mavis continued. 'Sheila, look. As a close friend of yours, I feel it is my duty to tell you about your Malcolm.' She leaned in closer, dropping her voice to not much more than a whisper.

'What about my Malcolm?' Sheila asked, beginning to feel uneasy.

'Well I'm really sorry to be the bearer of bad news. But, well how can I put this?' Mavis said, with a sympathetic, yet almost gleeful look in her eyes. 'He's having an affair with my next door but one neighbour. It's a well-known fact. I just think it's about time you knew the truth, my dear.'

Sheila stared at Mavis in disbelief, as she continued to inform her of Malcolm's comings and goings, at her neighbour, Brenda Hodder's house. According to Mavis, it had been going on for years and his van was parked there at all hours of the day and night.

Dumbfounded, Sheila made her excuses, waddling off as fast as her chubby legs would allow her.

Since that fateful day, the week had passed in a blur as she tried to digest the information she'd received. Her Malcolm was the love of her life and the only man she'd ever known. She truly believed that the marriage was forever and what she'd been told had rocked her to her foundations. The past few days had left her emotions all over the place, as she pondered on whether to question Malcolm about what she'd been told. He was such a loving husband and she didn't want to believe it could be true. How could there be another woman besides her in his life. If she asked him and he confirmed her worst fears, it would blow their loving family to pieces, and she couldn't bear that.

'Here you go Mum. Get that down you. Tea two sugars, just how you like it,' Judy smiled as she handed her mum the mug. But as she studied her mother's pained expression, Judy had an uneasy feeling. 'What's wrong Mum, are you sure you're okay?' she asked sounding worried.

Sheila looked up with a smile for her thoughtful daughter. 'Yes love, I'm fine. I'm just feeling a bit breathless, that's all. I'll be okay when I've had my brew.'

Judy looked at her mum's red face, covered with beads of sweat. It wasn't the right time to once again bring up the subject of her losing some weight. She would maybe try to speak to her tonight about it. She knew her mum couldn't carry on like this. It surely wasn't good for her health.

'I'm going to work now, Mum. I'll see you tonight, okay?' Judy waved as she was about to walk out of the door.

'Judy,' Sheila called. 'I just want to tell you; you're looking so lovely lately. Well done with your diet love. You should be really proud of yourself.'

'Oh, thanks Mum, that really means a lot,' Judy replied. 'See you tonight. Love you,' she called as she left.

'Love you too.'

One thing that made walking past her favourite chippy easier for Judy to bear, was that every Friday on her way home from work, she would call in at the Chocolate Box confectioners, for her weekly treat. Judy allowed herself her favourite indulgence once a week, which was chocolate. Knowing she had this to look forward to, actually made it easier for her to be disciplined, in her new healthier lifestyle.

Smiling to herself after bidding goodbye to the sales assistant, she popped the peppermint Aero into her bag and turned to walk out of the small shop. The bell above the door rang as she opened it, and her eyes locked on a familiar face. With the smile still on her face, she was met with a welcoming grin, in response.

'Hello Judy,' said Mark, as she stepped outside. 'You on your way home from work then?'

'Er, yeah.' Her heart began to race, and her legs suddenly felt weak. She couldn't believe he knew her name.

'I can give you a lift home if you like.' Mark said, nonchalantly.

His teeth were perfectly straight and looked so white against his tanned face and as Judy smelt a slight waft of dried cement, her hormones went into overdrive. That 'man' smell that builders have was well known as a big turn on for many women, and Judy was no exception.

Not expecting to be suddenly put on the spot, she panicked.

'I…I…I've got to call at my friend's in a minute,' she lied. 'So, it's okay, I'll walk…But thanks anyway.' She found she was unable to look him directly in the eyes but from the look on his face, she couldn't decide whether his expression was one of disappointment or not. She hurriedly made her excuses and began to leave, but before she could get away, Mark continued the conversation.

'That band, Morgan, are playing tonight in The Pineapple. Maybe I'll see you there?'

Before she could stop herself, Judy found she was readily agreeing. The Pineapple was the most central of pubs in the small town and was a great venue for bands to play at. It had a small stage and plenty of floor space for anyone who wished to dance.

'Great, I'll see you later,' Mark grinned, as they parted.

Walking the rest of the way home in a happy daydream, Judy couldn't believe what had just happened. Had Mark Devine actually just asked her out? Or was he making generalised chit chat? She was totally confused but totally ecstatic at the same time. Her two best friends may be away but come hell or high water, Judy would be in that pub tonight. She would find someone to go out with, if it was the last thing she did. Suddenly, her crappy day had turned into the best day she could remember, and she couldn't be happier.

She quickened her pace, in order to get home as fast as she could and choose her outfit for the night ahead.

Suddenly she could hear blaring ambulance sirens coming up behind her. As she turned onto her street, the sound continued to follow her.

Judy was alarmed to see a crowd of people surrounding her house. As she rushed towards them, she could see her brother wailing uncontrollably as his forlorn father attempted to comfort him.

'What's the matter? What's happened?' she screamed at them.

'It's your mum love,' her father began, as his face crumpled, and tears fell from his eyes. 'Dan found her collapsed when he came home from school. I'm so sorry love. She's dead.'

Chapter 30

'You can stop that bloody crying, before I give you something to cry for, lady!' Jackie Jenkins screeched, wagging her finger at her young daughter.

Carly Ann's bottom lip quivered as she tried to control her tears.

'Now get upstairs and out of my sight. I've had enough of you both today,' Jackie snapped.

'My God Jackie. What's wrong with you? She's only five. Don't be so cruel. What's got into you? You're not normally like this,' exclaimed a shocked Shelley, to her fraught sister.

'Oh Shell, you don't know the bloody half of it. God give me strength,' Jackie sighed, raising her palms towards the ceiling. 'I'm sick to the back teeth of it. I can't wait till they go back to school next week. These summer holidays are a killer. Six weeks is far too bloody long.'

'Hey, you weren't saying that when we were at school.' Shelley grinned, trying to lift her sister's mood, with no effect.

'Yeh, well if I'd have known then, what I know now, I'd have done things differently. Believe me,' Jackie continued, shaking her head.

Realising there was obviously more to the situation than just the twins playing her up, Shelley decided it was time for a heart to heart with her big sister. Shelley often called round for a catch up on Monday, which was her day off. It looked like today she'd arrived just in time.

'You put the kettle on, whilst I nip up and see Carly Ann. Poor little mite needs a cuddle from her Auntie Shelley.'

Already feeling guilty for shouting at her daughter, Jackie gave her sister a thankful smile. She was grateful that they'd always been close, and she could confide in her. She'd saddled the weight of her problems for long enough and she could already feel the relief wash over her, in the knowledge that she had her sister to talk to.

-

'She's going to have to go soon, Gerry. You'll have to have a word with her,' complained Carole, as she stubbed out the John Player Special, into an already overflowing ashtray. 'I love her, God knows I love her, but I thought we'd got shut of them both years ago. All this makeup staining my towels and hair clogging up the bathplug. I want my house back to normal. Do you know, I found a diamante dangler in the washing machine the other day? Could've broken the bleeding thing,' she tutted. 'How I ever coped when they were both at home, I'll never know.'

'I'll have a word later then,' Gerry replied, in a downtrodden tone. He would've agreed to anything at that point, just to shut his nagging wife up. 'I think you're being a bit harsh though, love. The kid's down on her luck. Her husband's run off with another woman and her confidence is down. She needs her mam and dad, at a time like this.'

Smirking at her husband, Carole shook her head.

'Her confidence is down? Don't you be bloody fooled, Gerry Barnes. She came home all sheepish at eight o'clock in the morning last Sunday. You're not telling me she was out dancing till that time. She needs to get her arse in gear. That bloody house she owns, with that Valentino ex-husband, well she's entitled to half of that. She needs to get the ball rolling and get back what she's owed. I can't tell her; she just thinks I'm nagging. You'll have to broach the subject, Gerry. And fast.'

Picking up his mug of tea and making his way back to his greenhouse, Gerry's heart felt heavy. He knew his wife was right about Shelley being entitled to half the house she owned with Chris, but he was enjoying having his youngest daughter back home. Her smile lit up the room and as far as he was concerned, she was a joy to have around. His life with Carole was not an easy one and he was henpecked, on a daily basis. He knew he had by no means been the perfect husband; he was a regular at the local bookies and any winnings he did make, which were few and far between, he often sunk in his local pub, The Commercial. He had sought comfort in the arms of other women, on more than one occasion. But in his defence, he knew, that if his wife hadn't been such a nagging thorn in his side, he would've been much more loyal.

Carole was only happy if she had something to complain about and their daughters' return to the fold was just one more thing, to add to her long list. Well, if she wasn't careful one of these days, he might well just shove off, like she was always telling him to. Deep down though, he realised that he was in their turbulent marriage, through thick and thin.

-

'Right, come on then. What's bothering you?' asked Shelley, as she pulled up the dining chair, in Jackie's council house kitchen.

'I don't really know where to start Shell,' Jackie sighed. 'Kev's working all hours and we can hardly afford to make ends meet. The kids are growing so fast and I've had to rely on hand me downs, for their school uniforms for next week's new term. It's embarrassing. It'll be Christmas before you know it, and I'm robbing Peter to pay Paul. God knows how we'll find the money for presents. It's not like when we were kids, Shelley. They want all sorts these days. It's making me ill, all this worry.'

As her sister's eyes began to fill with tears, Shelley leant forward to give her a big hug.

'You seem really hormonal Jackie. Is it your monthly time?'

At this, Jackie broke down completely.

'Whatever's the matter Jackie?' Shelley urged. 'Surely things can't be that bad?'

'That's just it though Shelley. To top it all, I think I'm pregnant. I should be on cloud nine, but the thought terrifies me. There's no way I can afford another mouth to feed. I wanted to get a part-time job when they went back to school, but now there's no chance of that.'

'Oh come 'ere, love.' Shelley beckoned her sister into her outstretched arms once again. 'Don't you worry. I think I might be able to help your situation a little. If you and Kev are in agreement, that is.'

'Why, what do you mean?' asked Jackie, looking up at her younger sister and wiping her red eyes.

'Well I know I've outstayed my welcome at Mum and Dad's. I can definitely sense that Mum's had enough of me. You know what she's like,' she added, as Jackie nodded raising her eyes and giving her a knowing smile. It was lovely for Shelley, seeing her sister smile for the first time that day. She just hoped her idea would be the perfect solution for everyone involved.

'Well what I was thinking was, that I could lodge here with you. At least till I decide what to do about my old house. I know that it's half mine and I should get in contact with a solicitor, but I'm just not ready to yet. So, what do you say? How does sixty pounds a month sound?'

Jackie's eyes lit up.

'Oh Shelley, why didn't I think of that before? It makes perfect sense. The twins are still sharing, and you can have the spare room,' she exclaimed, beaming.

'Will Kev be okay with it?' Shelley asked her suddenly very excited sister.

'You leave Kev to me,' Jackie grinned. 'He'll do as he's told. He always does.'

'Great, that's settled then. I'll go and tell Mum and Dad,' said Shelley. 'She'll probably put the bloody flags out.'

'I don't doubt it,' replied Jackie, as they raised their cups of tea in unison.

Chapter 31

'Who the bloody hell's that, now?' Ivy Doyle complained, shuffling down the hall in her slippers. 'Banging me pissing door down at this time on a Monday morning.'

Although it was hardly early, 10 o'clock in the morning was an inconvenient time to be knocking. Ivy was knee deep in washing and she did not take kindly to interruptions.

Standing at just 4ft 10", Ivy Doyle was known to everyone as, Little Ivy. Her height was a mystery as her parents had been tall, as were her nine brothers and sisters. It was often joked that her father was the milk man, and that statement may have been taken more seriously, had her mother Violet and father Tom, not been so in love.

Never had a couple been so devoted to one another. They had died five years previously, within two weeks of each other. Violet taken first from pneumonia and Tom dying in his sleep shortly after. Everyone who knew them, said that he had died of a broken heart and no one ever challenged that conclusion. They had been a quiet, gentle and kind couple, who were often remembered with great affection.

Ivy, on the other hand, was as different from her parents as day was to night. What she lacked in height she certainly made up for in character. Her heart was in the right place and she would help a neighbour in need, but woe betide anyone who crossed her. She had a fearless nature and a temper to match. The locals still recalled the time she'd marched into The Coach and Horses and smacked Harry Talbot around the head with a leg of lamb, after finding out he was the culprit, who had relieved himself in her front doorway on the previous night, as he'd walked home from his local in a drunken stupor.

A widow for the best part of twenty years, she had been mother and father to her four children, and after three daughters, her lastborn child, a son, was the apple of her eye. Darren could do no wrong as far as Ivy was concerned. He was the image of her late husband Brendan, with his thick, black hair, dark brown eyes and chiselled features.

Ivy and Brendan had fought like cat and dog every day of their married life, but she would have died for him. Although she never showed her feelings to the outside world, to this day there were still nights when she cried herself to sleep. She had never truly got over his sudden death, and the day that she'd been informed that her beloved Brendan had fallen to his demise from a 40ft high scaffolding, still remained the worst day of her life.

Yet, never one to wallow in her own self-pity, Ivy was a tough woman who had worked her fingers to the bone, in order to provide for her children. Dusting herself down, she continued with her life as best she could. Moreover, she had sworn that there would never be another to replace her beloved Brendan. True to her word, Ivy had never looked at another man since his death and never would.

'Is he here? I bet he is, 'cause he's not at bleeding work again.' Bernadette Kennedy barked, barging straight past her mother as she opened the front door.

'Oh, hello to you too.' Ivy replied, sarcastically, to her youngest daughter.

Following Bernadette into the kitchen, Ivy braced herself for the fallout, she was certain was about to commence.

Entering the room and setting eyes on her wayward brother, Bernadette let rip.

'Look at him. Stuffing his bleeding face without a care in the world. I knew he'd be here!' she shouted to her mother, whilst still glaring at Darren, who was merrily tucking into a full English breakfast, lovingly prepared by Ivy, moments before.

'What's with all the dramatics now, lady?' Ivy wagged a bony finger at her daughter. 'Don't you be coming around here, shouting the odds in my house. What the bloody hell's the matter with you. Have you lost your nut or somat?'

'It's him, Mum.' retorted Bernadette. In a lower, sulkier voice. 'He's not showed up for work again and I'm sick of taking the flack for it. Ian's threatening to come and give him a good hiding. Family or no family. I've had to beg him not to come looking for him. He'll get the sack for sure, this time,' she added.

At the mention of violent threats from the arrogant boss he hated, who just happened to be his sister's husband, Darren's anger suddenly rose.

'He can come and fucking well try,' he snarled, putting down his knife and fork and rising from his chair. 'Come on then, let's go and find your tosser of a husband, shall we. Let's see if he's still as cocky to my bleedin' face?'

Quick to intervene, Ivy turned to Darren.

'Now sit yourself back down son,' she said. Putting her hand on his chest and stepping between her grown up children, who both towered over her. 'There'll be no fighting today.'

Shaking his head at his now startled sister, Darren sat back down, continuing with his breakfast.

'See what you've started now.' Ivy said, turning towards her daughter. 'You can't just leave it alone, can you? They'd be brawling outside my front door, for all the bleeding neighbours to see, if it were left to you.'

'My God, Mother.' Bernadette began, staring at Ivy in disbelief. 'I can't believe you're siding with him, again! I've been warning him for weeks and this is the thanks I get.'

'But it's the way you go about it Bernie.' Ivy said, her voice softening. 'Look, I realise your intentions are good, but you can't come barging in here getting everyone's backs up. The lad's not well. He's cracked a rib playing five-a-side. He can hardly bend over. He's not fit to be in work and that's why he's here.'

'Oh yeah, that's what he's telling you, Ma. What about the other half a dozen Mondays he's skived off, in the last two months? It's not fair Mum. I'm stuck in the middle. My loyalties are torn.'

Bernadette felt herself becoming teary. There was only eighteen months between herself and Darren and until her marriage to Ian Kennedy, they had been extremely close. She knew he was her Mum's favourite, but he was *her* favourite too, and with him being the youngest sibling and the only son, that seemed to make it his privilege.

Ivy could read between the lines. She knew her son was no angel. She also knew that he wasn't coping as well as he'd have her believe, since the departure of his wife. Ivy had liked Tina. There were aspects of Tina that reminded her of herself, when she was young. When they'd first become a couple, Tina had been strong-willed and feisty. Ivy noticed the change in her daughter in law, happen gradually, and at first, she put it down to the miscarriage. Ivy herself, knew the despair that losing a child could bring.

She had experienced her own heartbreak when her first baby had been delivered, stillborn. It had been a boy, who she had named Thomas, after her own father. Following the event, it was never mentioned by her family, who thought they were sparing her feelings. This however, had further intensified the unhappiness she felt, after losing him. Making it impossible for her to grieve properly. Even her children were unaware of the loss their mother had suffered, prior to their own existence.

However, one unexpected day, Ivy found herself opening up to her young daughter-in-law, shortly after her own miscarriage. They had spent an unplanned afternoon drinking tea and sharing the sorrowful accounts, of their tragedies. It was Ivy who ended up doing most of the talking and although her visit to Tina was to initially cheer the girl up, it had ended up being the therapy that Ivy had needed. For this fact alone, she would be forever grateful, to her only son's wife.

What Ivy didn't know was the extent of Darren's violence towards Tina. She was unaware of the harsh treatment that her son had inflicted, many times upon his beautiful wife, and the confidence he had slowly drained from her. His conduct had sucked out the majority of Tina's lively and fun-loving personality. Until she'd been left a frightened shell of her former self.

Ivy was old school, believing a woman's place was in the kitchen, whilst the husband was responsible for providing for his family. She always backed up many of her son's ideas within his marriage. But if she'd known of it, she would never condone the violence he had shown to Tina, throughout their time together. She wouldn't think twice about giving Darren a thick ear, had she realised the extent of the misery he had caused. But his version of events were quite different, leaving Ivy feeling completely sorry for her beloved son. So, now believing his side of the story, she never missed an opportunity to bad-mouth the daughter-in-law, she had once taken to as her own.

Guiding her daughter towards the front door, Ivy lowered her voice, as she spoke.

'Listen Bernie. I'm not one to speak out of turn, you know that, but I'm worried about that lad. He's taken this break-up a lot worse than any of you lot realise,' she murmured, nodding towards the kitchen, where Darren was mopping up the remains of his bean juice with a Warburton's doorstep crust.

'Maybe he should've treated her a bit better, then,' replied Bernadette. 'She ran around after him like a blue-arsed fly, Mother. Lost all her friends and never went anywhere. I think I'd have left him too. These blokes don't realise how much we women actually do for them, until it's too late. My God, the amount of times I could've walked out on Ian, is beyond me. He never lifts a finger in the house and spends most of his time down the pub.'

'That's the difference though, Bern,' Ivy said, folding her arms and pursing her lips. 'You've made your bed and you lie in it. That's what we women do. From the information I've gathered from our Darren, there was a side to the lovely Tina that we never got to see.'

'What do you mean?' Bernadette enquired, interested to hear her mother's gossip.

'Well, this in strictest confidence, Bern. And I warn you, if this gets out there'll be trouble. I'm telling you. There's only me and you know this, so I'll know if it gets around, it'll have come from you.'

'It won't, Mother. Just tell me,' her daughter replied, in an exasperated tone.

'Well,' Ivy continued, almost whispering now. 'He thinks she's run off with another bloke.'

'No,' replied a wide-eyed, shocked Bernadette. 'I don't believe it. Not Tina, she worshiped him.'

'Mmm, well that's what she'd like you to believe. That lad's opened up to me. He had tears in his eyes when he told me how much he loved her. He said that whatever he did, was never enough for her. Apparently, there was nothing going on in the bedroom department either. She was denying him of his nuptials. So, you can hardly blame the lad for going out as much as he did. He also told me that he suspected, she'd been carrying on with some bloke from work,' added a stern-faced Ivy.

Bernadette gasped. 'I'm not having that, Mother. Tina isn't like that.'

Already on her soap box, Ivy continued. 'Well, it makes you think, doesn't it? We heard she'd been laid off at work, but after what Darren's said, she's probably been sacked, for carrying on at work! I bet that's why they've run off together, her and this bloke.'

Shaking her head at her mother's words, Bernadette responded, 'I think you might be getting ahead of yourself now, Ma. There's no proof to any of this, is there? As far as we know, no one, including her own family has seen her.'

Feeling annoyed at her daughter's dismissal, Ivy felt her blood boil, but managed to keep her voice low.

'Well I know my son, and if that's what he's said, then I believe him,' she spat. 'He might not be perfect, but he doesn't deserve that. So, you can tell that bloody husband of yours to lay off him, because I think he's close to a breakdown. Your brother needs his family's support at a time like this. Not pressure like Ian's been giving him. You tell him, Darren will be taking some time off, and if he's got a problem with it, he can come and see me,' Ivy finished, pointing a bony finger towards her chest.

Bernadette sighed. 'Okay, if that's what you think's best,' she replied, defeated.

She knew it was pointless trying to get her mother to see anyone else's point of view. She would back her son to the hilt, and there was no way that Bernadette was going to be the one to inform her mum of the gossip that was going around the local rumour mill, about the real reason her beloved son's wife had left him.

Giving Ivy a peck on the cheek, she left the house feeling as frustrated, as when she'd arrived. Going home to her husband, she could bet her life that she'd be entering another row when she informed him of her wasted visit. Oh well, as usual, she'd just have to suck it up.

'Families, who'd have 'em,' she muttered to herself, as her mother firmly closed the front door behind her.

Chapter 32

Extending her long, tanned limbs on the sun lounger, Mandy gracefully stretched and sighed.

'This is the life, hey Chris?' she said, smiling at her boyfriend.

'You're not wrong babe. Sun, sea, sand and plenty of sex. And if last night's performance was anything to go by, long may it continue.'

'Cheeky,' Mandy giggled. 'It was great though, wasn't it?' she grinned recalling their marathon session, the night before.

She knew exactly how to raise Chris's pulse, remembering how she had poured and seductively massaged in the Ambre Solaire coconut oil, all over her bronzed chest, whilst riding her boyfriend for all he was worth; he'd hardly been able to contain his excitement.

Seeing her enormous breasts glistening as they bounced up and down, was almost too much for Chris to take. He'd had to muster all the strength he could and divert his dirty thoughts in order for their passion to continue. Mandy was by far the sexiest woman he had ever encountered and this fact alone, made her hold over him a very powerful one.

'Fancy a Solero babe?' he asked, as he leant towards her, gently stroking her tummy.

Gesturing towards the pool bar, Mandy grinned. 'I'd rather have a cocktail. Happy hour's just started. Sex on the beach sounds more up my street.'

'Anything for you. You deserve as much sex on the beach as you like,' he smiled, blowing her a kiss before leaving to head to the bar.

Mandy sighed. Chris was a lovely guy, but a bit too wet for her liking. She wasn't complaining though. She hadn't spent a thing in the five days they'd been away. He had treated her to some Anais Anais perfume, in the duty-free shop at the airport and some gold earrings from a quaint little jeweller's in the old town. They were shaped like dolphins and were very pretty, but she knew she would never wear them back home, preferring the gold hoops or diamante danglers that were currently the height of fashion. Still, it was nice to be spoilt and

Mandy never refused the chance to have money spent on her.

Bending to turn her lounger to face the mid-afternoon sun, Mandy adjusted her bikini bottoms as seductively as she could, tracing the outline of her pert cheeks with her fingers as she rubbed in a little suntan lotion. She was aware that she had an audience and never missed an opportunity to play to the crowd. On several occasions, she had noticed the four young lads from the same hotel, gazing admiringly at her. She had affectionately named them 'The Quads', as they were all blonde and around the same height, with similar boyish slim physiques. Catching the gaze of the most handsome of the four, she gave him a cheeky wink, before lying back down on her lounger.

Mandy knew exactly what he was thinking. She had long since gained the ability to read men's thoughts. She was never insulted by them and loved the way she could manipulate her prey, and the power she held over the opposite sex. Getting comfortable she smiled to herself. If she was here with Judy instead of Chris, she would have been able to continue the flirting and probably ending up taking things further. There was a large, Club 18-30 party, staying at the hotel and Mandy found herself feeling envious of the fun and frolics that were going on amongst them. She knew, had she been here with Judy, that she would've been in the thick of it.

She smiled, thinking about Judy affectionately. She felt a little sorry for betraying her best and only true female friend. She had other girl mates who she could call on for a night out, but none were reliable like Judy was. Judy never complained and was always happy to allow Mandy to be herself. Enjoying all the limelight. Never one to dwell on her woes, Mandy decided she would seek Judy out, on her return from Ibiza. She would give it a couple of weeks, in order to allow the dust to settle. She was sure her loyal friend could not stay mad at her for long.

Briefly turning her thoughts to work, Mandy wondered how they were getting on without her. She hoped that Doreen had not managed to crawl her way back into Mr Cuthbertson's good books. She grinned when she thought of the letter, she had posted on the day she went on leave. She had addressed it 'Private and Confidential' to Kenneth Cuthbertson, pretending it was from a disgruntled client, who wished to remain anonymous. The letter suggested that Mr Cuthbertson, should address his rude and condescending secretary, Doreen, who had spoken to them in a most disrespectful manner. It went on to say that they were so unhappy with the treatment they'd received from her, that they were considering taking their business elsewhere.

Mandy smiled to herself, picturing her boss's face as he read the contents of the complaint. That would give old

Kenneth something to think about. Hopefully, in the not too distant future, Doreen would be out on her ear, and she, Mandy, would become his well-deserved, senior secretary.

She also thought about the interesting appointment she had seen in the diary, for Mark and Marion Devine. Next to their name in brackets, the word "(probate)" was written. Quickly scanning the files in Mr Cuthbertson's office whilst he was on lunch, Mandy soon put two and two together, realising that they were the acting lawyers for her ex-boyfriend and his mother. His father's sudden passing had left him inheriting a successful business, along with a tidy sum of money.

Thinking about what she had learned that day, Mandy also decided that the once penniless ex, she had readily dumped, was definitely worth a second chance. She smiled wryly to herself as she thought of her forthcoming plans.

'Here you go gorgeous. One sex on the beach for my beautiful lady,' gushed Chris, handing her the colourful cocktail.

'Oh thanks, babes. You're so good to me,' Mandy replied, smiling falsely. 'You're most definitely a keeper.'

Chapter 33

'Oh Jackie, you look gorgeous. And the sequins on that blue dress really match your eyes,' beamed Shelley, as her sister entered the living room.

Looking slightly nervous and a little uncomfortable, Jackie asked, 'You don't think it's too much; I don't look like a dog's dinner, do I?'

Shelley gave her sister a reassuring smile. 'Jackie, you look a picture. You really do. It's that long since you've got dressed up and been on a night out, you've just lost your confidence, that's all. Wait till Kev sees you. You look knock out. He'll be blown away.'

'Let's hope so. I've forgotten what it's like to get dolled up. That's what having twins does to you.'

Shelley grinned. 'Well, when he sees you looking like that, you'll be lucky if you make it out. I can see him wanting to take you straight up to bed.'

Jackie raised her eyebrows and laughed. 'Well after the scare I've just had, I'll settle for a couple of halves of lager, rather than a night of passion.'

'It must've been all the stress you've been under,' Shelley replied. 'That's why your period was late. It's a funny thing, stress and worry. It shows itself in all kinds of different ways. Remember that really posh lad in your class, Tim something or other? All his hair fell out when he was worrying about his exams?'

Recalling her school days, Jackie nodded. 'Oh yeah! And there was that woman dad used to tell us about, whose hair went white overnight when she saw her kid get run over by a steamroller, outside her house.'

Shelley snorted, nearly spraying the mouthful of the tea, she'd just gulped. 'You didn't actually believe that story, did you?' She sniggered, amused at her sister's innocence. 'Dad made that up when we were kids, to stop us from running in the road when we were playing out.'

'Really?' gawped Jackie, open-mouthed. 'All these years I've believed it.'

The girls began to laugh as they remembered their childhood fondly.

'Hey, I can't thank you enough for giving us the rent upfront,' Jackie smiled, enfolding her sister's hands in hers. 'It's a godsend you moving in here. I mean it Shell. I'm truly grateful.'

Shelley beamed lovingly at her older sister.

'Jac, I don't want your thanks. I'm just as grateful to you, for letting me stay. Anyway, see if you're just as keen when I've been here a few weeks,' she laughed, as she remembered the fights they used to have as teenagers, when they'd shared a bedroom.

Just then, Ben and Carly Ann came in from the back garden. Running towards their mother, they halted in their tracks as their auntie cried out.

'Ah ah ah, don't touch Mummy's dress with your dirty hands, kids.'

They looked up at their mum, as though it was the first time they'd ever seen her. Carly Ann was the first to break the silence.

'Mummy, you look like a beautiful princess,' she said, in awe.

Adding to his sister's compliment, Ben enquired, 'Are you going to a party, Mummy? You look lovely.'

Jackie's eyes began to fill up and she beamed with pride, but before she was able to answer, the twins both asked, in their excited voices.

'Can we come?'

Jackie and Shelley both laughed.

'Mummy and Daddy are going on a special night out,' Shelley told them. 'It's their wedding anniversary and they're going for a meal to celebrate,' she said, trying to explain to the bewildered pair. 'Now you've got ten minutes before you have to come in and get your pyjamas on. So, if I were you, I'd go back in the garden and make the most of it.'

She gave Ben and his sister's tummies a tickle as the giggling, pair ran out of the back door without a second glance. Smiling after her beloved twins, Jackie turned to her sister.

'My God, I love those two Shell, but I can't tell you how relieved I was when I realised, I wasn't pregnant, and it was just a false alarm.'

'I know, but you've got me here to ease the burden and now they're going back to school, you can look for a part-time job. I bet Littlewoods will be taking on soon.

There's bound to be some jobs going, and you've done packing before.'

Jackie nodded. 'Yeh, I've already decided I'm going to have a walk down on Monday, to fill out an application form.'

'Anyway,' Jackie said, changing the subject and narrowing her eyes as she looked quizzically at her beautiful sister. 'How do you know Irene and Bernard's grandson, Wayne?'

Shelley blushed, unable to hide her embarrassment.

'Come on then,' Jackie asked, grinning, realising she'd touched a nerve. 'I saw you both deep in conversation outside their house yesterday,' she nodded towards the living room window, which faced her elderly neighbours' house.

Taking a deep breath, Shelley decided to tell her sister about the one night stand she'd had with Wayne a few weeks before. Leaving out the graphic details, she recalled how they'd met and spent the night together, and how she'd told him she wasn't interested in meeting up with him again.

'I honestly thought that would be the last time I'd ever see him. I was gobsmacked when I was walking to yours and I looked up and saw him mowing his gran's lawn. I nearly had the shock of my life when he began walking over to me. My knees nearly buckled, and I got my headphones stuck in my banana clip. I couldn't find the stop button on my Walkman. I was so flustered.'

Jackie laughed at the scene her sister described. 'He does look fit with his top off though, Shell,' she giggled. 'You could do a lot worse.'

Shelley grinned. 'I know, he's really hot. I'd forgotten how handsome he was. He asked if he could see me tonight, but I told him I was babysitting for you.'

'You should've said you were out with your mates,' Jackie chided, offering her sister some words of wisdom. 'It'll do no harm, for you to treat him mean. It keeps 'em keen.' She nodded.

'You sound just like Mum.'

Wide-eyed, Jackie was quick to respond. 'Oh God, don't say that,' she laughed, as they heard Kevin's heavy footsteps coming down the stairs.

As he entered the room, doused heavily in Jazz aftershave; he couldn't contain the look of admiration on his face, when he saw his wife.

'Wow, Mrs Jenkins. You look bloody fantastic! I am one lucky man,' he added, beaming as he bent to kiss Jackie on the lips.

'Watch the lippy,' she scolded, offering him her cheek instead. 'There'll be plenty of chances for kissing later, when we're dancing the night away.' She winked, grinning at her sister.

Shelley thought to herself, how lovely it was to see her sister and brother-in-law so happy. It made her realise that the majority of what she'd had with Chris, had been based on material things. True love was a rare blessing that no amount of money could buy, and these two had it in abundance.

As she watched them walking down the path hand in hand towards their awaiting taxi, she could only hope that, some day she would find a man who loved her just as much as these two loved each other. For now, though, she was happy to find herself again and have a bit of fun. She decided that next time Wayne asked her out, she might very well say yes.

Chapter 34

The funeral was a sombre affair and as Judy said goodbye to the last of the mourners, she closed the front door and slumped to the floor.

Finally letting out the sobs that she'd been holding in all week, she continued to cry uncontrollably for the next hour. The reality of the life-changing events that had happened to her family, over the past few days were finally beginning to sink in. Judy felt as though the ache inside her chest, might actually break her heart in two. Friends and family had rallied round and on returning from their holiday, her two friends Kath and Jenny had shown her amazing support. But nothing could take away the hurt she felt, at losing her mum so suddenly.

Her dad had done a disappearing act a couple of hours previously and she was left with little doubt as to where he might be. Not knowing if she loved or hated her father at this precise moment in time, she was at least grateful that her younger brother Dan, was staying with their dad's sister, Joyce, in Halifax.

Judy was sure that she couldn't hurt any more than she did on the day she learnt about her mother's untimely death. But, on the night before the funeral, when she and her dad were reminiscing in the kitchen, he had dropped the bombshell which she'd never in a million years expected to hear.

They'd been laughing and crying together as they remembered her mother fondly and then after half a bottle of whisky, Malcolm began to cry. As Judy tried to be strong for her father and comfort him, his sobs became uncontrollable. Such was his guilt that he kept reciting the same words over and over. Telling her what a terrible husband he was.

'Ssshh, Dad. Don't say that. You were a wonderful husband and Mum loved you so much,' she hushed, as she held him to her.

Eventually breaking free from her arms, Malcolm stood with his head in his hands as he cried, whilst trying to speak.

'You don't know what I've done, Judy,' he wailed. 'You don't know, and you'll never forgive me when you do. Neither would your mother, if she'd known.'

Looking at her father puzzled, Judy knew she had to ask what he meant.

'Dad what is it? You can tell me. It can't be as bad as you think,' she said, in a comforting voice.

Letting out a loud cry, Malcolm Smythe shook his head and continued to weep. Eventually he removed his hands from his face so that he could look at his daughter.

'I have to be honest, Judy. I can't live a lie anymore!' he wailed, as his bloodshot eyes looked directly into hers. The tears soaked his cheeks as he continued and taking a deep breath he tried to compose himself. 'I loved your mum sweetheart, honestly I did. She was a wonderful woman, but I have to be truthful with you from now on. We can't start our new future whilst I'm living this lie.'

Terrified at what her dad was about to say, Judy held her breath, hardly daring to move.

Malcolm told Judy all about his love for Brenda and how he'd never meant to hurt his wife. 'It just happened Judy, and now your mum's gone I need to be honest with you. I want to be with Brenda. I can't live without her,' he sniffed. 'I don't expect you to understand, but please Judy, please find it in your heart to forgive me,' he begged.

As Judy tried to digest this latest information, the stillness in the kitchen seemed to go on for an age. Finally breaking the silence, Malcolm was the first to speak.

'Say something Judy. Please say something, love,' he pleaded, reaching his hand towards hers.

Swiftly pulling away, Judy glared at him with stony eyes.

'How could you?' she spoke. Her voice low and full of loathing, as she turned hurriedly and ran up the stairs to her room.

She hardly managed any sleep that night. Unable to forget the words her father had said, Judy could think about nothing else.

The house was busy the next morning with family and friends, meaning that Judy and her father had not spent any time alone, and for that much she was grateful. She knew she couldn't find the right words to say to him – she didn't even want to look at him, right now. Her poor lovely mum certainly hadn't deserved such a betrayal, from the man she had loved for so long. Judy's one consolation, was that her mum would go to her grave never doubting the love of her dutiful husband. Or so she thought.

Gazing upon all the leftover food in the kitchen, Judy realised that she hadn't eaten a thing all day. Kath and

Jenny had offered to help clean up, but she just wanted to be alone and they had been wise enough to sense this.

Sitting at the table, Judy poured herself a large glass of Blue Nun. She removed the clingfilm from a tray of egg and cress sandwiches and took a bite. She wasn't particularly hungry and couldn't even remember the last time she'd eaten a proper meal, but the buttery egg tasted creamy in her mouth and she could feel a sliver of cress caress her tongue. The bread was still soft, although the crust had hardened a little and the sensation and taste of the food in her mouth, along with the smell of the dough travelling through her nostrils, suddenly awakened Judy's taste buds.

Before she had fully swallowed her first mouthful, Judy stuffed a handful of salted peanuts in her mouth to accompany the sandwich. Greedily swigging a large mouthful of wine, she reached for a cocktail sausage roll and began to devour it.

Twenty minutes later, Judy sat crouched on her knees retching as she held onto the toilet seat. As her tears mixed with mucus and vomit inside the pan she cried aloud for her mum, which she always did when she was sick. Facing the variety of buffet food which she had just regurgitated, Judy felt disgusted with herself as visions of her ploughing through the food flashed through her mind.

She'd been like a human vacuum, devouring her way through the buffet; nothing had escaped her. Sandwiches, crisps, nuts and vol-au-vents were all consumed at a rapid pace. Then without hesitating she completed her mammoth spree with the consumption of a hefty portion of, black forest gateaux. Greedily spooning mouthfuls straight into her readily awaiting feeding tunnel, she hardly even tasted the rich, sweet dessert, before it was swallowed.

No sooner had the third and final glass of wine been downed, than the familiar watery sensation began to secrete in her mouth. Managing to reach the bathroom with seconds to spare, Judy emptied the contents of her guts into the awaiting toilet.

When she was fully spent, she lay down on her bed feeling disgust at her ravenous greed. Her only consolation was that she wouldn't gain any weight from her late-night gorge. With her stomach tender and her throat sore from retching, Judy finally closed her eyes, on what could only be described as the worst day of her young life.

Chapter 35

It was a surreal feeling for Tina to wake up in her old bedroom, as it was over two years since she'd left home, on what she thought was the happiest day of her life. In her room it was as though time had stood still. Everything remained the same. A room designed to house a teenage girl, whose dream was to marry her prince charming and live happily ever after. Even the fluffy toys that she'd been unable to part with as a young adult, still sat on the shelf. Tina closed her eyes sighing heavily, as the realisation that she was back living with her parents, finally hit her. Her life was currently one big disaster.

Her mum and dad had been brilliant, and she couldn't fault them in any way, but she was used to her independence and she knew for her own sanity that this arrangement would have to be a temporary one. She adored her parents, but it surely wouldn't be long before she would clash personalities, with her mum. After everything they'd done for her, she wanted more than anything to stay on good terms with them. Her vision was clear. She needed a job and a place to live, and to get her independence back. Getting a job was her first priority and as it was August Bank Holiday weekend, she decided she would begin her search first thing Tuesday morning.

She realised it wouldn't take too long before the news of her return reached the ears of her estranged husband. With the support of her family, Tina currently felt strong enough to deal with the fallout that she was sure Darren would create. Although she couldn't stop the worry that niggled away in the back of her mind, especially if she gave it too much of her time. She needed to think positive. She was back with the people who truly cared for her and with their backing, she was sure she could deal with whatever came her way. For now, she was just happy to let her mum spoil her.

Putting on her dressing gown and slippers, Tina opened her bedroom door, taking in the aroma of bacon that wafted onto the landing. One of her mum's cooked breakfasts was just what she needed right now, and she was determined to relax and enjoy her lazy Sunday, in the bosom of the family she had missed for so long. What she was blissfully unaware of, was that Darren had already found out about her return and was strategically deciding his next move.

-

Agreeing to have a quiet night in their local, Darren and his mates were playing pool in the Moulders Arms. It was August Bank Holiday weekend and the lads had decided to save their energy for a mammoth Sunday session, to end the summer with a bang. Dave was DJ'ing at an engagement party, so it was Wayne and Bryn who accompanied Darren, on this particular Saturday night.

'Fancy playing doubles?' Wayne asked, joining the lads at the pool table, with his first pint of the evening.

'Can do mate but we'll have to find another player as we've no Dave tonight,' replied Bryn.

It was still early, and the pub was pretty empty, with just a few teatime stragglers left in the tap room. Grinning slyly, Bryn nodded his head towards the corner of the room, where a lonely figure was sitting nursing his pint.

'What about Dopey Geoffrey? He's not a bad player.'

'That halfwit? You can pair up with him, Wayne. I'm not,' sneered Darren. 'He's thick as shit and dull as dishwater. All he talks about is trains. He always reminds me of a kiddie fiddler, in that anorak he wears.'

'Aw don't be tight. He's just a bit simple and lonely. He can't help it. You're not wrong though, he does look a bit suspect in that mac,' replied Wayne.

Known to many as the village idiot, Geoffrey Duncan kept himself to himself. School had been a very lonely, uninviting place for Geoffrey. He'd been bullied a lot and had come to realise, that it was better to remain in the background. Especially in the pub, where he was surrounded by lots of testosterone-filled males. As an adult, he was subjected to more light-hearted banter but the comments he received could be cruel and hurtful. Still, he tried to take them on the chin.

'Hey Geoff,' Wayne called out. 'Fancy partnering me against these two, in a game of doubles? I've heard you're a pretty mean player.'

Looking up, Geoffrey nodded eagerly. He loved being included and could think of no better way to spend the next hour or so, than with the popular Darren and his crew.

The game was running smoothly, and the lads were playing first to five. Darren and Bryn had just levelled the match at four all and everything, was riding on the final game.

'Rack 'em up Geoffrey lad, it's all on this one, mate.' Wayne winked at his partner.

Geoffrey was thoroughly enjoying himself, hoping that the lads might ask him to play, on a regular basis. He lived a lonely existence and was relishing being part of a group. He'd even chipped in a couple of times with the banter, and to his amazement, no one had laughed at him or made him feel foolish. This was the best evening he'd had in a long time.

'Right you two,' grinned Darren. 'If your pool's anything like your pulling skills, then me and Bryn have nothing to worry about. We've gone easy on you so far. Now it's time to separate the men from the boys.'

'Pffft, you obviously haven't seen me in action lately, mate,' Wayne chuckled. 'That blonde I copped off with the other week, was hotter than Samantha Fox. And she had a great set of knockers. I think it's you who's lost your touch, mate. The only birds you pull lately, are the likes of Leanne Dagger. Unless you count pulling yourself.'

They all started laughing at Wayne's quick wit, and shrugging his shoulders in surrender, Darren grinned.

'Okay, you got me, pretty boy, But I'll be back at the top of my game before you know it. And when I am, you'll have no chance.'

Deciding to share his input with the jokes, and wanting to get on Darren's good side, Geoffrey added to the banter.

'Hey Darren,' he chipped in. 'Now Tina's home, you'll show 'em. Bet you'll win her back in no time, won't you?'

As silence descended in the small tap room, Bryn and Wayne's eyes quickly shifted towards Darren, knowing how erratic his temper could be. Slowly putting his pool cue down on the table, Darren walked over to where Geoffrey was standing.

'What the fuck did you say, you, simple prick?' Darren's face twisted, in a menacing snarl.

A look of total fear clouded over Geoffrey's face, at the realisation that he'd obviously said something he shouldn't have. Taking in the scene, Wayne and Bryn hurriedly made their way towards Darren's side. Bryn was the first to speak to his hot-tempered friend.

'Leave it, mate. It's not worth it.'

'Yeah,' added Wayne. 'He's obviously not the brightest spark. I'm sure he didn't mean anything by it.'

Ignoring his friends, Darren continued, moving his face to within an inch of Geoffrey's.

'What the fuck do you mean, Tina's back? Grabbing Geoffrey's anorak, by the chest he questioned him again in a lower, more threatening tone. Tell me what the fuck you know, before I smash my fist down your throat,' he warned.

Frozen with fear, Geoffrey could barely breathe, let alone speak. He suddenly felt the warmth of his own urine, spreading across the front of his cords and down his legs, and through a mixture of embarrassment and fear, he began to cry.

'Please don't hit me,' he begged, raising his hands to protect his head. 'I didn't mean it. I just saw Tina going in her mum's the other day and I thought you'd be happy. I'm so sorry.'

Darren patted Geoffrey on the shoulder, going from angry to calm in an instant – but there was no emotion on his face, and his voice was no more than a whisper.

'I am happy, mate. You did the right thing telling me. Now get yourself home, you need to clean up.' Darren then walked out of the pub, without a look, or a word to his two bewildered mates.

Chapter 36

Shelley was in the back room cleaning the dye pots and brushes, when she heard the salon door open. They'd been surprisingly quiet for a Thursday and as Dawn was on holiday for the week, Shelley had let Tracey leave a little earlier than usual. Popping her head around the door, she was surprised to see Ross enter the shop.

At the sight of his warm, beaming smile and his toned, tanned arms, protruding from his fitted white T-shirt, Shelley felt her heart begin to race a little. She hadn't seen him since the day she'd bumped into him, whilst crying in the street on that fateful day she'd seen Chris and Mandy together, shopping in Chelsea Girl. Slightly embarrassed as she recalled the scene, Shelley felt herself blush a little. Before that incident, Jason had delighted in informing her that Ross liked her. But she imagined he now thought her, a foolish and silly young girl.

Although he was only a couple of years older than she was, Ross seemed like a real man in comparison to the other guys Shelley knew. He had his own place and a good job. He was established, and without even realising it, he made Shelley feel a little intimidated.

'Hi Shelley. Lovely to see you again. Is our Jason in the back?'

Realising that Ross had come to give Jason a lift to the dentist, it dawned on Shelley that he mustn't have received Jason's answer machine message.

'Oh Ross, he's taken an emergency appointment a couple of hours ago. He was in agony,' recalled Shelley, in a concerned voice. 'Poor thing was shaking like a leaf. He was terrified.'

Ross looked puzzled. 'He's only having a check-up. The appointment's in ten minutes. I know how scared he is of the dentist, that's why I said I'd go with him.'

Shelley began to explain. 'He tried to ring you. He thought you might be at home, but you must've been out. He left you a message on your machine. We've had a right drama in here this afternoon. Mrs Murray came in – she only wanted a dry fringe trim, and she was here all of ten minutes. Anyway, she's pregnant. It's actually her fourth,' Shelley gabbled on. 'Well, she's got a craving for nut brittle and she'd just bought a quarter from the sweet shop. She offered some to Jason and that was it. Crack. Half of his back tooth came away!'

Ross couldn't help wanting to smile as he pictured the scene. He also felt an undeniable affection, at the sincere concern this beautiful young woman showed towards his cousin. She was cute and funny, without even realising it and he doubted that she was remotely aware of the beauty she radiated, every time she smiled.

'I see. Looks like I've had a wasted journey then. Or maybe I haven't.' He looked at Shelley coyly 'There's something I want to ask you.'

Oh God, he's going to ask me out, Shelley thought, as her heart quickened, and she felt her cheeks redden. 'Er okay, ask away.'

'Well I was wondering,' he asked with a pleading smile, 'if you had time to give me a trim? I know you've cleaned up and everything, and I was going to ask Jason to do it tonight but if he's still recovering from his dentist ordeal, I'll not get the chance to get it cut before I go away.'

Feeling rather foolish, Shelley didn't know if she was relieved or disappointed. She fancied Ross like mad. He was so handsome and manly. But he made her feel childlike with his confidence and how comfortable he seemed in his own skin. He was nothing like any of the lads she'd known before and, for the first time in her life, Shelley felt like she'd met someone, who was out of her league.

'I can give you a lift home afterwards,' Ross smiled, interrupting her thoughts. 'It's the least I can do, as well as paying, obviously.'

Shelley returned his smile. 'Of course, I can. Sit yourself down and I'll get a gown and my scissors.'

Ross had glossy, thick, dark hair that had highlighted naturally with the summer sun, showing off subtle golden tinges. Shelley felt a tingle of excitement as she ran her fingers through it, to check the length before she began.

'So, where are you going? Is it a lad's holiday?' she asked, smiling at him in the mirror.

'Actually,' Ross replied, 'it's a weekend away, rather than a holiday. I'm going up to the Lake District. Windermere to be exact.'

'Oh,' Shelley said, a little taken aback. 'Who are going there with?' she asked. Shocked by her own directness.

'I'm taking my girlfriend,' he replied.

Seeing her surprised reaction in the mirror, Ross decided to explain.

'It's a long story. Me and Natalie had been together for about a year. Anyway, we split up a few months ago, mainly due to my shifts really. You know what I mean, unsociable hours and all that. It can be quite testing on a relationship. Well, I bumped into her last week, and we got chatting and decided to give it another go.'

Trying her best to sound happy for him, Shelley smiled. 'That's lovely. I love a happy ending. I really hope it works out for you both.' But inside, she felt disappointment. Here she was in her work scruffs, feeling less than glamorous, yet she'd actually believed that Ross was about to ask her out. When all he really wanted, was to look nice for his girlfriend. She felt like such an idiot, hoping to God that he hadn't sensed what she'd been thinking. 'There, you're all done. Natalie won't be able to resist you.'

'Oh, that's great, Shelley. I can't thank you enough,' he beamed. 'I owe you one,' he added, handing her £10. 'Keep the change, you've done me a massive favour.'

'Oh, don't be daft. It's on the house.' she replied. 'It's only taken me five minutes.' He thanked her grinning, and as he showed his lovely white teeth and the dimples that had appeared on his cheeks, Shelley felt her stomach flip.

'Right,' said Ross, finding his car keys, 'I'll drop you off home if you're ready.'

Suddenly feeling slightly sad, Shelley declined his offer, deciding she was going to stay at the salon for a while. As Ross closed the door, she locked it behind him.

Making herself a cup of tea, she sat down in the small kitchen area. How could she have been so stupid? Before today she hadn't thought about Ross in ages, and now she knew he had a girlfriend and was taking her away for the weekend, she felt truly miserable. She pictured Natalie in her mind, imagining her to be tall and slim with long dark hair and smouldering dark eyes. Shelley imagined her as a raven-haired beauty and thought of the pair together, looking like a stunning Hollywood couple.

Feeling as though she might cry at her own miserable love life, she knew she needed to have a stern word with herself. She'd never had any problems finding a boyfriend but getting the right one wasn't as simple as it seemed. She used to think she had the perfect marriage with Chris and look how that had turned out. She thought about Wayne and wondered if he would ask her out again. She liked him enough, she was sure of that, but she couldn't help feeling as though she'd missed her chance with Ross. Finishing her cup of tea, she decided to stop dwelling on it all and get herself home. Jackie would be wondering where she was by now.

On the drive home, Ross couldn't help feeling disappointed, that Shelley had declined his lift. He'd thought about her many times since the day she'd ran into him in tears. She was so beautiful, in such a vulnerable kind of way. She radiated allure and her smile could light up a room. Jason being Jason, had filled Ross in on all the gossip about Wayne, Shelley's latest flame. He couldn't help letting his mouth run away with him. It was just his way.

So, Ross led his cousin to believe that he was no longer romantically interested in Shelley. He also lied about not receiving Jason's answer machine message. He just had to see her again. He had to know if his feelings were still as strong as before. He needed to see for himself, if she still had the same effect on him. And she did. He thought about Natalie and their forthcoming weekend away. She was a sweet girl and he cared for her deeply, but he wasn't sure that getting back with her was the right thing to do. Was he settling for second best? Time would tell.

Chapter 37

'Shall we go and get some lunch, babe?' Mandy asked, turning onto her side on the sunbed, to face Chris.

'Can if you want,' came his curt reply.

Tutting and rolling her eyes, Mandy was beginning to lose patience, with her sulky boyfriend. She couldn't tolerate other people's drama and she had put up with Chris's smacked arse face, all morning.

'Right, forget it,' she snapped. 'I'll go and eat alone. I honestly don't know what's up with you, Chris. You're acting like a spoilt child. We've had a lovely holiday and you're ruining the last couple of days, by falling out with me over something petty.'

'Petty,' he cried. 'You call that petty? Showing me up, in front of a whole bar full of people? All those blokes leering after you and chanting obscenities! I hardly call that petty.'

'Oh, for fuck's sake,' Mandy bit back. 'It was just a laugh. Everyone else except you can see that. We were all having such a great night until you spoilt it for everyone. Deciding to go all, holier than thou on me. Andy, in his innocence was more than happy to tell me how excited you were, at the prospect of seeing loads of boobs, on display. You were keen enough to gawp at other girls getting their tits out, but not so happy for mine to be admired. That is so contradictory, Chris. In fact, I can't be around you right now,' she announced, pulling up her denim shorts. 'I'm going for a walk.' She flounced off, leaving a stunned Chris watching her go.

After a short stroll, Mandy stepped onto the sandy beach and made her way towards the shoreline, where the sand was much cooler. The warm, gentle breeze felt good against her face and as her hangover faded, she began to feel ravenous. There were numerous bars and restaurants along the beach, and she headed towards one, where she and Chris had enjoyed lunch a couple of days before.

Finding a table in the shade, Mandy ordered a coke along with omelette and chips. She was still on a high from the previous night's events and there was no way she was about to let Chris, rain on her parade.

Meeting Kelly and Andy by the pool, earlier that week, the four had decided to have a night out together. The fun-loving couple were from the Gorbals area of Glasgow, and to say they were a little rough and ready was an understatement.

The girls were getting on famously, but Chris and Andy found they had little in common. This fact didn't seem to matter to Andy though. He was in a permanent state of intoxication, sitting at the pool bar for most of the day, happy to chat jovially to anyone who would give him their time. His ginger hair and pale completion required him to stay out of the sun, and under the shade of the bar was where he was more than happy to spend his time.

Well-rounded and buxom, Kelly was loud, with a high-pitched laugh that always ended with a pig-like snort. Mandy thought she was hilarious, and it wasn't long before the pair were talking ten to the dozen. Much to Chris's dismay. The girls had arranged the night out, and when Mandy informed Chris, he was less than enthusiastic.

'They're a bit common,' he said, pulling his face in a sullen grimace. 'And there's no way I can keep up with his drinking. He downs them, like there's no tomorrow.'

'Oh, don't be such a snob, Chris. Once you've had a few yourself, you'll be fine. Lighten up a little and stop being so judgemental. You might have a laugh, if you'd only let yourself.'

After attending a few of the regular bars that they'd frequented during their holiday, the two couples decided to head to the very popular and trendy JJ's. It was owned by Jake and Jonathan, a flamboyant gay couple, who had decided to leave the British rat race, three summers earlier.

The couple were by now, a well-known fixture on the island and their bar had grown in popularity. They'd recently opened a new venue, to accommodate their ever-growing custom and Mandy loved the place, with its trendy vibe. She would've danced all night, if she could. Unfortunately for her, Chris's stamina tended to wilt well before hers and her night was often cut short. Kelly, on the other hand, loved dancing and was more than happy to boogie on down with her new pal, whilst the lads propped up the bar.

Deciding the only way to get through the night was to get well and truly slaughtered, Chris was suddenly surprised to realise, that he wasn't having as bad a time as he'd imagined he would. It turned out that Andy was very interested in computers too, so the pair finally found a subject that they both had in common. On hearing Kelly's excited shrieks, both lads spun round to see the buxom girl, bounding over to them.

'Oh god, oh god, Andy. You'll never guess what!' Kelly squealed in her high-pitched, excited, Glaswegian accent. Chris couldn't help thinking she resembled giant neon jelly, in her bright green, lycra vest top and matching skirt.

'What's up, doll?' Andy slurred his reply.

'Oh my god,' she shrieked again. 'They're only holding a Miss Page Three competition, here tonight! There's no way I can miss that,' she yelled, jumping up and down with enthusiasm. Grabbing her mammoth breasts, she exclaimed proudly, 'These bad boys are gonna win us five thousand pesetas, my hunny bun. That works out at about twenty-five quid, plus a bottle of bubbly too!'

Grinning his approval, Andy winked at his fiancée. 'That's my girl. Go and show 'em what you got, doll,' he chuckled.

Wide-eyed Chris couldn't believe what he was hearing. Did Andy not mind his wife-to-be flashing her wares on stage, for all to see? Chris was amused.

It takes all sorts, he thought, keeping his views to himself whilst the couple shared a lingering, sloppy snog, in front of him, making him feel slightly nauseous.

As Kelly made her way back through the dense crowd, Andy turned to him, grinning drunkenly.

'That girl's my world,' he announced, as pleased as punch.

Looking around for Mandy, Chris decided she must've gone to the ladies. He knew how long the queues got and fathomed she would join them soon enough. Chris was looking forward to the competition and could already see a few girls gathering by the stage, waiting to enter the contest. Seeing boobs on the beach throughout the day had become normality and he hardly gave them a second glance anymore, but the anticipation of these girls walking on stage and revealing their breasts began to get him slightly aroused.

As the compere announced each contestant, they mounted the stage, giving a quick account of their name, where they came from, and who they were on holiday with. Each girl was standing there in just her bra, and Chris couldn't wait to see what they had to offer.

As Kelly was announced as the ninth contestant, Andy screamed out a bellowing cheer, almost bursting Chris's eardrum. Chris could see her enormous breasts desperate to escape from their holster, as she bounced up and down in her excitement, introducing herself. When she informed the audience loudly over the mic that she was from Glasgow, another extensive applause erupted as her fellow Glaswegians cheered her on. It was obvious for all to see that she had a massive chest but she was large all over, and Chris did not like what he saw. He was however, looking forward to seeing number 2 and number 6 remove their tops. They were both slim, attractive blondes and he felt excited in anticipation.

Grinning at the audience, the compere announced the 10th and final contestant. Stating that she may be last, but she was by no means least. An almighty cheer erupted once more, as Mandy confidently sauntered onto the stage in her skimpy fluorescent pink bra and her micro, denim skirt. Her tiny waist and even tinier bra made her prize assets look even bigger than they normally did. Her tanned arms and chest glistened, as she had quickly applied some coconut oil, before heading onstage.

Staring, open-mouthed, Chris stood in stunned silence. The crowd were going wild and began chanting, 'Get your tits out for the lads.' Mandy's voice could hardly be heard as she introduced herself, but she didn't mind, as the cheers were recognition enough of the audience's appreciation for her.

Chris could not believe what he was seeing. He sobered up within seconds and began huffing and puffing, in a flustered manner as he looked to the crowd and then to his girlfriend, and then back at the crowd again. This was not acceptable behaviour as far as he was concerned. Mandy was his girlfriend and he wasn't going to accept other men openly leering at her. But there was nothing he could do. He just had to stand and watch, as the chanting became more raucous. The compere shushed the audience as he requested the girls remove the bras on the count of three. Another almighty cheer erupted, with Mandy loving every minute of the limelight.

The compere asked the crowd to cheer the loudest for their favourite, and it was soon clear for all to see that Mandy had won the competition, hands down. She was beaming from ear to ear. The first to congratulate her was Kelly. Snatching the mic from the unsuspecting compere, she drunkenly praised Mandy and informed the crowd that they were best pals, before having her speech cut short, by the none too pleased compere.

'Hey, put it there, pal,' said Andy, turning to Chris with an outstretched hand. 'You must be so proud of that wee girl.'

Not really knowing what to say, Chris half-smiled and nodded, as he tried to get his head around what had just happened.

It wasn't until the two couples later parted company, that Chris let Mandy know what he really thought of her performance. But she was too drunk to care, laughing in his face when he told her she'd acted like a cheap tart. Mandy's last words before falling asleep, were to tell

Chris to go and fuck himself. She added, that if he wanted to be with a boring woman with no ambition, then he should've stayed married to his perfect wife.

Mandy slept well that night, but Chris could not get her words out of his mind. His thoughts turned to Shelley and what she might be doing back home. She would never show him up like Mandy had done, and he longed for her arms to hold him like she used to do. She was so beautiful and good-natured and had treated him so well. He hadn't appreciated her the way he should have – he realised now, that he had treated her despicably. But it was too late…or was it? His eyes filled up as he listened to Mandy's gentle sleeping sighs, and a tear trickled down the side of his face and onto his pillow. He had made a real fuck up of his life, and he only had himself to blame.

Mandy wasn't one to carry on an argument, waking up the next morning as though nothing was wrong. That was, until she realised that Chris was still sulking.

Sitting in the bar, she finished her omelette and looked out at the beautiful blue ocean. She felt so at home here on this magical island and knew without a doubt, that she must someday, in the not too distant future, return.

Sitting on his sunbed, Chris too had plenty of time to reflect on the previous night's events. His mother was right about Mandy, that much was true. His eyes had been well and truly opened and he had seen a totally different side to her. But despite what had happened, he did enjoy being in her company. He decided that on her return, he would make amends with her. It was his holiday too and he didn't want the last couple of days to be unpleasant. He had no idea what the future held once they returned home, but he knew one thing for sure. Meeting Mandy Allsop had taught him a valuable, albeit painful lesson in life: to appreciate what you have, when you have it. He hadn't, but he would make sure, to never make that mistake, again.

Chapter 38

As the kettle boiled Tina heard the post drop onto the mat. Hoping it was the news she'd been waiting for she poured her brew, then taking a deep breath, headed down the hall. Just one white envelope sat, facedown, on the mat and as she picked it up, she saw that it had the Littlewoods franking stamp on it. From the living room, she could hear Wincey Willis from Good Morning Britain, announcing to the country that they were in for thundery storms, following the recent heatwave.

With a trembling hand, Tina tore open the letter. Glancing over the first paragraph, she heaved a sigh of relief as she immediately picked out the words, 'We are pleased to offer you'. On digesting the good news, she clasped her hands together, then looking up to the ceiling she mouthed a silent thank you. Reading the letter again in more detail, she realised that in just over a week's time, she would be starting her new job, which would be the first step towards getting her independence back.

As she had walked towards the huge building for her interview, Tina was overwhelmed at the size of the place. Littlewoods Distribution Centre was comprised of three mills in total, two of which stood side by side and could be seen from almost anywhere in the town. Nearly everyone knew somebody who worked there, and in some cases, there were whole families employed within the company.

Her assessor smiled, firmly shaking her hand as she introduced herself as the Personnel Manager, Miss Celia Bates. Although she appeared friendly and approachable, Tina was under no illusions. If Celia's handshake was anything to go by, she would not wish to incur her wrath, despite her primary school teacher appearance.

Nervous and realising she was beginning to talk too much, Tina was more than happy, when the interview was brought to a close and she once again shook the sturdy woman's hand as they said goodbye. Relief washed over her as she stepped outside, into the warm sunshine. Reflecting upon the last twenty minutes, she felt slight embarrassment when recalling how much gibberish she had waffled. Well, it was done now, and her fate lay in the hands of Celia Bates.

On the other side of town, Jackie was returning from the school run. Walking up the path to her house, the young postman smiled, handing her the letters he'd been about to push through the letterbox. The two brown envelopes needed no introduction, she knew instantly that they were the gas and electric bills.

Fingering the other letter with anticipation, she opened the drawer, taking out the butter knife and carefully slitting open the white envelope. She hardly dared unfold the paper, but when she did, she was overjoyed to read that her interview had been successful. She would start her employment in a week's time. She'd begin on a twelve-week rolling contract, with the possibility of being made a permanent member of staff after a year with the organisation.

Joining the company in September meant that she would be one of several new starters. The busy run up to Christmas meant there would be an influx of newbies throughout the following weeks. Her friend from school worked as a picker, and she'd told Jackie, that as long as she was willing to work hard and reached her departmental target, then there was every chance she would survive the post-Christmas lull, and be kept on.

Jackie suddenly felt very excited and yearned to tell Kevin her good news. She had no way of contacting him as he'd be on the shop floor, in the paint factory where he worked. His boss certainly wouldn't allow him to take a call, not unless it was an absolute emergency. Picking up the phone, she decided to ring Shelley at the salon. There was no way her good news would wait till her husband and sister got home, that evening.

Shelley was absolutely thrilled. She was overjoyed that things were finally looking up for her sister, and her brother-in-law. Living with them was such a comfort. They made her feel more than welcome, and she knew her rent money was a great help to the struggling young family. It was about time something good came their way, and hopefully this would be the beginning of a brighter future for them.

As predicted, the brown envelopes were the bills Jackie had been expecting. But even the prospect of shelling out more of their precious little money, was not going to take the shine off her day. Feeling overjoyed and contented, she hung out the day's first wash load in her small back garden, before making herself a cup of tea accompanied by two crumpets smothered with jam. Pressing play on the video, she settled down contentedly, to watch the previous night's recording of Coronation Street.

Chapter 39

Judy slumped exhaustedly onto the floor, resting her back against the side of the bath. She closed her eyes as the relief of her accomplishment washed over her.

Vomiting after she'd eaten was becoming an everyday occurrence for her, but the job in itself wasn't easy and Judy found that only by gorging herself beforehand, could she successfully achieve her goal.

She was brought back to the present, by her brother banging on the bathroom door.

'Come on Judy, I need the loo,' he urged, impatiently. 'You've been in there ages. Hurry up, before I piss meself.'

Quickly getting to her feet, Judy splashed and dried her face, taking one last look down the toilet, to check that there were no remaining remnants of her recent activity to give her away. As she opened the door, Dan looked her in the eyes.

'Were you puking in there?' he asked.

'What's it to you?' she replied, shocked that Dan had heard her being sick.

'Hey, you're not up the duff, are you?' he smirked, grinning at his own humour and knowing full well, that to the best of his knowledge, Judy had never had a boyfriend, let alone a sexual relationship.

'Don't be stupid you cheeky shit,' she barked, giving him a clip around the head. 'If you must know, I think I've eaten something that's disagreed with me.'

Dan sniggered. 'Well that would be everything in the kitchen,' he remarked. 'Pie, chips, peas and gravy. Then arctic roll. And if that wasn't enough, you polished off almost a whole packet of bourbons. You're like a human dustbin, Jude. The diet's obviously over then?'

Telling him to piss off and mind his own business, she went to her room, slamming the door behind her. The truth was, she felt thoroughly disgusted with herself. Her bedroom bin was filled with biscuit and chocolate wrappers and she knew she had to start hiding the evidence of her latest, secret pastime if she was going to avoid further suspicion. She realised that what she was doing was wrong, but she was continuing to lose weight, and right now, Judy felt that food was just about the only thing she could control in her life.

Her mum had died and left her to run the house and care for her brother. She no longer felt sad, she felt angry. And that in turn left her feeling guilty. Her dad was off with his fancy piece and it seemed to her that her parents' whole marriage had been built on lies. She buried her head deep within her soft pillow and began to cry.

'Why Mum?' she wept. 'Why have you left us in this mess? I can't do this, Mum. I'm not strong like you. I can't do this alone.' She continued to cry until she heard the soft knocking at her bedroom door.

'Judy? Jude?' the voice beckoned, quietly. 'Are you okay in there?' It was Daniel's voice. 'Can I get you anything?' he asked, a little louder.

'No, no thanks,' she sniffed. 'I'll be fine. I'm just not feeling very well,' she lied.

'Can I come in?' Dan replied, opening the door without waiting for his sister's response.

'Well, looks like you already are,' she responded, trying to hide the obvious fact that she'd been crying.

It wasn't often that the siblings had a civil conversation, but deciding to take the lead on this occasion, Dan sat on the bed next to his sister. Putting his arm around her, he looked directly into her bloodshot, swollen eyes.

'You're doing okay you know, Jude. Mum would be proud of you.'

Feeling embarrassed, Judy looked away and stared down at the crumpled tissue in her hand. She shook her head slightly; she doubted that very much. Her mum would be devastated if she knew what Judy's coping mechanism was. But even with this thought and the guilt racking her, she couldn't be sure that it was enough to make her stop. She turned to her brother and smiled.

'Thanks Dan. That means a lot.' Managing to lighten the mood, she ruffled his hair. 'Yep, coming from you that definitely means a lot. Now get out of here, before you spoil it all by insulting me,' she said, grinning.

As she watched him walk from the room, she realised he was turning into a young man before her very eyes. He'd be 15 in a few weeks and gone was the scrawny boyish frame. Standing at almost six feet tall, the results from the sports he was heavily involved in were beginning to show, with the muscles on his body rapidly forming.

Her thoughts turned to Mark. She wondered how he'd coped when his father had suddenly died. Was he angry too? Angry that he'd been left to run the family business alone, and shoulder all that responsibility? Somehow, she couldn't imagine Mark ever being angry. He seemed so gentle and carefree. But what did she know? She bet that no one she knew would ever imagine that she would end up with her head down the toilet, after almost every meal.

God, this is fucked up, she thought, realising that she had to sort herself out soon. But right now, she didn't know where she was going to get find strength. Suddenly, feeling very tired, Judy closed her curtains and got ready for bed. It was only early, but tomorrow was her return to work following her mum's death, and she needed to get a good night's sleep.

Going out like a light, Judy was sound asleep within minutes, unaware that her father had returned home. Looking in on her just as he used to when she was small, he felt nothing but love for his daughter, love and regret. Deep regret, for hurting her the way he had.

She was shouldering so much responsibility at her young age, and he had only added to her burdens by putting his own happiness first. It was his escape route from all the sadness that was currently surrounding their family, but he knew it wasn't right. He should be putting his children first. Judy had refused to speak to him since she'd learnt about his double life; he couldn't blame her for acting the way she was. His only hope was that someday she could forgive him for his actions. And that she might, just might, accept Brenda into her life. Blowing her a silent kiss Malcolm closed the bedroom door as a solitary tear fell from his eye.

Chapter 40

Finally reaching the eleventh floor in the high-rise block of flats, Tina stopped for a moment to catch her breath.

The stench of urine was overwhelming, and she made a point of avoiding contact with the banister or the walls. The lift was out of order and she'd tried not to curse too much, realising that for the residents of these flats, this was a daily hazard of their lives.

She had arranged her visit with Marsha the day before, and today she'd taken two buses and a short walk to find the flat. It was a dismal and depressing place, there was no doubt about that, but from the happy sound of Marsha's voice on the phone, Tina knew that living here was a better option than living with her abusive ex-boyfriend.

The door opened just as she was about to knock, and Tina was greeted by Marsha's beaming smile. The pair were truly delighted to see each other, hugging immediately.

The flat was humble, and Marsha didn't have much, but you could hear the pride in her voice as she showed her friend around the small accommodation. She was happy and that happiness radiated from every inch of her.

The girls chatted for the next couple of hours as Tina told Marsha all about her new job.

'I'm starting on Monday,' she said, with a nervous grin. 'I'm looking forward to it, I really am, but I feel like I've lost loads of confidence. Apart from you, I haven't really got any friends to speak of and I haven't worked in ages. I just hope I'll fit in and get the hang of it quickly. I'll probably recognise quite a few people there as it's a small town, so I know it won't be long until Darren hears about my return.'

'How does that make you feel?' asked Marsha, with a look of concern on her face.

'I'm not sure. I can say it to myself and I don't feel too worried, but I don't know how I'll react when the time comes. My mum and dad have been great and they're giving me loads of encouragement. I'm hoping I'll make some nice friends at my new place and get back to having some sort of social life. When I look back, I can't believe I gave up my friends, family, and everything really, all for a man.' Tina shook her head in disbelief. 'I must've been so weak-minded.'

Marsha leaned forward, holding her friend's hands in hers. 'You wanted your marriage to work love, there's no crime in that. Look how your family are supporting you now. They haven't held it against you, have they?

Anyone who's a true friend will do the same,' she said, nodding at her own wise words.

Shelley's face briefly flashed through Tina's mind as she listened to Marsha.

'I hope you're right,' she said.

Changing the subject, Marsha was filled with her own excitement as she began to tell Tina about the business course she'd enrolled on.

'I'm starting it in a couple of weeks. It's going to be tough, but I'm determined to succeed in it. I wanted to do it years ago when Jerome was in nursery, but Darnell had other ideas and put the blocks on it. But this time there'll be no stopping me,' she said, firmly.

It was obvious to anyone that Marsha was a bright girl. She'd loved doing crosswords in the refuge and always knew the answers to the teatime game-show questions. Tina had no doubt that she would smash the course and go on to bigger and better things, just as she deserved to. Marsha explained how she'd managed to get some part-time hours, working in the local off licence and hopefully she'd be able to work her job around her studies, with a little help from her mum, to look after Jerome sometimes.

'Sounds like you've got it all planned,' Tina grinned. 'This time next year you'll be one of them yuppies, working in the big city. There'll be no talking to you,' she laughed.

Both girls were really happy for the other, revelling in each other's good fortune. It was a wonderful feeling realising that their lives were on track and their futures both looked bright.

Putting down her coffee cup, Tina looked more seriously at her friend. 'Have you heard anything from Darnell?' she asked.

'Nothing at all,' Marsha replied. 'I'm miles from where he lives, and as far as I know he doesn't have any friends in this area. I realise that one day our paths may cross, but I pray that I can avoid him and anyone who knows him, for as long as possible.'

Tina nodded. 'I'll second that. Don't you know anyone in this area then?'

Marsha shook her head. 'Hardly anyone. I'm hoping to make some new friends at college.'

'And what about a new man?'

'Not a chance,' Marsha laughed, nearly choking on her coffee. 'I'm not interested. I've had a gutful to last me a lifetime. My boy and my studies come first. Then of course my career. A man is the last thing I need.'

'I really admire you, Marsha,' Tina said, looking sincerely at her friend. 'You've been through so much and now you're about to take on the world single-handedly, whilst still bringing up your lovely son. All that, added to moving to a town where you know no one and still you're smiling and always so positive about everything. You're a true inspiration.'

Feeling slightly bashful Marsha blushed a little, making her coffee-coloured cheeks glow.

'Oh, I don't know about that. The way I look at it is, you either sink or swim. I've seen loads of girls like me turn to drugs and prostitution, because of some lowlife bully who made them feel worthless. I refuse to be a victim, Tina. I believe everything happens for a reason and what's happened to me has made me a stronger person, and I know the same thing goes for you.'

'I'll drink to that,' said Tina, raising her cup and downing the last of her brew.

'Anyway, the people around here seem okay.' 'There's one girl who comes in the launderette, who I've been chatting to quite a lot. She seems really friendly. She's a bit rough and down on her luck, but she's okay.'

Tina's eyes lit up. 'That's good to hear – see, you're making friends already.'

'Yeh, her name's Kim, she has a little lad and I've managed to pass a few of Jerome's old clothes onto her. She was dead grateful. I was really nervous when I met her. She looks familiar but it turns out she's lived here all her life so she must just look like someone else.' Glancing at the clock, Marsha jumped up. 'Wow look at the time. Jerome will be coming out of school in ten minutes, I'd better get my skates on. Do you fancy coming with me?' she asked.

Tina looked at her watch. 'I can't believe we've been nattering for so long. 'Where's the time gone? The next bus comes soon, and I don't want to get stuck in teatime traffic, so I'd better not. Let's make it a weekend visit next time, so I can see little Jerome.'

'That would be brilliant,' said Marsha smiling and giving Tina the biggest hug.

Saying their goodbyes at the bus stop, both girls vowed not to leave it too long before they arranged another get together. When the bus pulled away Marsha waved frantically as it went sailing past.

Sitting back in her seat Tina reflected on her afternoon. It had been wonderful seeing her friend again and she felt really grateful to her. Meeting Marsha had been the first step on the road to getting her life back together. She was a true friend and Tina knew that she always would be.

Chapter 41

'What's the matter with your food, lad? You're not ill, are you?' Ivy asked, frowning at her son.

Darren had spent the last ten minutes pushing the pie and mash his mother had lovingly prepared around his plate.

'Nah. Just not really hungry Ma,' he replied, finally giving up and pushing his plate forward.

'Don't give me that,' Ivy said, squinting at him suspiciously. 'There's not a day goes by that you don't wolf your food down, so I'm not buying that one, Darren. As long as the Pope's Catholic, you'll have room for a hot meal. What's up? It's not that bloody Kev again is it, pestering you about going back to work?'

Darren shook his head. Ivy knew her son as well as he knew himself. He couldn't get anything past her. She had ears like a bat and eyes like a hawk. That coupled with a suspicious mind, meant that it would take a very clever person to lie convincingly to Ivy Doyle, and get away with it. Folding her arms, she looked down at her only son.

'It's Tina, isn't it? Is she back?'

A quick glance from her son was all the proof she needed to confirm her suspicions.

'When did that trollop grace the scene then? I knew all this gallivanting would blow up in her face,' she sneered. 'Pissing off with her fancy man, thinking she's too good for you. It's all backfired on her.'

Darren shook his head at his mother's vivid imagination. Part of him wanted to laugh. She loved playing judge and jury. She'd have Tina hung, drawn, and quartered if it was up to her.

'Mum, I've not even seen her. I've just heard that she's back at her mum's,' he replied.

'Well she'd better hope that I don't see her first, the little madam,' Ivy barked. 'I'll leave her with a flea in her ear. And that mother of hers too.'

Darren knew his mum was always likely to believe his side of the story, but he still needed to make out that he was the innocent party in all this. It would not help his case if his mother was to get wind of Tina's side of things. Especially if her mum, or anyone else were to back her up. Keeping them apart was high on his list of priorities, and he would go out of his way to do so, if needs be.

Look Mum. You know I'm not soft, but this situation is a real embarrassment for me,' he said, looking directly at Ivy. 'I need to know I can rely on you to let me deal with things in my own way,' he added, taking in her wounded expression.

Ivy's heart bled for her only son. Where Darren was concerned, she was like a lioness protecting her cub. She would die for him, if the situation arose.

'I can't have me ma, fighting my battles, can I? How would that look? I'd be mortified if anyone were to find out.'

His eyes pleaded with Ivy's solemn face. Shaking her head, she shrugged at him in defeat.

'I suppose you're right son. Anyway, she'll get what's coming to her one of these days, I'm a great believer in what goes around comes around.

Shuddering at the prospect of his own karma, Darren put his arm around his tiny mother.

'That's settled then,' he smiled down at her. 'I'll go and see her and find out where the land lies, with the house and stuff.'

At the mention of the house, Ivy was on her high horse once again. 'Don't you be walking away from that house empty-handed,' she ordered. 'You've as much right to that house as she has. In fact, you've more. She left you to fend for yourself and pay all the bills, whilst she was waltzing around living the life of Riley. It's not right. She pissed off and left you with hardly a teaspoon to your name. And if she thinks she's moving back into your house with her new fancy fella, she can think again.' Ivy's anger was rising, and her face was getting redder by the second.

Darren wished he'd never mentioned the house. 'Look Mum, Tina's at her mum's, so there's no way she's with any bloke,' he said, trying to calm his mother's fury. 'She won't be starting any funny business. I can assure you of that. If anything, she'll be really sorry and want us to get back together!' He only wished that that were true.

Looking horrified, Ivy began once more. 'Well don't you be going all soft on her, lad. That hussy's had you for a right fool. There are names for women like her, but I'm not going to be the one to say them. At the end of the day son, you have to carry the shame of folks knowing that you were married to her, and that she did the dirty on you. But you can rely on me to keep that information under my hat. My word is my bond,' she added proudly.

Darren had no idea where his mother got her wild imagination from. At no point had she been told that there was another man involved in his and Tina's break up. Planting tiny seeds along the way was enough to make Ivy to concoct her own version of events and Darren was always going to play the victim in her book. Having his mother by his side would always go in his favour and he knew he'd never go without good food and a place to live, as long as she was around.

'Right then, let's change the subject,' he suggested, giving his fiery mother a peck on the cheek to show his appreciation. 'Let's have a brew and see what's on the box.'

Chapter 42

As her son and his girlfriend walked through the terminal arrivals, Vivien Charlton was quite disappointed to see them still together. However, on second glance she could tell that Chris seemed somewhat forlorn. Hoping that was the case and that he'd had a rotten holiday with his money grabbing floozy, she smiled her sweetest smile as the couple approached.

'How was the holiday, kids?' Spencer asked, hugging an embarrassed Chris in an awkward embrace.

Mandy beamed at the middle-aged man, answering for the both of them.

'Oh, it was fantastic, Mr Charlton,' she gushed, planting a peck on the unsuspecting but delighted man's cheek. He was also subjected to more than an eyeful of her cleavage, as she leant towards him. 'You and Mrs C should get yourselves over there. It's a wonderful island, you'd love it. The nightlife's terrific.'

Vivien looked at her husband in shock; the brazenness of this young woman! She was fully aware that Mandy was trying to provoke a reaction from her, and if she could she would've given her a piece of her mind. But for now, biting her tongue was the only option she had. She needed to get to the bottom of what had really happened on the fortnight's holiday and playing the caring and non-interfering mother was the only way she was going to get a result. Chris could be a funny fish at times and had never been one to open up. Plus, she realised that he wouldn't want to hear 'I told you so.' No, she would bide her time and the truth would come out. Didn't it always?

Vivien could see that this little madam was all bravado and Chris's face said it all. It seemed that her predictions had been right and that her precious boy had chosen the wrong woman – again! Next time, he needed to go for someone with class and she knew exactly which direction to point him in. At least three of her friends had suitable daughters, who would surely give their high teeth to be with a wonderful man like her Chris. If he'd only allow her to work her magic, she could have them paired up in no time. The thought made her smile and for that much she was grateful, as listening to Mandy in the car for the next hour was not going to be a pleasant experience. She wasn't looking forward to it one bit.

Chapter 43

Entering the Bradford & Bingley Building Society, Tina smiled at the young clerk behind the counter, informing her that she'd like to open an account for her future wages to be paid into.

Providing the clerk with her personal details, Tina soon realised that the friendly young girl, who was around the same age as herself, was beginning to look concerned.

'Would you mind waiting here a moment?' the clerk asked, smiling nervously as she rose from her seat and disappeared into the back office.

Wondering what the issue could be, Tina began to have a bad feeling – but nothing could've prepared her for the truth. An older, scrawny woman in her fifties appeared, making her way to the front desk. She beckoned Tina towards the edge of the counter, so she was out of earshot of the young couple who had just entered the premises. Clarifying Tina's details, the older clerk, Marlene, who was still sporting a blonde 1960's beehive and far too much blue eyeshadow, leaned in closer to inform Tina of the bad news.

'I'm sorry Mrs Doyle,' she said, getting close enough for Tina to smell her strong tobacco breath. 'There's no way we can open an account for you, you're two months behind on your mortgage.'

Stunned, Tina looked at her with wide eyed disbelief.

'What do you mean?' she gulped. 'I've been away,' she continued, trying to explain as her voice began to rise in her panic. 'I thought my husband was taking care of the payments.'

'Well that doesn't seem to have been the case,' Marlene sneered sarcastically, beginning to tap her red-varnished, claw-like fingernails on the counter. 'We've already sent two letters to your address on Oak Street, and we haven't had any response from you or Mr Doyle. This is an extremely serious matter you know,' Marlene added, pursing her pencil-thin lips together.

Feeling her eyes beginning to water, Tina was about to protest further, when she heard a male voice coming from behind Marlene and her beehive.

'I'll take it from here, Marlene, thank you,' said the man.

Appearing before her was a grey-haired, slightly stout man who looked like he was around sixty. He reminded Tina of her late grandfather on her dad's side, and she instantly felt relief at his calming presence.

Allen, or Mr Price as the staff referred to him, was the manager at the building society and had worked there longer than any of them could remember. He was a caring and approachable man. A husband, father and grandfather. He ran a tight ship and, whilst he had a very kindly nature, his firm but fair attitude gained him respect and admiration from the staff he managed.

'Would you like to come into my office, dear,' he said, addressing Tina in a reassuring voice. 'Let's see if we can get to the bottom of things and sort this mess out, shall we? 'Marlene,' he said, turning to the clerk, who was slightly annoyed that she would not be allowed to continue with her high and mighty speech. 'Would you mind making this young lady a cup of tea with two sugars please? She's had a shock, and there's nothing like sweet tea, to cure a shock.' He added, nodding at his own words.

Feeling much more comfortable in the presence of Allen Price and his mahogany furnished office, Tina began to explain her situation. She felt at ease with this kindly gentleman as her story of woe began to unfold. She wasn't trying to gain sympathy, she just felt able to speak openly to the man before her, who listened intently, without judgement.

Allen Price felt protective towards the young woman seated in front of him, imagining his own similarly aged daughter being in Tina's situation. He shuddered at the thought. He wanted to help her, as was his nature, and he asked her if she was thinking of returning to the marital home she had shared with Darren.

Being honest and telling him that she hadn't really thought about it, Tina wondered where the conversation was going. Allen informed her that if she did want to live there and avoid repossession, then he would take the £50 that she'd saved and was about to open her account with, and put it towards the missed mortgage arrears, along with her future wages which would be paid into the account.

'But what will I live off?' Tina asked, looking worried. 'And what if Darren tries to take money from the account?'

Allen Price smiled. 'Don't worry my dear, we can set up a payment plan so that you will still have some money to yourself. And don't worry about your estranged husband. He won't be able to access any money from the account. We can put a stop on it. I will ensure that my staff are fully aware of the circumstances of the account. Using the utmost discretion required, of course,' he added, tapping his nose and giving her a reassuring wink.

Tina was beginning to feel a little easier about the situation, but her head felt light, as it was so much for her to take in. Her mind was in a whirl. She hadn't even considered moving back into the home she'd shared with Darren. But if he wasn't paying the mortgage, then what else was there left for her to do? One thing her father had always instilled in her, was to avoid debt like the plague. She had always been thrifty with money and getting her name blacklisted was not on her agenda. Darren would have to move out.

Walking slowly back to her parents' house, Tina realised that her situation and immediate future, were going to be a little different than she'd anticipated. The sincere Mr Price had offered her a lifeline, along with some very valuable advice, and for that she was extremely grateful. He'd also rung his good friend Mr Coupe, at Coupe & Co solicitors, to arrange a free consultation for Tina the very next day, and she couldn't thank him enough. Tina couldn't wait to start her job now and begin earning some desperately needed cash, to get out of what could've been a disastrous, long term situation for her.

She'd left out the fact that she'd only been taken on as a temp. But, if she did lose her job, she'd cross that bridge when she came to it. The thought of seeing Darren to discuss the situation of their home was not one she relished, but nevertheless, it was a conversation, that would sooner or later have to take place.

Chapter 44

Wayne got up and returned to the bar for a pint and a half of lager, just as the landlady rang the bell for last orders. Shelley smiled to herself, watching him walk from the table. His bum was so peachy, in his fitted Farah trousers. She couldn't help but admire his fashion sense as she eyed up the pure wool Lyle and Scott V-neck sweater, he'd matched them with. She sensed he was out to impress her and realised he was probably wearing his Saturday night clobber, but she had to admit that he looked and smelled, mighty fine.

Shelley didn't tend to drink alcohol mid-week, finding it virtually impossible to get up for work. On this occasion though, she'd decided to throw down the gauntlet and to hell with the consequences. This was her first date, since the break-up of her marriage and it was going far better than she'd expected.

She'd wanted to feel relaxed and carefree and the four halves she'd already consumed, were definitely helping her along. Shelley grinned dreamily, as Wayne chatted to her without reservation. There had been no awkward silences and the conversation easily flowed throughout the evening. It was as though the pair had known each other for years.

Also, a little Dutch courage from the alcohol was masking any shyness she felt, recalling the one night of passion the two of them had shared, on their first encounter. She knew it was bound to come up in conversation at some point, and the last thing she needed was to feel embarrassed. She found Wayne not only attractive but very funny too. He had her laughing till her sides ached, with stories of what he and his mates got up to.

As soon as she had entered the salon that morning, Jason had been upon her. Eager to share his latest news.

'Oh my god, darling. I've been waiting ages for you to get here. How come you're so late?' he'd said, taking the drenched brolly from her hand, so she could remove her jacket.

'The bloody bus broke down on Manchester Road,' she tutted. 'We had to wait ages for the next one. My nine o'clock isn't here yet, is she? Anyway, what's the matter with you?' she asked looking questioningly at Jason's excitable face. 'You're like a cat on hot bricks.'

Jason laughed. 'Have I got some gossip for you, lady! I was hardly able to sleep last night. I've been so looking forward to telling you. I need to take your Jackie's phone number. I could've done with preparing you for today.'

'Why? What's happening today?'

Jason didn't know where to start, but he continued with his news, hardly stopping for breath. 'Well, guess who came in here yesterday, when you were at college?' he asked, placing his hands on his hips. 'Oh, how was your first day at college by the way?' he added, without waiting for her to reply.

'Yes. Yes. Good. But never mind that. Tell me, who came in?' she quizzed, in anticipation.

Jason pursed his lips and widened his big blue eyes, before replying, 'Only that gorgeous A-ha lookalike,' he grinned. 'What's his name, you know, Wayne. Mmm-mmm, he is to die for.'

Wondering why Jason was so excited about Wayne's visit, Shelley shrugged, looking questioningly at her colleague.

'What did he want then?' she asked.

'He wanted you of course. He looked so gutted when I told him you were at college.'

Smiling at Jason's eagerness to matchmake, Shelley replied, 'Is that all? I thought something major had happened. What did he say?'

A little taken aback, Jason wasn't about to let Shelley's lack of enthusiasm put him off.

'Well, my girl. I hope you manage to find a smile for that beautiful face of yours and some of that sexy, Shelley spark. He's booked in for a cut with you at ten,' continued Jason, giving Shelley a cheeky wink. He was sure, that his little bit of additional news would change everything.

Shelley stared at him.

'Oh my god. Look at the state of me, Jay! I'm like a drowned rat, and my first appointment's already late. I'll have no time to sort myself out before he turns up. He'll run a mile if he sees me like this,' she gasped, looking at him frantically.

'Don't worry, my sweet angel,' he smiled, lifting her chin up. 'Your first appointment's cancelled, and I don't have anyone in for half an hour. So, let's get you under that dryer and slap a little tutty on that gorgeous face, shall we? I'll have you back to goddess in no time.'

Shelley smiled gratefully at Jason. He was such a wonderful person and he brought happiness to her every day, with his funny one-liners and kind gestures. He was a true friend in every sense of the word.

If Wayne was nervous it didn't show, as he entered the shop. He sat at the sink whilst Jason washed his thick brown hair, whilst making small talk. Massaging the shampoo into Wayne's head, Jason couldn't help feeling massively turned on, by the way his Adam's apple moved as they chatted. Well, if Shelley didn't want to go out with him, then he certainly wouldn't kick him out of bed. This man was gorgeous.

Shelley smiled as Wayne returned with the drinks. She'd readily accepted his offer of a date this time, and without having much time for her nerves to kick in, she was glad that they'd arranged to go out that very same night. Wayne was so easy to be around, and Shelley couldn't help being attracted to his wit, which at times bordered on cockiness. No-one would ever guess that Wayne was once the fat kid in school. He'd been shy and often the brunt of cruel jibes, which had left him very self-conscious. The ugly duckling, turned swan, had never fully adjusted to his now attractive exterior, using jokes to disguise the lack of confidence he still felt, deep within.

Reclining with his pint, Wayne watched Shelley's mouth as she laughed at his tales. She was as gorgeous as he remembered, from their first passion filled night and he couldn't wait to taste her once more. Hoping desperately that she liked him as much as he liked her, Wayne wondered if he was trying too hard. He seemed to be holding her attention and she was laughing at his goofy jokes, but could a girl of this calibre actually like him? She was stunning, and he knew that she could have her pick of guys. He just hoped, against hope that the night they'd shared had left a lasting impression, and that this first date would be the start of something special.

Chapter 45

Sitting at the typewriter, on her first day back at work, Mandy's enthusiasm was at an all-time low. She gazed out of the window at the early September drizzle. People were going about their business on the bustling street below. Their coats fastened up and shielded by umbrellas. She could hardly believe that only days before, her beautiful body was being drenched by the Mediterranean sun. How she longed to be back by the pool, relaxing on a sun lounger with a cocktail in her hand.

'These letters won't type themselves,' announced Doreen, interrupting Mandy's daydream. 'Come on, chop chop. You've still got a lot to do, and it's essential that they make tonight's post,' she added, spying over her glasses at Mandy, with a look of distaste.

As Doreen turned and walked back towards her own desk, Mandy stuck her tongue out, at her senior colleague. She hoped that the fake complaint letter, she'd sent prior to going away would have been received by now, and that Doreen would have been duly dealt with.

Having dared hope that Doreen may even have been dismissed, Mandy was certainly disappointed to see her still taking pride of place, in the office they shared. It seemed that the letter was not common knowledge within the company, and she had no way of knowing if it had ever arrived. It wasn't as though she could just come out and ask anyone.

She took her lunch that day with Wendy and Beth from accounts, asking them casually if, there had been any office gossip whilst she'd been away. If anyone would know, then these two would. To Mandy's dismay, there were no new rumours, and everything seemed just as before. To say she was disappointed was an understatement.

Back at her typewriter she sighed to herself. She needed to go back to the drawing board and come up with plan B. Come hell or high water, Mandy was determined that Doreen's job was going to be hers, and she'd prefer it to happen sooner, rather than later.

Chapter 46

The doorbell startled Tina, as she lay relaxing on the sofa. It was only mid-afternoon, but she found that doing nothing during the day to be so tiring. She couldn't wait to start work the following week and get back into a normal routine. Having the house to herself whilst her parents were at work had given her plenty of time to reflect on the last few months. She was looking forward to making new friends, without worrying what her controlling ex thought.

On opening the front door Tina's knees buckled. She reached out to steady herself on the wooden dado rail. Coming face to face with Darren was the last thing that she was prepared for, and the shock was written all over her face. In that split second, a mixture of thoughts and emotions ran through her mind. *What did he want? Was he going to hurt her? How would she escape if he tried to attack her?* But before she could react to her own thoughts, Darren spoke.

'Hello, Tina,' he said, holding up his hands in surrender, to let her know he'd come in peace. 'Please,' he asked.

'Please don't be afraid. I'm not here to cause you any trouble.' He could see her eyes wide with fear and her mouth half-open, as if the pause button had been pressed.

Even if she wanted to, Tina couldn't speak. Seeing her estranged husband standing on her doorstep, larger than life, was too much for her to take in. She knew that their paths would cross at some point but for him to actually turn up at her parents' house was something she'd never expected. He looked leaner than when she'd seen him last, but there was no question that he was still as spectacularly handsome. His deep brown eyes seemed kinder and his lips were full and soft. She couldn't help thinking how much he reminded her of when they had first met. His words jolted her from her thoughts.

'Tina, I'm not here to cause you any trouble,' he said. 'I want to apologise to you…For everything.' His words sounded so sincere and Tina was aghast.

She looked at him, waiting for the real Darren to appear, as he had so many times before. The Darren whose mouth would twist in anger and whose now kind eyes would turn to steel, before raining his fists down on her.

He smiled at her once more; 'be happy, Tina,' he said, in a voice not much louder than a whisper. 'I'll see you around.' Then, putting his hands inside the pockets of his leather jacket, he turned and walked away, down the street, without looking back.

Tina's heart was pounding as she closed the front door. She found the nearest chair and perched herself on the edge of it. Hardly believing what had just happened, she shook her head slightly, questioning her own senses.

Finally, after what seemed like an age, a solitary tear ran down her cheek. Darren had purposely sought her out. He had apologised to her. He had spoken the words that she'd wanted to hear for so long, and he genuinely sounded like he meant them. Could this really be true? Could the last few months have finally made him grow up and realise, that the way he'd treated her was wrong? Tina remembered the house, and the fact that she still needed to speak to him about it. Today would've been the perfect opportunity, but he'd caught her off guard. Plus, the timing was wrong. She wanted to savour Darren's apology and bringing the house up might've very well spoilt the moment.

His visit, if somewhat shocking and unexpected, had left her with a sense of relief. She dared to feel hopeful, that Darren might have finally taken stock of the past and that, maybe they could face an amicable future.

Chapter 47

Sitting in the bath, hugging her knees, Leanne finally became aware of how cold the water surrounding her had become. She couldn't recall how long she'd spent, sat staring at nothing. But she knew it was a long time. Touching her tender cheek, she felt the swelling beginning to appear and was dreading facing her reflection in the mirror. Her throat hurt when she swallowed, and the skin on her neck was sore.

Leanne Dagger had been subjected to sexual abuse throughout her short life and the ordeal she had just encountered, resurfaced many horrendous memories, which, for the majority of the time she managed to keep locked away.

After losing her mother to cancer at the tender age of six, it wasn't long before her father and main caregiver, began to sexually abuse her. The abuse continued until she was sixteen, after Leanne finally broke away from his clutches.

Leaving her native town of Gipton, in Leeds, Leanne came to Shaw, to live with her only true friend, Sue. The girls met the year before at Butlins, in Pwllheli. Coming from similar backgrounds, the pair gelled instantly. They had both suffered at the hands of the people who were supposed to love and care for them the most. Instantly recognising each other's plight, in a way that only two victims of these horrific deeds could.

It was through this shameful bond that a firm and indestructible friendship was formed. Leanne kept in regular contact with Sue, through phone calls and letters, and as soon as she was sixteen, she packed a holdall with her few belongings and moved to live with Sue and her grandmother in the small terraced house they shared, on Bowler Street. Sue's father and abuser had suffered a fatal heart attack earlier that year and she couldn't have been more relieved, at his departing.

Having grown up not remembering her mother, who'd left when she was a toddler, Sue finally left the council house she'd shared with her father, to set up home with her granny Eva. As much as she loved her gran, Sue never felt able to confess to her, the terrible abuse that her son had inflicted on her. Knowing this information would break her grandmother's heart. So, Sue had carried the burden of his heinous deeds with her for as long as she could remember.

In the few years since she'd arrived in Shaw, a lot had changed for Leanne and Sue. Eva sadly passed away, following an infection, which turned to sepsis. Sue was devastated, as was Leanne. She had only lived with Sue and her grandmother for a year, but she had become extremely fond of the old lady, who'd treated her with more love than she'd known since her own poor mother was alive. As Sue was her grans only surviving relative, she inherited her house, where both girls continued to live.

For some time, Sue displayed a lot of anger towards the world. She'd lost the only person, who'd ever shown her unconditional love, and she needed someone to blame. She began to shoplift and get in trouble with the police for other petty offences.

Both young women craved love and affection and their one-night stands, with numerous local men, had unfortunately left them both with a bad reputation. The girls didn't care. To them, sex was a meaningless task they endured, in the hope of receiving a small amount of affection in return. The more sex they had, the more short bursts of affection they were guaranteed to receive. Just like a dog begging for scraps from a table. It was merely a way of life for them both.

They continued on this destructive path for the next couple years, until Sue met the love of her life, Craig. A private in the King's Own Royal Border Regiment, Craig was on a stag do in Blackpool and Sue was on a coach trip with several women from their local pub. It was love at first sight for both of them. Having no knowledge of Sue's background, there was no pre-judgement towards her from Craig, and from that night on the couple were inseparable. They were married within three months, with Sue moving to Albermarle

Barracks in Newcastle, to live in the married quarters where Craig was stationed.

Suddenly finding herself alone, Leanne continued to live her life, the only way she knew how. Her job as a machinist in one of the town's local factories, allowed her to mix with lots of similarly aged girls. She was never short of a busy social life. However, none of these friends could live up to Sue. Still, Leanne had grown used to losing people throughout the years. The girls stayed in regular contact and Sue was happy for her friend to continue living in her house, and the arrangement continued from there.

Now, feeling numb, Leanne gingerly dried her slight frame. The rough towel hurt her delicate skin and her body ached, as though she'd completed an army assault course. She wanted to cry but no tears would come. Reflecting upon the last couple of hours, she resigned herself to the fact that the treatment she'd received was all she must be worth.

Opening the front door to find Darren standing before her, Leanne had been unable to hide her delighted surprise.

'Hello, stranger,' she'd said, with a big smile on her face. 'What brings you here at this time?'

She was usually only graced with Darren's presence after last orders, or at chucking out time, from Jaspers nightclub. 7pm on a weeknight was unheard of for him to call on her. Her first thought was that he must need an alibi, or place to hide out from the police. However, a tiny part of her dared to hope that he was beginning to have feelings for her. Leanne was desperate to find her happy ever after, just like Sue had. Could Darren finally want her in his life as a permanent fixture? Images flashed through her mind, of him introducing her to his family, spending his spare time with her and then finally taking her as his wife.

But before she could continue with her wistful thoughts, Darren ushered her inside, closing the door behind them. Grabbing her neck with his large hand, he pushed her none-too-gently up against the living room wall and began kissing her. As he clamped his wet open mouth over hers, Leanne could taste the alcohol on his breath and prepared herself, for what she realised was likely to be a bumpy ride. Darren liked his sex a little on the rough side and Leanne always obliged his wants willingly. The more accommodating, she was, the longer time he might spend with her.

Tonight however, he seemed different. There was no conversation from him and by the glazed look in his eyes, she could tell he'd had more than enough to drink. Leanne wasn't completely naive. She knew that when Darren turned up at the weekend, after closing time that he wasn't there for chit chat – although in the past, he had at least engaged in small talk.

Not thinking too much of it, Leanne went along with what she believed was one of Darren's little games. She responded to his kisses passionately until he bit her lip hard, drawing blood.

'Ouch, she shrieked, shocked. Don't do that, you bastard,' she stared, pushing him away.

Feeling her bottom lip with her fingertips, and tasting the blood on her tongue, Leanne suddenly saw Darren's face twist in anger, as a menacing glint appeared in his eyes. Tensing up, she prepared herself for the fallout of his rage. He'd never been violent towards her, but in the past, she'd witnessed how he'd made mincemeat, of men in the pub. She had always been wary of incurring his temper.

'I'll show you who's a bastard, you fucking slag,' he spat, grabbing her by the hair and roughly throwing her to the ground.

'No, Darren. Stop,' she yelled, in panic.

But before she could cry out again, Darren punched her face, instantly drawing blood where his signet ring connected with her cheek. Then clamping his hand over her mouth, he unbuckled his belt. Leanne knew what to expect, and just as she had years before, she didn't fight it. There was no use. She must try to relax and let her mind take her to a better place.

Dragging her to the ground, Darren mounted Leanne, spreading her thin white legs with his muscular own. As she felt the crotch of her knickers being dragged to one side, he forced himself inside her as a silent tear fell down the side of Leanne's face, running into her ear. The memories, of the years of abuse she'd endured, instantly came flooding back and all she could do was close her eyes, waiting for it to end.

Before reaching his climax, Darren let his hand slip from Leanne's mouth to her neck, where he pressed his palm tightly until her eyes bulged. Finally spent, he let out an almighty groan, finally releasing her to cough and gasp, until she caught her desperate breath. When she finally managed to sit, Darren was already dressed. Walking away, he turned to her and winked.

'I think that was our best yet,' he smirked, as he left the room.

Hearing the front door slam, Leanne staggered to her feet, locking the door and bolting it. As she felt the semen slide down her leg, she raced upstairs, turning on the bath taps and realising that, once again, she would be able to scrub the filth of man from her body, but never from her mind.

Chapter 48

Walking home, Tina couldn't smile widely enough. The first week in her new job was over, and she'd loved it. The days had flown by and she already felt as though she'd worked there for ages. She'd been introduced to lots of new people and on the whole, everyone seemed very friendly. So much so that she was meeting some of her new colleagues that very night, to celebrate one of their birthdays. Thinking back to her first day, she couldn't believe how nervous she'd been.

Waiting in the large reception, with over twenty other people, Tina wondered if the others felt as anxious as she did. Looking around they seemed at ease, chatting amongst themselves and sharing pleasantries. Coming from a small town, she recognised a couple of faces, but she didn't know anyone enough to talk to, that was until she heard a familiar voice call out her name.

'Tina?'

She turned around.

'Tina! What the heck are you doing here?' Before she had a chance to answer, the woman spoke again, shaking her head as she laughed at her own question. 'Well, obviously you're here to start a new job, but I'm just so surprised to see you. It must be two years.'

Tina smiled with glee, recognising the woman before her. 'Oh my god!' She squealed with delight, before remembering where she was. 'Jackie! How wonderful to see you,' she said, beaming excitedly. 'I can't believe it. So, you're starting here today too? That's brilliant.' Tina was ecstatic to see her once best friend's older sister, and she was bursting with questions to ask her.

But just as she was about to continue chatting, two official-looking women approached the group, introducing themselves as the training managers who would be taking that day's inductions. The months running up to Christmas were the catalogue's busiest time of year, and this week's intake was at an all-time high. Therefore, the group was to be split into two.

As the employees' names were read out, Jackie and Tina couldn't hide their dismay at being separated. As Jackie's group was led away, she gave Tina a wave, mouthing that she would see her soon.

Tina was thrilled at their reunion and hoped that it wouldn't be too long before the pair saw each other again.

Following her induction, Tina was led into a large and bustling department, known as Central Packing. Along with two other new girls, she waited at the front desk for the supervisor. Tina eagerly watched the staff busily packing at their benches. They were chatting and laughing with one another, and she couldn't help but feel a buzz of excitement in her stomach. She had a good feeling and a sense of exhilaration, instantly knowing that she was going to be happy here. She noticed people looking over and nudging one another, obviously interested in the department's newbies.

'Right girls, who've we got here then?' asked the approaching, blonde woman, jolting Tina back to the present.

As they informed her of their names, she ticked them off the list on her clipboard, suspiciously eyeing them up and down for what seemed like an age, making Tina begin to feel slightly uncomfortable.

In a haughty tone, she finally introduced herself. 'I'm Bridget Hornbrough,' she announced, meeting each pair of eyes. 'I'll be your supervisor and I run a tight ship. So, keep on my good side and we'll get along just fine.'

Her voice was high-pitched and nasally. Tina imagined that her husband, if she had one, probably kept the TV volume quite loud, to drown out her screechy tones.

'You two girls wait here for your trainer – and you,' she said, looking directly at Tina, 'You follow me.'

As they walked down the packing aisles, passing a sea of faces, Tina nervously smiled at the busy workers. Most of the girls smiled back in a welcoming manner, and Tina began to relax. As Bridget's heels clip-clopped along the asphalt floor, Tina noticed that at the sight of their supervisor, the staff hurriedly stopped chatting and began busying themselves with their work.

'Have you done any packing before?' Bridget asked, without turning to look at Tina.

'Sort of,' she replied. 'I used to work at Sandy Mill, stuffing handbags.'

'Was it piece work?' questioned Bridget, eyes still forward.

'Oh yes. I worked to a target,' Tina responded, upping her pace as she tried to keep up with the swift-walking woman. 'I did it for two years,' she said, smiling, whilst thinking of the job she used to love.

Bridget turned around, eyes locking on Tina's. 'Good. Well, I expect you not to have a problem reaching your target on my department,' she said, slowing down to approach one of the benches.

Tina could tell that this woman was a tyrant, and she vowed to herself, to do her best in order to keep in her good books.

'Norma?' Bridget's nasally voice called. 'Where's Norma?' she asked, questioning an older woman on the opposite bench.

But before the woman could speak, a voice behind them answered.

'I'm here, Bridget,' said the small young woman, hurriedly taking her position back at her bench.

'I hope you've not been for a fag, Norma,' Bridget said, looking at her questioningly over her glasses. 'It's only forty minutes till your lunch break. You're paid to work, not fag it.' Her voice was like nails down a blackboard, and Tina hoped that she wouldn't have to spend too much time in her supervisor's company.

'I just nipped to the loo,' Norma said, winking at her co-worker. 'Less than two minutes, I was.'

'Mmm,' Bridget remarked, disbelievingly. 'Well, this is Tina. I want you to train her up. And don't distract her with your gossiping.' Turning to Tina, she briefly smiled, before her stony expression returned. 'Norma's one of our best, so I'll expect you to learn the ropes pretty quickly,' she quipped, before tottering off in her heels, leaving Tina wondering if she was ever going to see a softer side to Bridget Hornbrough.

'So, where do you live?' asked Norma, before Tina had a chance to gather her thoughts. This was to be the first of her many questions and pretty much depicted how the rest of the day followed.

As Norma quickly ran through the job, she continued with her friendly interrogation. Tina liked her immediately. She was very nosey, that much was true, but in a friendly, getting to know you kind of way. Instantly put at ease, Tina even found herself spilling details of some of the private accounts, in her recent life.

Some of which she hadn't even divulged to her closest family.

Norma was tiny. Standing under 5ft tall. She was of medium build, with enormous breasts, that made her look as though she might topple over at any moment. She also had an enormous personality to match. Tina's mum would have referred to her as 'a right, character' and Tina couldn't help but smile to herself as the chatty woman continued to babble. Never had she witnessed someone talk and work in unison, at such speed. But to Norma it was as natural as breathing, and she hardly came up for air.

The day was going so fast. Tina couldn't believe how much she was enjoying herself.

'Right, come on then,' Norma said, downing tools and glancing at her watch. 'It's brew time. And more importantly, fag time,' she grinned, shaking a packet of Benson and Hedges.

As the girls took a seat in the large canteen, Norma sparked up, taking a long, satisfying drag of her cigarette.

'I wish I could pack these in. Costing me a bloody fortune, they are' she moaned. 'I need to start saving some cash. I've just applied for a mortgage on a house I've viewed, on Shaw Road in Royton. It's just a little terraced, but it'll do me,' she exclaimed, sounding chuffed at her achievement.

'Are you going to live alone?' asked Tina, thinking how lonely it would be.

'Yeh, and I can't bloody wait. I'm nearly twenty-seven, it's about time I got a place of my own. I left me Mam and Dad's when I was sixteen, and I've been flat sharing ever since with different mates. It's time to go it alone' she said, blowing smoke towards the ceiling. 'All my close friends are getting married these days, but I don't think Mr Right exists for me.'

'Well, husbands aren't all they're cracked up to be,' Tina smiled, knowingly.

'Hey, and don't I bloody well know it,' Norma replied, shaking her head. 'Liars and cheats, the majority of blokes are. There's only one man who ever treated me proper,' she gazed wistfully into space. 'Pete, he was called. He really loved me, and I never realised how much, till I let him go.'

Tina saw the sadness in Norma's eyes and momentarily reflected on how their positions weren't too dissimilar. They had both loved and lost and were both about to move into their own homes as single women, living alone. The thought scared her, and she was relieved when Norma swiftly changed the subject.

'Hey, don't look now, but Flat Pat and Hissing Sid are coming over,' she whispered.

'Who?' Tina asked, a confused look appearing on her face as she automatically turned around, to see two women approaching.

'Who's your friend, Norma?' asked the first woman, who was in her 30's and sporting a short blonde perm, along with a Princess Diana style, frilly blouse.

'This is Tina. She's just started today,' Norma responded, in a less than enthusiastic tone. She didn't care much for the pair standing before her and she wasn't at all bothered if her feelings showed.

'Nice to meet you, Tina,' said the blonde woman. 'I'm Yvonne and this is Pat,' she nodded towards the smaller, stout woman with the short dark crew cut. 'Do let us know if you need anything, won't you? You're part of the gang now and we always help our own. Don't we, Pat?' she stated, eyeing her so far, mute friend. Pat nodded without uttering a word as the pair made their way towards the vending machine.

'Listen, stay as far away from those two as possible,' Norma said, in a low voice.

'Why, what's up with 'em? And what's with the nicknames?' Tina laughed.

'Because they're the biggest backstabbing gossipers in this place,' Norma replied, eyes wide. 'More faces than the town hall clock. They're also that far up Bridget's arse, they could tell you what she had for breakfast.'

Tina sniggered. 'You're so funny, Norma. You've got nicknames for everyone.' She said, recalling all the people she'd been introduced to throughout the day.

'Yeah, well if anyone deserves their names, it's those two,' she nodded towards the vending machine, where the women were standing. 'Hissing Sid is on account of the fact that Yvonne's the biggest snake on our department,' she sneered.

'What about Flat Pat then?' Tina enquired.

Norma giggled. 'I'd have thought that was obvious,' she said, pointing to the back of her own head. 'Look at hers, it's as flat as a pancake. And not helped, I might add, by that god-awful haircut.'

Tina laughed aloud – she felt like she'd known Norma for years. Getting back to work, was just what she had needed.

'Well, we can't sit 'ere all day,' Norma exclaimed, standing up. 'Let's get back before Brigadier is on the warpath. You don't want to get on the wrong side of her, I can tell you.'

Zipping up her coat, Tina continued the short walk home. It was only just after 4pm but now that the clocks had gone back, the dark nights were drawing in. The wind was brisk and biting and autumn leaves were swirling in all directions.

Turning the corner onto Crossley street, Darren's face suddenly appeared in front of her. Startled, Tina jumped in shock. Before she could react further, he spoke.

'I'm so sorry, Tina, I didn't mean to frighten you,' he said, gently placing his hand on her arm. 'I need to talk to you about the house, so I thought I'd see if I could catch you on your way home from work.' Realising, by the look on Tina's face, that she was wondering how he knew where to find her; he already had his answer prepared. 'You know what small town gossip's like. Someone in the pub told me, you'd started at Littlewoods, so I just thought I'd try my luck. I hope I've not upset you. I realise I should've mentioned the house the other day, but the timing didn't seem right.'

His smile seemed genuine and Tina wanted to believe him, but months of abuse and beatings had taught her to be wary. Her barriers were up but, at the same time, she realised, that to get the house proceedings underway, this conversation had to take place. Icy raindrops began to fall, and she shuddered as a droplet of water fell down the back of her neck.

'Look, we can't talk here. The pub's just across the road. What do you say?' Darren asked, gesturing towards the stone bricked building, facing them.

Hidden in the corner, Tina sat at the small round table. The Moulders Arms was littered with tradesmen in their work gear. Friday meant a lunch time finish for most of them and the majority wouldn't make it home to their wives before closing time. Tina was glad of the warmth but kept her coat on, feeling a sense of unease. She desperately wanted Darren to agree to her taking the house on alone, but knowing his unpredictable temper as she did, she was terrified of saying the wrong thing.

As Darren returned from the bar, Tina was shocked and secretly surprised, to see that he'd ordered himself an orange juice. Seeing her puzzled face staring at his pint of cordial, he smiled.

'I've knocked it on the head in the week now,' he explained. 'I might nip out for a couple tomorrow night, but it was getting out of hand, Ti,' he continued.

Watching his full mouth and perfect white teeth as he spoke, then hearing him call her Ti as he had in the old days, made her heart lurch. She hated this hold he still had over her, and she hated herself, for allowing him to make her feel this way. Deciding she needed to keep this meeting as brief as possible, she took a deep breath, in order to begin the speech that she had previously prepared.

But before she could begin, Darren cut in. 'Tina, I want to ask something big of you.' With baited breathed, Tina felt as though her heart might beat out of her chest, as she waited in anticipation, for him to continue. 'I want to ask if you'll take on the house. On your own, obviously,' he added.

She gasped, staring at him disbelievingly, her mouth half-open.

'Shit!' Darren said, aloud, shaking his head in annoyance. 'I'm sorry, Tina. It's too much of me to ask, isn't it? I've not upset you, have I?'

'No. No. Not at all,' she replied, finally finding her voice. 'I just wasn't expecting to hear that.'

He continued to speak in a low voice, as he looked intently at her. 'I need to be honest with you, Tina. I was a total wreck when you left. All my own fault, I know,' he said, holding his hands up. I went on the booze for a while and nearly lost my job in the process. But since then, well, I've had a wake-up call.'

'It's my mum, you see. She's been very ill. We thought she was a goner at one point,' he added, breaking just long enough to take in the pitying, concerned looks that his estranged wife was showering on him. 'Anyway, with all the upset and everything else that was going on, I let things slip a bit. I've missed a couple of payments on the mortgage. We're in danger of losing the house if you can't take it over,' he rambled, now looking down at the floor. 'I've been living at me mams. And now, well, I just can't leave the old queen. Not when she's been so poorly. So, I didn't know what else to do, but to ask if you could take it on. If it gets repossessed, we'll both get blacklisted, and that'll do none of us any favours.'

Seeing Tina's body relax, he knew he was onto a winner. He shook his head slightly. 'I'll be glad to be shot of it, if I'm honest. It's been like a noose 'round my neck.' After a moment's pause, he looked directly into Tina's eyes. 'So, what d'ya reckon?'

Tina wanted to jump up and down with glee. She couldn't believe her luck. The house was going to be hers, and she hadn't even had to ruffle Darren's feathers to get it. Of course, she was sorry to hear that Ivy had been so ill, and she genuinely wished her a speedy recovery. But knowing she could have her home back, was music to her ears. She couldn't believe the change she was seeing in Darren. He was almost unrecognisable from the man she'd been married to. Maybe her going away had done them both a favour. She smiled at him.

'Well, I've got a full-time job now, Darren,' she said. 'So yes, of course, I'll take over the house. The money will be tight, but I'll manage somehow.'

Quickly thinking on her feet, Tina decided she'd better not milk it too much. She was getting what she wanted. The last thing she needed was for Darren to think she was basking in his hardship. He might change his mind just to spite her and then they'd both lose the house; she couldn't take that chance. As Tina waved to a couple of her new colleagues, Darren stood up.

'Right, I'll love you and leave you then, Ti,' he smiled, once again touching her arm.

The familiar lurch in her stomach came again and she wished she could just turn off her feelings for him. Why couldn't he have been this way when they were together? It was so sad. All she had ever wanted, was for him to love her the same way that she had loved him.

Leaving the pub, Darren walked the hundred or so yards to the nearby working men's club.

"Ere, Dianne,' he called to the droopy-breasted old barmaid, who was wearing a tight top that she should've discarded ten years earlier. 'Get us a pint of Stella and a whisky chaser,' he grinned. 'I'm celebrating.'

Darren was very pleased with his performance so far. He had Tina eating out of his hand. She was falling for his 'Mr nice guy' act and it was working a treat. He realised by now that she'd have been into the building society and found out about the mortgage. He knew that she'd be wanting the house back and he was giving her everything she wanted, on a plate. Allowing her to believe that he was doing it all, of his own accord. He'd have her back before Christmas at this rate, he thought, checking out his handsome reflection in the mirror behind the bar. At the same time, he clocked the two fit blondes that had just walked in, giggling, arm in arm. Yes, tonight Darren was celebrating.

Chapter 49

With his head in his hands, Chris sat on the edge of the bed. He'd hardly managed to catch any sleep and getting up at this early hour on Saturday morning, was normally unheard of. Turning around, he viewed Mandy in all her glory. She was laying on her side with her back to him, exposing her tanned body, tiny waist and the top of her pert bottom. This sight would normally have Chris erect within seconds, but after what he'd learned, all he could do was put on his jeans and sweater and go down to the kitchen to make himself a strong coffee.

Mandy was already asleep when he arrived home the night before, and that was probably a good thing. A full-scale row was more than he could handle after the night he'd had. He had a lot of soul searching to do and staring at the bedroom ceiling hadn't given him any inspiration at all.

Last night had been a total embarrassment for him. It was the wake-up call that, in his gut, he knew had been coming. But to have his good reputation dragged through the mud like it had been, was almost too much to bear. Chris prided himself on being a cut above. His career was going full pelt and he had the capabilities to make something of his life. His darling mother had always pushed him to do his best, and his good education and hard slog were starting to pay dividends. Her snobbery was also beginning to rub off on him. These days he tended to look down on some of the lads whom he'd mixed with when he was younger. Most of whom were not as privileged and did not have the opportunities, that he'd had. But thinking back to the way those same guys had mocked at him last night, made him cringe.

Ross and Shane had proposed they meet in The Pineapple. It was centrally located in the small-town centre, and an obvious choice. Chris was not a fan of the place, finding the clientele a little too downmarket for his liking. There was bound to be at least one fight break out, and he would no doubt get a drink spilt on his new chinos. His suggestion was to get a taxi straight to Manchester. His preference for the new style, trendy wine bars, rather than backstreet pubs, was becoming all the more evident lately. City centres were creating a newly established breed that the media referred to as Yuppies, and Chris wanted to be part of this work hard, play hard crew.

Having recently been approached by large marketing company, on Deansgate in Manchester City Centre, Chris had the feeling that his small-town days were numbered. He enjoyed his job at Cuthbertson's, but it was only a stepping-stone until the right opportunity came along.

As soon as he walked into the pub, Chris had the feeling that he was the target of other people's humour. As he waved to Ross and Shane, he noticed crowds nudging one another and sniggering as he walked past them. Wondering if he had something stuck to his shoes or clothes, he checked his appearance, but nothing seemed untoward. On approaching his friends, he was aware that they had sheepish looks on their faces, which were coupled with stifled grins.

'What's the matter with you two,' he asked, feeling unnerved. 'And what's everyone grinning at?'

Shane spoke first. 'Sorry, mate,' he said, in a low voice. 'There's a sort of tape, doing the rounds.'

Looking confused, Chris responded, 'A tape? What kind of tape? What you on about?'

'It's a sex tape…..of Mandy. Your Mandy,' he blurted out.

Chris' face was a picture of disbelief and confusion. Ross looked to his left at the group of guys of a similar age, who were openly pointing and laughing at his mate.

'Come on, pal,' Ross said, taking hold of Chris's arm. 'Let's get out of here and we'll explain.'

But Chris was having none of it and aggressively shrugged Ross's hand off him.

'Fuck off,' he snapped. 'Tell me what the fuck he's on about. And tell me now.'

Everyone turned to stare. Some of them had pitying looks on their faces, but just as many were grinning with delight at Chris's downfall. These were people who, nowadays, Chris turned his nose up at. Men and women who he'd been friends with, since he was a child, but whom he'd recently decided were beneath him, and didn't warrant his time. Most thought he was getting too big for his boots, with his good job and flashy clothes. It was safe to say that a lot of people were happy to see him being brought down a peg or two.

'Hey, Chrissy boy,' a dark-haired bodybuilder type shouted over. 'You wanna know what's up, mate? You'd better have a word with Dobbsy,' he sniggered, nodding towards the bar, where the wiry-looking man with greasy hair, was sitting. 'Didn't think the dirty fucker had it in him, pulling a bird like her,' he taunted, looking round at his mates for further encouragement. 'Hey lads, remember the porno, "Debbie Does Dallas", how about "Mandy Does Manchester"?'

With this, the whole pub erupted in laughter, as Lenny Dobbs raised his pint and grinned, showing his yellow teeth. He was loving his newfound fame, as usually this rowdy lot didn't bother to give him the time of day. He would teach that bitch to ignore his calls and cast him aside as though he meant nothing. After all he'd done for her. Taking her photos and making sure her portfolio was more than impressive. She'd had her chance. Well now, this was his time to shine.

Chris couldn't fight his way out of a paper bag, but Ross and Shane, saw the rage on his face and realised they needed to get him out of there, before a full-on brawl took place. Grabbing Chris with both arms, they dragged him out of the pub and clambered straight into a passing taxi.

'Take him back to your place,' Ross hissed to Shane. 'I can't chance taking him to mine. Our Jason might be home, and I don't want him getting wind of this.'

Shane was well aware that Jason worked alongside Chris's ex, Shelley. He also knew that Jason couldn't hold his own water and would have no problem letting the cat out of the bag. Shane was also the only person who knew that Ross was head over heels in love with Shelley. He would do anything to spare her blushes. The last thing he wanted for her, was any more reminders of what her estranged husband or his girlfriend had been up to.

Shaw was a small town and she was bound to get wind of this little bit of shenanigans sooner or later, but the longer she was kept in the dark the better as far as Ross was concerned. His weekend away with Natalie had been a disaster. He couldn't even make love to her. They were surrounded by the beautiful landscape of the Lake District, and the plush extravagance of a luxury hotel, but all Ross could do was think about Shelley. The thought of her beautiful smile and the memory of her soft hands running through his hair, made his loins tingle and his heart ache. He knew it wasn't just lust. He had deep feelings for her, and yet here he was, pretending to still be friends with Chris. Acting as though they were still best mates.

In truth, Chris had begged him and Shane to go out. Neither of them had much time for him these days. He couldn't believe they used to be so close. When he'd married Shelley, Ross had been so envious of his friend's happiness. The couple were so in love. They seemed made for each other. But that hadn't been enough for Chris. He didn't deserve someone as thoughtful, kind and beautiful as Shelley. Ross decided he was no longer going to feel guilty about his feelings for her. Chris had had his chance and he had well and truly blown it. If it meant choosing between them, Ross decided that after tonight, he wasn't bothered if he never saw Chris again. He made a lame excuse and left him in Shane's capable hands, much to Shane's dismay.

'Come on, mate, it's time you got yourself home now,' said Shane, looking at his watch for the tenth time.

Chris had gone through the best part of a bottle of Shane's Jack Daniels, as he continued with his sob story. After Shane had filled him in on the full details of the sex tape video, in which his girlfriend was playing the starring role, Chris's emotions had turned from anger to sadness, to embarrassment, and then to self-pity. And the more he drank, the more emotional he became. If it was up to Shane, Chris could've slept on the couch but when his girlfriend Simone returned home around midnight, she gave him a look that told him, in no uncertain terms, that there was no way she would allow it. Simone ruled the roost and Shane wasn't about to argue.

Mandy had her own key to Chris's house. He prayed that she would already be in deep slumber, following a boozy, girls, night out. He needed to be sober and compos mentis, when he gave her, her marching orders.

Chapter 50

Crying out, Judy woke up with a start. Sweat was pouring from her as she scrambled for the lamp switch. As the light flooded her bedroom, her panic began to subside, giving way to a flood of tears.

Within seconds, her door was thrust open as her concerned father burst in. At the sight of his face, Judy held out her arms like a child and openly sobbed. The feeling of her dad's embrace was overwhelming. She had missed him so much and her emotions were reciprocated. The pair clung to each other for what seemed like an age, with Malcolm gently stroking the back of his daughter's head, as he comforted her.

'I'm sorry, Dad,' Judy managed to say between her sobs.

'Ssshh, ssshh, no need for an apology from you, my love,' he replied, with a lump in his throat. 'It's me who's the sorry one,' he whispered, as his own eyes filled with tears. 'Hey, this takes me back to when you used to have bad dreams as a little girl,' he said, reaching for her Teddy Bear and passing him to her. 'I can't believe you've kept him after all these years. Still a little girl at heart, aye?' Giving her a kiss on the cheek, he then held her at arm's length, looking her in the eyes. 'Now listen, we've had a big shock today, with our Dan. But he's in the best place. The doctor said he was very lucky indeed and that he'll be good as new in no time. I don't want you stressing about him, love. I've been so worried about you lately,' he said, with a look of concern clouding his face. 'You've gone to nothing, love. You're disappearing before my very eyes.'

Judy looked down, to hide her shame. 'I've just been so frazzled with everything, Dad,' she replied. She felt so ashamed. If her dad knew that she'd been making herself sick after every meal, he'd be so upset. She vowed to herself right there and then, that she would never, ever do it again.

'Look. From now on, me and you are going to be here for each other. Dan too, when he comes home. You two are my world, and you will always be my priority. Okay?'

'Okay, Dad,' Judy nodded, feeling calmer and happier than she had in a long time.

'I'll go and do us a Horlicks,' Malcolm said, squeezing her hand. 'I'll be back in two ticks.'

What a day it had been. When the police had arrived at the house, informing them that Dan had been in an accident, Judy immediately feared the worst. He'd been knocked off his bicycle, by the 181 bus, in front of the war memorial. He was very lucky to only suffer a mild concussion. Thankfully, he'd landed on the grass verge instead of the concrete pavement and it was also fortunate that the accident had happened outside Crompton Health Centre; with some quick actions from one of the GPs, Dan had received the first aid he required, until the ambulance arrived.

It had been a long, exhausting day, and Judy had fallen into a deep sleep, within minutes of going to bed. What occurred next was the reason she'd cried out, waking up in such a panic. Whether it was a dream or something more, she'd never know, and couldn't begin to explain. Judy could only say that it was the most surreal and emotional thing, to ever happen to her. She would treasure the memory, for the rest of her days.

As she lay in a deep slumber, her mother had appeared to her in a dream. She seemed so real and so close, that Judy recalled, being able to see her hairline and the pores on her skin. She felt her mother's arms embrace her, and as she wrapped her own arms around her mum's neck, she felt the clasp on the chain of the St Christopher, that Sheila had always worn. No words were spoken aloud, but in her mind, Judy sensed her mother telling her that everything was going to be okay. She told her that she loved her and that she was extremely proud of her. It was at that point that her mum's vision began to fade, forcing Judy to cry out in her sleep.

Bringing her back to the present, Malcolm, entered the room, carrying the mug of Horlicks.

'Here you go, love. I've topped it up with a bit of cold milk, so it should be ready to drink. I know how you hate it when it gets a skin on,' he chuckled.

Judy took a sip. 'Mmm, it's almost as good as Mum's,' she said, smiling lovingly at her dad.

'Well that's good enough for me then, love,' he replied, kissing her on the forehead.

Chapter 51

'Oooh, get yerself in, Shelley. You must be bloody frozen. It's brass monkeys out there,' Jackie shivered, ushering her sister through the front door. 'I've done you gammon, egg, chips and beans for your tea.'

Shelley smiled. 'Oh, you do look after me, Jackie. But if I keep eating like this, I'll be the size of a house end, before long.'

'Ey it, were grand,' beamed Kev, rubbing his ever-expanding belly, as he sat watching the news. 'I had three breads wi' mine. My wife certainly knows the way to a man's heart,' he grinned, winking at a proud Jackie.

Shelley laughed. She loved staying at her sister's, they made her feel so welcome, but their eating habits were so different from hers. They had chips with almost everything and, now winter was here, Jackie always made sure there was no end of stodgy food, spared.

Since marrying Chris, Shelley had been introduced to a whole new plethora of different cuisines. Gone were the pie, chips and peas dishes, that she'd been brought up on; these days she was used to cooking for a much more diverse palate. Chris's mother had given Shelley some of her old cookbooks and she thoroughly enjoyed experimenting with the recipes, within them. Some of which she had never even heard of before. At home, her cupboards were stocked with pulses, herbs and spices, which she regularly used, to produce numerous, exotic and nutritious meals. Shelley had offered to cook for the family, but Jackie wouldn't hear of it. When she suggested making them a risotto, Kev's face had been a picture.

'I'm not eating that foreign muck,' he grimaced.

Shelley realised that sometime soon, she needed to address her future. She'd buried her head in the sand for long enough. She must go and see Chris about the house and get the divorce wheels in motion. She was feeling much stronger of late and going out with Wayne had really boosted her confidence. He showered her with compliments, and she enjoyed his company. However, finding some alone time with him, was proving to be somewhat difficult. He lived with his sister and her family, with what seemed like no intentions of getting a place of his own. For Shelley, living with her sister was a stepping-stone, until she got some money behind her. It wouldn't be long before she had her independence back, she would make sure of it. Wayne, however, seemed quite happy in his rut. Shelley was in no hurry to rush their relationship, so for now she would just go with the flow.

'So, have you seen Tina yet?' Shelley quizzed her sister, eagerly.

It was becoming a daily question between the women as Shelley had been stunned and delighted when Jackie told her about their brief meeting. She couldn't deny that she missed Tina's friendship dreadfully and she often found herself wondering, what her once best friend was doing these days.

'No, I've not seen or heard anything,' Jackie shrugged. 'And I'm far too busy with my own job, to go looking for her. I'm struggling to reach the target, as it is,' she moaned. 'I'm run off my feet.'

Jackie was employed as a picker, on floor 6. At first, she'd hated it. The target was high, and she was not used to the physical aspect of the job. However, as the weeks flew by, she was beginning to feel much more positive. She was now managing to keep up with the work demands and she'd also made some new friends. Working part-time suited her family life and the extra money, certainly came in handy.

'I think I'll nip round to her mum's again this weekend,' Shelley continued. 'Hopefully, there'll be someone home this time.'

Since Jackie had told her sister that she's seen Tina, Shelley couldn't stop thinking about her oldest friend. So much so that she'd called around to the house Tina had shared with Darren, hoping to find her there. Shelley was more than surprised at what she'd discovered on her arrival. After waiting at the door for a few minutes with no response, Shelley decided to have a sneaky look through the front window.

What she saw, left her in no doubt of her friend's absence. The living room was littered with empty cans of lager, and plates with half-eaten Chinese food, lay on the floor. There was no way Tina would live in that state. Either the couple no longer lived there, or Tina and Darren had split up, just as she and Chris had. If that was the case, she couldn't say she was surprised. Shelley had always known Darren was a wrong 'un. If only she had realised the same about her own husband.

Chapter 52

Judy's feet were freezing as she stood waiting in the precinct doorway. Huddling her shoulders, she pulled her coat in tighter, protecting herself from the biting wind. Looking at her watch once more, she began to get a sinking feeling in her stomach. Having waited for forty minutes already, she decided that she'd been well and truly stood up. How could she be so stupid, believing that Mark Devine, actually wanted a date with her? But surely, he wouldn't be so cruel as to phone her at home, ask her out and then just not show up. That didn't seem his style at all. But all she could do was resign herself to the fact that he'd changed his mind.

The phone call had come completely out of the blue and Judy still didn't know how Mark had obtained her number. Once she realised it was him on the line, she'd acted like a gibbering wreck. She was dumbfounded when he asked her, outright, to join him on a date. In a daze, she agreed to a time and place. Replacing the receiver, she couldn't believe what had just happened.

That was Tuesday, and Judy had been on cloud nine ever since.

The first thing she did was ring her friends, Kath and Jenny to tell them her good news. Joining her in her bedroom that evening, the three of them excitedly chatted about what Judy could wear on her forthcoming date. She'd lost over two stone in the last few months and realised that she no longer had anything suitable for such an occasion. She would have go shopping for a new outfit, before the big night.

'What about my hair though? It's a right state,' she moaned, looking at herself in the mirror and lifting the lank, mousy strands in her hand.

Kath and Jenny looked at each other awkwardly, then back at Judy. Neither girl wanted to agree, but they didn't have to. Judy's hair was a mess and she knew it. It was flat and lifeless, sitting limply on her shoulders. She tied it back the majority of the time, so she didn't have to attempt to style it, as she had no idea, when it came to hair products. Weight had always been Judy's biggest issue and she preferred not to draw attention to herself, doing her best to blend into the background, whenever possible.

Jenny smiled at her friend. 'I know exactly what you need. A trip to the hairdresser's, is just the ticket. Once you've had your hair done, then that pretty face will look twice as lovely. I know just the place. Let me make the call' Jenny grinned, nodding at Kath, who was in total agreement.

Entering, Colour Chameleon hairdressers, Judy felt extremely nervous. She hadn't visited a salon in many years. Her mum had trained as a stylist, after leaving school and was always the one who'd previously trimmed her hair. Walking into the trendy salon, Judy could feel herself blushing, on announcing her arrival at the counter. True to her word, Jenny had arranged the appointment for her, giving her stylist, Shelley, the heads up. Saturday's were always busy, but as this was a mercy mission, Shelley made sure she'd managed to book enough time out for her client's friend.

Looking at Judy's face, it was obvious that she was terrified, poor thing. But apprehension wasn't the only reason for Judy's trepidation. Instantly, she recognised Shelley, as Mandy's boyfriend's estranged wife. Judy's heart sank, recalling how she and Mandy had once hidden from her behind a clothes rail, giggling, in the busy boutique in town. Thank goodness Shelley hadn't seen them.

Shelley soon realised that Judy didn't have a clue what look she wanted to achieve. So, with some gentle suggestions, which Judy readily agreed to, she went to get a streaking cap.

Judy was surprised how at ease she quickly found herself. Shelley was lovely and so easy to talk to, that she began to open up about her forthcoming date, and even some of the recent events of her life. She found Shelley to be a genuine girl and nothing like the bitchy money-grabber that Mandy had described her as. It didn't take a genius to realise that everything Mandy had said about her was a pack of lies.

When Shelley finished the look with a final spray of Insette, Judy could hardly believe that it was her own reflection in the mirror. The transformation was amazing. Shelley had given Judy a concaved bob style, after adding lots of blonde streaks. Poor Judy was nearly in tears when her hair was being pulled through the streaking cap. She had wondered if beauty was really worth all the pain she was enduring. But now, admiring herself in the mirror opposite, she decided that it definitely was.

'Wow. It looks just like Elaine Paige's, in the, I Know Him So Well, video,' Judy gasped, gently teasing the tips of her soft locks with her fingers.

Shelley couldn't help but smile. She was really pleased with the outcome and always looked forward to this aspect of her job. Realising she was ahead of schedule, she suddenly had an idea, telling Judy that she was offering free makeup trials for her beauty course.

'Would you mind being my guinea pig?'

Judy was thrilled. 'Yes,' she agreed, hastily, 'I would love that!'

Shelley studied her soft features, along with her beautiful pale green eyes, which she couldn't wait to transform. Judy's limit on makeup was mascara and maybe a touch of lipstick, now and again. Shelley realised this, deciding to go for a very subtle, look that managed to maintain

Judy's natural appearance. Unable to thank Shelley enough for the finished result, Judy forgot her shyness and hugged her tight.

'Oh Shelley, consider me one of your regular clients from now on,' she beamed. 'You're amazing, I can't believe the difference in me.'

Shelley was thrilled at the compliment. 'Thanks! I hope he's worth it,' she giggled. 'You'll have to let me know next time you come in.'

As the minutes continued to tick by, Judy decided to give up waiting. It was obvious that Mark wasn't coming, and if she had to endure one more pitying look from another passer-by, she felt she might cry. Her feet were almost numb inside her black court shoes, and she longed to get into a warm bath and forget that Mark Devine ever existed.

Making her way down the steps back onto the pavement, she gasped in surprise as she suddenly came face to face with a panting Mark, who'd sprinted around the corner, almost knocking her over in his haste. Bending forward, resting his palms on his knees, he tried to catch his breath.

'I'm so sorry I'm late,' he gasped. 'I thought you'd have gone. Thank God you're still here,' he added, finally looking up and managing a smile.

Judy was so relieved to see Mark that she forgot all about the cold, placing a concerned hand on his shoulder.

'I was just about to,' she said. 'Are you okay? What's happened?'

'An old lady slipped on some black ice, near the Big Lamp, roundabout. I had to wait with her until an ambulance came,' he answered, standing upright and finally beginning to breathe normally. 'Other people arrived but I was the one that found her, and she wanted me to stay with her. I couldn't just leave the old girl.' He smiled at Judy, hoping that she'd understand. 'I ran the rest of the way here.'

'No, of course, you did the right thing,' Judy exclaimed, thinking how thoughtful Mark was. *What a gentleman.* 'I hope she's going to be alright.'

'Yeh, I'd say so. She seemed in pain, but the ambulance man said she'll be okay. It's possibly a broken hip, poor lass.' Finally recovered, Mark managed to take a proper look at Judy, as they stood under the streetlight. 'You look lovely,' he exclaimed. He could see that she'd had her hair done and her face looked positively stunning, albeit frozen.

Judy smiled coyly. She wasn't used to receiving compliments and was unsure of what to say. Aware of her embarrassment, Mark suddenly felt extremely protective towards her.

'Come on,' he urged, 'let's go around the corner and get a taxi up to the Black Ladd. They've got a roaring log fire there. We'll have you warmed up in no time.'

Chapter 53

Reaching into the drawer of her bedside cabinet, Leanne studied the small piece of paper. Still in shock, her eyes filled with tears as they did every time looked at it. However, they were not tears of sadness, but joyful disbelief. Staring again at the box the pharmacist had ticked confirming she was pregnant, Leanne felt she should pinch herself, to be sure that the last few days were not a dream.

She had long since resigned herself to living a childless life, after a diagnosis of endometriosis as a teen had supposedly left her infertile. According to her gynaecologist, her chances of ever becoming a mother were virtually non-existent. Already on a path of self-destruction, Leanne felt her fate was a license to continue with her promiscuous and damaging lifestyle. She figured that God must really despise her, to have sent her all the shit that she'd endured throughout her short life. Therefore, it seemed natural that she too should despise herself. She believed that if she expected nothing from life, then she couldn't be left disappointed.

But this new turn of events had changed everything. Gently caressing her stomach, Leanne closed her eyes, portraying a smile that made her lean, gaunt features seem almost pretty. Life was growing inside her. A life that she believed would never exist. In just a few days her future prospects had done a 180, and she found her new, good fortune somewhat overwhelming.

Every morning since her pregnancy had been confirmed, the first thing she did was look at that piece of paper. She had to be sure that it wasn't all some dream that would be cruelly taken from her upon awakening. But the morning sickness she felt was an immediate reminder that her pregnancy was not fictitious. She thought about Darren. It had briefly crossed her mind to tell him about the baby, but that idea was quickly discarded.

As though Leanne's blinkers had suddenly been lifted, she now clearly saw Darren for what he was. A bullying predator who manipulated people weaker than himself for his own advantage. His last visit had made her realise this. She had no future with him. Just as her father before him, he saw her as an object, to use for his own desires. She had been intimidated by him for the last time and she wasn't prepared to become his victim.

Never before believing that her existence was worth a thing, the life now growing inside of her, suddenly gave her the strength to fight a thousand armies. This baby would have every bit of love that she never had, and once she was in Newcastle, Darren wouldn't even be aware of its existence. Sue was selling the house and her offer for Leanne to move to Albermarle, whilst Craig was on exercise in Belize for a year, couldn't have come at a better time.

Chapter 54

The office rumour mill was in full swing and Mandy decided to try and act normal and ride it out. Couples split up all the time, so if anyone asked, then she would just tell them that she and Chris had decided to go their separate ways. Thankfully, Chris had handed in his notice as promised, accepting the job offer from the company in Manchester, and he would be leaving any day now.

She supposed she should be grateful that he'd kept his word and not outed her to their colleagues. Mandy was brazen but even she couldn't be sure she had enough neck to ride that storm. Gossip was one thing, but hard evidence was something else. If anyone at work were to find out about her recent film role, then she would have to leave her job for sure. Her dreams of promotion would be out of the window. Living in a different town to Chris certainly had its advantages, and the fact that they worked a few miles away was also in her favour.

One thing was for certain though; Lenny Dobbs would not be getting away with what he had done to her. She was happy to bide her time for now. What was it they said? Revenge is a dish best served cold. She had some pretty undesirable cousins living in Salford and Moss Side. One phone call to them was all it would take, to ensure that Lenny Dobbs paid for his double-crossing behaviour.

-

Mandy realised that Chris was in a strange mood as soon as she came downstairs. Wearing just his T-shirt, which barely covered her arse cheeks, she offered to make him a coffee.

As she bent to retrieve the cups from the cupboard, he didn't try to ravish her as he normally would, and it was at this point that she was aware that something was amiss.

As he sat motionless at the small dining table, the cold steely look in his eyes was different to any she'd seen from him before. His face was expressionless as he stared ahead. In front of him was an envelope addressed to her, but before she had the chance to question him about it, he rose from his seat and handed it to her.

'Mandy,' he said, quietly but firmly, looking directly into her eyes. 'I want you to get dressed, collect all your belongings and leave my house for good. Everything you need to know is in this letter. I am going out now and will return within the hour. When I do, I want every trace of you gone from my life. Do you understand?'

She didn't, but she was wise enough not to question him, as he grabbed his keys, before closing the front door behind him. This was not the man she knew and could wrap around her little finger. This man meant every word he said, and after tearing open the letter she realised why.

'Shit,' she repeated numerously, as her eyes scanned the words he'd written.

It explained about the tape and how she had made him a laughingstock. Going on to say that he totally blamed himself for allowing her to tempt him with her forbidden fruits in the first place. He explained that he had been offered another job, which he would be taking, and that he would not be telling anyone at work about the tape. It would damage his reputation just as much as hers. There was, however, an underlying warning in his words when he explained how he had paid Lenny Dobbs off and now had the tape in his possession. So, for her sake, he warned that she would be wise to think twice, before badmouthing him to anyone. Surely, she didn't begrudge him some damage limitation.

Mandy stood frozen, staring at the letter in disbelief. This was the first time in her life that she felt outsmarted and outwitted, as well as embarrassed and humiliated. Those feelings would pass, but the realisation that she'd been backed into a corner frustrated her more than anything. There was no sweet talking her way out of this one.

Stuffing her clothes into a bag, she used the house phone to ring for a taxi, deciding to use an out of town firm just in case she was recognised.

Fuck knows how many of these, small town idiots had seen the bloody tape, but she wasn't about to take any chances. Spotting the £20 note along with some change on the table, she decided it would be in her best interests to leave it where it was. Chris was serious, she was sure of that, and she wasn't going to call his bluff by pissing him off any further. She could not chance that tape getting out at work.

As the taxi pulled away, she took one last look at the modern little semi, where she'd enjoyed playing lady of the manor over the last few months. At least it would save her having to buy him a Christmas present, she thought, looking on the bright side. Knowing she was the subject of ridicule bothered her slightly, but she'd get over it. As far as her relationship with Chris was concerned, that ship had sailed, and she wasn't going to dwell on it. Her sights were set higher, so onwards and upwards.

As she sat back in the taxi, Nick Kershaw's 'I Won't, Let The Sun Go Down On Me' came on the radio. Mandy smiled to herself. She had no intention of letting that happen.

Chapter 55

Doreen's screams could be heard echoing throughout the Victorian terraced building, and within seconds a small crowd of her colleagues were gathered, staring in horror from the top of the cellar steps.

'Don't just stand there gawping!' 'Somebody phone for a flaming ambulance,' Kenneth Cuthbertson bellowed, as he barged through the onlookers and made his way down the cellar steps to where Doreen lay.

The day had begun much like any other, but as midday approached most of the office had stopped work and were winding down, preparing for the staff Christmas lunch. A tradition that Kenneth Cuthbertson and his junior partner Crispin Healy, undertook each year, taking their staff to the ever popular, Giuseppe's Italian restaurant. It was an opportunity to show their appreciation for the loyal, hard work that their employees had shown the company throughout the year. This was, however, on the understanding that they were back at their desks by 3pm.

Looking up from her desk Mandy spotted the girls from accounts pass her office, making their way to the toilets to get ready for the forthcoming merriment. Some of them had been allowed to book the rest of the day as leave and would be going onto a night of drinking and dancing. Unfortunately for Mandy, she wouldn't be joining them. Doreen had seen to that.

'I'm sorry,' she'd replied in a snooty tone, when Mandy had asked for the time off. 'There are still letters that need typing up. Tonight, is the last post before Christmas and its business as usual, as far as I'm concerned.'

'Fine,' Mandy replied, smiling through gritted teeth.

She could live with missing Mad Friday, but what she couldn't stand any longer was Doreen's power trip attitude. As long as that bitch stood in her way, Mandy would never be anything more than a lackey, in this place. She decided it was time to put her plan into action, determined to start the New Year as Mr Cuthbertson's senior secretary. Now was the time to act.

Giuseppe's was bustling with celebrating crowds. It was a popular restaurant and many firms had tables booked, which were already filled with tipsy workers, geared up for the Christmas festivities. Mandy looked across at the girls from accounts as they sat pulling crackers and gulping wine. Normally she would be sat amongst them, but she had decided to place herself beside Doreen, with Mr Cuthbertson facing them. This was not where she wanted to be, but if she was going to be convincing, she must ensure that she was surrounded by people who could see that they appeared to be one big, happy team.

'Let's have your glasses, ladies,' Kenneth instructed, raising a bottle of house red.

'Oh, just a small one, if you insist,' gushed Doreen, coyly.

'Thanks Mr Cuthbertson,' Mandy smiled sweetly, spotting him peeking a good look down her cleavage as he stood to pour her drink.

Clearing his throat, Kenneth raised his glass. 'Merry Christmas, ladies,' he said. 'Thank you for all your hard work, it doesn't go unnoticed.' Kenneth wasn't a man of many words, let alone compliments, and he was glad when their starters began to arrive, abruptly ending his brief toast.

On finishing her prawn cocktail, Doreen took a sip of her wine and, seizing her chance Mandy lifted her glass, turning towards her senior colleague.

'I'd like to raise a glass to you, Doreen, and wish you a Merry Christmas.' Mandy smiled, sincerely.

Doreen eyed her suspiciously.

'I know we didn't really get off to the best start,' Mandy continued, 'and you may find me a little flighty and feckless at times. But I just wanted to say that I do appreciate everything that you've taught me. I want to thank you for having patience with me. I know how much experience you have, and if I become half the secretary that you are, I'll be more than happy.'

It took a moment for Doreen to process Mandy's words. This was the last thing she expected from the girl, and to say she was surprised, was an understatement. Eventually breaking into a smile, Doreen raised her glass, clinking it against Mandy's.

'Merry Christmas, my dear, that's a very noble thing to say, and I appreciate your kind words,' she replied a little stiffly, still in shock at Mandy's compliment.

Kenneth lifted his eyes from his turkey. Just as Mandy had hoped, he had heard her words and was very impressed by her humbleness. *Hopefully*, he thought to himself, *this might soften the ice queen and she would begin to cut the girl a bit of slack.* Mandy was a good worker, and he for one certainly didn't have a problem with her. She certainly brightened up his day, that was for sure.

The festivities continued and as Mandy had hoped, Doreen was becoming putty in her hands. To Mandy, it was more than obvious that she was a threat to the older woman, and the reason Doreen had instantly taken a dislike to her. But after plying her with almost a bottle of wine and many more compliments, Mandy had Doreen wrapped around her little finger.

The two women linked as they walked the short distance back to the office, and it was clear for all to see that Doreen was less than steady on her feet.

'I'll make you a strong black coffee,' Mandy insisted, as they got back to the office.

Kenneth raised his eyes in distaste as Doreen plonked herself, back at her desk, grinning like a Cheshire cat.

'Don't worry, Mr Cuthbertson,' said Mandy, quietly. 'I think it hit her when she stepped into the cold air. Once she's had a strong coffee she'll sober up.'

'Well she'd better,' he replied, marching into his office and slamming the door behind him. If there was one thing Kenneth Cuthbertson couldn't stand, it was a drunken woman.

That was the last thing he heard until Doreen's screams echoed throughout the building, making him jump from his seat like a scalded cat. Just as Mandy planned, Doreen had walked straight into her trap.

Doreen was a stickler for routine and without fail, always archived the completed files on Friday afternoon. Mandy decided that this was her perfect opportunity to strike. Before they'd left for the Christmas lunch, she'd nipped into the cellar, removed the bulb from the ceiling cable, and replaced it with a dud one that she had saved in her drawer, ready for this very occasion.

On heading back up the stone stairs, she'd placed a pile of carbon papers halfway up, knowing full well that once stepped on they would create a slippery friction causing a tumble for sure, especially as Doreen would have her arms filled with files. No one would suspect for one minute that foul play was afoot. Especially if the whole office were to witness Doreen's intoxicated conduct, prior to the event.

The whole thing had gone exactly to the letter and Mandy couldn't believe her luck. Her heart was pounding with nervous excitement as Doreen left the office, armed with files, headed for the cellar.

'See you in a tick,' she'd called as Doreen left the room.

The minute that followed seemed to last an eternity, until Mandy heard the bloodcurdling screams coming from below. As she charged from her office, she came face to face with a wide-eyed, startled, Kenneth Cuthbertson on the landing. The pair, along with a number of stunned co-workers headed in the direction of the bawling cries that echoed beneath them.

Mandy, couldn't help but smile to herself the whole way home, watching from the bus window as the crowds enjoyed the hectic, Christmas celebrations. As a rule, she loved to party, but the exhilaration she felt at that very moment was better than any night out she had ever experienced.

From the look of Doreen's leg, she wouldn't be returning to work any time soon. Mandy had a strong stomach but even she felt a little squeamish at the way the older woman's limb was twisted behind her crumpled body. Once the ambulance had taken her away, the whispers about how tipsy Doreen was, had already begun to circulate. Mandy was home and dry. She would go back to work on Monday, sure of an inadvertent promotion. She could then finish for Christmas with the reassurance of returning in the New Year, as Mr Cuthbertson's senior secretary. She couldn't wait to get home and celebrate. Her mum was sure to be out with her new boyfriend and Mandy had a chilled bottle of Blue Nun, and a box of Milk Tray just waiting to be devoured.

Chapter 56

Sitting in the toilet cubical with her head resting against the wall, Shelley grinned drunkenly to herself, closing her eyes for a brief moment. She was having a great night and best of all, she was happy. A thing that a few short months ago, she thought she would never be again. She could hear Slade's, Merry Christmas Everybody, playing in the heart of the pub, along with a chorus of singing punters who were celebrating Mad Friday. Tomorrow was the salon's busiest day of the year, but she would worry about that when her alarm went off the next morning.

As Shelley said goodbye to the day's last customer, she was feeling envious watching crowds in happy groups, singing as they staggered past the shop in their Santa hats, with tinsel around their necks.

'Aw, I'm jealous,' she'd said, turning to Jason who was watching behind her. 'I wish we didn't have to work tomorrow,' she moaned.

'Me too,' he sighed, as some of the revellers shouted Merry Christmas to the forlorn pair. 'Oh, stuff it,' he said aloud. 'Come on, girl, get your coat. We're going for a drink with the rest of them. We can have a couple without getting plastered,' he urged.

Shelley grinned. 'Right, you've twisted my arm. But don't let me have too many, will you?'

'No, don't let her have too many,' Dawn repeated, from the back of the shop. 'I want you two in this shop at 8am, sharp. And no hangovers,' she warned, in a playful tone, which they knew had an underlying warning. 'Go on, get gone and have a good time,' she smiled as they giggled, waving goodbye.

That was three hours and seven vodkas ago. The external toilet door opened, and Shelley made no attempt to move. She was comfortable and felt that she might nod off, right where she was. That was, until she heard a familiar voice amongst the giggling chatter.

'Oh, let me borrow some of that lippy. Is it Heather Shimmer? I love that shade.'

Shelley sat bolt upright; she'd know that voice anywhere. She listened again, as the other girl spoke.

'I could do with some hairspray,' the girl complained. 'My hair's as flat as a pancake.' Not recognising the second voice, Shelley waited with bated breath.

'Here, I've got a small Insette in my bag. I always carry it,' the first girl replied.

Shelley pulled her ski pants up quickly, in an urge to confirm what she hoped was true. If this was who she thought it was, she couldn't let her get away. Opening the cubical door in eager anticipation, her eyes instantly locked with the owner of the familiar voice. Both girls shrieked in unison, at their recognition. As Shelley and Tina clung to one another, Norma stared, smiling at the pair, who had obviously not seen each other for some time.

'I can't believe it's you,' Shelley cried. 'I've missed you so much.'

'Me too!' replied Tina, as the girls hugged one another again.

The next five minutes were spent in a whirlwind of chatter, as they exchanged phone numbers and gave each other a brief overview of their lives, since they'd last spoken.

'You were right all along, Shell. Darren was a wrong 'un and I had the bruises to prove it,' Tina said, in a serious tone.

'Well I know just how it feels to be betrayed,' replied Shelley. 'Who'd have thought that the wonderful Chris would turn out to be a cheating bastard?'

'Hey, let's not dwell on that now. This is Norma. We work together at Littlewoods,' she said, introducing the pair. 'Come and have a drink with us and you can get acquainted.'

'Better still, let's have a boogie,' Shelley squealed, as the DJ began to play, Elton John's, 'Step into Christmas.' 'I want you guys to meet my friend, Jason. He's brilliant. You'll love him!' she cried, as they all made their way out of the ladies and back into the bustling pub.

Chapter 57

What a hectic weekend. Tina muted the TV on The Two Ronnies' Christmas Special. She wasn't really watching it, but she was trying to act as normal as she could, even though the evening was far from ordinary. It was her first night back in the home she'd shared with Darren and she was completely alone for the first time. Shelley had called round in the afternoon, then Tina went to her mum's for tea, arriving back home in the evening. She had planned an early night and should be shattered after days of cleaning and unpacking, but there was no way she would be able to sleep. Her mind was filled with the events of the last few months and she hardly dared to believe that things could be going so well. Everything in the house was in place, and it was as homely, as if she'd never left. However, she couldn't help but notice how still and quiet it was. When they'd lived together, Darren had hardly been there, but his belongings had filled the place, making it feel lived in. Now it felt eerily silent, and as happy as she was, it made Tina feel a touch uneasy.

I'll soon get used to it, she thought, deciding to go upstairs and have a relaxing bath.

Once soaking in the bubbles, she sighed, feeling peaceful. In her wildest dreams, she wouldn't have believed she'd be back in her own home, now the sole owner. Meeting back up with her oldest and best friend was a massive bonus too. But topping the lot, was that she'd been made permanent in her job. This took a great weight off her mind and secured her future. Money would be tight, but Tina was a fighter and would work all the extra hours she could, to make a success of her life.

The Friday before had been a nervous one, and as well as being referred to as the 'Mad Friday' before Christmas, in the workplace it was commonly known as 'Black Friday,' due to the amount of temps that received their finishing letters, as the busy Christmas period came to a close. Many of them were expecting it, as the letters were issued throughout the day, but the tears were still plentiful, and Tina's nerves were in shreds. A few people received new contracts, securing another three month's work, but their joy was bittersweet as many of their friends were being finished.

As Bridgette Hornborough's nasally voice bellowed Tina's name across the packing hall, many of the workforce watched her walk to the office to seal her fate.

'Good luck,' said Norma, giving her a wink as she set off, hoping against hope that her new friend would be kept on. Tina was a brilliant worker and Norma had a good feeling that she'd be one of the lucky ones.

Once in the office, Tina took a seat as Bridgette continued to write at her desk. In what seemed an age before she looked up, Tina sat wringing her sweaty hands, willing the whole thing to be over with. Everything depended on her keeping this job, and the next few moments of her life meant the difference between a good or bad Christmas for her. She had been liberal with the truth to her solicitor and building society manager in order to take the house on in her name. She just wanted a chance to prove herself and failure wasn't an option.

'There you go, Tina,' said Bridgette, handing her the white envelope.

Her stern face gave nothing away, and as Tina opened it, her hands trembled with nerves. Scanning the lines, her eyes were immediately drawn to the words "permanent contract". Her heart lurched with excitement and she started from the beginning, reading the words slowly, fully digesting them. When she finished, she looked up at Bridgette, who she swore was half-smiling.

'A permanent contract, Tina,' she said. 'What do you think about that?'

Tina was speechless, and Bridgette could clearly see the happiness along with disbelief on her face.

'You've made quite an impression with high management,' Bridgette continued. 'The monthly figures have once again shown that there have been no returns errors packed from your bench and your target levels are excellent and very consistent.'

Tina's face must've shown her bewilderment. She wasn't even aware that anyone could see if errors were occurring. She'd always had good attention to detail and naturally worked at a speedy pace, never struggling to meet the high demands of the departmental targets, unlike some of her co-workers.

'But why a permanent contract?' she uttered, finally finding her voice.

'As I said,' Bridgette replied, 'you've made quite an impression with Frank and Lynda. They came to see me to ask about your timekeeping and attendance, which I told them was excellent. It was from that meeting that the unusual steps were taken to make you permanent.'

Tina's eyes lit up. Lynda was the production manager for the packing hall and Frank was systems director for the whole building. She wasn't aware that they even knew her name.

'Tina,' Bridgette said, looking into her eyes. 'It was on my recommendation that you have been taken on permanently. I know a good packer when I see one, but at the end of the day, it's my neck that's on the line here, so don't let me down,' she added, sternly.

'I won't,' Tina replied swiftly, hardly able to contain herself. If she could've, she would have thrown her arms around her supervisor's neck and kissed her, but she was sure Bridgette would not appreciate that. 'Thank you, Bridgette. You won't regret it,' she said, grinning.

'Now, it's up to you what you tell the others but bear in mind there's quite a lot of tears and sad faces out there. So, I'll leave it up to your discretion,' Bridgette advised, knowing full well that she needn't worry about Tina on that score. She would keep mum about her good fortune. She'd sussed Tina out right from the start and knew she could be trusted. 'Now off you go back to your bench and keep up that good work.' Just before Tina turned to walk out of the office, Bridgette spoke once more. 'Who knows, you might be sitting where I am one day.' She winked, giving Tina a rare but very warm smile.

As Tina slid down under the warm bubbles, she decided she needed to stop stressing about the future. Life couldn't be going better, and Darren had been as good as his word, signing the house over to her without any drama. The nightmare was over, and the pieces of the jigsaw were finally in place. She was happy and contented and looking forward to Christmas, and the New Year ahead.

Outside, a lone figure watched from the dark backings, looking up at the bathroom window. As he eyed Tina's distorted shape though the frosted patterned glass, stepping out of the bath, he could clearly see the pinkness of her naked skin. He had been sat on the bollard for almost an hour and although the temperature was below freezing, he hardly felt the cold, such was his obsession with his estranged wife. She could have the house, he didn't care about that kind of responsibility, but he wasn't giving up on her that easily.

The time would come when she would want him again, he was sure about that. So, for now he was happy to bide his time. The frosty weather didn't stop his erection tightening in his jeans as he pulled his collar up, deciding to make his way to the pub in time for last orders. A visit to Leanne after closing time would satisfy his frustrations. The thought made him smile as the light went out in Tina's bathroom and he walked away.

Chapter 58

It was still dark as Kenneth Cuthbertson fumbled with his keys, in front of the Victorian building's large wooden door. He was startled upon hearing footsteps, approaching behind him.

'What the hell are you doing, creeping up on me like that?' he barked. 'You nearly gave me a coronary,' he added, a little calmer, once he recognised his companion.

It was 07:30 in the morning and as he did every day, Kenneth arrived at the office before any of his employees. Business hours were 9 to 5, but each day he took the opportunity to begin his working day in peace and quiet. Managing to get more done in that hour and a half, than he did throughout the rest of the day. The stillness made it easier to think, giving him a chance to prepare for his appointments.

'Sorry, Mr Cuthbertson,' Chris replied, hurriedly. 'I didn't mean to make you jump. I just wanted to catch you before any of the staff arrived.'

'Well, you'd better come inside then, hadn't you boy?' said Kenneth, glaring intimidatingly. He hadn't had many dealings with Chris in the past, but he seemed a likeable sort of fellow. Therefore, Kenneth was prepared to hear him out.

As a man in his late fifties who considered himself as very much 'old school', Kenneth wasn't keen on familiarising himself with computers. If truth be known, he was scared to death of them. The less involvement he had with them the better. No, he would leave it up to the youngsters to embrace this modern, fast-paced, way of living. Soon it would no longer be his problem, as his dream of retiring to his beloved cottage on the beautiful Cornish coast was becoming much more appealing recently. He suspected that Chris's early morning visit, was due to having second thoughts about his resignation. Arriving there, cap in hand to ask for his old job back. But he couldn't have been further from the truth.

'So, let's have it then, son. What brings you here at this time in the morning?' he asked, posing the direct question to a nervous-looking Chris, as he leaned forward on his leather and mahogany chair, peering over his spectacles.

Eyeing the boy suspiciously, he couldn't help thinking what a marvellous head of thick blond hair he had. Just like the one that had adorned his own head, some thirty years earlier. The thought made him a little envious.

'Spit it out, lad,' he boomed, as Chris sat hesitantly, still saying nothing.

'It's…it's the accident,' Chris blurted, clearing his throat with a small cough. 'With Doreen,' he added. 'I don't think it was an accident at all, and I believe I know who's behind it. It was Mandy,' he announced, trying to hold his voice steady and sound as confident as he could.

Kenneth's eyes widened like saucers at Chris's admission, then narrowed in quizzical disbelief as he processed Chris's words. Finally, he bellowed his response, in a voice so loud that Chris jumped up in alarm.

'Sour grapes! Sour grapes, that's what this is!' Rising from his seat, Kenneth placed the palms of his large hands on his desk, leaning so far forward that Chris could smell the sourness of his stale breath. 'If you think you can come to my office, throwing wild accusations around, you're very sadly mistaken, boy. This is slander, and I for one won't have it. Do you hear? You lot think I don't know what's going on under my very nose, don't you? Well I do. I know that you and Mandy were carrying on, and I also know that you have recently split up. Just the same way that I know Brian in accounts sleeps here when his wife kicks him out, and Joan the cleaner steals toilet rolls!' he finished, smugly.

Small flecks of spittle were hitting Chris directly in the face and he wanted to turn and run, but his mother had always insisted on him telling the truth and he could not let what he knew, go unreported. He had been guilty of too much deception in the last year, which he would never be able to undo. But his weekend had been an unsettled one, and if he could put one thing right, then he must do so. Mustering all his courage, he looked at Kenneth Cuthbertson's puce, red face. Directly into his sagging eyes.

'I am speaking the truth, and I implore you to hear me out,' he stated, firmly.

Standing up straight, Kenneth took in the young man before him. He was a good judge of character. Hadn't thirty-five years as a solicitor forced him to be? Chris was a handsome man, well-groomed and certainly clever but, he would need an incredible amount of confidence and self-assurance to believe for one minute that he could pull the wool over Kenneth's eyes.

'Let's hear what you have to say then.' The words were delivered much quieter than before, as the old man sat back, waiting in anticipation for Chris's revelation.

Chapter 59

As more of his employees arrived for work, Kenneth gulped the last mouthful of the single malt from the Waterford, crystal glass. Locking away the bottle and solitary tumbler in his desk drawer, he reached for his coat and scarf. It was Monday the 23rd of December and he could hear the excitement in his staff's voices as they chatted about the forthcoming festivities. It was tradition that they were allowed to leave an hour early on the 23rd however, today was unlike other years. Today would be different. But first, he had some people to see and there was no time like the present.

He had no appointments booked that day. It was just a matter of tying up loose ends before the Christmas break. As he left his office, making his way onto the landing, he could see Mandy hanging up her coat in the office she shared with Doreen.

Poor Doreen, he thought to himself, shaking his head as he spied the nonchalant young woman fixing her hair in the mirror, before heading towards her desk.

As he left the building, he passed his junior partner's secretary.

'Please let all the staff know that I've had to go out,' he informed her. 'I'll be back by lunch time,' he added, without looking back.

Sitting in the busy Christmas traffic, Kenneth pondered on the morning's events, which in a million years he could never have predicted.

Chris had told him how throughout their relationship, Mandy bore a vengeful hatred for her senior colleague. He spoke of how her mouth would twist in distaste, whenever she mentioned her. At first Chris had laughed it off, until the day she'd asked him to post the letter.

'What letter?' asked Kenneth, wondering where his story was going.

'Mandy typed a letter. It was the day we finished for our holiday,' Chris recalled. 'She asked me to post it on my way home because she wasn't going to the Post Office that day. It was addressed "Private and Confidential", to you,' he said, looking directly at Kenneth now, with much more confidence. He could tell that he had captured the old man's attention and was aware that there was definite intrigue in his eyes. 'The letter was an anonymous complaint, made about Doreen, from a very disgruntled client. Mandy hoped that after you received it, you might see your way to dismissing Doreen, so that she could step into her shoes. Especially after all the typing errors she's been making lately.'

Chris saw the penny drop in Kenneth's eyes. He knew Mandy had been to him about Doreen's lapsed typing. He could also see that this was exactly what the old man was now recalling.

'But I didn't receive any letter.'

Chris pulled a folded white envelope from his pocket.

'You didn't receive it because it's here, still sealed. I never posted it. I loved Mandy, well, I thought I did. But I knew this was wrong, and I never actually thought she would go through with it. I swore to her that I'd posted it, but I could never sink that low,' Chris added, solemnly.

Kenneth's face was a picture as he reached for the envelope. He opened it, scanning over the words, whilst shaking his head in dismay.

'If you hold it up to the light, you'll see it has the company name in the watermark of the paper. A fact I don't believe Mandy realises,' added Chris, now looking intently at the shocked face before him. 'I felt compelled to come and see you today Sir, as I met up with some of the team on Friday, following your office meal and, of course, Doreen's accident. They told me what happened. I was horrified, and I couldn't get out of my head, the words that Mandy said when she gave me the letter. She was laughing when she handed it to me.

She was very pleased with herself. Her exact were,' he hesitated for a second before quoting his ex-girlfriend, "If this doesn't get rid of the bitch, I'll see to it personally that she has herself a nasty little accident on those very hard cellar steps."

Thoughts flashed through Kenneth's mind. He couldn't believe what he was hearing. How could this be – what if it was Chris who was behind all this, in a vengeful attempt to discredit his former lover? But those thoughts were quickly dismissed. He could see in the eyes of this young man standing before him, that he was trying to do the right thing. That it was his own conscience that wouldn't let him keep what he knew to himself. This sorry mess needed to be sorted out today. And sorted out it would be!

'Mandy! Finish your letter and then I'd like a word in my office please,' said Kenneth, popping his head around the office door.

Mandy looked up from her typing. Her heart began to pound in her chest.

This is it, she thought. *This is my time to shine.* Her whole weekend had been filled with thoughts of this moment. She could smell promotion, along with a substantial pay rise, to mark the occasion. What a wonderful Christmas this would be after all. *Who needs a boyfriend,* she thought excitedly?

Kenneth took off his coat and sat at his desk. His morning had been productive, if somewhat different to the one he'd had planned. Now, there was just one more thing he had to do before he could conclude his mission.

As Mandy entered the office, the beaming smile she was wearing, slipped slightly from her face.

'Take a seat please, Mandy. I'd like to introduce you to my sister, Cynthia.'

Looking at the grey-haired, heavy-breasted woman sat in the chair at the side of Kenneth's desk, Mandy had an uneasy feeling, that she was not going to like what she was about to hear.

Cynthia Cuthbertson-Parker was tall. Even in her flat, sensible, Clark's leather shoes, she was a beast of a woman. Her long, pleated, tweed skirt was shorter than it would be on most women, but still covered her knees in a respectable fashion. As Mandy took in her short, grey, wavy hair, spectacles and firm mouth, she was instantly reminded of the dog trainer Barbara Woodhouse. Cynthia's eyes bore into hers and Mandy half expected her to command she 'sit' in the same way, that the popular, TV personality was famous for doing.

'Ahem.' Kenneth cleared his throat as he prepared to address the young woman before him. 'I have been to see Doreen this morning,' he said, looking directly into her eyes. 'With all things considered, she has decided to retire and move to Lytham, to live with her sister.'

Mandy's eyes widened, as she held her breath, preparing herself for her moment of glory.

'There's no point in dressing up what I have to say, Mandy,' Kenneth announced. 'I have also decided to retire, with immediate effect. Cynthia will be taking over the practice in my absence. Starting with the company in the new year.'

Mandy's heart began to race. She was shocked at his announcement. She would prefer to work for a man any day of the week, but she was sure she would be able to work her charms on the stuffy-looking woman before her. She would just need to use different tactics.

'Does that mean Doreen won't be coming back at all then?' Mandy asked, in an eager voice.

Kenneth's eyes slowly closed, as he bowed his head slightly, realising in that instant that the woman before him really was an unscrupulous individual, who only had her own interest at heart. That one question spoke volumes to him. There was no concern and no pity shown for her senior colleague. Chris was unfortunately right. All Mandy was interested in was Doreen's job.

His visit to see Doreen that morning had been sombre to begin with. She was still highly embarrassed at her display of drunkenness and completely blamed herself, for her unfortunate tumble down the cellar stairs. Thankfully, she was unaware of the malice that was really behind it. Her injuries were not as serious as they had first appeared, and she was lucky to escape with a dislocated hip, along with some bruising.

But her remorse was the first thing that struck Kenneth, and she was quick to inform him of her resignation. She was actually under the impression, that his visit was to dismiss her from her position, and she was surprised to find that he was actually there because he was merely concerned about her. That, however, had no effect on her decision to resign.

Doreen may have outwardly appeared to her colleagues as a confident, no-nonsense kind of woman, but this fall had taken the stuffing out of her. When her sister Marjorie had arrived to take care of her, their talks had been lengthy, with Marjorie finally convincing her to sell up and move with her to Lytham St Anne's. The invitation of waking up and breathing in the fresh sea air every morning, seemed too good to pass up. A telephone call to the estate agents, putting her bungalow on the market, had been made first thing that morning.

Once back in his car, Kenneth's vision was clear. His wife would be thrilled. He never thought this day would come, but suddenly, the timing just seemed right. His sister would be delighted to take over his position. As an established solicitor in her own right, she had left her previous position, to nurse her husband through cancer, until he passed away some months before. She was chomping at the bit to get back into her work and would see this as a fantastic challenge. After all, she and his wife had dropped enough hints over the last few months. He was sure they were conspiring together. The thought made him smile.

Maureen Cuthbertson was a wonderful wife and mother. A successful accountant, she was loyal and steadfast and his greatest ally. Their relationship had always been a partnership, more than a conventional marriage. Their lives were quite separate, as were their sleeping arrangements, and this suited them both. Kenneth had been allowed to attend his gentlemen's club, with no questions asked. On paper, it was a marriage that seemed disastrously flawed, but for the Cuthbertson's, it just worked.

They visited their holiday home in Cornwall as often as they could and for some time now, Maureen had expressed a wish to retire there, full-time. In the past, Kenneth had always been reluctant. His work was demanding and until now he'd had no desire to call time on it, but in light of today's events, his mindset was suddenly changed. The time was now!

'Ahem.' He cleared his throat once more. 'I realise that the timing is somewhat unfortunate, but this means that your position is now redundant,' he said, watching the smile slip from Mandy's face. He could tell that she was shocked, but he continued without wavering. 'To begin with, Cynthia's workload will be somewhat smaller than mine, and Mr Healy has agreed for his secretary to take on any extra work, for the foreseeable future.'

'But what about my promotion?' blurted Mandy, aloud. 'Doreen's job was supposed to be mine.'

Kenneth decided not to get into a debate with her. Knowing what this girl had done infuriated him, but he could not prove that she was behind it without a confession, and he knew that he was never going to get one.

'As I said, your position is now redundant Mandy. There was never going to be a promotion. Along with this month's wage, you will be given three month's pay, which is more than fair, seeing as you have been with the company, less than a year.'

Mandy's mouth dropped open. This was the last thing she'd been expecting, and tears pricked her eyes as she took in her boss's words.

'I shall be announcing my retirement to the rest of the staff shortly, but I completely understand if you wish to collect your things and go now,' he urged. 'I wouldn't expect you to work the rest of the day.'

Mandy stood up and began to make her way to the door. She was shell-shocked and in disbelief at the conversation that had just taken place.

Chapter 60

Closing the front door and stepping out into the familiar cul de sac, Shelley breathed a sigh of relief, exhaling warm breath that instantly turned into a swirl of smoky mist as it hit the afternoon's icy climate. Today was as crisp as a winters' day could be, and just as one would expect for a frosty Christmas Eve. As she made her way back towards the main road, small flakes of snow began to fall around her. Christmas was finally here. She stepped up her pace, eager to get back to Jackie's, where the children would be excitedly awaiting her return.

The salon had closed at two, and once she'd bid Jason and Dawn a Merry Christmas, she walked the short distance to the bus stop. The 59 would take her to the end of her old street, giving her a couple of minutes to compose herself before coming face to face with Chris, and entering the home she loved, but had not set foot in for seven months.

Her phone call to Chris the night before to arrange the meeting had been brief and almost business-like. Gone were the emotions that he'd previously stirred in her. She was ready to get the ball rolling on the next chapter of her life. After spending Sunday afternoon with Tina, Shelley realised that it was time to get her independence back and take stock of her life. Living with her sister was fine but she was on the cusp of new beginnings. Her beauty work in the salon was taking off and she wanted to start the New Year with a vision, which meant unsaddling old baggage. She wanted a divorce and her share of the home that she had once loved so much.

The girls had swapped phone numbers on the previous Friday and, as arranged, Shelley arrived at Tina's just after lunch, as she was unpacking the last of her boxes. They'd embraced once more, just as they had on the Friday, and the next couple of hours were filled with excited chatter. They were both ecstatic about rekindling their friendship, with each of them apologising for allowing to let a man to come between them.

'How do you feel about moving back in?' Shelley asked.

'I'm not going to lie, Shell, I was so nervous about coming back here. As soon as everything was signed over, me and my mum began gutting the place. It was a right mess. Mouldy food and cans of lager everywhere. Pretty disgusting really,' she said, wrinkling her nose as though a sour glass of milk was being held beneath it. 'He must've been living like a pig. But it was nothing that a can of Jiff and some elbow grease couldn't shift.'

Shelley smiled. 'You've done amazing, Tina. You should be really proud. You've got your little palace back.'

Tina smiled her thanks. 'He's left all the furniture and pots and pans. He's back at his mum's, so I haven't had to buy anything. Although there was one thing, I definitely wanted rid of.'

She paused, as Shelley looked at her with inquisition – and then, realising what she was referring to, they both said in unison, 'the bed!', and laughed aloud.

'Mum and dad gave me theirs; they've only had it twelve months. My dad said it's too soft and making his bad back worse.'

'Jason turned up trumps,' said Tina. 'He came around yesterday after work, just as he said he would, to help me shift all the rubbish to the tip. He brought his cousin Ross, who's got a trailer.'

Shelley's eyes lit up at the mention of Ross's name. 'Did he mention me?' she blurted out.

Tina looked at her, knowingly. She might not have seen her best friend for over two years, but she could immediately sense when she fancied someone.

'He did, as a matter of fact. He said he was happy that we were back as mates. He also said he thinks you're the hottest girl he knows and that he can't wait till you split up with Wayne so that he can ask you out.'

Shelley's eyes were like saucers.

'Did he really say that?' she asked, eagerly.

Tina chuckled, 'No, but you wish he had, don't you? I can see right through you, Shelley Barnes,' she said, using her friends maiden name. 'And I don't blame you either, he's gorgeous. Seems like a lovely guy too.'

Both girls giggled, feeling as though they were sixteen again.

'I'm going to have to tell you, before I burst,' Shelley grinned.

'Tell me what?' quizzed Tina.

'Well, it's Ross. On Friday after you left, I saw him as I was getting into the taxi to go home. He ran towards me with his mistletoe and asked me for a Christmas kiss.'

Tina's eyes widened.

'And?' she asked.

Shelley was grinning from ear to ear. 'Oh Tina, it was fantastic. In fact, it was electric, I'm not kidding. I've never felt a kiss like it,' she added, dreamily. 'I can't stop thinking about it.'

'Well, what are you going do about it, then?'

'Oh nothing, I suppose,' Shelley sighed. 'It was just a Christmas kiss, and the last I heard he was back with his long-term girlfriend...Natalie.' She pulled a face as she said the name. 'Plus, I'm seeing Wayne and, I do like him. He's a decent lad.'

'Well, we'll just have to see what the New Year brings,' said Tina, winking at her friend who still had a wistful look on her face.

It was great to have her old friend back in her life. She could certainly see Jason becoming a good friend too; they'd hit it off immediately and she felt as though she'd known him for years. Tina secretly hoped that Shelley and Wayne would end up going their separate ways. She realised this was selfish of her, but he was Darren's mate and if she and Shelley were going to get close again, she was worried about him becoming Darren's spy. Darren had been as good as his word, but what she needed was a clean break from him. She had to draw a line under their marriage. The legalities of the house had been dealt with, and as far as she was concerned, that was the end of the matter.

As Shelley approached the driveway to her marital home, she paused. Her heart was now hammering in her chest, and she was sure Chris would be able to hear it. What if Mandy turned up? Shelley shrugged the thought from her mind. Jason had already told her the gossip about the sex tape and the couple's break up, even though Ross had sworn him to secrecy. Shaw was a small town and gossip like that wasn't going to escape her for long, especially as she worked as a hairdresser. Shelley was shocked but glad at the same time. She felt a sense of karma, after all the upset she'd endured. But what if Jason had got it wrong, what if it was just a silly rumour and they were still together? So, she had made it crystal clear to Chris on the phone that the meeting was just to be between the two of them. Her own assertion surprised her. Outwardly, she sounded confident, but inside she was nervous.

This was her husband, yet it felt like he was a stranger. Her utmost fear was that, if she saw him, she would fall in love with him all over again. Her life was finally on track, but what if she saw his smile and smelled his familiar scent, and was unable to resist him? True, she no longer went to bed crying over him, but what if after one short meeting with him, all the months it had taken her to heal, were wasted?

As she approached the front door, Chris opened it, giving her a coy but welcoming smile, showing his perfect white teeth. To her surprise, Shelley felt no excitement or butterflies. As he moved aside to allow her to enter, she could honestly say that he was having no effect on her, whatsoever. It was as though she was being greeted by a mere acquaintance. Her home instantly looked familiar, but it lacked presence. There was no life in it, and it felt cold, even though the central heating was on.

'Would you like a brew?' asked Chris, as he beckoned for her to take a seat in the armchair. 'You look really well,' he added, before she had the chance to answer.

'Thanks,' she smiled slightly, at his words. 'Yes, please, I'll have a cup of tea.'

'Still two sugars?' he called, as he entered the kitchen.

'No, just a half please,' she replied, looking around. There were no signs of her nemesis, or even that another woman had ever been there. The awkward politeness between them was obvious and to be expected, and although she had been worried about coming back to see her estranged husband and the house she had loved, Shelley felt strangely calm and quite comfortable. If anything, it was Chris who appeared a little anxious.

'There you go,' he said, handing her the cup, whilst taking a seat on the settee opposite her. 'So, how've you been?' he asked, making small talk, at the same time as trying to gauge the reason for her visit.

'Yeh, I've been good,' she answered, politely. There was a pause and it was Shelley who decided to speak first. 'I've come to speak to you about my share of the house,' she announced. 'And a divorce,' she added.

It was as much as Chris had been expecting, but he couldn't help feeling disappointed at her words. Looking back on the last year, he would be the first one to admit that he'd made a massive mistake. The woman before him had loved him with every breath in her body. She was beautiful, kind, and so easy to love, but it hadn't been enough for him. He wished he could take it all back, but he couldn't. It was the hardest lesson he would ever have to learn.

Now, as Shelley walked towards the town centre, she could hear the distant chorus of the carol singers outside the Blue Bell pub. Hark The Herald Angels Sing was her favourite carol, and as she made her way towards the direction of the choir, she felt a nostalgic buzz of Christmas excitement, taking her back to her childhood. A divorce was no account for celebration, but she couldn't help feeling slightly elated about her immediate future.

Her meeting with Chris had gone smoothly, and as happy as she was with the outcome, she also felt a little sad and somewhat sorry for him. He had wronged her, in the worst possible way and many people would've taken pleasure in, just desserts being slowly spoon-fed to their ex, but not Shelley. She only wished the best for him. She could see on his face that he was genuinely sorry for his actions.

He'd tried his best to appear unaffected by her words, but she knew him too well for that.

'Yes, I suppose we should get the wheels in motion,' he'd said, replying to her request for a divorce. 'I've got a new job,' he added, trying to sound light-hearted. 'It's in Manchester.'

'That's great,' she responded, smiling genuinely.

'Yeah, It's a big step up for me and should open a lot of doors. It's a great opportunity. So, I suppose if we're going to sell this place, it makes sense for me to move there. There's nothing keeping me here.'

'What about your mum?' Shelley asked.

At the realisation of what she'd just said, they both laughed, rolling their eyes.

'I think it's time I cut the apron strings, don't you?' he said, nodding at his own words. Pausing, he took a deep breath. 'Shelley,' he spoke, this time, looking directly into her eyes. 'Before we get the ball rolling on all this, I need to ask you something.'

She returned his stare, holding her breath, whilst awaiting his question.

'I know I have no right to ask this, but…is there any way back for us? We could be just how we were. No, we could be better. We could start a family and have the things we always dreamt of.' His words were tumbling out at speed, as he babbled without pause, too afraid to hear her response.

Her eyes fell to the floor, immediately letting him know her answer. It seemed an age before she looked back at him.

'I'm sorry, Chris, there's no way back for us. We have to look to the future now.'

She could see the tears forming in his eyes and she took no joy in it. Her marriage had meant everything to her, and she wasn't giving up on it lightly. But the bridge between them had been well and truly burnt. Shelley knew that moving on with her life was her only option.

Chris said goodbye, whilst watching her walk down the drive and out of his life forever. Taking a seat at the kitchen table, the radio began to play Mud's, It'll Be Lonely This Christmas. He broke down and began to cry, like he had never cried before.

Chapter 61

Judy sighed, sinking her head into the soft, duck down pillow of the single bed in the spare room of Marion Devine's, four bedroomed, detached, house. The chink of light from the landing, that was shining through the door went out, and all around her became still.

What a day, she thought. *What a Christmas!* It was like none she had ever experienced or could ever have predicted. As her eyes adjusted to the darkness of the room, they spied the outline of the gold watch she had carefully placed beside her on the bedside cabinet. Just looking at it made her heart leap, recalling the moment she had unwrapped it on Christmas morning. It had taken her breath away, with its slim gold strap, safety chain, and long black oblong face, with the tiniest diamond placed in the number twelve position.

Placing it on her arm, Mark snapped the clasp shut and she turned her wrist to admire it.

'Oh, Mark, it's the most beautiful thing I've ever owned,' she said, flushing a little with happy embarrassment.

They were only two months into their relationship but were already a well-established couple. This, however, didn't stop Judy still feeling a little coy at times. Mark was her first real boyfriend and the emotions and experiences she was going through were totally new to her. Mark had never been short of girlfriends, but with Judy it was completely different. He knew he loved her. She was so unique.

Judy was still getting used to her new shape. She wasn't one for wearing much makeup or getting dressed up unless it was a special occasion, but that was exactly what Mark loved about her. She had, however, kept up with her new hairstyle and had taken great pleasure in sharing her newfound happiness with Shelley, who was thrilled to hear that the date had been a success.

On the surface, most outsiders might have seen Judy and Mark as a bit of a mismatch, with his smouldering good looks and her plain Jane appearance; they weren't a couple that most people would have put together. Judy was in awe of Mark and often wondered what he saw in her, but he didn't see it like that at all. To him, he was the lucky one. He thought she was stunningly beautiful, inside and out. Happiness radiated from her, making her glow. She was funny, kind and quirky, and he wouldn't have her any other way.

Judy knew that the gold watch must've cost Mark a pretty penny, but it was the gesture and thought behind it that made her love him. He'd then gone on to surprise her with a second gift, a bottle of Opium perfume. She was speechless. No one had ever made her feel so loved and cherished. It had made the jumper she bought him from Top Man look a little poor in comparison. But Mark was thrilled with it, immediately putting it on and parading around as though he was on a catwalk. Making them both fall about laughing.

Their lovemaking had begun three weeks earlier, when Mark had stayed late one night at Judy's. These days, her house was almost always empty at the weekends. Dan was staying over at his mate's and her dad was at Brenda's. The topic was still a little delicate and Judy was yet to meet her dad's lady friend, but it was obvious to see that he was genuinely happy with her; a fact that no one could argue with. She knew he missed her mum in his own way, but Judy wasn't about to deny him his happiness. How could she when she was enjoying her own so much?

As she and Mark made love for the first time, they climaxed together, falling exhaustedly into each other's arms. Gazing into Judy's eyes, Mark whispered.

'I love you, Judy Smythe. You're amazing.'

Blushing, she looked away. Then affording herself a shy smile, she returned his gaze.

'I love you too,' she whispered.

There they stayed for the next three hours, just holding each other, until Judy begrudgingly suggested that it was time for Mark to go. Even though she was sure her father wouldn't return home until the next day, she couldn't risk him finding Mark in her bed. She was still his little girl at the end of the day, and that embarrassment would be too much to bear.

'I want to stay like this with you forever,' he said, stroking her hair.

'I wish we could,' she smiled up at him.

'One day,' he grinned, kissing her lightly on the lips.

The touch of the kiss sent electricity running through their bodies, and in no time at all, unable to hold back their urges, they were making love once more.

Mark's mother Marion, and sister Cassie, had welcomed Judy into their family with open arms. Both taking an instant liking to her. They could see how smitten Mark was with her. As a close-knit family, it meant everything to Marion to know that Mark and Cassie were happy. They had all been through so much this last year, and it was obvious to her that Judy was a genuine girl whose only agenda was to make her son happy.

Following his father's death, Mark was now heading the family business and he was doing a fantastic job. Marion knew his dad would've been extremely proud of him, just as she was. He would be a wealthy man one day and to some girls, this fact would make him an attractive catch. Marion could tell that Judy was not one of them. The same couldn't be said for the girl he had been dating prior to Judy; Marion had only met the brazen, busty brunette once but thankfully the relationship was short-lived, and her concerns had been extinguished.

Judy spent the whole of Boxing Day with the Devine's, and she couldn't have felt more like part of the family. Marion had even invited her dad and brother, and although she was grateful for the kind gesture, Judy was glad that they had politely declined.

Some of Mark's aunts and uncles visited, and although it was a day that had been spent not really doing anything, the plentiful eating, drinking, and socialising had made Judy very sleepy. As she was about to close her eyes, the quiet squeaking of the bedroom door made her raise her head from the pillow. As Mark tiptoed towards her, he put his finger to his lips.

'Shhh,' he whispered, grinning.

Judy's eyes widened with astonished excitement.

As he slid into the single bed, the two of them snuggled close.

'I couldn't go to sleep knowing that you were under the same roof and I hadn't given you a proper goodnight kiss. I just had to come and see you,' he whispered in her ear.

As the pair kissed lovingly, Judy whispered, 'I'm so glad you did. Thanks for the best Christmas ever.'

Chapter 62

Shelley looked around the pub; it was dead. Christmas had come and gone in a flash and tomorrow the salon was back open. Fortunately for Shelley, she was taking another day off, as the shop would be quiet, and Dawn had allowed her an extra day. As the newest staff member, Jason would have to go in and Shelley could just picture him dragging himself to work, bleary-eyed from all the partying. God, that boy drank vodka like it was going out of fashion. The image made her smile.

Her thoughts turned to Ross. What an effect he'd had on her since the Friday before, when they'd shared a rushed but intense Christmas kiss as she was getting into her taxi. His lips were so soft and full, and when his hand held the small of her back, it sent shockwaves throughout her entire body. That certainly wasn't the feeling she'd got when Wayne kissed her.

She smiled at Wayne as he turned from the bar, looking at her, like a puppy seeking out its master. He was lovely and so sweet, but even though they were the same age, she felt so much more mature than him. They'd come to the pub to escape his hectic household. His family were great, real salt of the earth kind of people, but there were so many of them and, with it being Christmas week the partying was non-stop. They could've gone to Jackie's, but it was much the same there, with the twins and all their new toys. It didn't seem to bother Wayne too much, but Shelley had already enjoyed the independence of owning her own home, and she was beginning to feel smothered.

She thought of her marital home. Chris had phoned, leaving a message with Jackie to say that there were two viewings booked for the following day, so maybe it wouldn't be long before she'd have enough money to put a deposit down on a little terraced house of her own.

The idea excited her, but as she watched Wayne sharing a joke with the landlord, she knew there and then, that he would have no place in her future. She thought of the bath set he'd bought her for Christmas. She wasn't ungrateful. But, come on. That was the sort of present you bought your mum when you were twelve, not your girlfriend. And since she and Tina had reconnected, she'd discovered that Wayne and Darren were good friends. Even though she didn't like to tar them with the same brush, the thought unnerved her.

As Wayne returned to the table with the drinks, Shelley decided to make it her last one of the night. Once home, she'd have a chat with Jackie and see if she had any advice on how to finish with someone, without hurting their feelings too much.

Chapter 63

Replacing the receiver, Tina stood in a state of shock and disbelief. She had not been prepared for the news she'd just received, and she was finding it difficult to take in. Her beautiful friend was dead, murdered by her ex-boyfriend. It was a fact she couldn't comprehend. A beautiful life wasted, for nothing.

As she pictured her lovely friend lying there, killed in cold blood, the tears began to well in her eyes. They'd only spoken on Christmas Eve, and Marsha's voice had been filled with hope for the New Year ahead. Her college course was going great and Jerome loved his new school. She had such a promising future, to then have her life cruelly snuffed out, just like that! It wasn't fair.

The girls had planned to get together on Saturday the 28th, but Tina had been trying for two days to get hold of Marsha to reschedule. Her mum had decided on throwing a pre, New Year's party. Calling upon Tina to help with the buffet and balloons. Under normal circumstances, Tina would've told her mum to find help elsewhere, but after all her parents had done for her since she'd left the refuge, it was the least she could do. She knew Marsha would understand, as she and her own mother were extremely close, and as she would often say to Tina, 'you only get one mum.'

After two days, with no joy, she had decided to ring Marsha's mum, Deana, who was the one to sadly inform Tina of her daughter's death. She explained how Darnell had found Marsha, through some girl in the launderette, who had shopped her for a bag of weed. Turned out, the girl had lived near them years ago, and on the promise of free drugs, which she had decided was worth more than her new friendship with Marsha, she'd spilled the beans of her whereabouts, to Darnell. Somehow, late on Christmas Eve, he'd made his way into the flats and tricked her into opening the door. The police weren't entirely sure what exactly happened, but a fight must've broken out and Marsha was stabbed 38 times. Poor little Jerome was the one who found her on Christmas morning.

As the terrible scene played out in Tina's mind, she began to cry. She was in terrible shock, hardly believing what had happened. Through her sobs, she suddenly heard a light tapping against the front window. Looking up she was faced with Darren, peering at her with concerned confusion. She quickly tried to disguise her upset as she made her way to the front door, but it was obvious to see that she was distraught. As she opened the door, he held his arms out to her and she fell into them, without hesitation.

Deciding to call round, to see if he could borrow the ladders, from the outhouse, Darren couldn't believe his luck on finding Tina in such a vulnerable state. He had no intentions of using the ladders. It was just an excuse and a lame one at that, but his visit was working to his advantage, much more than he could've imagined. Here was, his Tina, in his arms. She needed him and he would make sure, she was left in no doubt, that she'd be better off with him in her life than without him.

Sitting her down, he poured her a glass of sherry. A Christmas raffle win and the only alcohol she had in the house. It was sickly sweet, but the warmth comforted her. As she explained the basics of what had happened to Marsha, and how they'd come to know each other, it suddenly dawned on Tina that it could very well have been her that had been murdered. It sounded extreme, but hadn't she found herself in the women's refuge, for the exact same reason that Marsha had? She studied the man who was sitting on the settee with his hands wrapped around hers, reassuring her with comforting words, and she froze. Why would she think he could ever change? What did he want from her – in fact, what was he even doing here?

Abruptly, Tina stood up. She wanted Darren to leave and she wanted him to leave right now. He had no place in her life and she didn't need him. She certainly didn't owe him anything. Suddenly, she felt strong. She felt like the old Tina, who wasn't afraid of anyone.

'Listen, Darren, I think it's best if you go,' she said. 'I'm upset and I need to be by myself right now.'

'Darlin', you've had a massive shock,' he soothed. 'I can't leave you like this. You're my Tina and you need me right now. As he went to cup her chin with his rough hands, she hastily shrugged him off.

'I'm not your Tina, and I never will be again. You lost that privilege the first time you beat me black and blue. Leave it, Darren, and leave me alone. It's over between us and it's best you don't come around here again,' she added, looking him directly in the eyes.

He stared at her in disbelief and out of the corner of her eye, she saw his fists clench. In that split second, she knew that Darren would never, ever change, and she had been a fool to believe that he could. Well no more. That was the last time she would be taken in by any man. The old Tina was back, and she was back to stay.

As Darren marched from the house, he slammed the front door so hard that the bottle of sherry, sitting on the sideboard fell off, spilling the dark, sticky liquid all over the carpet. Tina quickly ran to the kitchen to get a bowl of soapy water to clean up the mess. This was her house and her life, and no one would disrespect either of them, again.

Chapter 64

Banging his fists on the door once again, Darren began to lose patience.

'Leanne,' he hissed through the letterbox. 'Leanne' he said again, louder this time. 'Open up, I know you're fucking in there.' When, after a further minute, no lights came on and the small terraced house remained still, Darren bellowed, 'Slag!' giving the door a kick, before striding off angrily down the long street. This was the third time he'd called round to Leanne's house and there had been no answer. He was desperate to take out the sexual frustration that Tina was causing him, and he was beginning to think that the bitch was avoiding him.

Hearing Darren's footsteps walk away, Leanne began to breathe normally again. With the sheets held tightly under her chin, as though acting like a protective layer, she hoped he wouldn't return. Her eyes focused on the porcelain lightshade which was barely visible in the darkened room and as relief washed over her, she began to relax a little. How she prayed for the next few weeks to fly by. She couldn't wait to pack up her few belongings and move to be with her best friend. She and Sue spoke daily on the telephone, about the move and were clearly as excited as each other about it.

Sue had also made a decision regarding the money from the house sale and Leanne was thrilled to hear that she was planning to open her own business. Even better, was that she wanted her best friend to work with her. Already employed in a florist, Sue had been to night school to learn the trade. The owner was selling the business, and the thought of opening her own shop was her reason for selling the house she'd inherited from her gran. Sue could think of no one she trusted more to help her build her dream.

Chapter 65

'What are you thinking of wearing tonight, Shell?' Jackie asked, as she began filling the washing machine, with its second load of the day.

'Well, I wasn't thinking of getting too dolled up, it's only a house party. In fact, it's not even a party, is it? More like a small gathering,' Shelley replied, finishing her mug of tea.

'Yeah, but its New Year's Eve, Shell. If that's not a reason to put your glad rags on, I don't know what is. Kev's not too happy, he wanted to get tickets for High Crompton Con club. They've got three artists on tonight, and the bingo prize is a hundred quid. You should've seen his face drop when I told him we were going to me mam's.'

Both girls chuckled.

'Oh God, I bet he weren't happy, was he? To be honest, Jackie, I don't really like New Year that much. All that pushing and shoving to get served, and then the taxis charge double fare. It's all a big hype.'

'Oh, don't be such a misery guts,' retorted Jackie, looking at her sister with surprise.

'I'm not. I just think it's a farce. Strangers kissing you and everybody thinking that next year's going to be a new start, and better than the one they've just had. It's a load of bollocks if you ask me. I'm glad we're only going to me mum and dad's,' she shrugged.

Jackie closed the washing machine door and sat at the table with her sister.

'What's up, Shell? You've had a face like a wet weekend all morning.'

Shelley smiled, realising her sister knew her only too well.

'Oh, I'm just feeling a bit guilty, that's all. I finished with Wayne last night and I left him in tears. I feel really bad.'

Jackie sighed, relieved that it was just a triviality that her sister was getting herself in a state about.

'You really need to toughen up, you do, our Shelley. You've had a crap year and things are starting to look up for you, so don't start feeling sorry for some lad who you've only been seeing for two minutes. He helped you get over Chris, didn't he?'

Shelley nodded.

'Well then, he served his purpose, love. I know it sounds harsh, but all's fair in love and war. You of all people should know that. Now let's see you smile,' Jackie urged. 'You're putting me off my donut,' she grinned, stuffing the rest of it greedily into her mouth.

Shelley couldn't help but smile as the raspberry jam oozed from Jackie's lips.

The evening before had unnerved her a little. She'd decided earlier on that day that she would give Wayne a second chance. He was very handsome and such a lovely guy; maybe she had been trying to find fault with him, because of how the kiss between her and Ross, had left her feeling. But as the night wore on, it was all the more evident that she and Wayne had no future together. Even his laugh was beginning to irritate her, and when he continued to drone on about his beloved Cortina and how he was going to get a sticker for the windscreen with Wayne and Shelley on it, she knew enough was enough.

'I'm sorry, Wayne,' she blurted out, 'I think we should split up.' Once she'd said the words, there was no going back.

His eyes looked at her, pleadingly. 'Why, Shelley, what have I done wrong?' he asked.

Shelley was unprepared and didn't know what to say. 'It's just not working,' she said, in a small voice, wishing that his bedroom floor would swallow her whole.

As the two of them sat on his single bed, saying nothing for the next minute, Shelley looked around her. She felt like a sixteen-year-old, sneaking up to her boyfriend's bedroom whilst the rest of his family were downstairs watching Coronation Street. It wasn't Wayne's fault that he didn't have his own place. But it was obvious that they were poles apart in their outlook. He was happy with his lot, whilst she was striving to achieve so much more.

There had been a lot of interest in the beauty salon, and even though the treatments were still limited until she'd finished her training, her makeovers were going down a treat. She was doing special offers on make-up trials with every perm or colour and her clients couldn't get enough. Her best seller was eyelash tints, and for the first time in her life she felt like she was a success in her own right. It was exhilarating. She'd already decided that she would train in massage therapy next. Women worked hard and they wanted to be pampered, and Shelley was going to make sure that she could provide exactly what they wanted.

'Can you at least give me a reason?' Wayne eventually asked, staring at her.

Shelley smiled weakly. She didn't want to blame him, so, put on the spot she decided to use the fact that his relationship with Darren was coming between them, and if she had known they were best mates, she wouldn't have gone out with him. Now her best friend, Tina was back in her life, there was no way she would risk losing her friendship again. It was far too important to her. The excuse was feeble, and she knew it, but she was surprised and taken aback at Wayne's reaction. His face began to turn red and he shook with fury.

'That fucking bastard's done it again,' he spat. 'He spoils everything for me, that fucker.'

Shelley was shocked. She had never even heard Wayne raise his voice, never mind lose his temper. He was usually so placid.

'Everything I've ever had he's ruined for me,' he continued. 'Ever since we were at school, he always had to be top dog. Coming up smelling of roses, whatever shit he fell into, whilst I'm left shovelling it for him. Well I've just about had enough of it,' he ranted. 'You're the only girl I've ever loved, and now I'm losing you, because of that bastard.'

Shelley was genuinely frightened. This was nothing like the man she thought she knew, and to hear Wayne say he loved her left her feeling very uncomfortable. He'd always been keener than she was, that much was clear to see, but love was the last thing on her mind.

'I'll kill him,' Wayne snarled through gritted teeth, making her jump as his features twisted in anger. 'You see if I don't.'

Finally finding her voice, Shelley grabbed her coat and headed towards the door.

'I've got to go, I'll see you around,' she said, hurrying from the room and down the stairs as fast as she could. Thankfully, none of Wayne's family were in the kitchen, and as she ran from the house into the cold night air, she breathed a sigh of relief.

Grateful for the fact that she was wearing flat shoes, she turned once to check that she had not been followed. Then ran most of the half mile home.

Chapter 66

As Mandy replaced the receiver, she realised her New Year's Eve options were becoming more limited by the minute. That was the third person who had declined an offer to join her in Hogmanay celebrations. She was beginning to wonder if word had spread further afield regarding her role in the infamous sex tape. Mandy didn't really have friends as such, more acquaintances that she called upon when she needed a girls' night out.

As she sat at the small telephone table in her mother's hallway, she tapped her glossy red nails against the mahogany wood, turning her thoughts to Judy, whom she'd been considering contacting, more and more lately. She missed her loyal friend and the fact that she'd always been there, to pick up when she was needed. Judy never let her down, and Mandy wondered what she was doing right now. More to the point, she wondered what she'd be doing that very night. Mandy bet that whatever it was, Judy would change her plans for her oldest and best friend. Not that Mandy considered for one minute that if the boot were on the other foot, she would do the same in return. It had been months since they'd spoken, but Mandy was sure that by now, enough time had elapsed to allow her to pour oil, on the troubled waters between them.

The sound of the key in the lock of the aluminium-framed front door broke her thoughts. She could see the outline of her mother, Gloria, through the frosted glass, along with what looked like a dozen shopping bags.

"Ere, help us in, our Mandy, before I trip over all these. I'm dying for the lavvy.'

Mandy stood up, taking the bags from her mother's arms.

'Bloody hell, Mum. Looks like you've bought half of C&A with this lot,' Mandy said, peering into the bags.

Her mum grinned as she passed her, taking the stairs two at a time.

'Well, why not?' she called from the bathroom. 'The sales have started, and I wanted to get myself something nice for tonight. Ronnie's taking me out for a posh meal to that new French bistro, and then we're going to a casino,' she exclaimed, excitedly, racing back down the stairs to show Mandy her new purchases.

There were shoes, handbags and lots of clothes. Gloria was in her element as she held them against her, showing them off to her daughter.

'Hey, you can borrow any of these, love, I'm sure they'll fit you,' she said, admiring herself in the, long hall mirror.

'I just might do,' replied Mandy, studying the price tags of the, high quality merchandise. 'This lot must've cost a fortune,' she said, raising her eyebrows.

Gloria winked. 'Yep, and all thanks to my lovely Ronnie. That five hundred quid he gave me for Christmas has come in very nicely, thank you very much. He treats me like a queen, and it's not before time. Decent men are hard to find, my girl, and I'm hanging onto this one.'

Ronnie, Gloria's latest flame was a local businessman and, well-respected Mason. His wife had passed away ten years previously and the last six months he had spent with Gloria, had been the most sexually active of his life. Fat, grey and balding, he was a bit older than her usual type, but Gloria could sniff out money like a bloodhound and she was thoroughly enjoying herself. At forty-six, she was still very attractive, if a little careworn. Her all-year tan was thanks to her canopy sunbed, which was used on a daily basis, and her trim figure was kept in shape with the help of regular aerobics classes. She had the same large chest that her daughter had inherited, even though it was no longer quite as perky. Together, the women were like two peas in a pod.

'Oh, you'll never guess who I bumped into,' Gloria announced, removing the stuffing from the tan leather handbag she'd bought from Marks & Spencer.

'Who?' Mandy replied, whilst standing in front of the hall mirror, admiring the red leather mini skirt that she thought would look much better on her, than her mother.

'Only Judy, and she was with her boyfriend.'

Mandy dropped the leather skirt at the sound of Judy's name. Giving her mother her full attention.

'I swear I honestly didn't recognise her, love. I would've walked right past her, if she hadn't let onto me first.'

Mandy looked surprised, and her eyes questioned her mother for more information.

'She's as slim as you and me, Mand, and that's no word of a lie. I couldn't believe it. And her hair, it's all streaked and cut into a bob. She looked lovely. She even had a bit of lippy on! It really suited her.'

Mandy stared at her mother in disbelief. 'You mean, Judy, as in my Judy? Big Judy, who's never had a boyfriend in her life?' Mandy added.

'Yes, that's exactly who I mean. Judy who used to come here all the time and eat all the custard creams. Well I'm telling you, our Mandy, there's not a custard cream passed her lips in many a month. 'She looks bloody fantastic.'

'Who's this boyfriend then?' Mandy enquired, hardly believing her ears.

'Well how should I know?' said Gloria. 'I didn't actually see him. She was outside the shop waiting for him.'

Mandy smirked. 'Oh, so you didn't actually see him, this boyfriend of hers? I'm telling you, Mother, she's making it up. She's never had a boyfriend in her life, and if by some miracle this boyfriend does actually exist, I can guarantee he'll look like he's fallen out of the ugly tree and hit every branch on the way down.'

Gloria looked at her daughter, open-mouthed. 'Mandy, that's a bloody awful thing to say about your friend. Sounds like you're jealous to me.'

'Get real, Mum. As if I'd be jealous of two-tonne Tessie!'

Gloria was about to open her mouth to protest, but Mandy continued on her rant.

'And if you think for one moment, that I believe Judy's as slim as I am then you must be deluded mother. Judy will never be as slim as me. She loves her food too much.'

Gloria was shocked at her daughter's outburst. Mandy had always been a selfish piece of work, but to talk about her good friend like that, made Gloria dismay at the kind of daughter she'd raised. It was true they were cut from the same cloth as far as looks were concerned, and there was also no denying that when it came to men, the pair were always on the lookout for what they could take rather than give, but that's where the similarity ended. Gloria was popular with both men and women, and she had no end of friends, that she could call upon at any time.

Seeing this mean streak in her daughter instantly reminded her of the father that Mandy had never known. Gloria shuddered at the thought. Petey Jones had wined her, dined her, then taken her for everything she had. And as soon as she was pregnant with Mandy, he'd moved on to her best friend, leaving Gloria in debt up to her eyeballs and holding the baby, literally. It was a tough lesson that she was thankful she'd learned at an early age. Vowing never to be taken for a fool by any man or woman again.

As Mandy slammed the front door behind her, Gloria shook her head, continuing to admire her new goods. She'd spent her life scrimping and working and for once she'd met a man who truly wanted nothing more, than to make her happy. Ronnie was no oil painting, that much was true, but the more time she spent with him, the more she could honestly say that her feelings for him were genuine. He was loving and generous and they made each other happy. Gloria was not going to let her selfish daughter get in the way of that. If her relationship with Ronnie continued like this, she could see good things coming her way in 1986. The thought gave her a warm glow as she carried her purchases upstairs and began to run a bath, ready for the big night ahead.

Chapter 67

The knock at the door came just as Tina was washing the teatime pots. The cottage pie she'd made could've fed the whole street, and she realised she needed to start cooking smaller portions. Making her way down the hall she felt apprehensive. She wasn't expecting anyone and wondered who the caller could be.

Scanning the distorted male figure through the front door glass, she could tell it wasn't Darren, and heaving a sigh of relief she went to answer it. She was shocked and surprised to see Jason standing before her.

'Hello, love,' she said warmly, 'what brings you here on New Year's Eve?' It was early evening, but the temperature had plummeted to freezing, as the icy wind circled through the narrow streets. 'Come on in,' Tina beckoned, as a blast of cold air entered the hallway.

On hearing her friendly voice and kind words, Jason's face crumpled, and his tears began to flow.

'Oh my god, what's the matter, love?' Tina cried, instinctively putting her arms around him.

'I've been dumped,' he sniffed, allowing her welcoming arms to hold him.

As Tina closed the front door, the lone figure, standing in the darkened ginnel across the street, clenched his fists. There was a tight knot in the pit of Darren's stomach and as the anger soared through his body, he tried to breathe through it in order to suppress his rage. His instincts were telling him to charge over and beat the living crap out of his rival, but his logic told him that it wasn't a good idea.

Following his last visit to Tina, he realised that something was amiss, and his intuition told him there could be another bloke in the frame. After what he'd just witnessed it seemed his suspicions were correct. Ever since Tina had dismissed him, asking him to leave her alone, Darren had been like a bear with a sore head. Even Ivy was getting fed up with his moods. That very night, she'd told him not to bother coming back until he changed his attitude. That in itself was extremely unusual as Darren rarely did anything wrong in her eyes. She also told him that he'd better start back at the garage in the New Year. Ivy adored her son, but she was not about to let him take her for a fool. It was obvious that he was swinging the lead, and she wasn't prepared to put up with it any longer. He ate like a horse and it was about time he started bringing some earnings home. The fridge wasn't going to stock itself.

Settling down to a New Year, shared with her neighbour Elsie, also a widow, and Lillian, her bingo buddy, Ivy let rip at her son. Shocking her pals, who were under the impression that Darren couldn't put a foot wrong. As he'd entered the house, slamming the front door behind him, Ivy bellowed from the kitchen.

'Watch the bleeding hinges on that door, lad. What d'ya think you're doing, charging in 'ere like a bull in a bloody china shop?'

Darren was in a foul temper and certainly not in the mood for his mother and her cronies. She'd been getting on his case more and more of late and he was wondering whether moving back home had been such a good idea. Unbeknown to him, Ivy was beginning to question how well she actually knew her son. Her neighbour and closest friend, Elsie, had been the one to break it to her about Darren's heavy-handed activities towards his wife throughout their marriage. If it had come from anyone else, Ivy would have told them to sling their hook, but coming from her friend of over forty years, it was a different story. Elsie didn't gossip, and when she revealed to Ivy that her source had been Tina herself, with the bruises to prove it, Ivy felt she had to take note.

Darren's afternoon session in the Moulders Arms had not gone without incident. He loved New Year and was looking forward to seeing his mates and arranging the night ahead. The nagging doubts he had about Tina having a new man, were still in the back of his mind, but he was prepared to put them on hold for a good piss up to see the New Year in. The atmosphere in his local was buoyant and the lads were on a high as they discussed the almighty session ahead of them.

That was until Wayne appeared. He was drunk and unable to walk straight, which was unusual for Wayne as he was not known for getting wasted to the point of incapacitation. A few of the lads began to laugh, nudging one another as Wayne stumbled towards the bar.

'Fuck me, Wayne,' Dave chuckled. 'What's all this? Bit early to be pissed, mate. You'll have nowt left for tonight.'

Darren sniggered at Dave's joke, shaking his head and wondering what had got into their good friend.

'What's up, pal,' he asked jovially, putting his arm round Wayne's neck. 'Not like you to get totally wankered at this early hour. Who're you with?' he asked, looking around to see if Wayne had a companion.

'You mind yer own fucking business,' Wayne slurred, turning to Darren and trying, with drunken eyes, to focus on him. 'I'm fucking done wi' you, yer tosser,' he continued. 'Sick of yer ruining everything for me. Yer a bullying bastard and I'm gonna teach you a fucking lesson.'

At this point, Darren realised that Wayne was deadly serious. He had the attention of most of the pub and Darren was not happy with the showdown he was causing.

'What the fuck you on about?' he asked, still trying to remain light-hearted, hoping he could diffuse the situation before he lost his rag with the best mate he adored like a brother. 'Come on mate, I think you've had a few too many. Let's get you home, to sleep it off, so you'll be ready for tonight.'

'Don't you fucking touch me,' Wayne hissed, shrugging off Darren's arm. 'And don't ever call me mate. You're no fucking mate. You're a using bastard and a fucking wife beater.'

No sooner had the words left Wayne's mouth, than the fist, hit his chin straight on, knocking his already unsteady legs from under him. Knowing that Wayne was in no capacity to fight his corner, a few of the bigger men jumped in to split the pair up, before he took a major kicking. The regulars, seeing the look on Darren's face, realised that if he got his hands on, Wayne there was no telling if he'd ever stop. They'd all heard the rumours about how Darren had treated his wife, and although no one, but Wayne had had the guts to say it to his face, the majority were pleased to hear him being publicly exposed.

Shelley's break up with Wayne had affected him enormously. He'd never felt as much for any woman as he had for her. Hearing that Darren's reputation was the only reason she could give for splitting up with him had made him hate the friend he used to look up to. But it had been a long time coming.

Since the rumours had begun to circulate about Darren's wife beating, Wayne found his feelings changing towards him. As a child, he'd often witnessed his mother on the receiving end of his father's punches, and he despised men who hit women. Seeing Darren's temper flare many times in the pub, Wayne was sickened, imagining what Tina had been through. He'd seen her bruises with his own eyes, and over time, he'd also witnessed her shrinking personality. Once such a feisty sort, Tina had turned into a frightened mouse when he used to call round to their house. He'd begun to have his suspicions, but the thought that his own mate would behave that way, seemed unimaginable to him. It was only after she'd gone AWOL that the truth had started to emerge, and the puzzle pieces began to fit together.

The belated Christmas card from the father he hadn't seen in years had arrived that morning, a week too late. The cheap and flimsy acknowledgement to his son lacked sentiment, simply reading 'to Wayne, from Dad', and as the unhappy memories of the drunken bully who'd made his, his mum, and his sister's lives a misery, came to the forefront of his mind, Wayne had begun to feel angry. It was an anger that wouldn't begin to subside until the first large whisky burnt his throat. Downing it in one, he'd immediately poured a second. He was on a mission, and as the negativity in his mind turned to Shelley and their failed relationship, the comparison between his father and Darren grew. Two hours later, he had only one thing on his mind. He wanted revenge, and if he couldn't give it to his dad then his mate would have to take double the punishment.

Wayne wasn't a fighter, never had been, but after almost a bottle of scotch he felt like ten men. Staggering to his feet, he lunged towards his enemy, who had now turned his back on him. As the half brick that he'd been hiding under his coat left his hand, several men ducked reflexively. The brick whistled past Darren's right ear, landing clean on the pool table, leaving the debris of crumbling cement behind it as it rolled.

Darren turned to stare at Wayne. The room was still, and the air was thick with his menacing aura. As Darren finally spoke through gritted teeth, his mouth twisted in anger, as a now horrified Wayne suddenly realised the enormity of the situation – but still drunk and fuelled with anger, he was prepared to fight the goliath before him.

'Get that fucking' cretin out of my sight,' Darren snarled at the men surrounding the pair, arms waiting to intervene on the inevitably explosive situation. As a few of them pulled Wayne towards the entrance, he managed to half turn in his struggle.

'This isn't fucking over, Darren. Do you hear me?' he shouted.

-

Jason took a seat in Tina's cosy front room, wiping his eyes and feeling a little embarrassed.

'I'm so sorry for turning up like this, but I couldn't go home to my empty flat. I needed to talk to someone. You said you weren't going out, so here I am. I hope you don't mind,' he explained as his face crumpled again in his sadness.

'Oh Jason, of course I don't mind,' said Tina, taking the seat beside him and putting her arm around his shoulder. 'Tell me what's happened.'

'God, I feel really daft,' he said. 'You and me only met a couple of weeks ago. The last thing you need is some blubbering gay boy turning up on your doorstep on New Year's Eve.'

'Not at all. Shelley's friends are my friends and you can come here any time.'

'Thanks,' he replied, drying his eyes once more.

'Would you like a cup of tea? Have you eaten?' Tina asked. 'I've got loads of cottage pie, if you're hungry.'

'Oh God, I could murder a plate of that,' said Jason, perking up a little. 'But first things first, have you got any drink in?' he asked, hopefully.

'I've nothing in,' Tina sighed. 'But I tell you what, there's an off-licence around the corner. You nip down there for a couple of bottles of wine and I'll warm the food up.'

As the front door opened, Darren watched the hooded figure leave the house he'd once shared with his estranged wife. He hid himself, peeking from behind the corner of the adjacent property. After the stream of traffic passed, he crossed the road, trying to blend in with the other pedestrians. It was only early evening and there were a few people dotted around. Most were making their way to parties with friends and relatives for a night of celebrations. He didn't recognise the man ahead of him; he was certain it wasn't anyone he knew.

'Alright, Darren,' said an elderly man, stepping out of number 78 and straight into his path. 'What brings you round here? Thought you moved back to your mum's?'

As Darren came face to face with his old neighbour, he cursed under his breath. That was all he needed, old Joe stopping him for a chat.

'Yeah, just passing through, Joe,' he said. 'Sorry, I can't stop, I'm late,' he waved, leaving the old man standing alone on the pavement.

All Darren could now see before him were a young couple and a man walking his dog. His prey was no longer in sight. Anger gripped his stomach. His adrenalin was pumping, and he had an urge to punch something. As he stepped up his pace, he approached the corner of the street, but the man he was following had disappeared.

'Fuck,' he said aloud. 'Where the fuck, did he go?'

Approaching the high street, Darren was still looking around in bewilderment as though the mystery man might pop out from one of the alleyways, but there was no one else in sight. He thought about turning back and confronting Tina, but his instincts told him not to. She was alone and he knew what he was capable of, in the mood he was in. It was the man he wanted, and as the thought of beating him to a pulp flashed through his mind, Darren clenched his fist once more. Walking past

Russell's off-licence, he debated on whether to get some fags. Looking through the window, the shop seemed empty of customers, but his thirst for vodka was greater than his need for nicotine, so he decided he'd make what he had last him. He could see the Duke of York pub in the distance and there was only one thing for it; he needed to get pissed on an almighty scale. The day had been a fuck up from start to finish and he was determined to end it obliterated.

In Russell's off-licence, Jason stood up from his crouched position, cursing at why the cheapest wine was always on the bottom shelf. He'd taken his time, seeing himself as quite the connoisseur these days. Still, if you knew what you were looking for, you were able to go cheap, whilst still managing to purchase a palatable vintage. Thinking about his day from hell, he thanked the Lord for Tina and wine, as he hurried back for his first glass and a hearty plateful of homemade cottage pie. What a rock 'n' roll way to see out 1985.

Chapter 68

With less than an hour to midnight, Gerry Barnes lifted the needle off the record, abruptly interrupting Cilla's, You're My World.

'Aw, Dad, put it back on,' Jackie called, 'I love that one.' She grinned drunkenly at her husband, Kev, as she continued swaying with her arms around his neck.

The twins had exhaustedly been put to bed, hours before, and Jackie and Kev were making the most of their time without them. Shelley nibbled on another sausage roll even though she wasn't hungry. 1985 was coming to a close and she wasn't at all sorry to see the back of it. She had no reason to feel melancholy as her house had now sold, and everything in her life was looking up, but she still felt a twinge of envy as she watched her sister and husband in their blissful happiness.

'Why's the bloody music stopped?' cried Carole, strutting in from the kitchen, 'I was enjoying that. I love Cilla. Ey Gerry, remember when we used to go to the

Three Cellars club, in our teens? Everyone used to call me Cilla, didn't they?' she reminisced, looking wistful as she fondly recalled the images of her youth.

'Aye, they did, love.'

She had been a flame-haired beauty in her day and never short of admirers. They'd had their troubles but deep down, Gerry loved her with all his heart.

'Right you lot,' Gerry exclaimed. 'I want you all in here, sitting down. I need to talk to you.'

Carole tutted. 'Sod that. Put the music back on!' She drew on her cigarette with her pink-painted lips. 'It's almost New Year, we want to dance! Your little chat can wait,' she said, leaning over him to reach the stereo needle.

'No,' said Gerry, firmly, moving her arm away. 'What I've got to say is important.'

The four of them looked at each other and then at Gerry.

'What is it, Dad, are you okay?' asked Shelley, with a look of concern.

'Yes love, I'm fine. But I have something important to talk to you all about.' Aware that he had their full attention, Gerry began.

Chapter 69

Tagging along with the large crowd of girls she hardly knew; Mandy was relieved she'd finally found someone to go out with. The wild bunch, headed by Tanya, an old school acquaintance, had readily welcomed her. The more the merrier as far as they were concerned. Mandy and a handsome tall guy in a red leather jacket had been exchanging flirty glances for the past half an hour, and when he finally made his move, she was more than relieved. Mandy had soon decided that Tanya's crowd weren't her type. Watching each girl battle with the next in order to see how many men they could attract, wasn't what she was used to. And she certainly didn't like the competition for male attention.

After a little small talk and a quick dance with the man in leather, he went in for the kill. As his tongue entered her mouth the taste of cigarettes was overwhelming. He was certainly handsome, there was no denying that, but he kissed like a washing machine on full spin. Mandy pulled away with distaste, wishing she had not separated herself from the crowd.

When her admirer went to the bar, she looked around to see if she could spot any of her acquaintances. The pub was packed, and Mandy couldn't see anyone she knew. Suddenly, she hated New Year. It was only forty minutes away and she was still relatively sober. The night was flat, the crowd were overbearing, and she just wanted to go home. Deciding to escape before the man in leather returned, she ducked under some of the revellers and weaved her way towards the entrance.

As the cold air hit her, she shivered and began tottering towards the taxi rank. At least it was before midnight so the chances of getting a cab wouldn't be too bad. She only lived ten minutes away, but there was no way she was walking home in 5" heels. The temperature was below freezing and without a coat, Mandy's nipples protruded through her skimpy lace top.

Two men shouted from across the road.

'Want me to keep you warm, love?' one called out.

'Hey Phil, I know where to go if I need to hang my coat up,' chuckled the other.

Normally Mandy would've seen the funny side of this, but tonight she was cold and lonely and just wanted to be snuggled up in her bed. It was at that point that she spotted him, standing outside Mario's Italian restaurant, with his toned, tanned arms and wavy, treacle brown hair, which she instantly recognised. Her heart leapt. Maybe the night wasn't going to be a disappointment after all. As he began to walk towards the parked taxi, she called out to him.

'Mark,' she called out, waving as she approached. 'Fancy seeing you here!'

Mark and Judy had decided to go for a meal instead of battling the pubs and bars. Mario's was a family favourite, holding precious memories for Mark. His father was friends with the owner and had taken the family often. Mark couldn't think of a better place for him and Judy to be on New Year's Eve. As his mum was at home alone, the pair had decided to go home to join her, seeing in the new year together. It was her first as a widow, and Mark realised it would be a difficult time.

'Oh, hi Mandy,' he said, smiling awkwardly, surprised to see his ex-girlfriend. 'Fancy bumping into you.'

Mandy rushed towards him in excitement.

'It's fantastic to see you,' she gushed, throwing her arms around his neck. 'This must be fate.' She smacked a kiss on his cheek.

Their previous relationship had been mostly dictated by Mandy. She'd called the shots and Mark had obligingly followed. She was full on, in your face, downright sexy, and saying no to her was a difficult plight for any red-blooded male. Mark had certainly never encountered anyone like her before, but after a couple of months of dating, he had to admit that she'd exhausted him. She was spontaneous and exciting in a demanding kind of way, with a sex drive that he was struggling to keep up with. When she cut their relationship short, his emotions were mixed. Mandy was certainly the type of girl most men would dream of having on their arm, but the reality was somewhat overbearing, and Mark looked back on their time together as a two-month long party. And all parties have to end at some point.

'Is this your taxi?' Mandy asked. 'Can I share it with you?' she purred, tilting her head to one side, in a puppy dog fashion, whilst batting her eyelashes at him. She reached out and stroked his collar with her slender fingers, brushing past his chin. 'We could see the new year in together if you like,' she grinned. 'For old times' sake.'

Mark felt flushed. Her protruding nipples were inches away from his face, and memories of licking and nibbling on them sprang into his mind.

'You, getting in mate?' the taxi driver called through his window.

'Yeah coming now, just waiting for...' Mark stopped mid-sentence as he heard Mandy screech, in a loud and extremely high-pitched voice.

'Oh my god, Judy, is that you? No fucking way. Look at you! Where the hell have you gone, you're half the size!'

It was difficult to tell who was the most shocked between the three of them. Walking out of the restaurant, the last thing Judy had expected to see was her ex-best-friend, inches away from her boyfriend. Instinctively, the old feelings of betrayal came flooding back to her. But overshadowing them, was an instant sudden lack of confidence and self-worth.

At the beginning of the night, Judy couldn't have felt happier. The black velvet dress she'd ordered from the catalogue fitted her beautifully. With its square box neckline and perfect length, resting between her knee and thigh. It looked as though it was made for her. The fashionable court shoes she'd matched with it made her legs look extremely shapely, and Mark had been bowled over, waiting in the taxi as she'd walked down her path.

Her whole night had been spent being showered with compliments from him, and Judy was revelling in it. Her hair had been trimmed and re-streaked by Shelley the day before, sitting perfectly on her structured, jawline. She'd even learnt how to use heated rollers, styling it with a subtle wave, set in place with Bristow's hairspray. Judy was in her element when a fellow diner followed her into the ladies' asking her where she'd bought her dress.

The night couldn't have been going better, but now she was faced with Mandy, her once fair-weather friend, and her boyfriend's glamorous, large-breasted and extremely sexy ex-girlfriend. Judy's legs turned to jelly. She felt sure of Mark's love for her – he adored her as she did him. But this was a situation that suddenly stripped her of any of the confidence, she'd built for herself.

She smiled uneasily at Mandy, trying to disguise her fears, but Mandy's thick skin prevented her awareness of any underlying issue, and she threw her arms around Judy.

'Oh, it's so good to see you, Jude. How've you been?' Without allowing Judy to answer, she continued. 'Well, you've obviously been doing great judging by the look of you. I've never in my life seen such a transformation.'

Her mum had been right, and she couldn't believe her eyes. Judy looked amazing, and there was definitely a twinge of envy coming from Mandy. Her loyal friend's once dowdy persona was gone, and if they were to become pals once more, Mandy briefly worried that she might not get as much male attention, as she used to in the old days.

Her thoughts quickly dissolved. Her old friend looked great, but Mandy was sure that Judy's classy, understated look was no match for her own glamour. Men wanted sexy, alluring and confident and she was oozing with the lot. It wasn't something you just developed, from weight loss and a new hairdo. It was something you were born with. The thought made her smirk to herself.

'It's nice to see you, Mandy,' said Judy, finally finding her voice. 'Where are you heading?'

Mandy grinned. 'Well as luck would have it, I've just bumped into my knight in shining armour,' she gestured towards Mark. 'We're about to share a cab, aren't we?' she winked at him. 'Hey, do you guys remember each other? Well maybe he doesn't remember you, Jude. It was a while ago, and you were obviously a lot bigger back then. But you must remember him! Once seen never forgotten,' she gushed, squeezing his biceps.

Judy swallowed hard, feeling the tears prick behind her eyes. She wanted to protest but she couldn't find the words. What if Mandy's cocksure presence was so appealing, that Mark was tempted to start seeing her again? It was difficult to shake the thought.

'Well it's been great seeing you,' gushed Mandy, giving Judy an unreciprocated hug. 'I'll give you a call in a couple of days, and we can arrange a proper catch up. Are you ready, Sir Lancelot?' she beamed, turning to Mark.

Mark was aghast at the scene before him. He knew Mandy was cavalier, but who the hell did she think she was? He heard the way she blatantly tried to belittle Judy, and he didn't like it one bit.

'I think you've got the wrong end of the stick, love,' he said, shaking his head. 'There's only one Guinevere for me, and it's certainly not you.' Walking over to Judy, he took her hand and led her towards the waiting cab.

As her eyes flitted between the pair, Mandy was speechless. Not for one moment, had she suspected they might be together. She was stunned and in complete shock.

As Mark held the car door open for his girlfriend, Judy finally saw Mandy how Mark had just seen her, and it was a sorry sight. Feeling totally exhilarated at the way he'd dropped his ex from a great height, she no longer felt any kind of threat from her rival. Mark loved her and she never needed to doubt it.

'Don't bother to ring me Mandy,' she said. 'I won't be home to take your call. The taxi rank's further down the road,' she added. 'Be careful that your heels don't break under the weight of your big head.'

As the doors slammed and the taxi drove off, Mandy stood there in stunned bewilderment. She looked around her, unsure if anyone had witnessed the scene. To think that Judy would ever have had the guts to speak to her like that – and what was worse, was that Mark, her once boyfriend whom she'd cast aside and was now running his own successful company, actually preferred boring old Judy to her.

In her typical blasé fashion, Mandy shrugged her shoulders in disbelief at what had just occurred, but she could not deny the hurt she felt in the pit of her stomach. It was as if she had been railroaded, and the feeling was totally new to her. There was a lump forming in her throat, and she was suddenly aware of how cold it was. Glancing at the town hall clock, she could see that there were twenty minutes to go before it struck midnight. If she was quick, she may be able to get a cab and be in bed before twelve. She would take one of her mum's sleeping tablets and pretend that this sorry night had never occurred.

Chapter 70

'Don't fucking move and I won't have to use this,' hissed the menacing voice in Tina's ear.

Waking instantly, she felt the cold blade pressing against her throat. She lay totally still, frozen with fear. The room was black, but she recognised the owner of the voice, in an instant. The smell of alcohol was overwhelming and his laboured, heavy breathing was the only audible sound, moistening her ear with the warmth of each exhalation. She was lying on her side with her perpetrator leaning over her from behind; the radio alarm clock staring at her, was illuminated at 02:12. Her eyes were transfixed on it, willing it all to be a bad dream. But as involuntary images of Marsha's murder flashed through her mind, Tina truly believed that tonight could be the night, her life ended.

'I'm surprised to find you alone, Tina,' hissed Darren. 'I thought you'd be sharing the bed with your new fucking boyfriend. Yeh, that's right, you thought I didn't know, didn't you? Thought you were too fucking clever for me, didn't you?' he accused, jabbing the tip of the blade against the soft skin of her neck, with each taunting question.

Tina swallowed, feeling the edge of the knife move with her neck muscles. Terror paralysed her entire body and Darren could smell fear oozing from her every pore. He had been expecting to find his ex-wife in bed, with her lover. The knife was meant for him. But as Darren crept into the darkened room, the landing light displayed Tina's single silhouette, alone in the double bed.

Throughout the entire evening, he had been plagued by thoughts of her with another man. Drinking, laughing and finally making love, in the house they had shared, as man and wife. The visions tortured him and as the rest of the pub continued in their merriment, Darren sat alone at the bar, drinking pints of larger with vodka chasers. Anyone who knew him could tell his mood was black and apart from the occasional nod in his direction, he was mostly avoided. As the New Year chimed and punters hugged and kissed one another, he decided he could take no more.

Making his way out of the bustling pub, he trekked through the lonely streets, listening to a chorus of Auld Lang Syne getting quieter in the distance. He'd had his plans all sewn up. What could go wrong? He was going to win Tina back. He would show her what she wanted to see. He would be kind, caring and loving. He would be the man she had wanted him to be, and then she would be his once more. How could he fail? But her meeting someone else was never part of the plan and this thought angered him like never before. He hadn't once imagined that she might not actually want him back. That she had begun a life that didn't include him, and that she could be happy alone.

Creeping into his mother's kitchen, he opened the cutlery drawer, removing her sharpest veg knife. He could hear the three women in the living room, singing along to Tom Jones's Delilah, and he was sure there wasn't a chance of him being heard.

With its four-inch blade, the knife was perfect for what he had in mind and he could carry it quite easily in his jacket. No one else was ever going to have his Tina, and if it meant snuffing out both of them, then so be it. His rage was such that the consequences of his actions were way beyond his considerations, and as he left the house to enter the frosty night once more, the excitement in him was beginning to build. His penis was becoming erect at the thought of the violence that lay ahead, and there was one place he knew he could go to satisfy his needs, before the grim deed took place.

Chapter 71

Leanne's house was on the way to Tina's. Approaching the small terraced, Darren could see a light on upstairs and his excitement grew. He'd not clapped eyes on her in a number of weeks; she seemed to have dropped off the face of the Earth. Usually, it was a guarantee that she could be found at closing time, pissed out of her head, always willing and able. The thought gave him a wry smile. She was a goer, that was for sure, and he had secretly missed her. The fact that she hadn't answered the door to him on his past few visits did not deter Darren's eagerness, to give her what he considered as, a good seeing to. Neither did he think for one minute, that she may actually be avoiding him. Filled with a combination of testosterone and raging anger, Darren was on a deadly mission, and he was heading Leanne's way.

Without knocking, he first tried the door handle, wanting to surprise her, and to his delight it opened. Quietly gaining entry and heading silently up the stairs, he could hear Leanne humming to herself as she finished cleaning her teeth in the small bathroom.

Her evening had been a quiet one and probably the first New Year she had ever spent at home since she was in her early teens. After phoning Sue and wishing her a Happy New Year, she'd decided to make her way up to bed to read her Jackie Collins novel, leaving the door unlocked for her young work colleague, Helen, who was staying over to avoid her parents' early curfew. Recalling the days when she had first felt the same excitement of illegal drinking, Leanne only wished that she had been fortunate enough to have caring parents to look out for her. Instructing Helen that the door would be locked at 1am prompt, she expected her friend's arrival any time, and she was sure that the younger girl wouldn't let her down.

The evening had been rather unsettled one. She was experiencing a lot of backache and some stomach cramping. Still in her first trimester, Leanne was also aware of how very tired she was, and she was looking forward to getting in bed. Turning out the bathroom light and stepping out onto the small landing – with a sharp intake of breath, she came face to face with Darren, who was approaching the top of the stairs.

He grinned at her appearance. She was wearing an old, baggy, once white T-shirt that was just long enough to cover her dignity. Taking in the image of her thin, lily-white legs, Darren's urge to expose what was under the greying material became stronger.

'Happy New Year, Leanne,' he said, wryly. 'Bet this is a nice surprise for you.'

Leanne's heart was suddenly pounding. She could see the glazed look in Darren's eyes and was immediately panicked. But it was more than that. He was intoxicated, that much was obvious, but his eyes had a steely, almost crazed look about them which frightened her immensely. Heading towards her, his hand began to reach under her T-shirt, as he pushed her against the wall with all his weight. Instantly she felt his rock hard, penis pressing against her groin.

'You can't be here, Darren,' she said, trying to sound assertive, pushing at his chest. 'My friend's coming home any minute, you need to leave.'

His body froze as he pulled his face far enough away, to focus on her eyes.

'What fucking friend? You fucking slag,' he raged, forcing his hand around her neck and banging her head none-too-gently against the wall. 'You dirty, fucking slag. You've got another bloke on the go? No fucking wonder you've been on the missing list for weeks.' Darren's anger suddenly escalated; he gripped Leanne's hair in one hand, yanking her head back whilst he unbuckled his belt with the other. She prepared herself for what was to come, closing her eyes and allowing heavy tears to fall.

Then, as the unexpected blow struck her stomach, Leanne's automatic reflex was to crouch to protect her precious cargo, but with Darren holding her up by her hair, her belly was fully exposed to the second punch.

This time she slumped to the ground, leaving great chunks of hair in her attacker's clenched fist. Her only fear was for her unborn child and as Leanne's fight or flight instinct kicked in, she realised that her only option was to try and flee from this monster.

Stunned and dazed, she knew that her only escape was down the stairs and through the front door into the cold night. With Darren standing before her, beginning to undo his jeans, she took her only opportunity. Rising from her crouched position, Leanne unsteadily got to her feet, ducking past his huge frame and gripping onto the banister, before attempting to take to the stairs. Sticking out his foot in a bid to halt her getaway, Darren forced her to fall to her knees, and as she tumbled face first down the fourteen steep terraced steps, everything went black.

The image of Leanne's crumpled frame, lying lifeless in the hallway simultaneously shocked and excited Darren. Descending the steps, he was aware that she was out cold, and for a split second, considered that he might even have a dead body on his hands. Realising he needed to get out of there and fast, he stepped over her motionless frame, reaching for the front door. Glancing behind him as he departed, he was shocked to see thick red blood seeping from her privates, covering the insides of her pale white thighs. The horror of the blood excited him further, and as he left the scene, he was sure to wipe the door handle with his sleeve, before fleeing into the night.

Chapter 72

'Jeez Shelley, you frightened the life out of me, sat there in the dark,' Jackie said, switching on the living room light.

'Oh, I can't sleep'

'Me neither. I've been staring into space for the past hour, whilst Kev snores his head off. I'm making a cuppa. Do you want one?'

'Yeh, might as well, Shelley replied. I can't get my head around it, Jackie. It's unreal. It's massive.'

'I know, love, I'm the same. I keep going over it all in my mind.'

As Gerry sat before his family, he urged them all not to worry. 'It's okay, I'm not ill or anything. I just need to talk to you. Together.'

They glanced at one another in bewilderment as he began.

'Do you remember I had a brother who moved away, Howard?'

'Phuh, that toe-rag,' sniffed Carole in disgust.

'He's died,' continued Gerry, without acknowledgment.

Carole lowered her eyes in slight embarrassment, but readily addressed her husband as soon as she'd digested the news.

'How do you know? I thought you'd not heard from him since he left?'

'I hadn't,' he replied, quietly. 'I was contacted by a solicitor, in Birmingham. Turns out Howard's left us some money in his will. Along with his house, as well.'

Four pair of eyes stared at him in wonderment, hardly believing their ears.

'How much?' said Carole, breaking the silence.

'Well after the house is sold, it'll be around eighty thousand in total,' he announced, to his open-mouthed audience.

Gerry had not seen Howard for many years, and the news of his death was a complete shock. After a family dispute, over a business venture the pair had decided to embark upon, Howard had been disowned by his brother. They were skilled cutters and had planned to branch away from the firm they currently slaved for, to open their own company. Their skills were in high demand, but when the compulsive Howard found a new love interest, he secretly squandered the business's profits, leaving the company and Gerry, high and dry.

Unable to recover, and with his love for the job deflated, Gerry gave up the business and his attachment to his brother. He had lost his anger and hatred for Howard years ago, but by then he had no idea of his brother's whereabouts. Since their parents had passed away, Gerry often felt alone without the sibling he'd once been inseparable from. So, when he was contacted by Taylor & Taylor Solicitors in Birmingham, instructing him that he was the sole beneficiary to Howard's will, he was deeply shocked and saddened by the news. Having known about his brother's death for over a month now, Gerry had even attended the funeral in secret, whilst he'd tried to come to terms with the loss.

'Woohoo,' Carole suddenly cheered, raising her glass. 'This is cause for celebration!' She was already spending the money in her mind. 'We're rich, Gerry,' she laughed. 'Finally, Lady Luck has shone down on us. Cheers, Howard!' she cackled, looking towards the ceiling and raising her glass once more.

'We're splitting it,' Gerry continued. 'The money's been left solely to me and I want our daughters to take twenty thousand each,' he added.

Carole's faced dropped. She'd already been planning a new house, car and a cruise, as well as giving up her jobs.

Jackie and Shelley sat in stunned silence, whilst Kev listened intently to what his father-in-law was saying.

'Twenty each for the girls and forty for us. It's fair and it's what I want,' Gerry said, firmly.

Carole opened her mouth to protest, but Gerry continued. He looked at his wife with loving eyes, and as if reading her thoughts, he spoke gently to her.

'You've been a wonderful wife to me, Carole, and a cracking mum,' he added, with a quick wink in his daughters' direction. 'But we don't need a fancy new house to make us happy. Half of that money is more than enough for us. I know I've been a bit slack on the work front, but you wouldn't know what to do wi' yerself if you gave up work completely. These two are just starting out,' he added, nodding towards his girls and taking Carole by the hands. 'Just think how different things could've been for us, had we been given that kind of boost at their age.'

Carole nodded, smiling awkwardly at him. She had no doubts that he was right and suddenly felt embarrassed at her obvious greed.

Jackie handed the mug of tea to Shelley. 'Here you go, love, I've put a nip of whisky in there to help you sleep. What're you thinking about doing with your share then?' she asked her younger sister.

'If I'm totally honest, Jac, what I really want more than anything is to stay in my house. Redecorate it and wipe away every trace of Chris's existence. I adore that house and it pains me, having to sell it. I'd also like to put something into the salon, now it's expanding,' she added, 'but I'd have to discuss that with our Dawn.'

Jackie smiled at her. 'You've grown up before my very eyes in this last year, you have, our Shelley. I'm so proud of you.'

Shelley recoiled in slight embarrassment, but she was fully aware of what Jackie was getting at. A year ago, she'd relied on Chris for everything from paying the mortgage and bills to deciding where they went on holiday. Aware that she was finally happy, she felt sudden gratitude for every positive thing that her life offered, realising that it didn't matter if she was in a relationship or not. What mattered was that she was in control of her future, and she had the support of her much-loved family and friends.

'Happy New Year, Uncle Howard,' she said, clinking her mug against Jackie's.

Both girls grinned, raising the cups in unison.

Chapter 73

Hammering on Wayne's front door, Darren shouted through the letterbox.

'C'mon, Wayne, I know you're in there. Please mate, open up. I need your help.'

Aware that Wayne's sister and husband were away for New Year, Darren had decided to hide out at his best friend's house.

Now totally sober after sleeping through the whole of New Year's Eve, Wayne was sitting at the top of the landing in his boxer shorts, terrified that Darren had come to beat his brains out, following their showdown in the pub the previous day. But he could hear in Darren's pleas, that he wasn't his usual self; his voice was desperate, and Wayne was aware that if he continued to shout, he would wake the neighbours.

As Wayne cautiously opened the door, Darren barged past him.

'Help me out of these clothes and wash them, mate. I need to stay here for a couple of nights,' he said, visibly shaking.

'What the fuck's happened?' asked Wayne, with wide eyes, staring at Darren, who was now holding his head in his hands. 'What. What is it? Tell me!' he repeated.

Darren moved his hands away from his tear streaked face, looking directly into Wayne's eyes.

'I think I've killed Tina!'

Chapter 74

The unplanned, if somewhat unconventional New Year's Eve, had been a tonic for Jason and Tina alike. The pair felt as though they had known each other for years and talked freely about anything and everything. Jason confided in Tina about his relationship with a married man, who had been promising for some months to leave his wife for him. Jason hadn't told any of his friends, including Shelley, about the affair. But after the relationship had finally broken down that day, with his lover breaking it to him that he couldn't go through with it, Jason had found solace in opening his heart to Tina.

She listened intently, offering him the comfort he needed. In return, she unburdened herself to him. She told him everything about Darren and their marriage, her friendship with Shelley and how glad she was that they were back together. One thing Tina was totally clear about was that she had no room for a man in her life anytime soon. Jason second that, and the pair continued with their heart to heart until the wine was finished and the New Year was toasted.

Covering him up on the settee, Tina left Jason gently snoring as she made her way up to bed. He had drunk most of the two bottles of wine they'd shared, and he looked contented lying on the three-seater velour couch.

But awakening for the toilet about an hour later, Jason was aware of another man's presence in the small terraced house. His voice was low and barely audible, but Jason realised instantly that the tone was male, and it was coming from upstairs. The landing light was on and as he made his way to the bottom of the stairs, he could see that whoever was in the house had used their own key, entering through the front door. The night had turned wet and from the freezing rain, there were traces of dirt on the carpet from the trespasser's shoes.

After telling Jason about Marsha, Tina swore that as soon as the Christmas break was over, she would get a locksmith in to change the locks. She didn't believe it was Darren's style to break in, but she wasn't taking any chances, and Jason had fully agreed with her.

Everything was quiet now, and as Jason crept up the stairs he hardly dared to breathe. A bath towel was hanging over the banister, blocking his view into Tina's bedroom, but the door was open, and he was suddenly able to hear the voice once more.

'I'll fuckin' cut your throat from ear to ear if you lie to me again, Tina,' Jason heard the menacing voice threaten. 'Tell me who he is, just tell me his fuckin' name!'

Hearing Tina's terrified whimper, Jason realised that she must be trapped by Darren and in fear of her life. Now standing on the landing by the side of the open door, he had to think and act fast. If Darren had a knife, he needed to be cautious. If he were to act on impulse, Tina could be hurt, or even worse, killed.

'Who is he, Tina?' Darren raged once more. 'Tell me who the fuck he is!'

Suddenly finding some courage, Tina cried out, struggling with Darren and managing to break free from his grasp. If her life was going to end tonight, then she decided she wasn't going down without a fight. 'It's no one!' she shouted, turning to face him in the faint light. 'It's all in your fucking head, you moron! But I'll tell you something,' she spat, 'I would rather be with any man on this Earth, than be with you again. You repulse me, I hate you!' she shrieked.

Enraged, Darren lunged forward with the knife, instantly aware of the warm liquid which spilt, as the sharp blade pierced its target.

Rushing into the room, Jason grabbed him from behind, grappling with him in a frenzy as Tina slumped to the floor. The room was dark apart from the dim light coming from the landing, and Jason could not tell what state she was in. With the karate moves that Ross had taught him years earlier, he floored Darren, sending the knife reeling across the room.

Rising to his feet, Darren's only concern was to get himself out of that house and into hiding. He had no intention of continuing with the attack, following the realisation of what he'd just done. He had stabbed Tina and if she died, he would go down for murder. He needed to get out of there fast, and without hesitation he scurried down the stairs and out of the front door.

Jason's heart was pounding as he switched on the bedroom light to assess the extent of Tina's injuries. Turning to look at her, he heaved a massive sigh of relief, as he saw the shredded hot water bottle, still in her hands.

Taking her in his arms they sat side by side, no words between them, as Jason held her tiny frame for what seemed like hours.

'I'll make us a brew,' said Tina, finally, pulling away from Jason's embrace.

'I'll make it,' he replied. 'Then I'll run you a nice hot bath before we call the police.'

Tina shot him an urgent look. 'No police, Jason. I mean it. No one can know what happened here tonight.'

'But you can't let him get away with this, Tina! He needs to be punished. He could've killed you,' he replied, shocked at his friend's request.

'And he will be punished,' she said, in a low voice, 'but it has to be my way. I beg you, Jason, I don't want another soul to hear about this, do you promise?'

He nodded in response as Tina left the room. He had never seen someone look so determined before. If Tina had some form of revenge planned, then he would stand by her, whatever happened. She was his friend and she deserved that much from him.

Chapter 75

Lying in the hospital bed, Leanne stared numbly at the ceiling. The admissions ward was busy with nurses running around, attempting to attend to a multitude of patients. The elderly lady in the bed to her right was repeatedly calling out for her mother. Leanne's heart went out to her, realising she must have some sort of dementia. There was a woman in the bed facing her, who was still drunk from the night before, shouting obscenities and threatening to walk out if she wasn't given some pain relief soon. Leanne wished she would give them all a rest and carry out her threat. She could hardly hear herself think; it was total mayhem.

Her whole body ached, but the biggest ache came from her heart. She'd lost a lot of blood since arriving at the hospital and she feared the worst for her baby. Another tear rolled down the side of her face at the thought. This baby meant everything to Leanne. It was her hope and her lifeline to a better future, and the thought of losing it filled her with indescribable grief.

As the stern-looking, middle-aged nurse approached the bed to take her obvs, Leanne greeted her with a weak smile. It was Helen who'd called 999, after returning to find Leanne unconscious at the bottom of the stairs. The ambulance had brought her straight to Boundary Park Hospital, where she had been immediately admitted.

She'd told the doctors she'd lost her footing and fallen down the stairs, but that didn't account for the big chunk of hair that was missing from her scalp and the bruising around her neck.

'Do you know what's going to happen next?' Leanne asked the nurse, desperately. 'I need to know if my baby's okay.'

The nurse looked up from the blood pressure machine, directly into Leanne's pleading eyes.

'They'll send you for a scan, love,' she replied. 'But from the amount of blood you've lost, I wouldn't bother. If you take my advice, you'll leave the bastard, and fast. That baby didn't deserve to be born into a life like that.'

Leanne looked at her in shock, but there was no love in the older woman's eyes. She had seen this situation too many times and it was beyond her why any woman would stay in a violent relationship.

'You deserve all you get,' she said, shaking her head as she wheeled the trolley away.

With the realisation that her baby was no more, Leanne began to sob, but her cries were lost amongst the bedlam of the noisy ward, where she lay, contemplating her life.

She couldn't remember how she got home, only that she had left the ward unnoticed. As she lay on her settee two days later, her sadness turned to anger. Darren Doyle had robbed her of her only chance of happiness. Leanne wanted revenge and she would not leave for Newcastle until she got it.

Chapter 76

Returning from the off-licence, Wayne unscrewed the cap off the cheap whisky and poured himself a large measure.

Darren had stayed for almost two days and Wayne was annoyed, to say the least. He was annoyed that Darren had once again used him for his own means, to save his skin, but he was equally annoyed with himself, for not having had the courage to stand up to him.

Lying on his bed, he could hear his sister and her husband downstairs, laughing at something on the telly as he gulped his drink and poured another shot. The police hadn't been round yet, but surely it was only a matter of time, and if Darren was in the frame for whatever crime he'd committed, then surely Wayne would go down as an accessory.

Looking around at his small bedroom, he shook his head. What the fuck did he have in his life? Twenty-four years old and living with his sister's family. He should be having the time of his life, with the girl of his dreams, not living in a box room waiting for the police to knock. His hand squeezed around the glass as his anger grew. In his mind, all his woes began and ended with Darren. He had to be stopped, and Wayne needed to find the courage to stop him.

Chapter 77

Four weeks later – January 1986

Surrounded by the topless posters, which adorned the walls of the garage, Darren cupped his hands, blowing his warm breath onto his cold, numb fingers. He couldn't wait get out of this town, with its small-minded inhabitants. He found it impossible to escape the rumours regarding his estranged wife's return and each time he walked into the pub or a shop, he felt as though everyone was talking about him. True, they tried to disguise their gossip for fear of riling his temper, but he could see through them. He thought about Tina and New Year's Eve. How had she escaped the knife he'd lunged towards her? He was sure he'd stabbed her. He shook his head slightly with confusion. She was alive and kicking, he knew that for certain. Several people had informed him of her presence. Even his mother had seen her walking to work. She then proceeded to give him a two-hour ear bashing, about how Tina was lucky that she hadn't been close enough for Ivy to have asked her a few choice questions, as to where she'd been hiding all these months. Something didn't add up and come hell or high water, Ivy would get to the bottom of it. Darren knew that if his mother found out the truth about the beatings, he was rumoured to have given Tina throughout their marriage, then he would be out on his ear. Ivy always had his back, but trouncing his wife? Even she couldn't overlook that. Darren was flummoxed as to how Tina had avoided injury, but in the cold light of day, he'd been extremely relieved to hear she was unharmed. A murder charge was not something he intended adding to his attributes.

The same thing couldn't be said for Leanne. She had vanished into thin air. Darren had kept a low profile since New Years' Eve. He could only recall snippets of what happened within the bouts of his rages. But the one clear vision he couldn't get out of his head was Leanne's lifeless and bloody body, lying at the bottom of her stairs. He shuddered, thinking of how out of control his temper had been. Taking a detour on his way home from work the day before, he'd walked past Leanne's little terrace. It was pretty obvious that the house was empty, and he was in total bewilderment as to where she could be. He shrugged. It was no longer his concern. That slag could've fallen off the face of the earth for all he cared. It was freezing and when he blew onto his hands again for warmth, he wistfully sighed, thinking of his forthcoming plans. He couldn't wait to get away from this poxy garage and the mundane job he hated. He'd signed up to join the Army and in a week's time, he would leave this god-forsaken hole, to begin his training. He knew army life would suit him and he couldn't wait to leave. He had nothing left here. Tina's return was a constant reminder of how he'd fucked up his marriage. His greatest ally Wayne never showed his face anymore and Darren had a feeling that the bridge between them had been well and truly burnt. That much was evident after the two awkward days, following New Year, which he'd spent cooped up at Wayne's house, whilst hiding from the police. Army life beckoned and he couldn't wait for it. He hadn't mentioned his departure to anyone, and he decided that he would only let Ivy in on his secret, the day before he left. It was best that way. As he bent his head beneath the bonnet of the Vauxhall Astra, to finish off, before closing the garage for the weekend, he felt extreme satisfaction on the embarkment of his new life plans.

As the hammer struck his head, Darren slumped to the ground. He was unconscious immediately, but his attacker would not be satisfied with that. As the second blow struck, the sound of his skull shattering echoed through the small garage, and as the blood began to trickle under the car he was working on, his assailant calmly walked away. Leaving him dying in a pool of blood.

Chapter 78

16 months later - May 1987

'I'm sorry, Mrs Doyle,' the young nurse said, welcoming Ivy onto the ward. 'He's not had a very good night. The seizure was quite severe, and he's had some swallowing and breathing difficulties since. He's back on the ventilator, but he's stable.'

Ivy thanked the nurse and sat by her son's bedside. Just as she did every day. His vegetative state was apparent quite soon after the attack, with him barely showing any signs of improvement since. Some days he could signal using his eyes, which mostly pleaded to his mother, for what she could only guess was an end to his misery and suffering.

Friends and family rallied round following the attack, but only Ivy had been his constant companion.

Keeping a continual vigil, she had often wondered who had despised Darren enough to do this to him. Her son was no angel, but to bludgeon and leave him for dead was an act of pure evil.

Numerous people had been questioned, but they all had alibis that stood up, and after a search of their homes, no evidence had been found and the police were no closer to charging anyone.

Poor Wayne, thought Ivy, *he was a troubled soul.*

She had been shocked and saddened to learn of his suicide the year before. His sister had been the one who found him one morning, hanged in his bedroom. Ivy was aware that he and Darren had fallen out not long before the attack, but the lads were as close as brothers and she supposed that afterwards, when Darren showed no signs of a recovery, the pain was too much for Wayne to bear. It must've felt like he'd lost a member of his own family. Others weren't so convinced.

The small-town rumour mill had gone into overdrive, with many believing that the guilt of bludgeoning his once best mate, was too difficult for Wayne to live with. There were many stories circulating and there had also been many people in the pub, who witnessed Wayne threatening Darren on New Year's Eve. Of course, Ivy had heard the gossip, but she'd known Wayne since he was a baby and wasn't buying it.

One thing she was sure of though, was that something had definitely occurred between the lads. Darren hadn't returned home for two days, and when he eventually did, he was shiftier than she'd ever known him. A knife from her drawer was missing but she'd been prepared to wait for the truth to come out, as it always did. Now, with Wayne gone and Darren looking like he'd never be able to tell her, she could only wonder.

-

'Have you brought your veil?' Shelley asked, grinning in excitement as she looked at Judy's reflection in the salon mirror.

'Oh wow, I love how you've done my eye makeup, you're so talented,' Judy said, praising Shelley as she studied herself. 'You could make the bride of Dracula look like Cindy Crawford.'

Both girls laughed as Judy handed her the white veil, which was encrusted with pearls and diamantes. Shelley gasped in awe at the lace and netted headpiece.

'This is absolutely stunning, Jude. I can't wait, to see you in your dress later.'

Jason and the rest of the stylists came over to admire it.

'You, my dear, are going to look absolutely divine,' he gushed. 'Just like a princess. Oh, I do hope I meet my Prince Charming one day!' he said, wistfully, gazing up with his hands on his heart.

The rest of them laughed.

'I'm sure he's just around the corner,' Shelley winked at him.

On her birthday, the previous year, Mark asked Judy to marry him and their wedding had been eagerly anticipated by everyone in the salon, where Judy was now a regular.

'The shop's closing early today, so don't worry about us being late,' said Shelley, who was honoured to be invited to the whole wedding.

She briefly cast her mind back to her own wedding day to Chris, when she'd been just as excited as Judy was. She no longer felt sad at thoughts of her past marriage. She'd learnt so much from it, and her main focus in life now, was the shop. Following her inheritance, Shelley bought into the business, making herself and Dawn equal partners. 'Material Girl' the beauty salon she now managed, continued to flourish with great success. She was now a fully qualified and established beautician and running this additional side of the business meant more to her than anything. Wedding makeup was in massive demand, and she'd even had to employ a junior therapist to meet demands.

She currently felt that there was no time in her life for a romantic relationship. But that didn't stop Jason constantly trying to play cupid between her and Ross. If there was one man, she would ever consider giving her heart to, it would be him, and she was fully aware that he felt the same. They occasionally shared secret rendezvous, which no one apart from Tina knew about, but the timing never seemed right, and Shelley was completely happy to keep things as they were for now.

Hearing on the grapevine that Chris was now running his own I.T. company and living in a large house in Alderley Edge, she honestly felt no ill will towards him, wishing him all the happiness that she had found. They'd both been so young when they'd married, and she only hoped that he treated his next lady better than he had treated her.

Judy was on cloud nine. She couldn't wait to become Mrs Mark Devine. Their love continued to grow and getting married was the icing on the cake. Mark had planned a lavish honeymoon to a secret destination as a wedding gift to her, and on their return the pair would be moving into a detached house he'd just finished building for them. Judy couldn't wait.

Her life was amazing and sharing it with her soulmate was a dream come true. She decided she would wait till after the ceremony to give Mark his wedding gift. Suffering bouts of nausea over the past few weeks, Judy had put it down to wedding nerves, just as she had with her missed period. But with no signs of her next one appearing, on the morning of the wedding she'd decided to do a pregnancy test. Waiting in her bathroom at her dad's house, where she'd spent the night to avoid seeing her future husband before their big day, Judy had been stunned and elated when the two blue lines appeared on the test stick. This was going to be the best news she could ever give him, and she knew without a doubt that he would be overjoyed.

With joy and excitement bursting within her, Judy decided to confide in Brenda, who was making a cup of tea in the kitchen. The women had become close over the past year, and on hearing the wonderful news, Brenda hugged her tight. Despite still missing her mum, Judy could clearly see that Brenda was a wonderful match for her father. She was great with Dan and looked after them all with love and kindness, and that was good enough for her.

-

'Please tell me there's no overtime on tomorrow,' Norma asked, peering round the office door.

Tina looked up from her paperwork, shaking her head. 'No, it's been cancelled,' she said, grinning. 'You look as relieved as I am.'

'Just a bit. I was dreading having to set my alarm after tonight's shenanigans,' she laughed. 'Shall I come for you in a taxi, about 7.30pm? We can nip to the pub for one first if you like.'

'Sounds good to me,' said Tina, giving Norma the thumbs up. 'I'll make sure I'm ready.'

Both girls were invited to Judy and Mark's evening reception and were planning to make a full night of it. Meeting Judy through Shelley, the group had become firm friends over the past year and were overjoyed to celebrate with her.

Looking at the clock, Tina decided to begin wrapping things up. There was only ten minutes to go until it was time to clock off and she needed to collect the staff timesheets before they left for the day. Saturday morning overtime usually flew by, but today had dragged, due to the fact she'd been clock-watching. She was really looking forward to Judy and Mark's wedding, and all she really wanted to do was go home and pamper herself, ready for the big night ahead. Sitting in her office, she leant back on the big leather chair, looking around her, and smiling with satisfaction. Being promoted was a major boost to Tina's self-confidence. Taking the place of Bridgette Hornborough, Tina had thrown her heart and soul into the role. Bridgette had been side-lined following an altercation with one of her staff, where it was reported that more than just insults were thrown; so, she had been swiftly moved to one of the picking floors.

Tina was stunned when the management approached her, advising her to apply for the supervisor position. The interview was extremely nerve racking, but she'd held her own, answering all the questions diligently. When she was offered the position, she was astounded and thrilled in equal measures, although she was slightly worried that the friends, she'd made in the packing hall might resent her and begin to treat her differently. But that didn't happen. Every one of her colleagues was happy for her. She was a natural manager, firm but fair, showing empathy and consideration to her staff. She treated them with respect and in return they were always happy to go the extra mile for her.

That was almost a year ago, and to say her bosses were pleased with her was an understatement. Figures were up, returns were down, and absence was at an all-time low. She'd begun a college course in business and management, which the company were funding and her knowledge and confidence were growing daily.

When she looked back at her life only a couple of years before, she was extremely proud of what she'd since achieved. She briefly thought about how, back then, she'd been a virtual prisoner in her own home. She thought about Darren and the night he'd broken into her home, with the intent to harm her. She had been desperate to keep the whole thing a secret and, true to his word, as far as she knew, Jason hadn't broken her trust. She couldn't stand the thought of being a victim and, although she didn't like to admit it, revenge had often crossed her mind back then. But violence wasn't her style. True, she had a feisty streak, but the thought of physically inflicting pain on another human being was beyond her.

No, the only way to get her revenge was to prove that she was a survivor. To succeed in whatever, she decided to do with her life, and that was what she implemented. It was what drove her every single day, and even though Darren wasn't around to see it, she had proved to anyone who'd ever doubted her, that she was capable of whatever she set her mind on.

Tina had no idea who'd attacked Darren and left him for dead. She felt sorry for his family, but she found it difficult to sympathise with him. The way he'd lived his life, it was inevitable that karma would come looking for him one day. She used to wish she'd never met him but in reality, he was probably one of the reasons she'd turned into the person that she was today, and in a backhanded way, she was grateful for that.

-

Laying her beach towel onto the fine golden sand, Mandy sat down and began applying Ambre Soleil to her golden skin. After six weeks on the island, she'd acquired a sun-kissed glow and was down to factor 2, sunscreen oil. She adored Ibiza and never wanted to leave. This was her second season working on the island and nowhere had ever felt more like home. Winter months were spent in England doing various degrees of mundane jobs in order to get by, but as soon as April came around, Mandy had her flight booked, looking forward to a season of hard work and hard play.

After being made redundant from her job at Cuthbertson's solicitors, she got a job in her local chippy. The work was smelly, and the pay was a pittance, with each shift melting into the next. Mandy soon realised that she couldn't put up with it for much longer. One day, as she was serving, she overheard a customer talking about her daughter, who was going abroad to work in a bar. In that instant she had a lightbulb moment, wondering why the hell she hadn't thought of it before.

Hadn't Jake and Jonathan, the owners of JJ's bar in San Antonio, always said there'd be a job there if ever she wanted one? That afternoon, she walked into the local travel agent's and booked a, one-way flight, leaving the very next day. Both boys had welcomed her with open arms, and Mandy was soon a permanent fixture in the trendy hotspot.

It was tough graft, but she loved it so much that it didn't feel like work. She was still as lustful as she'd ever been, but now she didn't have to worry about stealing other women's boyfriends or husbands. The relationships she encountered were over within a week or two and that was just how she liked it. She learnt to never again mix business with pleasure, and as Jake and Jonathan were gay, there was no worry on that score.

Today was her day off and as she stretched out on her towel, she afforded herself a smile. All in all, life couldn't be better, and she didn't care if she never clapped eyes on the shitty English weather again.

-

The small house was filled with young mums and their babies and toddlers. Leanne was in her element. All the birthday gifts were piled on the dining table in an array of coloured wrapping paper, in varying shades of pink. The chatter of the women and cries and squeals from the children made the room a hive of activity, and she loved it. Turning around, she saw Sue watching the scene and gave her a broad smile. Without her best friend, none of this would've been possible.

Sue returned it with a wink. Seeing Leanne so happy was wonderful, and it was more than she had ever hoped for, recalling how she'd been just eighteen months before.

Hearing her friend sobbing down the phone had been heart-wrenching. It was difficult to tell what she was saying at first, but it soon became apparent what had happened. The attack. The loss of her baby. The, fear she was living in. Sue could only imagine what she was going through, and alone, too. When she, her best friend was so happy all those miles away.

Arriving back in Shaw, Sue was horrified when Leanne came to the door. She was thin, gaunt and ever so pale. As they sat on the small sofa, Sue cradled her like a child as she wept. She knew Leanne could cope with the attack and the physical brutality, and even the sexual assault she'd experienced. The girls were made of the same stuff, and they knew how to survive. They'd always had to. But to lose the child she never thought she'd ever have, that was too much to bear, and Sue could feel the pain seeping out of her friend like a fog.

In the months prior to the attack, when the girls spoke on the phone, Leanne had mentioned that she'd been casually seeing someone. The fact that she'd never mentioned him by name wasn't particularly unusual to Sue. Names had never been important to them. In the past, they'd always figured that using names meant developing feelings, and feelings weren't something they were comfortable with. Easy come easy go, meant you were always in control.

Sue held Leanne in her arms, listening to her friend relate the story from start to finish, about how she'd come to know Darren Doyle. She knew he'd been embarrassed by her and that he'd kept her from all his friends as his dirty secret. Yet he'd keep on coming back to her, time and time again. Until, she finally hoped, even allowed herself to consider that she might have begun to mean something to him. None of that was important now. All that mattered to Leanne was that she was no longer pregnant and that the last few weeks' joy she'd spent, imagining her wonderful future, was now just a cruel memory.

At the sound of his name, Sue's heart lurched and her stomach instantly knotted. She had not thought about him in years, but his name immediately made the anger rise within her. Once upon a time, he had been her saviour, or at least she thought he was. He'd made her feel loved. He was her shining light in a world that was dark. The man who would take her away from a torturous life, spent with the father everyone thought to be a wonderful parent and pillar of the community. How wrong she had been.

As a shy 15-year-old schoolgirl, Sue considered herself as plain and uninteresting. She was not comfortable with her appearance, hating the curly brown hair that she struggled to style. Friends told her she'd be really pretty and could have loads of lads after her if she wore makeup and kept up with the latest trends. But Sue wasn't interested in being noticed. She was happy to blend into the background. Her ripe breasts that had swollen to double their size in the past year, were not welcome. And the curvy hips she was developing only reminded her of the woman she was becoming. Lately, she'd become aware of teenage boys and even men eyeing her body wherever she went, and she did her utmost to shield herself from their stares.

The molestations from her father were part of her everyday life now. She had lived with them for as long as she could remember and she coped with it, but what she didn't want was to have to re-enact those scenes with anyone else. Whilst all her friends were discussing the, boys they fancied, Sue remained silent. Some of her friends had experienced sexual fumbling's with spotty youths of their own age, and a couple of them had even had sex. They'd often ask her why she didn't fancy anyone, and would sometimes make fun of her, but she didn't care.

One day, whilst boasting about her steamy relationship with her new boyfriend, one of her more experienced friends told Sue she didn't know what she was missing – Sue wanted to scream. She wished she could confide in them and share the horror that was her home life, but she wouldn't know where to begin. They couldn't attempt to understand what she was going through.

Sue never wanted a boyfriend. The thought of a sexual relationship with anyone made her feel physically sick. That was, until she met Darren Doyle. He wasn't like the spotty teenage boys at school, with their crude comments and vile jokes. He was older, funny and caring and didn't look at her as though he was undressing her with his eyes. He was strong and protective and knew just the right things to say, and that's why she fell for him.

The first day of her Saturday job at Della's Café, was nerve-racking. Sue wasn't confident like many of her mates, and she blushed whenever anyone spoke to her. Della Jones, the café owner, could see this a mile off. It was one of the reasons she'd given Sue the job. The last thing Della needed was an idle, teenage girl who saw waiting on tables as an opportunity to flirt with the regulars, leaving all the donkey work to her. No, Sue was plain, studious and not afraid of hard work. Della had been in the café game long enough to know a good waitress when she saw one. She threw her in at the deep end and it was just what Sue needed.

Most of the regulars were labourers who were looking for a hearty fry up to set them up for the day ahead. The café was a no nonsense, greasy spoon that supplied a full English at a good price with a mug of tea thrown in.

As Sue leaned across the table to hand out the four large breakfasts, to Darren and his colleagues, his boss, Ian Kennedy gave her round bottom a hearty slap, making her almost jump out of her skin, spilling tea all over the white tablecloth. Sue's face went as red as a tomato. Darren chastised Ian, trying to spare her blushes and that was her first encounter with him.

Sue certainly wasn't Darren's usual type. She was shy and awkward, and he had no idea what the hell it was about her that he liked. But she was elusive, not even giving him so much as a second glance, unlike other girls of her age. She also appeared so very vulnerable and he had an overwhelming urge to protect her. It took over a month before he managed to get more than two words out of her, and over six months before she finally agreed to go out with him, but once Sue finally fell, she fell hard.

Darren was so handsome and confident. She wasn't foolish enough to think that he wasn't inundated with female attention, but she couldn't ignore his persistence and as much as she tried not to show it, his cheeky humour eventually won her over.

After trying to kiss her on their first date to the cinema, Sue very firmly told him, no. Darren wasn't used to being treated that way, which made her seem even more desirable.

After three blissful months, Sue was madly in love. Darren would be her husband some-day, she was sure of it. He said the sweetest things to her, telling her he would always look after her and that they would be together forever. Remarkably, their first sexual experience was a pleasant one for Sue. She was a one off, and Darren instinctively knew she needed to be treated with kid gloves. She was the polar opposite of the girls he usually dated, who were always eager to please him sexually. It surprised him how much these young girls knew, and he shuddered with disgust at the thought. He was more than happy to sleep with them, but considering one of them as a permanent fixture, was a definite no-no.

Once Sue had given herself utterly and completely, Darren became her entire reason for living, but her feelings weren't reciprocated in the same way. True, he cared for her, but once he'd tasted her forbidden fruit, his interest waned. He still saw her on a regular basis, but the sweet nothings began to diminish, as his attentions where once again drawn to the long line of girls, eager to throw themselves at him. Sue didn't have a clue. She was too wrapped up in her dreams of a rosy future with her wonderful boyfriend, who'd promised her the earth. So, when she first saw Darren's aggressive side, she was floored with shock.

Telling him she was pregnant wasn't easy, but Sue was sure he would be happy. He wanted their future as much as she did; he'd told her often enough. It was a total shock to her when she first found out. She'd been on the pill for over a year. Her father had told her she needed to get on it, now that she was of a certain age. What he really meant was that he didn't want her getting pregnant as he continued with his wicked ways. Sue had obediently obliged, just as she always did, and the subject was never mentioned again.

Since she'd been with Darren her father had all but left her alone, and it was a huge relief. She at last felt a little bit in control of her home life, and it was empowering. Thinking back to a tummy bug she'd had a few weeks before, Sue could only assume that it was during her sickness bout, that her contraception had become void.

Feeling Darren's large hands around her throat, Sue began to gasp for air. His black eyes stared into hers until they began to bulge. When he released her, she fell to the ground, coughing. Looking up at him, large tears began to fall from her eyes. This wasn't her Darren. The Darren she knew was loving and gentle. He would never hurt her. Yet, here he was, standing before her, ordering her to get rid of the child she'd already bonded with. A baby that was desperately wanted by its mother and would be adored and loved so much.

As she sobbed, Sue felt Darren's arms surround her. Lifting her to her feet, and gently kissing her head as he held her to him. Telling her how sorry he was for hurting her and explaining how he'd just freaked out because he was scared. He told her they needed to be realistic. She was only just 16 and they were too young for children. It just wasn't the right time for them. They had forever together, and they shouldn't rush things. They needed to do everything in the right order, and he promised her they would. When the time was right, they would be married and have a whole football team, if that's what she wanted. Sue was crushed, but just as with her father, she found herself submitting to Darren, and when one week later he drove her to the clinic for an abortion, she had to keep reminding herself that it just wasn't the right time for them to have a child. It was the only way she could get through it.

When he picked her up afterwards no words were spoken, and the drive home continued in silence. As he parked up outside her house, all Sue could remember was Darren telling her that it would be better if they didn't see each other anymore. After that first sentence, the rest of his speech was a blur. Through her tears she watched as the Ford Cortina sped away, along with the man she'd loved with all her heart. Her trust had been broken and Sue was distraught. She stumbled up the drive and round to the back door of the house.

Seeing her father on the kitchen floor, clutching his chest and gasping for breath was the first thing that Sue encountered on entering the house. It took a moment for her to register the scene as he held an arm out to her, mouthing the word help. With his face ashen grey, he pleaded with her, to call for an ambulance. She stood frozen for a moment just staring into his eyes. Then, as though he wasn't there, she turned to lock the back door and walked straight past him and up to her bedroom. Leaving him to die on the cold kitchen lino.

In the days that followed everyone assumed Sue's tears were for the loss of her father, but only she knew her despair was for the baby she'd lost and so desperately yearned to keep. The anger she felt towards Darren was nothing compared to the self-loathing she harboured towards herself, for trusting and believing in him.

Over time, and since meeting Craig, she learnt to forgive herself, but never a day went by that she didn't think about the child she was tricked into terminating. She tried her best to bury her hatred for Darren Doyle, considering it as wasted energy that would take over her life if she let it. But sometimes it wasn't that easy. Especially as she and her lovely husband had continued without success to create the baby they desired so much.

As she watched Leanne holding baby Jessica's podgy fingers, guiding her as she took five unsteady steps towards her, she grinned. Everyone clapped the little girl, who was scooped into her mother's arms, and Leanne beamed with pride, kissing her daughter's head.

Jessica was adorable. From the top of her curly blonde hair to the tips of her little pink toes. Everyone loved her. Her eyes were the palest blue and her lips were rosebud red. Her nature was placid and her laugh infectious, capturing the affections of everyone she met. Today was her first birthday and lots of Leanne and Sue's friends, many of them army wives, had come to the small house party with their children, to celebrate the event.

It was three months after Leanne moved in with Sue that she found out she was still pregnant. Her reaction was one of shock and disbelief, as was her best friends. Upon reading her notes, her new doctor told her that her previous hospital confirmed that she had lost a baby and the only explanation he could give was that she must have been carrying fraternal twins.

It was a week before the news began to sink in and both women were ecstatic. Jessica was here before they knew it and on a sunny, Friday afternoon in May, she was born with Sue by Leanne's side every step of the way. In the months that followed, little Jessica received more love from Leanne and Sue than any baby could've hoped for, and both women delighted in mothering her.

When Craig returned from Belize, Leanne was ready to move into her own rented flat and, within a month, Sue was ecstatic to discover she too was finally pregnant.

As she stood watching the party before her, she caressed her growing bump. She was five months pregnant now and life couldn't be better. The florists was thriving and both women managed the shop, whilst taking turns to look after Jessica.

If Sue had known how good things were going to turn out, would she have still done what she did? Being honest with herself, she believed she probably would. Leaving Darren for dead had left her with a sense of calm. All the anger she'd tried to keep locked away for years, suddenly left her. They say revenge is a dish best served cold, and hers was positively frozen.

As she'd walked to the garage where Darren worked until midday on Saturdays, she'd had no intention of bludgeoning him. She didn't even know if he'd still remember her, but she remembered everything about him, even all these years later. He was a creature of habit. Men often were, and she figured that he'd probably be alone, just as he used to be years ago, when he would complain that his boss and brother-in-law always finished early, leaving him to tidy the place and lock up.

Leanne and Sue's train was scheduled to leave Shaw at 12:20pm, where they would travel to Manchester and catch their connecting train to Newcastle. Contracts on the house had been exchanged the day before and neither of them looked back as they left it. With Leanne's few belongings, they sat in the small cafe, waiting for the minutes to pass, whilst watching the world go by.

The urge to confront Darren had been nagging Sue from the minute she woke up that morning. She'd said nothing to Leanne and kept brushing it aside, telling herself it would do no good. But as they sat there, nursing a pot of tea, Sue suddenly stood up, informing Leanne that there was someone she needed to see before she left. Leanne didn't question her friend; Sue's eyes told her not to and, as she left the café, her friend picked up a magazine, so that she didn't have to dwell on her sadness.

Walking the short distance to the backstreet garage, Sue's heart was pounding. She had no idea what she was going to say, or if at all, she'd actually get to see Darren. But before she got on that train, leaving this grimy mill town for good, she needed to look into his black eyes once more.

As Sue turned onto the side street, she saw Darren's boss, Ian Kennedy, leaving the garage. Darting behind a side wall, she heard him telling Darren to lock up when he'd finished and that he would see him in The Moulders Arms later. As Ian walked away, he didn't look back, and Sue felt the adrenalin beginning to pump around her body. Snow was in the air, and she was glad she was wearing her winter coat and gloves.

Approaching the open garage, she spied Darren directly in front on her. He had his back to her, with his head under the bonnet of a Ford Fiesta, singing along to Wham's, I'm Your Man, which was playing on the transistor radio. Her eyes flitted around the garage, which was adorned with topless posters of page 3 girls and playboy models, and as Sue watched Darren, gyrating his hips to the music, the anger in her began to rise. The man before her was the cause of so much pain, and here he was, without a care in the world. He sickened her and as the feelings of hatred and loathing for him grew, a red mist descended before her eyes.

All she could remember was picking up the ball-pein hammer from the shelf and swinging it as hard as she could in the direction of Darren's head. He immediately fell to his knees, and as the hammer swung down on him again, he fell to the ground, without witnessing a thing.

Since that day, the women had never discussed the event. Sue didn't even know if Leanne was aware of the attack and the police, had never questioned them. The weapon was left at the scene and as there were no fingerprints or witnesses. It seemed as though the enquiry had gone cold. Apart from their first sexual encounter, Darren's relationship with Leanne had always been his dirty little secret. She was just one, in a long line of women that he had slept with and used along the way. She certainly didn't qualify as a police suspect.

Sue had wondered if, in time, she would ever feel any guilt for what she had done. She knew he was still alive and in a vegetative state, but she continued to feel no remorse for him. Just like her father, Darren had got what was coming his way.

Life was better than it had ever been and as long as the people she loved were happy, then that was all that mattered to her.

-

Getting off the 59 bus outside the Railway pub, Ivy walked the short distance to her terraced house. It was the middle of May and yet it felt like March. The air was damp, and she was perished. It had been a long day at the hospital, and she was gasping for a cup of tea. Turning the front door key into the Yale lock, she could hear the telephone ringing in the hall. Darting through the door, she picked up the receiver in haste.

Upon hearing the news from the doctor on the other end of the line, Ivy dropped to her knees, expelling a wailing howl, as she was informed that her son had died during a seizure, a few minutes after she'd left the hospital. Her precious boy, Darren was dead, and the pain she felt was like nothing she'd ever experienced. But although awash with sorrow there was also a sense of the relief. Her beloved boy was now devoid of pain and finally at peace, with his dad and, Wayne. It was this thought that gave Ivy the comfort she would need to carry on living, without her most treasured and favourite child.

The End

Printed in Great Britain
by Amazon